SUPER BORN II

World on Fire

Keith Kornell

Super Born II: World on Fire

Harper Landmark Book, Willoughby, 44094

© 2015 Keith Kornell
All rights reserved. Published 2015.

Cover image by
Editing and production by Indigo Editing & Publications.

Printed in the United States of America.

ISBN: 978-0-9826452-7-7

Library of Congress Control Number: TK

CONTENTS

ONE

Building a Nest

LOGAN

I hoped they wouldn't kill him until I got my chance to give him a good swift kick right in the...ribs. The three victorious super-women were looking down at Dr. Jones with disgust, as if he'd just eaten their last piece of pizza *and* drank their last beer. Jones had kidnapped one Super Born, tried to catch another, and battled the third with his two now-deceased minions. Even worse, he had betrayed yours truly and discarded me like a stale donut. Other than that, he was a great guy.

Jennifer Lowe's eyes glowed red; she looked intently at Jones as he sat bewildered on the rooftop. You could tell by the way Jones scanned the three women but always returned to Jennifer that he feared her the most. She studied him like a street fighter trying to decide where to stick her knife while she slowly closed in on him with the others. Her casual clothes and running shoes belied the power she had just unleashed on Jones' stooge, transforming her from a tower of energy into a lump of ice drained of her power. I'm sure Jones had other thoughts on his mind, but even with my commitment to Allie, I couldn't help but marvel at the way Jennifer filled out her jeans. There was a hypnotic sway of her hips...of course, I had the luxury of such thoughts. It wasn't me who kidnapped Rebecca or tried to capture Allie or ate the last damn piece of pizza.

Allie looked at Dr. Jones with calm resolve. My girl was a vision with her skintight black jumpsuit and long, windblown blond hair, and suddenly all I could think about was getting this over with so we could "fly" home together. But the cool determination on her face brought fear to Jones' eyes. He must have wondered which punch or kick of hers was going to hurt him most.

Yet it was skinny Rebecca who seemed the angriest. She wore the B.I.B.'s black cape and Zorro mask tied over her short auburn hair and had her arms folded, a bitter sneer on her face. Dr. Jones and his two minions had captured Rebecca, locking her in energy bands that covered her mouth, wrists, and legs. And it was Rebecca who had vaporized the second of Jones' superwomen after being freed by Jennifer. So I thought it would be her who would strike first.

Me? The broken arm hanging at my side was reason enough for me to desire revenge on Jones. When you add in how he had betrayed and used me, I should have felt more bitterness than I did. But once…once he had been a friend. Not a great friend, mind you…I don't kick great friends in the ribs…too often…well, once…but Jones had been a friend nonetheless.

I moved past Allie and Jennifer to get my kick in before Rebecca could finish him off. Jones took no notice of my approach. Through the darkness of the night, Jones' eyes scanned the roof of the Bank Towers building, which was cluttered with the shadowy shapes of ventilation ducts and utility boxes. The poor fool was trying to put together what had happened since I'd clocked him under the chin, putting him out on his back and releasing a flock of tweety birds to circle his head just like in the cartoons. Jones had been out like a light during the entire battle between Allie and the girls and his minions. He looked over, finally, and gave a start upon seeing the ice sculpture that had once been his powerful groupie. He gave out another when he saw his Interrupter gun, an invention he had used to control the Super Born, lying smoldering and broken nearby. That's when he realized there was no one left to help him.

As predicted, Rebecca reached him first. Her eyes began to turn black, just like they had before she vaporized his sidekick.

"Nice mask, Rebecca. Is that new?" he said.

Really, Jones? Was that the best you could come up with?

Rebecca ripped off the mask, exposing the red burn marks around her eyes. "Look familiar, Doctor Jones?" she asked, closing in rapidly on Jones before showing him the same burn marks on her wrists. She pointed toward the melting ice statue that, until a few moments ago, had been a potent superwoman. "Your little friend over there gave me these. Like 'em?"

He began to shake his head no, but then realized that was the wrong answer. "What? I don't see anything. I didn't mean you any harm."

"You kidnap and imprison all your friends, I suppose," taunted Rebecca.

"What? You don't?" He tried to laugh it off but stopped when he saw that no one was laughing with him. "It was all with your best interests in mind, I assure you."

Rebecca shook her head and sneered at him. "Not from where I stand."

Thinking that Jones would soon be toast, I hurried past Rebecca. Each movement sent a gush of pain from my arm, but I lived with it just to get at the little bastard. (Ever try really hurrying with a broken arm? It's sort of a step, *oooh*, step, *oooh* affair, but you get the idea.) When he saw me approach, he seemed to somehow forget how he had betrayed me. His face lightened, as if I were there to help him.

"Ah, my friend…" he said, smiling as I approached. But then his joy drained from his face as I sent out a poorly aimed, rushed, and painful kick, which missed. "What did I do to you?" protested Jones. "You were my friend. I made you wealthy, befriended you, and confided in you my greatest theories!"

"Wait!" Jennifer moved up assertively beside Rebecca. "Let's think this through carefully."

Jones nodded ferociously up and down in agreement. "Very carefully, good idea," he said.

Rebecca turned toward Jennifer, puzzled. Allie moved in beside them with a thoughtful look on her face, as if she was already considering the possibilities. And I took another half-assed kick at him, though the pain from my broken arm seriously hampered my accuracy.

"Dude!" Jones complained, easily avoiding me.

Jennifer brought her palms together and raised them over her mouth, tapping her fingers against one another. She took a couple of steps before saying, "Tonight has taught me that there's a lot we don't know. We don't know where we came from, why we have these powers, what's going to happen to us next, or who's after us. My powers keep changing. Problems keep appearing that I have to overcome. It scares me sometimes. Is that happening to any of you?" she asked, looking from Rebecca to Allie. They both nodded in agreement. "Well, if that's true, does it make sense to kill the person who knows the most about us?"

"It does if the bastard just tried to kill you!" Rebecca said. I nodded and tried to line up for another attempt at a kick. That made Allie step over to me, put her hand on my aching shoulder, and shake her head.

Jones raised himself to his knees as unthreateningly as he could. "I can help you. I can help you all," he said, smiling sweetly. But when he briefly turned toward me, the smile disappeared. "Well, except maybe you." He gave me a friendly pat on the arm, which caused me to yelp. "Oh, sorry," he said dusting off my arm with his fingers, as if that would make up for the pain he'd caused me. "We can work together. I would be glad to share my research with you. This would be far better than that silly plan I had before about trying to control you." But the word *control* seemed to ignite something within Jones.

His body became more erect, and his face hardened. He tightened his fists. "And controlling the world, crushing all that opposed me," he said in a strange voice. Then, realizing his mistake as he looked around, he slumped his shoulders and pushed up a cutesy smile.

"You're not falling for this, are you?" Rebecca asked Jennifer. "How could we ever trust this guy? He would turn on us the first chance he got. The plans for that...that Interrupter thing are in his head."

Jennifer wore a big smile—it was clear that she already had the answer. She slowly walked up to Jones, who raised his arms defensively. The two other Super Born shared a questioning glance before comprehension dawned over their faces. Jennifer turned back to them and awaited their approach.

"What? What are you doing?" Jones asked. He backed away from them. "Surely you have no plans to harm good old Dr. Jones? I can be of great service to you all, very great indeed!" They didn't say a word, just moved in close and stared at him as if they all were imagining him munching down that last piece of pizza. He turned to me. "My friend, certainly you cannot let them...hurt me?" He swallowed hard. My silence offered him no solace.

Jones turned back to the Super Born. But as he opened his mouth to speak, he was suddenly blinded by flashing beams of light: blue then green from Allie's eyes, crimson red then violet from Jennifer's, and yellow then orange from Rebecca's. He staggered back and then slowly crumpled to the ground unconscious with an idiotic smile on his face. The little flock of tweety birds returned to circle his head, but you could tell they were reluctant and pissed off, feeling overworked for one night.

* * *

I had been elected to be there to explain things when Dr. Jones awoke, as he would no doubt be confused. I'd taken his shoes off and pushed him onto his bed, which was covered with Penn State sheets and blankets, but that's as far as this man would go. If a guy wanted to get tucked in with a lullaby, he'd have to find another dude to do it. It had been a few hours since we arrived at his apartment, and I checked in on him every twenty minutes or so, watching his pillow distort his face, drool forming in the corners of his mouth—you know, fun stuff—when all I wanted was to be in the general vicinity of Allie. At least thoughts of her in that tight black outfit helped pass the time.

The pain from my arm in its new partial cast and shoulder sling wasn't bad, and the break turned out to be less serious than I'd thought. Maybe if Jones' minion who'd broken it—the one I'd named Toughy—had used two fingers instead of one to hit me, it would have been worse.

With time to kill, I turned to Jones' laptop to see what sort of entertainment I could find, anything to divert me from the snorting sounds Jones made while sleeping in the next room. In his files, I found an endless parade of papers and theses he had written regarding the environmental impacts of epsilon radiation on Scranton and the Super Born. (Zzzzzzz.) One looked interesting—"Psychological Control of the Inferior Mind." The paper was about someone he called "subject 1," who was a journalist and sounded like a real moron. I was glad I'd never met that loser.

Looking for lighter fare, I moved on to the video files. The first started with a good closeup of Jones' nose and then widened out to show the empty lot behind O'Malley's Bar and Grill to document how he was taking his soil samples. That had me on the edge of my seat and wishing for popcorn, let me tell you. The next video started out with a close up of Jones' eyeball as he set up the camera. When he moved out of the way, a striking young woman was standing naked in his living room with her hands on her hips. I stared for a moment, transfixed, until the spell was broken by the woman's squeaky, gum-snapping voice: "This is just for research, right? You're not gonna put this on the internet, are you?"

"I assure you as a gentleman and a scholar, no one but me will ever see this tape," said Jones off camera before running into the frame bare assed and chasing the woman around the room. They knocked over the camera, and it lay recording the empty sofa. After a few moments filled with the sounds of giggling, kissing, and general sexual contact, Jones and his partner's faces fell into the camera's view (unfortunately for me). The woman's long brown hair flowed over Jones' face as she moved down his chest until her head was out of frame. All I could see then was his face going through various contortions of ecstasy or pain; it was hard to tell which. After a few moments, he went cross-eyed and sang out the first few bars of "God Bless America" before falling instantly asleep.

Compared to one moment feeling Allie's petite back during a hug or even one gaze into her gray eyes, this sexual escapade was so lame. Still, not for the first time, I wondered how a guy like him managed to get girls like that. Obviously, he was right: in a town like this, where the men didn't know a pussy from a piñata and the women were all sexually frustrated, just about any man could get lucky. Which was great. I just had no desire to see it happening for him, let alone to him. I closed Jones' homemade porn without even the hint of a hard on—in fact, I think seeing cross-eyed Jones getting all patriotic made me go a little negative in length.

I stood up and began pacing in front of his living room window, staring out at the sunny day I was missing. Bored, I plucked up a violet thong panty lying innocently ownerless on his desk and began twirling it around my finger. Then, remarkably, I found a red pair of bikini briefs on the arm of his desk chair—I paused for a moment and then began twirling both of them. To my dismay, a gigantic pair of white flowered granny briefs also lay nearby. I let that one sit. But not the black lace bra, which I found hanging off a lamp. I was running out of fingers to hold them faster than Jones' apartment was running out of underwear to be discovered. I looked around the room, imagining all of these panty-less women running around with Jones in hot pursuit. I started to feel violently itchy all over. With all the action he was getting, it was amazing Jones found the time to be an evil genius. But with the girls having marked him, all that was over now.

Just then I heard the genius groan. I made my way around the islands of books and papers in his living room and down the short hallway to his bedroom. When I rounded the corner and looked into his doorway, Jones was squeezing his Penn State pillow and humping his covers. "Who yur daddy is now, shorty girl," he mumbled in his sleep, making my skin crawl and making me swallow a bit of vomit. That was enough for me. I hurried in to shake him. "Wake up! Now! Please!"

Jones' eyes slowly blinked open. "What is this?" he mumbled. He stared blankly as his mind tried to piece back together what had happened. His gaze slid from side to side, and then he looked over at the saliva-enhanced pillow he was clutching. He quickly let it go and sat up. "My friend, what is going on?"

I could tell that he was trying to put things together but was missing a few fragments.

I dropped the panties and the bra to the floor. Compared to all the sexual activity for Jones they represented, I felt a little sorry for him in his current condition. Still my leg had the desire for a quick kick, one right in the ribs. "You're okay, back at your apartment."

He looked around for a long moment, and at that point I could tell flashes of memory from the rooftop battle were coming back to him. He had a look of dismay. "Where are the Super Born? Was that a dream I am remembering?"

"No," I said, beginning to pace around the room, "it's no dream. You were stupid enough to mess with Allie, Jennifer, Rebecca…and me. And we kicked your ass and the two Super Born you rode in on," I said, smugly victorious.

"My…my Super Born are," he stammered with an amazed look on his face before he swallowed hard, "gone?"

"Poof! Took the Interrupter with them."

He quickly looked down to inspect his body. "They…your friends did not kill me as well?"

I patted him on the shoulder. "You don't remember, do you?"

Dr. Jones shook his head, his copy of the book still missing a few pages.

"You captured Rebecca and made me bring you the B.I.B. Remember that?"

He nodded with an embarrassed smile.

"Remember the rooftop battle?"

Jones appeared to strain his memory here. "I remember all of you standing around me, but nothing after that till I woke up here. I thought I was going to die."

"You don't remember the deal?"

"Deal?" Jones stared up at the ceiling.

"Your promise?"

Jones went to a cutesy smile and then shook his head.

"You," I said, sitting down on the end of the bed, "told the Super Born that you would share your research with them and help them understand their nature, their origins, and their destiny."

"I did? That's right, I did," he said nervously.

"That, my friend, is why you are alive right now."

"Oh," Jones said, his eyes moving rapidly in their sockets.

"No, no. Don't even think of betraying them," I said waving my finger back and forth. "I see your scheming little mind working. Your plans to control them are over."

"They are?" he asked sheepishly. "Why?"

I patted him firmly on the shoulder, wishing it was a kick. "Because you, my friend, have been marked by all three of them with some kind of hellacious power that knocked you out for twelve hours. Their eyes flashed, and you went down faster than a mug of beer on St. Paddy's Day. Try as you like, you won't be able to do anything that will hurt them—any of them. They will expect you to continue your research. There are a lot of questions they need answered by the Great Dr. Jones, Super Born expert. Your ability to find answers for them is the only thing keeping you on this earth after that little kidnapping plan. And they are serious. Better give them what they want. Remember, superwomen equals super hormones."

"Really? Is that it?"

I just laughed, picked up the two pairs of panties, and began twirling them around my fingers as I left. "You'll find out."

"Tell me, what will I find out, my friend?" he asked, standing up to follow me to the front door.

My answer was to give him a knowing smirk as I closed the door behind me, leaving him to his thoughts for a brief second. Then I suddenly opened the door and slingshotted the panties back at Jones one at a time. It wasn't a swift kick in the ribs, but at least I hit him with something. *That'll teach him for getting more than me.*

Ah, but I was on my way to Allie; have all the panties you want, Jones.

* * *

You could call it journalism. Personally, I would call it great journalism, and the best part was, I was the only one with the story. My website, specializing in all the Super Born news fit to print, broke the story as I had witnessed it in my apartment and on the rooftop of the Bank Towers building. It revealed that the diabolical forces behind recent troubles in Scranton had all been defeated by the Super Born. The city was not just under the protection of the B.I.B., the Bitch in Black, but a triumvirate of unbeatable superwomen.

I detailed the amazing events that had transpired and tried to back them up with as many facts as I could to make my story believable, which was always a problem when explaining the actions of the Super Born. I referred to Allie as the B.I.B., Jennifer as Super Born 2, and Rebecca as Super Born 3. I told how I had watched as

Rebecca vaporized Carmine Camino in my apartment. I described how the crime boss had slowly disappeared before my eyes while trying to kidnap Rebecca and make me eat a lead sandwich. When news of Camino's disappearance blossomed in the conventional news media, my credibility grew, as only my story accounted for why no one could find his body (or those of several of his workers). Hundreds of people had heard the weird sounds of the Super Born battling on the roof of the Bank Towers—the clashing of power shields was heard from miles away—and thousands had experienced the bizarre localized electrical blackout that had occurred when Jennifer battled Dr. Jones' superwomen.

Of course, official news outlets expressed skepticism, but I responded to all of their points of contention, even bringing Dr. Jones in as a witness. In reality, most of what he had witnessed was the six-square-inch section of roof where his head had lain, and he himself was one of the defeated diabolical forces—both facts I neglected to reveal—but his professor-like statements added to my believability, 85 percent according to most polls. (And Hungarians.)

The coup de grâce came four days into the article series when I published a picture of the three Super Born who now protected Scranton. It wasn't easy to get that picture, because it meant the women had to agree on their costumes.

Jennifer insisted on the red-bustier-bare-arms-bare-midriff-tight-pants outfit of her dreams, along with a mask to disguise her face. Allie had her black costume already. That left Rebecca, who remained unhappy with a green outfit and cape that Jennifer had pushed on her. "I look like a frog," she bellowed. After a brief rebellion, she realized she couldn't come up with anything better. I took the picture in the back bedroom of Allie's apartment one night while Allie's teenaged daughter, Paige, was on a field trip. Despite numerous takes, Rebecca's face always managed to convey her lack of excitement over her outfit, and with each one, Allie and Jennifer battled for the middle position. As I was the photographer, the ultimate choice was mine, and I chose a photo with Allie in the center with her hips cocked, one hand on her hip, the other on her thigh. The lens of my camera was fully extended, if you know what I mean.

Can you imagine the poster revenue and photocopy rights for that one picture alone? And everyone said I would amount to nothing! (That's right, everyone: Mom, Dad, Aunt Mary, even my childhood dog who ran away from home.)

When that photo hit the website, all hell broke loose. Everyone wanted interviews. But I soon found out that, even in elementary school, Allie had always bordered on being violently ill whenever she spoke in public. (There was a nasty Christmas program incident in third grade involving a vomit solo in the middle of "Jingle Bells," among other things.) A sweating, nervously belching superhero, she claimed, was not what the people wanted to see. Jennifer too preferred to exercise her power from behind the scenes. And Rebecca, by her own admission, was more at home with machines than people.

Nevertheless, we had to establish our credibility, so I talked them into doing just one interview with a local morning TV show, which the station could then syndicate across the nation. We agreed on a list of questions. I coached the Super Born on their answers at Allie's apartment for a full frustrating night before the show. It was like herding cats, all claws and hissing. All three of them refused to follow the script I had prepared, letting their answers drift off on their own personal tangents. So when the morning of the interview arrived, I was full of confidence…and alcohol.

When the time came, I led them onto the set, which had been prepared with four chairs beside a desk where the interviewer, Katie Thompson, sat. She was a thirtyish chameleon with one eye on Scranton and one on the job she obviously longed for in New York City. I'd sold her on this being the story that did it for her, and she bought it.

I greeted our host and the cameras with a gigantic smile before ushering the Super Born in with a dramatic wave of my arm. Jennifer led the pack by four or five lengths while Allie beat out a slumping Rebecca by a nose. Jennifer wore her red outfit with golden bands on her arms and in her hair. Allie wore her black, tattered B.I.B. jumpsuit and cape with Zorro mask, while Rebecca, despite her protests, wore the green outfit Jennifer had forced on her. We all sat in the order we had entered in, with me closest to Katie. Jennifer looked from camera to camera as the director changed the angle of the shots, while Allie stared straight ahead, swallowing as if her breakfast kept trying to escape, and Rebecca sat like a lump, looking at her feet.

"Good morning, Scranton. This is Katie Thompson, and with me here today live are the three women who call themselves the Super Born, along with Logan from the wildly popular B.I.B. website. Good morning to you all."

"Thanks for having us this morning," I fluffed.

"Let me start with you, Logan. May I call you Logan?"

"No, Katie, I would prefer to be called Logan."

Katie paused for a moment then moved on. "According to the reports you have published on your website, these are the women who have virtually ended crime in Scranton and are responsible for ending the criminal reign of Carmine Camino."

"That is correct, Katie," I said. "Mr. Camino and his henchmen were holding automatic weapons to our heads when the green Super Born"—here Rebecca raised her hand slightly and gave Katie a feeble wave—"put an end to them all."

Katie's expression suddenly became cynical, and I could sense that she had decided to ambush us despite having assured me earlier she was planning no such thing. "Really? Her?" Katie gestured to Rebecca then smiled to the audience in disbelief. "She finished off a gang of thugs and killers?" Katie said, nearly laughing.

I nodded. "It wasn't pretty, but it was either them or us." Then

I paused and gave Katie a long hard look. "You have any other explanation where good ol' Carmine went? I hear he's not answering calls these days."

Katie smiled at the audience and then turned to Allie. "You must be the B.I.B. then, the great crime-stopper vigilante."

Allie nodded while keeping her mouth closed, staring into the camera like a deer frozen in headlights, then appeared to swallow back a bit of vomit.

Katie laughed. "Her?" she exclaimed. "Seriously? Sorry, Logan, but I find this whole story a little hard to believe! Really, if you had brought some better actors, maybe....but you expect us to believe *these* women are the *real* Super Born? Do you have any proof, or are we supposed to just take your word for it?"

Rebecca extended her legs and tapped her toes together. Allie stared wide-eyed. Like them, I tried to remain cool, but Jennifer glowed with anger.

"Listen, bitch, you want a little proof?" Jennifer stood up and sent out a red beam of light with her hand that lifted Katie a full two feet out of her chair.

Katie flailed her arms and legs. "Let me down!" she said in panic.

"Things look a little different from up there, do they?" asked Jennifer.

I took hold of Jennifer's arm, shook my head, and convinced her to lower Katie, which she did slowly at first before letting her drop the final foot with a thud. Katie tried to straighten out her hair and regain her composure while wearing a fake smile for the audience.

Allie began convulsing, apparently reminiscing about her breakfast, and ran off camera.

Rebecca rose and walked over to one of the cameras, put her hands on the housing, and looked into the lens. In a second the image the station was broadcasting became full of wavy lines with sporadic flickers of cartoons, game shows, and news reports. We could all see this clearly from the monitors.

I looked up at the director in the control booth, held out my arms, and said, "Cut! I guess." Then I mumbled to myself, "Just the way we rehearsed it."

Of course the video went viral.

From then on, there were no more interviews for the Super Born. It was up to me to be the front man. Suddenly, I was like a rock band manager. That role took me all over Scranton and then soon to New York. They wanted me on the morning shows and the news shows, clearly only half believing what I was selling, but it was a story everyone wanted to hear. Overnight I became Scranton's superpimp, and I did more to promote the city than the Chamber of Commerce ever did. The only drawback was leaving Allie behind whenever I had to make an appearance. Even out of costume, any dim bulb would have been able to put together the blond accompanying the "B.I.B. expert" and the B.I.B.

Meanwhile, in Scranton changes were already afoot. My story about the superwomen was just the ticket. Crime seemed to have vaporized just as Carmine Camino had. With little in the way of lawbreaking to report, TV news suddenly focused on positive events. By all accounts, everyone in Scranton felt good about themselves, having something, someone, to believe in. A new sense of community was in the air.

And it seemed everyone now wanted to live in a town protected by superwomen. After years of fighting its reputation as a Rust Belt city in decline, Scranton became a hot place. New people brought income, and income brought more people. Real estate boomed overnight. With the economy struggling and crime on the rise across the country, Scranton was thriving, drawing hopefuls to its Super-Born-safe shores. Men immigrating to Scranton for work suddenly found what Jones had: a large population of potent, undersatisfied women. (To hell with LA, Paris, and Rio—if you were a man, the place to be was Scranton.) Scranton's best-kept secret was a secret no more. Just as Dr. Jones and his bizarre theory had predicted, two half-lives of epsilon radiation later, Scranton's decline was over.

That was why no one could believe that I would sell the website, which was the hottest source of news on Scranton's Super Born. Merchandising was at an all-time high, and we were getting hits from all over the globe, yet it felt right to move on. I was reluctant to tell Rebecca the news—after all, I owed much of the site's success to the brilliant way she had set up and managed it for me. But when I told Rebecca what I inteded, she was totally behind me. She explained that she was ready to move on to new and better things anyway and just hadn't had the nerve to break the news to me.

Miner's Lite, the B.I.B.'s favorite brand of beer, was more than happy to fill my bank account and take over the site—paying a hefty premium, I might add. They brought in a crew of hotshot IT people from New York, but let's be honest—the site went downhill the second Rebecca left. I gave Rebecca a hefty cut of the sale despite having no agreement or obligation to do so. (Hey, I'm not an ungrateful pig, despite what Sarah might have told you, or Denise, or Nicole…oh, Nicole.) With the rest of the money I planned to buy a house in the area I called New Scranton and start a nest egg, as I now hoped to have a career as a legitimate writer.

Of course, *legitimate* is a somewhat subjective word. Some, my mom included, would say my exposé in the *Scranton Times* on the pigeon feces problem in the downtown parks was legitimate; others called it crap about crap. But hey, I thought I could do this writer thing.

What's more, the website had fulfilled its purpose. It had brought me Allie, and now it had no meaning to me. I kept the trademarks and T-shirt rights, though. I wasn't a total moron. (At least not anymore.) A woman like Allie deserved the best, and starving writers lose their appeal after a while. Believe me, I know.

I called the area where my house was located New Scranton because it was at the center of the new construction that had begun right after the Super Born had reignited the city. Having learned some things from Jennifer, I planned to buy the house in the name of a real estate trust I'd created. I needed to show Allie the house before I signed all the papers, though—it would be a package deal with Allie and Paige included or no deal at all. I was buying the house so that we could be a family together. Up until then Paige only knew of me, with Allie protecting her as she always had. So far in our relationship, Allie and I had enjoyed a mixture of sneak-away meetings at my place or hers and incredibly romantic flights to getaway locations only a fool would complain about. But you guessed it—that fool was me. Here I was, applying for the hardest job there is…okay, the hardest *jobs* there are: being a superhero's boyfriend and being a surrogate father to her daughter…willingly…on purpose…and with my extensive (not) history of success at either. What a schmuck!

Allie didn't question me when I pulled into the driveway of a large new house. She wasn't even curious when I asked her to come inside, only asking, "Whose place is this?" as she looked around. I started pointing out the furniture-less, neutrally painted rooms—the foyer, the great room, and the main hall. You could still smell new wood, carpet, and the freshly dried paint. "What, you into real estate now?" she asked, trailing behind me. When I reached the end of the hallway I took a step into the large, empty bedroom with an attached bath and said, extending my arm, "And this is Paige's room."

First she said, "Uh, huh," her mind elsewhere. Then her head snapped quickly to attention. "What?"

"I thought Paige should be down the hall. You know, private, away from our room. You have been getting loud recently."

She tapped me on the shoulder, but being a little excited now, forgot her strength, so the blow nearly knocked me over. "You love my being loud, and you know it."

"And your incredible orgasms, and you flying over the bed when you get really excited, yes, but I'm not sure Paige will."

"This," she said, turning to face me. She put her arms around my neck. "This is ours?"

I nodded. "No more running between cracker-box apartments, no more you having to leave to get home to Paige."

"No more sleeping on dirty sheets and horse blankets…" she muttered.

"Okay, I won't bring the stuff from my apartment…no matter how you beg. Those blankets have character."

"And fleas," she grumbled.

"That was never documented! But hey, seriously, I thought this would be great for us, and I think we're ready to do this. We both have something the other one needs, so we'll all be great here, like a little family."

Allie let go of me and began pacing the room. "Are you sure you're ready for this? Paige doesn't even know who you are. The only men she's been close to are in my family. I don't know how she'll take it. How are you with kids?" she asked, returning to face me.

I remembered horrible things my mother had told me about having children (something about them needing food, shelter, and attention every day), a few painful run-ins with my nephews and nieces, someone once saying to me, "The thought of you breeding scares me," and one nasty summer coaching kids' soccer…that kid had to have healed by now, don't you think? Anyway, he had it coming. "I'm okay with kids," I told her, hoping she wouldn't notice the new length the comment had added to my nose.

"It's not easy," she said shaking her head. "And a girl, a *teenage* girl!"

"Let me try."

She breathed heavily, walked away, and then turned back to me. "We'll have to take it slow. Do a trial run before we dump this on her," she said, gesturing around the room.

I corralled her in my arms. "Does this mean I'm officially your boyfriend?"

She laughed. I gave her a long kiss, and her delicious, willing lips had their usual effect on me. (What does she eat anyway? She always tastes great, like strawberries or something; must be a Super Born thing.) "Come on, let's test out the acoustics in here," I said as the argent moonlit glow and feeling of warmth that always occurred when our bodies met encircled us. I pressed the kiss as our bodies began their light show.

I guess it wouldn't surprise you to hear that we had experimented (a lot…no, a lottttttt) since our first encounter with Super Born sex, flying over Scranton that summer's night. That magical act of levitation was driven by our bodies merely touching and rubbing over one another. We soon learned how to magnify the experience, taking it to another, higher level. It's hard for me to describe the feeling. It was like we were something more than human when we were together, immersed in a pool of warmth, exhilaration, and a feeling of connection with the universe…and each other. Okay, I know that may sound a bit sappy, but it's true.

She laughed at my ardent attention before quieting to a purr as my fingers slid under her skirt and between her welcoming thighs; the moonlit glow was really flowing down there, if you know what I mean. We drifted up and down, floating off the ground a little. Then she looked up at the ceiling. "You know, the ceilings are a little low in here," she said, only half joking.

I signed the papers the next day, though the bruise on my head reminded me to add a clause requiring the sellers to knock out and extend the ceilings in our bedroom up through the attic…or maybe a little higher. It should be easy for them, I figured—my head had started the ceiling modifications already.

TWO

The Magnets Collide

ALLIE

I remember being nervous when I introduced Logan to Paige at Charley's, her fave restaurant. Paige was very reluctant, seemingly ready to jump on any little problem that might arise. Knowing how much hung on her opinion, I was prepared for a battle. I had seen her like this before, and it wasn't pretty. But when we reached the table and she saw his face, it was like two opposing magnets had suddenly found each other. *Clang*!

Her pout turned immediately into a grin. "Wait! Aren't you the guy from the B.I.B. website? I've seen you on TV! I read your site every day!" Then she turned to me almost angrily. "You didn't tell me this guy you met was *him*! This is the B.I.B. expert!" She said this as if I didn't know who he was. Right away, they began talking, Paige sliding her chair as close as possible to him. He loved the reaction; he knew he could stop worrying now.

I'll admit I was surprised. I thought he had lied to me about being good with kids. Who knew? He shrugged an apology to me and then turned back to Paige and began telling tales of my adventures and talking about actually meeting the B.I.B. herself.

As the B.I.B. was the favorite subject for both of them, they went on all night talking about her while I sat across from them in silence, ordering soda refills, doubles. And I got to count how many times she asked him, "Do you think I could meet her? Could you arrange for me to meet her?" Seventeen. I wanted to remind her that she met me this morning and wasn't too excited about my telling her to clean her room. At least I got to eat my dinner, part of theirs, and an after-dinner snack…well, two. I made a couple of attempts to join the conversation, which Paige dismissed by saying, "Mom, she's not much of a B.I.B. fan." I had a friggin' B.I.B. T-shirt, didn't I? Hell, I even had a B.I.B. costume and a B.I.B. body, for that matter, not that she cared. I wasn't sure why it bothered me. Somehow it didn't even seem like they were talking about me, just some made-up character. Yet here I had a man and a daughter who loved and admired what I had become. Why wasn't I thrilled? I guess because we had a new house and moving to plan.

By the end of the evening—as Logan escorted Paige to the car, arm in arm, laughing—I thought I had lost my man to a younger woman. He looked at me periodically with a smile, assuming I was glad things had gone so well with Paige. Which I was, but also kind of annoyed that they'd ignored me all night. Is this what it was going to be like, living with the two of them?

Later, at home, all she could talk about was how dreamy he was, how much they had in common, and how he was going to try to introduce her to the B.I.B. It had started to get pretty irritating, so I saw no reason to hold back on the news of the three of us moving in together. I expected silence and concern, maybe an "Is it that serious?" but instead got hugged and mauled as if I had given her the keys to an expensive car, a credit card with no limit, and a backstage pass to her favorite pop star's concert all at one time. She was texting before she even turned around, excitedly skipping to her room.

THREE

I'm a Father and I'm Abandoned

LOGAN

I was excited but mellow, almost content (who, me?). After leaving the restaurant, I drove back to my lavish new estate, watching the city lights flash by. HellFuck, was I doing something right…again? I felt lucky that I happened to be the B.I.B. expert, which covered for my lack of parenting skills. But it wasn't exactly lucky, was it? I had earned my status as an expert. It was not an accident but my directed plan that had put me and Paige on the same page, so to speak. (Was that too many pages, Paiges?)

Then I thought of Allie's face, quiet mood, and lack of her usual sarcastic humor. It finally dawned on me that she was pissed. Crap, I had ignored her all night.

I began to reach for my mobile phone to call her when the flashing lights appeared in my rearview mirror. With my thoughts having drifted away on the girls, I had failed to notice my ever-increasing speed. *Damn! This will be a fast $150 picked out of my pocket,* I thought as I pulled over and watched the cop begin his slow I'm-the-boss walk to my car. *And another $200 in increased insurance rates,* I realized.

Scranton cops were the worst. They had a reputation for all carrying a chip on their shoulders and even eating stale donuts, tough hombres. Maybe it was the town, or maybe it was the times, but they were all nasty. I made a mental note not to be a smart ass. (Yeah, right.)

The middle-aged, overstuffed officer paused behind my car for a minute, making me wonder if someone had hit me in the parking lot. Then he appeared at my window. By then the girls were a faded memory, and so was mellow and content. "Could you open the trunk of your vehicle, please?" he ordered.

I paused and stammered, thinking, *You need a warrant to search my car, pig!* But then considering my ass in a jail cell, I popped the release just the same. "There you go, Officer." I listened to him digging around in the trunk and began to wonder if he wasn't an RFD, one of the men in Scranton afflicted with Reduced Functionality Syndrome—the feebleness that was the yin to the Super Born's yang, or vice versa, whatever. But the officer seemed around fifty, too old for that to be his excuse. I really wanted to get out and see what was happening. When I cracked the door open, his head appeared around the back of the car.

"Just stay in your vehicle, sir," he ordered me with an extended palm. After a minute, he again paced slowly to my window. "Remain here, please, this will just take moment," he said before strolling to his patrol car and tapping the radio on his shoulder, mumbling something into it.

I couldn't help myself. "Officer, was I speeding or something?" I called after him.

He stopped, annoyed, as I had interrupted his radio call, and gave me another extended palm. "Just remain in your vehicle. I will be with you shortly."

His tone told me that any further comments would risk my spending a romantic night with Guido in the county jail, so I reluctantly shut up, began to sweat, and watched the officer in my mirrors. People in the cars that drove by smiled, glad that I had been plucked from the herd instead of them.

What the hell is he doing? I thought as I watched him open the trunk of his patrol car, still talking into his radio. Then he disappeared behind the lid of his trunk, and all I could see was the blinding flash of his lights.

I took a deep breath when I heard his trunk lid slam. Had someone backed into my car, placed a dead body in the trunk, and filled it with a million dollars in drugs before slamming the lid? Stolen diamonds? For…some reason? I briefly scanned the gearshift and accelerator, contemplating a Bonnie-and-Clyde. Then he began digging around in my trunk again. I heard popping, banging, him saying, "That's not right," and then a couple more slams and the trunk lid closing again and again. I really had to get that fixed.

Once again, he began that slow authoritative pace to my window with his hand on his gun hip. *This is it. This is fucking it!* I thought. The gearshift was already in my hand.

"That should do it, sir. Have a good evening and drive safely," he said with a thin smile.

I was stunned…freedom? I was free to go? Then I realized that I hadn't done anything. I was no criminal; I'd just been made to feel like one. Starting out strong, then remembering cellmate Guido, I was polite and mild by the end of the sentence when I said, "Why did you stop me then, Officer?"

He looked off into space for a moment before shaking his head and releasing a sigh. He turned back to me and put his head in the window. "Your taillight was out on the driver's side." He raised his hand to show me the light bulb he had removed from my car.

"You're not giving me a ticket?"

"Ticket? My heavens, no. Why should I give you a ticket when I have a box of the bulbs you need right in my trunk? I can't have you hurrying off to the auto parts store in the dark without a taillight. That would be dangerous. No, it's better to take care of things right here and now. I'm sure the bulb just burned out since the last time you inspected your taillights."

You're supposed to inspect those? I thought.

"You're in Scranton. This is a town where we protect each other. You have to ask yourself, 'What would the B.I.B. do?' Simple rule. I live by it, and it gets me through the day. Protect your citizens and treat criminals without mercy, just like she does. Drive safely." With that he paced back to his car, mumbling into his shoulder radio. A moment later he was whistling as he looked up at the stars.

It took me at least a minute to move. I was in shock. Where was I? I needed to know that I was still in Scranton. Had I mistakenly driven over the border into Canada? What else could explain…nice…caring? But I didn't remember the cop saying anything Canadian like "eh?" or "aboot" or talking about hockey.

Then I smiled, remembering the theory he lived by: "What would the B.I.B. do?" The Super Born had brought change to Scranton more profoundly and quickly than I could have imagined possible. In a few short months, the B.I.B. had turned the police from the picketpocket highwaymen on commission we all feared to the kind of protectors we wanted them to be. Realizing all that, I think I drove more slowly and proudly home with fully functional taillights.

* * *

In the last few years—that is, before I'd met Allie—I had gotten used to waking up in unusual places, places that sometimes took me a minute or two to figure out. There was that dark morning trapped behind the sofa, waking up with a beer bottle in an unexpected orifice, and the unfortunate snuggling incident with my friend's dog. (That mutt still hasn't called.) But this one was by far the most unbelievable I had ever experienced. I sat up in bed in my new house, wondering how a guy like me could have stumbled into a place like this. It was totally amazing work on my part or maybe just some dumb luck. You know, even a blind squirrel eventually finds a pepperoni pizza (extra cheese), or whatever it is they say.

But in the sunlight of a wonderful fall morning, what amazed me most was the form of the B.I.B., the most wanted woman in America, lying in bed beside me. From years of past training, my first instinct was to get the hell out of there. But then it dawned on me that I lived here. She wanted me here, and this was no hungover Sunday morning…it was Monday.

The flight instinct quickly drained away, and a contented smile lifted my cheeks. I slowly pulled back the crisp, clean covers to reveal her lying on her side, her back and that marvelous curve from her hip to her waist—you know, that thing only women's bodies can do. Disbelief hit me again. *Flee, you asshole! Get out of there before you're found out! You don't belong here!* But I did.

I ran my fingers lightly along her hip and up to her waist, marveling at how my hand and her skin began shimmering with that molten silver glow wherever I touched. The warmth of her skin traveled up my hand and my arm and then down…to somewhere…else. My confidence grew…that too, which reminded me that I really did belong here. She stirred but did not awake, rolling over onto her back. The sight of her feminine form and smooth, exposed skin forced me to swallow hard. There was no escaping now. My goose was cooked, there was no turning back…whatever phrase you wanted to use, I had to have her and right now.

Slowly, yet totally gleefully, I drifted down between her thighs as she sighed deeply but did not awake. We glowed together for a long time while I continued wishing her a "good morning." When her moans quickened and the moonlit glow surrounding her hips pulsated wildly, I knew she was close. It was inspiring…very inspiring, almost too inspiring, if you know what I mean. When she climaxed, I knew she had gotten my message.

What? Your partner doesn't moan helplessly and shudder in your face during a five-minute orgasm that takes you up to the ceiling and through a twisting set of laps over the bed? (Glad I had the ceiling raised when I bought the house.) She lay back down in the glow with a contented smile on her face. "Good morning to you too," she said in a sleepy voice.

Then came the footsteps and the knock on the door. "Mom? Are you up?" called Paige.

The mother in Allie took over, and she was instantly alert, pulling the covers over her body. I, on the other hand, sighed in disappointment, struggling to pull the sheet over an erection I hoped Paige wouldn't notice. Lying on my side was the only answer.

"What is it, honey?" Allie said, straightening her hair.

Paige stepped warily inside the room. "Can someone drive me to school? I've got that art project due today, and it's so heavy."

I smirked. "You mean your B.I.B. statue?" I said as Allie whacked me under the covers.

"Yeah," answered Paige. "I hope the paint's dry…put on three coats last night."

"Sure, I'll take you in. Just give me some time to get ready," I answered, rubbing myself across Allie's thigh under the covers from the other side of the bed.

Allie laughed and took firm hold of me under the sheets. "Yeah, he'll be out in a minute."

As her hand spread its warmth all through me, I thought, *Just a minute?*

Paige saw the smiles on our faces, turned, and walked out the door, closing it firmly behind her. From the hallway, we heard her stop to say, "Eww, old-people sex!"

Exactly fifty-nine seconds later, I tried to muffle a surprised moan. I had never been a minuteman before, but somehow Allie had managed it. The sound made Paige "eww" all the way from the kitchen. So much for the sound-proofing package I'd bought with the house.

A few minutes later, I drifted into the kitchen, fully dressed, to find Paige with her chin in her hands staring at the B.I.B. statue she had painstakingly made. "Do you think I'll ever meet her?" she asked.

I put my hands on her shoulders reassuringly. "You know, Tiger, I have a really good feeling you will."

We'd become our own little B.I.B. support group, and it seemed as if this had made Paige's life with her mother easier as well. Who knew I could deal with children so well? Certainly not me or anyone who had ever met me…or the kids I'd pissed off in the past…or my mother. I was shocking myself left and right.

"One day soon you're going to be as close to her as I am now. She's going to smile, give you a big hug, and thank you for believing in her," I reassured Paige.

"I hope so," she said still staring at the statue. Then she turned and gave me a quick hug. "Thanks…now let's get this sucker loaded up!"

Just then Allie came into the room in her robe, smiled, and gave Paige a big hug. "Have a good day—whoa, that statue is really cool! I bet the B.I.B. would love to see that."

Paige smiled. "Yeah, it was a lot of work."

Behind us the small TV was playing the local news when a report from the national network broke in. A sober-looking middle-aged man sat at a news desk with a picture of the White House on the screen behind him. "Our Washington bureau is reporting that at 8:12 this morning a lone man wearing a bomb vest climbed over the fence of the north lawn of the White House and managed to run unchallenged toward it until he was confronted just inside the entryway. At that time the suspect detonated his vest, wounding several Secret Service officers and White House staff. Information is still incomplete, but there are reports of ten dead or injuried, including the suspect himself. Also, the White House sustained damage and broken windows from the blast. The president and the first family were not in residence at the time. It is unknown if the suspect acted alone or if this was the act of a terrorist organization. We will bring you further updates as they are available. We will now return you to your regularly scheduled program."

"Do you believe that?" I commented. "With all the heightened security these days, how does someone just run into the White House?"

Allie shook her head. "Some people just want to burn the world to the ground."

"Somebody should stop 'em," I added casting Allie a direct look.

Paige pointed a finger at the TV. "If this were Hollywood, that guy would have been shot by snipers and eaten by guard dogs the minute he dropped down from the fence, like in all the White House movies."

"Well, Paige," Allie said, "this ain't Hollywood."

"We better get you to school," I said, lifting the statue and moving toward the garage.

Allie and Paige laughed as I struggled with the statue, lightening the mood.

"Need some help?" Allie taunted me in her usual sarcastic tone.

I gave her "the look." The look I had had to develop, being the man of the house with a woman I knew could twist me into a pretzel at any time. She could have carried the statue with one finger while doing her makeup, stopping a bank robbery, and putting a loaded train back on the track with her other hand—I just had to learn to live with it.

Allie responded with a look of her own as she wobbled after me with her arms outstretched, imitating me as I carried the statue through the garage to my car. I ignored her, placing it on the floor at Paige's feet in the front seat of the car. I closed her door and then came around to join Allie in front of the car. Even if she looked matronly in her robe, I knew how hot she was underneath. I gave her a hug and a warm good-bye, I-wish-it-was-hello kiss.

"You wait for me just like this till I get back?" I whispered in her ear.

She surprised me by pulling away and shaking her head. "I have to go. The girls will be here any minute."

Since we had moved in, the house had become the base camp for the activities of the Super Born. Jennifer and Rebecca had been introduced to Paige as friends from work who hung out with Allie and worked on various charity causes, and who joined her on shopping trips and girls' nights out. We had a big garage and empty basement, both of which had become the Super Born's den.

"Oh," was my well-thought-out reply. I pulled away and turned toward the car. "Okay, then."

She pulled me back. (Believe me, when a Super Born "pulls you back," she really pulls you back.) "I may be gone a day or two," she said, almost as if an apology. "Can you take care of things...of Paige while I'm gone?"

"Of course," I answered, getting worried that she seemed so dramatic. "Where are you going?"

She lowered her eyes and shook her head. "Can't...don't wanna say. Just take care of Paige, okay? I told her we were going to New York—shopping and a show, just the girls."

Then Paige opened her door. "I would like to get to school...today!"

A hurt part of me wanted to know why I was the last to know about her leaving. I looked at Allie and saw concern in her eyes, but I had to respect her for doing what she did.

I took hold of her shoulders and squeezed as hard as I could. "Paige and I will be here waiting. You do what you have to do. There are at least three or four bars Paige and I have been wanting to hit." Then I thought about it. "Anything you wanna tell your favorite journalist about, though?"

She laughed. "Oh, is that what you are? Don't worry, I'll have a story for you. Soon. Better get this girl to school."

I looked into her eyes. "You take care."

"And you take care of Paige!" Allie instructed me. She walked over to Paige's side of the car, and Paige lowered her window. Allie reached in and gave Paige a long hug. "I'll be back in a couple days. Don't worry, and try not to give Logan too hard a time."

"I won't…much," Paige said, glancing over at me. "Have fun in New York, and say hi to Jennifer and Rebecca for me."

"Will do."

I watched Allie as I backed out of the drive. Judging from her body language and the look on her face, she was planning something new, something she had never done before, and it worried her. For a second I felt a flash of concern for her safety, until my unquestioning faith in her blew that away. However, it did bother me that she had left me out of the loop for the first time. After all, I was the front man for the Super Born group—but I knew it was useless to press her.

Apparently I watched her a little too long, because I wasn't looking where I was going and almost smacked into an approaching car while backing out of the driveway. The soccer mom in her SUV slammed on her brakes and shouted "asshole!" through her open window while her little daughter in the back flipped me the finger. I wonder where kids these days get that from. It was okay, though, as Paige and I responded with fingers of our own.

* * *

That night Paige and I had a great time. We cooked our own dinner together: pizza, of course, and she made some kind of salad-like pasta-vegetable thing. It tasted good if you put enough sugar in the dressing, which I did. It made me think back for a minute to my mother's cooking—the dry turkey, the gross shredded-chicken sandwiches, the ham I was convinced you could make shoes out of, and oh, the greasy spaghetti sauce. In comparison, this food was gourmet.

We ate our dinner in the media room in front of the big-screen TV I'd bought to fill one wall, sitting on the sofa I had bought, which was big enough for all of us to sit on together. The sales-man had separate recliners or studio chairs in mind (and a bigger commission), but for me, togetherness was sitting on the sofa, sandwiched between my superhero and her daughter. Now that's livin'!

Crap, did I just say that? Who was this clown? Maybe it was the chemically contaminated air in the new house or all the chick food. Wait, I hadn't had a beer in days. Was this what it was like to be…sober? Anyway, even with my macho side, I had to admit, watching TV and movies with Paige, cracking jokes, and just being goofy together was something that I loved about my new life. And the popcorn, don't forget the popcorn and the popcorn fights. (I'll deny all this in court, though.)

FOUR

Girls' Night Out

ALLIE

This godforsaken area of Pakistan or Afghanistan or wherever the hell Rebecca brought us looked more like the dust balls I pull out from under my refrigerator than a place people could live. The mountains were just piles of anemic dust piled on top of more dust. It covered my hiking boots, my clothes, and my hair and eyes, coated my skin, and motivated me to get the job done so I could get the hell of out here. No flashy jumpsuit here—we all wore khaki shirts, pants, and boots. All of Rebecca's information told us that the guy we were looking for and his terrorist operatives would be here after they made a run from the shelter of one of his urban hideouts to this mountain pass in the middle of nowhere. It had been my idea to come here, but I let Jennifer take the lead.

As planned, Rebecca and I positioned ourselves out of sight behind some massive rocks across a narrow stretch of land from the opening of the cave. Jennifer made the first contact by boldly walking up the slight grade to our right until she confronted the first line of men guarding the entrance. She knew she would get an immediate reaction from these conservative Muslim men— her ponytail, bare arms, and khaki shorts were not quite burqa attire. Plus, there was her open, forward attitude, marching at them alone with a confident look that said she knew she definitely looked hot. It worked: Men came out of their hiding spots, revealing themselves from out of nowhere, like moths drawn to a light—a light they planned to stone, dishonor, and mutilate. In fact, they were coming from all directions now, shouting and shaking their fists, abandoning their concealed positions, revealing their numbers. After all, what threat could a lone woman be to them? They did not even sound an alarm to alert the others who were in the nearby caves. She had clearly inspired their rage, this brazen infidel so openly challenging their laws regarding the place of women in their social structure.

Jennifer stopped and faced the opening of the main cave while Rebecca and I stayed concealed in the boulders behind her. They surrounded Jennifer—some picked up stones while others readied the butts of their AK-47 assault rifles, continuing to rant at her. I became worried for Jennifer and my muscles flexed, beginning to move, when Rebecca grabbed my arm and shook her head. I peered between the boulders.

With a slight wave of his hand, a short, bearded Muslim man gave his men permission to begin the assault on Jennifer, and then he began a slow return to the cave opening. Two men yelled at Jennifer and lunged toward her with the butts of their rifles. Instantly, with a loud thud and the sound of a massive engine whirling, a column of red lava light surrounded Jennifer, not only shielding her from their blows but sending a dozen men flying around her, who fell hard fifty feet away, cratering into the dust. The leader turned back at this and yelled to his men by the cave. They suddenly rose, each firing a rocket-propelled grenade capable of destroying a mammoth tank in Jennifer's direction. All three rockets exploded, sending up fountains of flame, which made Jennifer disappear. But when the flames died down, there she stood, laughing at them. To taunt them further, she smiled and waved. Six more men readied RPGs, leveling them at her. Now Rebecca and I joined Jennifer in the fight. At Rebecca's direction, the rockets merely popped off the end of their launchers and dropped to the ground like the cork at the end of a child's popgun.

The men stood in amazement. They were veterans who had fought both Russians and Americans. They were lethal, violent men, no strangers to combat, and yet it was clear that this experience was like nothing they had ever seen. Twenty or more men stood trying to clear their rifles, which Rebecca had turned useless. Then the fallen RPG shells' tail fins popped out, the explosives armed, and the men all leaped for cover just as the rockets exploded. That was when panic ensued, and the alarm was spread into caves and other fortifications—unfortunately for them, too late. It only took a couple of minutes for me to say "good night" to all of them. Their feeble hand-to-hand skills and small blades put up little resistance. Soon all the terrorists guarding our target were kissing the dust. Dr. Jones was right: when we supported each other, our powers were magnified, our weaknesses were covered, and we were unbeatable.

Jennifer moved to the cave opening and raised her arms, and a massive beam of searing red light shot into the cave's entrance and then bounced throughout the cave, escaping back out through every other tunnel, air shaft, or cave opening connected to the main shaft. Suddenly, the mountain was aglow with crimson beams of light shooting out into the sky. There were screams as men came running out of all the cave exits to escape the heat of Jennifer's beam, men with their clothes, beards, and unibrows smoldering. As they appeared, I flew from one opening to the next, dealing each escapee a good hammer fist. It was like that arcade game where you hit gophers with a big mallet as they pop up. I had taken Paige to play that game so many times when she was young, and now I was realizing why she thought it was so much fun.

When the gophers stopped popping out of the caves and our target still did not appear, Jennifer turned off her lava beam and joined me on a reluctant trip into the main tunnel. It was an eerie place, with the feeling of danger around every turn, and the cave walls still radiated steamy heat from her lava energy beam. Finally, we found the tall, bearded Saudi we were looking for surrounded by a group of his followers. He was staggering at the end of the main shaft, wobbling, supported by men on either side who wobbled as well. Unlike the weak minds he had sent to their deaths as suicide bombers, he seemed to have chosen staying alive rather than martyrdom.

We strode up to him, confident we had found our man. He offered no resistance, just looked at us, surprised, clearly wondering who the hell we were. He appeared too weak to resist, so I put out his smoldering beard with two fingers and in short order rendered them all unconscious. When there was no more movement in the cave, Rebecca joined us, and we quickly sorted through those we wanted to transport and those little fish that we would have to throw back for the US military to collect.

I was glad that we had accomplished our goal and could now get out of this hellhole. Rebecca multitasked preparations for our departure while notifying the military of the coordinates where they would find a large collection of America's most wanted. But Jennifer was all smiles. She seemed to get off on how little resistance these trained murderers, murderers for God (yeah, right), had offered her. She stood proudly with her hands on her hips, surveying the site. A moment later we collected those we wanted and in a flash were gone, leaving the wind to raise the dust over the fallen terrorists and their weapons.

FIVE

Anyone Want to Raise a Flag?

LOGAN

During the day, I managed to write some freelance things the new owners of the B.I.B. website wanted, as well as some pieces for the paper and a magazine that, like everyone else, wanted "the Super Born." But evenings with Paige were more fun. I soon learned, as she became open and goofy with me, that she had own unique sense of humor. I noticed that she even blew off texting and emails (maybe homework too) to spend time with me. It was an unspoken thing. We just congregated in front of the TV or into the kitchen without much fanfare, planning, or effort, or we went out to dinner at Charley's. With her mother and my B.I.B. as subject matter, there was no lack of conversation or entertainment. Paige made Allie more real for me. You could tell they had their fights and trials, but that under it all was a great affection.

Still, I didn't sleep well those nights when Allie was gone. Every couple of hours, I would look over at the flat new comforter, which was supposed to be shaped like her curves, as I drifted in and out of sleep. But this time when I awoke, it was different. My blurry eyes cleared to the image of Jennifer's wicked smiling face looming at the foot of the bed. She was totally nude, her breasts swaying as she climbed up the length of my legs on her hands and knees, and her wicked smile grew…more wicked. As she reached my waist, she stopped and sat back, looking down at me like an eagle gliding over a mouse….well, not a little mouse, a big nasty one. You know, the bad-boy type that mouse chicks dig. Then she laughed and hit me with the red then violet flash of her eyes.

I was petrified. Was she planning the old Spinderella move, the sexual position that Russian Super Born Olga Settchuoff had used to kill Dr. Jones' associate Demetri? Was this it?! I didn't run, didn't do a thing but lay there. She rose up again and came slithering down, her thighs swallowing my entire length in one fluid, easy stroke as she sighed contently, hissing, "Finally…" She continued moving in long, slow strokes and then began to pound me with intense, quickening fury. Jennifer lifted her arms up through her hair behind her head, closing her eyes with a look of ecstasy as her legs lifted off the bed and she began to spin, a move no man's equipment was made to handle for long.

I woke up, my heart pounding as I looked around at the shadowy room and the shapeless comforter beside me. I took deep breaths and calmed down, my sweaty body going cold and clammy all over. *Just a dream, thank God, just a dream*, I thought, feeling like I really had come close to the same death as Demetri. I closed my eyes, but after sliding in and out of sleep for the next few hours, wary of another visit from Jennifer, I finally realized there was no rest to be had.

The sun was just coming up as I went into the kitchen and made some coffee, amazed that there were coffee and filters right where you expected to find coffee and filters, cups right where you expected to find cups, clean ones too! I sat at the island in the kitchen tapping my fingers on the stone counter, starting to feel pathetic: me, sitting here, waiting for a woman…in my boxers. (*It's okay*, I told myself. *Paige won't be up for a couple hours*.)

Was I worried or was I pining? *Is this what they mean by pining? What the hell is pining, anyway?* I wasn't sure, but I thought that's what I had a case of, a bad one too. There was this aching hole in my chest all the friggin' time. Writing, drinking, or chillin' couldn't fill the hole. It just caved in like grains of sand, washing away like a kid's sand castle in a breaking wave, leaving this…abyss. I tell you, this caring business, this sober business, this having a purpose in life was a tricky thing that no one had warned me about. I was sure I never got the memo or a warning sheet about it. You buy a friggin' hair dryer, you get ten pages of warnings: "Don't stick this up your nose," and "electrocution hazard," etc., but caring…not a friggin' word—bubkes, zero, not even a leaflet.

* * *

Pining me and my hollow abyss grabbed the coffee when it was ready. I drifted around the kitchen and then pined my way out into the great room, staring at the sun, which was pink, orange, and rising in the front windows. Strange that this was happening when I had just gotten out of bed. Normally, I saw this sort of thing when I was getting *into* bed. Somehow, beginning my day with a "Hi, how ya doin'" from the universe seemed to make more sense. I sipped my coffee, and it actually steamed, making me feel like I was in a coffee commercial. Man in boxers contemplating the sun rising, drinking steaming coffee, pining, with an abyss in his chest and a little shrunken something sad in his boxers—now, that's a commercial. How could it fail to sell tons of Columbia's finest? (Coffee, I mean.)

I was improving my pose for the commercial when the charter bus came to a whooshing, air-brake stop at the end of the driveway in front of the house…my friggin' house! The door opened, and Rebecca emerged, wearing khaki clothes and a layer of dust. Suddenly, I heard the garage door rattling open, and Allie appeared, leading a column of men, wobbling and haggard, dressed in dusty Arab clothing, their eyes downcast—one, I noticed, much taller and wobblier than the others. She directed them onto the bus; none of them showed any signs of resistance. My coffee cup and

I watched the procession outside the window. (I think I was even more amazed than the cup, or maybe he just handled it better.) Allie stood by the bus and looked back as Jennifer shepherded the long column inside. Jennifer seemed to be enjoying her job. She'd give one terrorist an encouraging push and send him cascading into those in front of him, sort of a group nudge. When the violent killers acquiesced, she smiled.

I blinked, but just once. All this was coming from my friggin' garage? I briefly thought of running out there to find out what was happening, but remained frozen in my coffee-commercial pose (never know when Hollywood might call). Besides, the image of me displaying my hairy crack while questioning the girls just didn't seem to fit the situation. I never saw a news anchor interviewing the president while scratching his ass in boxer shorts.

As the terrorists—at least, I assumed they were terrorists—began climbing into the bus, I could see two of them becoming animated with panic. As they reached the bus, they exploded off in separate directions in an escape attempt. The B.I.B.'s arm shot out, clothes-lining one, flipping him head over heels to the ground, and Jennifer shot out a red lava beam that grabbed the other and lifted him back into line. The rest of the prisoners took notice and continued to board the bus, eagerly now, without incident.

Allie turned and saw me, a smile growing on her face. She brushed back her I-haven't-had-a-shower-in-days ponytail, said something to Jennifer, who nodded, and then ran into the garage. I meet her as she burst into the hall. She hesitated, but I didn't, wrapping her in my arms and spinning us around. I started with an intense kiss that turned lighter and more sensuous as it matured. Her kiss started off weak but then grew welcoming. We stayed together for a long moment after that with no words, just sighing, laughing, happy sounds.

After a long moment, I asked, "Is that who I think it is?"

She kept a straight face for a second or two and then smiled and nodded excitedly.

"He's supposed to be dead!"

"Come on, you really believed that burial-at-sea story?" She said putting a finger over her lips to cover a little laugh. "You still believe in the tooth fairy too?"

"Holy crap! Are you serious? The tooth fairy's not real?" That made her laugh.

Just then Rebecca burst through the door from the garage. "Not good! They don't believe me!" she said, shaking her mobile phone at Allie.

"What?" Allie turned away from me, rapidly shifting gears.

"They don't believe we have them. They think it's some publicity hoax! The plan was to get them to Washington! Now Washington doesn't want us!"

"What? Those assholes can't even find him when someone is trying to deliver him? And I voted for that dick!" Allie began to scratch her head and pace. "Yeah, but who knows us in Washington? No one. Outside of Scranton, we're a joke. Besides, the plan wasn't to have fifty of them to schlep around and feed," Allie said, continuing her tirade. "It was supposed to just be him! We go through all this, and no one believes us?"

"You can thank little Ms. Fireball for that one," Rebecca said, pointing her thumb toward Jennifer, who was standing in the driveway now. "Bringing all these terrorists here was her idea."

"Who thinks it's a hoax? The FBI?" I asked.

Rebecca nodded, giving me a quick look over. "Nice boxers," she said.

"Nice mud collection," I fired back.

"Come on, this is serious," Allie added to the fray. "Do you know anybody?" she said, turning to me. "Can you help us?"

Moi? Little old moi? I handed muddy-pants Rebecca my phone. "Get me his picture."

Rebecca nodded and turned away, but then turned back to me with a sour face. "Eww, why is it sticky?" she asked, dangling my phone from two fingers, "You ever clean…anything?" she said before turning away.

"I could say the same about you, mud ball!" I fired back after her.

"What was that colonel in Afghanistan's name? They can check our story with him," Allie added.

"Samuels," Rebecca said before running off to the bus for the picture and still dangling the phone.

I did have one contact at the local FBI office, Ed Baker. We had worked together on the racketeering case against ex-Mob boss Gregorio Gambrelli; I'd alerted Ed of Gambrelli's limo always parking in my spot being critical to the investigation, I think. Anyway, I'm certain my cutting exposé on Mob parking habits helped in some way. Then, later on, we worked on a horrific kidnapping/interstate flight/hate crimes case. (What that raccoon had done to be carried off into New Jersey like that and how they knew he was of Asian descent, I'll never know.) Somehow, every time a big case like that appeared, Ed and I were always in the thick of it. After a couple years surviving under fire in the trenches, we had formed somewhat of a bond of brothers—and a long tab at the local bar. Speaking of survival, the weekend Ed and I spent with the Nelson twins came to mind, what I remember of it. I recalled Ed saying he had finally figured out how to tell the mischievous minxes apart, a trick that I never mastered.

But when I called Ed that morning, he was pissed about being woken up. (When you're on call, it does mean that you're going to get called, okay?) Ed was the kind of young man who had ambition but was greedy and lazy, always looking for the quick score (and a free drink). I had to appeal to the gambler in him, explaining that this was big and if it hit, there would be a promotion in his immediate future. He battled inertia and then finally referred me up the ladder to the bureau chief. As it turned out, the chief was a B.I.B. Pub Crawler video-game champion whose daughter was going through a B.I.B. phase herself, and who had just seen me on the early morning network show from New York talking about the Super Born. When I told him who was sitting in a bus in front of my house and who had brought him there, I had instant credibility. (You wouldn't have wanted to be standing behind him at the time though, because I think he soiled some underwear.) When I sent him the photo Rebecca had taken and called him back, I could already hear the whirling of gears in his head. He could see himself on the evening news taking credit for it all, and he began wondering which tie he should wear...after a change of underwear.

"Put one of those Super Born on the phone—the B.I.B., preferably. I'll arrange the security, everything."

So I gave him Rebecca. I didn't like the way he figured he could just talk to my girl. Besides, she was busy...with me.

"That's right, sir, his name was Colonel Samuels. He can verify everything about the others we left behind. It's one big package for you, all tied up with a bow. You just need to take it from here," Rebecca said, heading back into the garage.

He spoke loudly enough for me to hear him through Rebecca's phone as she walked down the hall. He was asking questions about playing Pub Crawler, and Rebecca was giving him tips.

I held out my hands to Allie with open palms. "See? All done." I took her in my arms again and whispered in her ear, "Paige won't be up for another hour. Care for a few laps over the bed?"

She rubbed my thigh in a way that put me instantly at attention. "When I get back," she said, giving me a kiss. "I *really* need a back rub."

"I'll rub more than that," I said stroking her her thigh in return.

She laughed wickedly. "Maybe a back rub in the Jacuzzi. You wouldn't want me all covered in dust and sweat."

Oh yes, I would, I thought. I wasn't pining anymore. (Huh, imagine I had ever done that.) Abyss? Ancient history.

When the women had donned their costumes and I had warned Allie not to make any attempt at public speaking, reminding her of her nauseating Christmas program in third grade, the bus pulled away. I went back to the great room, picked up my cup, and assumed my coffee-commercial poise, trying to comprehend the magnitude of the story that was unfolding with the Super Born. But something else was demanding my attention. I vogued proudly in front of the living room mirror. Anyone need to hang up a coat or raise a flag? Now that's a coffee commercial.

SIX

I Am Iyla and We Are Here…Live with It

IYLA

I am Iyla Settchuoff, daughter of Olga, the famous Russian film star, model, and cosmonaut of the 1970s. Also Mommy was the World Champion Cheese Roller from 1974 to 1980. (She never lets me forget that one.) No one knew Miss Wonderful was a lousy mother who abandoned me and left me to be raised by others who had the parenting skills of rocks and bad breath. Well that's what I deserved for not being the daughter she expected…but I'm not bitter. "One day we'll rule the world together," she used to tell me. Then she'd pat me on the head like a good little dog and flash away back to her world of fame in a shiny car. She'd leave me behind with Aunt Zora, who smelled of sardines and treated her mangy dog better than me. Well, Mother dear, you can take that cheese and roll it right up…but enough for introductions.

Standing in a long, slow-moving line for US Customs was not what I had in mind after a trying flight from Moscow. There were many in my party, and each passing moment was unleashing little demons in my mind. I could hear the customs agent's thoughts as he checked the passport of Valeria, the bitchy blond in front of me whom I knew all too well. He had little mental vacations while stealing glances at her. His thoughts were so easy to hear, I wished I could turn down their excruciating volume in my head.

"Good morning," Valeria said with her thick Russian accent as he looked over her passport. She batted her gray eyes and smiled as she vogued for him.

The agent's mouth actually hung open for an instant before he returned to his businesslike demeanor. I don't want to share what he was thinking, but I can tell you it involved Valeria's backside. He glanced once more at Valeria's passport and then scanned the line waiting beyond her from that morning's flight from Moscow, shocked by the line of beautiful women. His eyes lingered on me, of course. *My god*, he thought, *Russian women are supposed to look like male weight lifters, like the ones in the Olympics, not babalicious hotties like these.* He took a deep breath and tried to steady himself. When he glanced back at me, though, I knew he had already lost control, as most men do. I may be far from the most attractive, but I am always the one drawing the most puppy eyes, as I am, how you say, unique. My short black hair with red highlights is wild and unkempt. My clothes don't always go together but are always provocative, with plenty of my glorious tattooed skin exposed at my bare midriff, shoulders, and arms. What can I say? It's a curse, just like being the daughter of a champion cheese roller.

"Good morning, welcome to the United States. Are you here for business or pleasure?" When Valeria just stared at him, uncertain how to respond, he added, "You a model, an actress, or something like that?"

Valeria looked self-conscious for a moment. "No, not model. I am here to see a man...as you say...for pleasure."

I sensed the agent twinge as she spoke, like he had never felt the full power of the word *pleasure* until he heard this foreign woman say it. Something about the way she dragged it out and played with it sent his thoughts racing so fast I could barely make them out. But then there was the part that I could make out that I didn't understand. Why did he want Valeria to bust a twerk? What is *twerk* and why did he want her to break his? And why was he interested in hiding his salami? Sometimes hearing everyone's thoughts is a curse.

"Is this Scra…Scran-tone Penns-illvonia?" Valeria asked struggling with the unfamiliar words.

"No, this is JFK International Airport, New York. You need another flight or a rental car to get to Scranton. It's not far. Boy, everyone seems to be going to Scranton these days, quite a boomtown."

"Yeeeeessss, boom, very, very bigga boom in Scrantone. This way to Scrantone?" Valeria asked, pointing to the left.

"Yes, you can get a connecting flight that way. Are all you women…together?" he asked, gesturing to the line behind her.

Valeria's face soured as she turned back to look at me and the other women from our flight. "That one," she said pointing at me, "the one with the pig nose is with me, but not the others."

Just then Demetri pushed himself into the mix, saying in his heavy Russian accent, "No, she is not with them. She is with me. Now, if you would be so kind," he added, pushing his passport into the agent's hand. "I am Demetri Zeelo, and that is a diplomatic passport. If you would be so kind as to stamp our documents so we can be on our way." There was something magnetic about Demetri's confidence that made you overlook the black, lifeless eyes that never betrayed his emotions. He was tall and thin, with graying hair. He was also ruthless, selfish, pushy, arrogant, and incorrigible. So, needless to say, I found him irresistible.

The agent handed their papers back over the counter and, in passing, felt the fiery warmth of Valeria's hand. "Welcome to the United States," he said quietly as she gave a false smile and moved on. Valeria made him feel uncertain and disoriented. The poor man broadcast his thoughts in loud waves. Suddenly he was thinking about taking "old one-eye to the optometrist." Who was that poor, vision-impaired man? And then there was the salami business again. Just how many salamis did this man have, and why did he want to hide them all?

"Next."

I stepped up to him knowing that he was the only thing standing between me and Scranton. He studied my face and papers longer than I liked, longer than I felt was necessary. Suddenly his thoughts turned to static and white noise. I struggled to tune back into him, but the thoughts of those around me were all colliding together, keeping me from finding his frequency. The middle-aged agent stared at my eyes. What was this delay? I could clearly hear Demetri's frustration and Valeria belittling the mismatched outfit I was wearing, but not the thoughts of the agent. Had he found something wrong with my faked passport? When I finally found his channel, his mind opened like a book, and I could tell for sure that he was flirting, delaying the process while he stumbled for the perfect thing to say. What a child. *Yes, my eyes are beautiful, aren't they?* I thought, sending the words deeply into the customs agent's mind.

He repeated my thoughts exactly, like a shy thirteen-year-old. "I'm sorry, I don't mean to stare, but your eyes are just beautiful," he said sheepishly.

Give me my papers; they are all in order. Wish me a good stay in your country, I thought. *Oh, and tell me how beautiful you think my hair is.*

The customs man stamped my passport. "Well, everything seems in order," he said with an overfriendly smile. He made a point of brushing my hand with his as he handed my papers back. Then he looked at me again and shook his head. "I'm really sorry, miss, I don't mean to sound forward, but your hair is just beautiful, so unique, so wild. I've never seen red streaks in black hair like that before. Most women couldn't pull off a look like that, but on you…" he said, noticing the large tattoo of vines and roses that covered my right arm. I sensed his mind swirling and his blood racing. Playing with his thoughts was so easy it made me shake my head and smile, yet it was somehow confusing. Why exactly was he thinking about "pounding the duck" or "wild monkey love"? Did he really like animals that much? "Well, have a good stay in the USA," he said.

"Thank you," I answered in my excellent English, which bore only a slight hint of my Russian upbringing. *But you can keep your salami and pull your own train*, I thought. I could feel the customs agent's eyes following me as I left, hear his longing thoughts as he stared at me swaying away from him. His imagination created a pressure I could feel in the air. I stopped for a moment, angered by the man's continued attention. Then a wicked thought entered my mind. *Is this what you want?* my thoughts asked the agent while I planted feelings and sensations in his mind. I continued on my way as the agent muffled a moan and nearly doubled over in his booth from the sudden genital release. He took several deep breaths and eventually righted himself, hoping the counter was high enough that no one would see the growing wet stain on his pants. *What am I, twelve?* he thought in disgust. *I need to get out more.*

I smiled and laughed to myself. I joined Demetri and Valeria, who waited nearby and spoke to me in our native Russian.

"What is it you find so comical, my dear?" Demetri asked, noticing my smug look.

"Just having a little fun."

"She'll ruin everything with her risky stunts! I told you not to bring her!" exploded Valeria like a hissing cat.

"You told? *You* told! Who are you to tell anyone anything!" I countered.

"Quiet, both of you," Demetri commanded in a calm, level tone that made us both pay immediate attention. "We are here to find Dr. Jones. You two can enjoy your petty bickering once the job is done. Little do I care what happens to you after that. Until then shut your mouths, or I will shut them for you."

I could tell by his thoughts that he meant every word he said. So I became quiet and followed them down the concourse. Behind me I could hear the agent welcome his next visitor.

"Is this Scrantone?" asked another tall Russian beauty with a welcoming smile and luminous gray eyes.

SEVEN

Jones Gets the Bad News and I Get Some Roomies

LOGAN

I was still smiling when the girls returned home. When they arrived under the radar in Rebecca's low-key economy car, I had a lavish lunch ready for them. (Takeout, of course, which I had brought in from the outside, so maybe it was really take-in.) Anyway, I put it on the plates, and to show you just how pussy whipped I've become, I even put out silverware, glasses, and napkins—not paper towels I'd torn off, but napkins. Knowing how Super Born can eat—and hoping to get a bite to eat too—I ordered six large pizzas, two family spaghetti dinners with salads and garlic bread, four roasted chickens, five pounds of mashed potatoes with gravy, four pounds of corn, four apple pies, and a case of guilt-relieving Diet Coke. Not that it did me much good; before long, they'd polished it all off, and when Allie started nibbling on my plate, I was forced to go out to grab a quick burger for myself. When I returned and they asked me where I'd been, Jennifer asked, "Did you get us anything?" The three of them split my burger, but I got the fries—some of them.

After they had their fill, Jennifer crashed in one of the spare bedrooms. Rebecca never made it beyond our couch in the great room. And I kept my promise to the B.I.B. and gave her a back rub in the

Jacuzzi. She nearly fell asleep, but her contented sighs and moans were great to hear. Hey, I still had my imagination, the feel of her soft skin beneath my hands…yada yada.

I got her into bed and watched her slowly drift off to sleep. Somehow, this woman who had just out-dueled an army of violent terrorists seemed almost childlike to my eyes as she nestled into her pillow. It made me wonder if my image of her was dangerously naïve. But seeing her contented face put a quick end to that.

I knew she was exhausted, but I was far from it. I crept into the great room, sat in my recliner, and began to consider how I would cover their story. It wasn't long before I intercepted Paige when she came home, warming her up some Chinese leftovers the girls had somehow missed, and asked her to text without any loud editorial comments. While the Super Born slept, Paige and I watched a movie in the media room. Paige did have to run to the great room and pile some pillows over Rebecca's head, though, when she started to snore. A half hour later, she added another layer, to no avail. Later, after Paige drifted off to her room, my phone chimed with the caller ID identifying Dr. Jones.

"Yeah?"

"I'm at the Banshee," Jones said in an uninspired monotone.

"Oh yeah, ladies' night. Having any luck? Not!"

"I need to speak with you in person. You got a few minutes?"

"I just sat down," I complained.

"Please?"

I sighed and shook my head at the thought of expending the energy necessary to move from my comfortable spot. I would rather be dealing with the swirling thoughts in my mind than Jones' problems. "Okay, give me twenty minutes," I said in resignation. Why am I such a schmuck?

* * *

"Super Bowl? What the fuck are you talking about? It's October! I thought you wanted to party!" said the short brunet with long hair wearing half a dress and way too much jewelry. "Whatever…" she said, stalking away with her pink drink.

Dr. Jones stammered, "But I meant Super Born…" He appeared frustrated, like he couldn't believe his reliable pickup banter had failed him here at the Banshee, his never-miss hunting ground. "I'm a fucking PhD, goddamn it!"

"Strike out, did ya?" I asked, amused as I approached and sat in the booth across from him.

"I had already added her to my panty collection," he said before dropping his chin into his palm. "Red lace, I'm certain," he said whimsically. "But now her thong and heart-shaped behind are swaying away toward that tall guy," he said pointing. Then he shook his head, "This cannot be happening. Three times I have been rejected already. How can this be? And where the hell did all these tall guys come from?"

"It happens," I said slapping him on the shoulder. "Not to me, but it happens. So, what's up, big guy? What did you call me about? I don't have much time. The girls have something big brewing."

Jones looked at me in shock and dismay. Even in the dim light of the Banshee, I could see his pupils looked large and black behind his thick glasses. "What did I call you about! What did I call you about! You see that hot brunet over there?"

"The slutty one with the tall guy? Nice choice."

"Well, she just blew me off, and not in a good way. And that one," he said, pointing to a tall blond vixen, "and that one," he said, indicating a slightly overweight but extremely friendly looking blond lying back in her seat with her face raised to the sky and eyes smiling. She was either visiting her gynecologist in a back booth or being pleasured by someone under the table.

"Happens to the best of us. What's your problem?" I don't know why I am so sensitive and reassuring. It's a curse.

"To you, maybe," he said, pointing at me, "but not to the Jonester!"

"Jonester? Fucking Jonester? That the best you got?"

"You don't understand! This cannot happen! I have scored here like a pinball machine ever since I came to this town! Never once," he said, holding up an emphatic finger, "have I failed. And it's ladies' night, goddamn it!"

I had the answer but wasn't sure if I had the heart to give it to him. I patted him on the shoulder. "What are you drinking?"

"How about cyanide, and make it a double!"

"Don't move," I said before disappearing into the frothy mob. God, I hate battling for a bartender's attention on a busy night. It was like you had to know someone to get a friggin' beer around here, and I knew the B.I.B., for Christ's sake. After four shouts and waving arms had failed to get a bartender's attention, I tried a different approach. At a small table behind me, a couple had just been delivered two beers. I slipped by in the mob, left a ten, and took the two Miner's. Those two, I figured, would never miss their beers. They hadn't even touched them yet, too busy touching something else, if you know what I mean. I returned to our booth and put the two Miner's down on the table.

"So what is it that is going on with me, my friend? At my apartment you said I would find out. Find out what?"

I took a long sip of my beer and then spun the bottle. "You've been marked."

"So you have said. Just what the fuck does that mean?" said Jones, more disturbed than I had ever seen him.

"Remember how I told you that Allie, Rebecca, and Jennifer had all marked you and you now had to share your research with them?"

Jones paused. "You were serious about that?"

I looked at him, surprised I had failed to impress that point on him, shook my head, and laughed a knowing little laugh. "Dead serious. If you don't give them what they want, they'll have no reason to keep you around. "

"But I'm a new man. I haven't considered world domination for...days."

"Believe me, Rebecca is still pissed, and I've seen that little sweetheart off five people already. You should see the nasty bastards she caught today."

Jones swallowed hard. His night just kept getting worse.

I didn't know what to say, so I looked Jones in the eye and tried to be honest. "I was marked by the B.I.B. last January, and I didn't have sex again until I met her in July."

Again Jones' Adam's apple made a long descent, his face crumbling like I had just told him that he had been given a life sentence in prison. "So that is why..." he said, his eyes drifting off to look longingly at the lovely group of women at the next table.

"Yeah, that's why you can't score. But it gets worse—they own your sexuality. They're the only ones you can do it with, and just to remind you, they don't want you."

Jones' eyes opened wide and his mouth dropped. "Holy crap!"

"You better believe it. You, my friend, are forlorn on the prairie."

"The prairie?"

I nodded. "The friggin' prairie! A place where everything is terrible! Forlorn, maybe even five-lorn."

Jones took one last look at the women at the next table, lowered his head, and began to cry like a little girl.

I wanted to be sensitive and all that, but my eyes were drawn to the large TV that hung over the bar, caught by a flashing image above the title: *FBI Headquarters, Scranton, PA.* A short video clip ran of a charter bus—my friggin' charter bus—pulling into an underground parking facility, and then a minute later, the blurred image of something flew out of the garage and was gone. Following that was a large mug shot of the tall man on the bus—withered, haggard, but still beaming evil out of his defiant, dead eyes. Everyone in the bar cheered and clanged glasses or bottles with their neighbors, whether they knew them or not.

Then came the image I'd expected of the Scranton FBI chief standing at a podium with a blue curtain and the FBI seal behind him, taking credit for the day's events, the apprehension of "fifty top terrorists," he called them. I was glad to see he'd chosen the conservative blue tie. Somewhere in Washington, someone who had turned our delivery down was hitting his head against the wall repeatedly or being given a new asshole by his boss—ex-boss, probably—for not having accepted the Super Born's offer.

I smiled, not so much because of the event, which was cool, but because of the effect it would have on the people in Scranton and the town itself. All this was happening in Scranton because of Scranton's superhero protectors. It was like a dream, like a town winning the Super Bowl every other day (with one day in between to party). The bar was packed, and you could feel the life in the air, the confidence, the smell of optimism mixing with the smell of spilled beer, a little vomit, and the fragrance of something else. (It wasn't me this time.)

After I had finished consoling Jones and tried to leave, I got wedged into a group of merry people leaving the bar. The next thing I knew, I was part of a giant conga line that joyously wove its way through downtown. Public celebration had become commonplace in the new Scranton, with everyone offering you a beer. I couldn't be rude. Needless to say, it was late when I finally got home and quietly slipped my key into the lock. I tiptoed into the great room to find Rebecca still snoring on the couch with her laptop and phone on the coffee table beside her, flashing away. I crept up to her computer to see what looked like an official Russian government website, from which files were downloading. Apparently, Rebecca and her machine friends had spliced into a secure website, having found something of interest. The girl never stopped multitasking, even when she was asleep and snoring like a pro.

Then I crept into the media room to find Paige asleep on the sofa before the widescreen TV, her phone still nestled in her fingers, showing a half-completed text. I covered her with a blanket and clicked off the TV, whispering, "Good night, tiger."

I was checking in on Allie when I heard one scream and then another coming from the first guest room down the hall on the other side of the great room. I bolted down the corridor...okay, I was apprehensive at first, so maybe it wasn't an actual official bolt, but it was boltish. When I got to the guest room, the image I saw froze me just inside the doorway: Jennifer sat up against the headboard screaming with a terrified look on her face. Floating above her over the bed was a flashing red energy storm sparking and hissing like a broken high voltage line. A red flash of energy lashed out of the storm and threw Jennifer out of the bed to the floor. Then another bolt of red lightning picked her up and tossed her against the wall, flattening her face into it.

I stood helplessly, not knowing what to do. I shouted something stupid like, "Jennifer, are you okay?" when obviously she wasn't. But somehow it did the trick. The red storm flickered and then faded away slowly until the flashes and humming were gone. I waited for a second—better safe than sorry—before I found Jennifer's dark form in the corner and knelt down beside her. She was shivering and sobbing uncontrollably, dressed in one of my oversized B.I.B. T-shirts, which she'd apparently lifted from my closet, and nothing else.

"Jennifer, are you okay?" I repeated.

She leaped into my lap like a small, frightened child and wrapped her arms around me so tightly it hurt. She shivered and blubbered without making any coherent sounds, burying her face in my chest. So I wrapped my arms around her and waited for her to calm down. Eventually she stopped sobbing and began taking deep breaths. Finally, she lifted her head and looked up at me with a faraway expression on her face.

"They came at night just after we'd had dinner—two escaped lifers, desperate men with nothing left to lose. I was just sixteen. I came down the stairs just in time to see it happen. My dad was the first to go. He had no idea what was happening. He was such a good man—how could he know? I screamed as I watched him drop to the kitchen floor in a red puddle. The two men turned their attention to me and smiled. One thug took hold of my arm. I remember his horrible, rancid breath. He said, 'Lookie what we have here.' He dragged me through the living room into my parents' bedroom. When I resisted, he slapped me across the face so hard I saw stars. When my mother screamed and tried to stop them, she was the next to go. They tied me to the bed and took turns with me. Men are such fucking bastards."

As I listened to her speak, images of newspaper articles I had seen of men found tied to beds claiming to be sexually abused by a beautiful woman flashed through my mind. It suddenly made sense. And another connection occurred to me: the red storm that had drifted over her bed reminded me of the bolts of crimson energy Jennifer had used to defeat Jones' Super Born. It made me wonder if she had turned them on herself.

"I listened to them talking in the living room. They just ignored my parents lying on the floor around them like trash. I tugged and twisted on the ropes holding my arms, then finally began pulling my right hand loose. It got so close, but wouldn't come free until I heard the pop of my thumb dislocating. See," she said, holding her hand out for me to see.

I nodded. "Yeah, that looks messed up," I said, wondering why she wanted me to hear this story, feeling amazed at what a different person she seemed now, crumpled in my lap.

"My hand's still not right. One of the bastards was busy dousing the house with a can of gas they'd found in our garage while the other was out starting our car. I took my dad's softball bat from the corner and crept into the living room behind the one spreading the gas. The first blow made him look around, trying to figure out who hit him. After the second blow, he would never be able to look at anyone again."

I ran my hand over her hair. "My God, what you went through."

Her next words brought a savage look to her face. "The second thug came running through the kitchen into the living room when I struck. I remember his saying, 'We have to gooooooo,' just when I clobbered him in his chest. The word *go* seemed to last forever. I think the next uppercut swing finished him, but it didn't make me stop. He'd killed my dad, the slimy bastard. He got what he deserved. When my muscles burned and I couldn't lift the bat one more time, I finally stopped."

Her face seemed to soften, and I tightened my arms around her in an attempt to be empathetic. I thought her story was over, so I tried to think of what a normal person would say after hearing something like that. (Of course, normal was a stretch for me.)

But then her eyes went blank. "What was left of him lay beside my dad. I dropped to my knees and then fell over my father's body. But when I felt that rigid mass, it scared me. This was not my dad anymore. After a minute, I lit the match myself and watched the gas erupt in front of me and spread like a wind of fire."

"My God," I erupted involuntarily.

She took a deep breath and paused. "I don't remember, but I was told a fireman carried me out just before the house collapsed. Now and then the memories come back to haunt me, and I live it over again—every time, it seems so real. I feel better knowing you understand what I'm dealing with every day. "

She got up, seeming calmer now, and began pacing beside the bed.

I stood up too and gestured to the spot where the energy storm had been. "That? That was a nightmare?"

She took a moment and then turned to me and tapped her chest. "No, I'm the nightmare."

I reached out to console her, thinking she'd want some support, but she pushed me away. It was the first time I realized the Super Born were not in complete control and their powers might not be benevolent. I remembered all the people I'd seen Rebecca vaporize and these additional people I now knew Jennifer had offed and tried to reconcile my warm feeling for the Super Born with their apparent realities. I thought of Allie lying safe in her bed and wondered if she truly was. "You're not the nightmare. You're the victim," I said, trying to be supportive, and this time I think I was.

"How's that for my survey, Tom?" she asked, referring to the fake psychological survey I had used as a way of originally meeting her.

"Yeah, you never did turn in that survey. We only finished a few questions."

"You see why?" She sat on the bed and seemed to be regaining her composure.

"You okay?"

"Yeah, peachy."

"Is there anything I can get you? Some water? Quart of bourbon?"

"I wish you could help me sleep," she said, rubbing her hands over her hair and down over her face, giving me a wicked look. "Maybe a back rub, foot massage…or you could rub somewhere else. I'm sure it would help." Then when I failed to leap at the offer, her face soured. "Oh, I forgot, you belong to Miss Goody-Two-shoes."

I said nothing, though her offer sent a tingle from my head to my toes…and a few places in between. "Good night, then," I said, turning to leave. "I'll just keep the bourbon for myself."

"You do that. Logan, thanks for being there for me tonight," she said almost sweetly.

"No problem."

"Don't ever fucking do it again," she added without the hint of a joke.

I smiled and left, knowing she was back to being herself. I slid back into the dark hallway as I heard Jennifer plop down on the bed and mumble "fuck" into her pillow. I had no way of knowing then that my exit had been watched by Paige as she stood one-eyeing me from the doorway of the media room.

* * *

The next morning when I awoke, my hand found a rumpled sheet where Allie's chest should have been. Right—you can imagine the disappointment of that hand.

I got out of bed, slipped on a B.I.B. T-shirt and jeans, and went out to find the real thing. All I had to do was follow the drone of conversation to the kitchen. Allie was sipping a mug of joe with both hands while she leaned against the stove, doing her best to avoid the nook where Jennifer and Rebecca were seated. Paige was there too, dumping an empty yogurt cup in the trash and grabbing her backpack for school. The conversation I had heard was coming from the breakfast nook, which was located behind the kitchen. Outside the tall glass walls of the nook, the sun shone and birds merrily chirped. Inside the nook, Rebecca and Jennifer sat at the table embroiled in what appeared to be a heated discussion.

"Hey, tiger, you need a lift to school?" I beamed at Paige way too broadly for the early hour.

Paige just kept her head down and passed me, mumbling, "No, Kelly's pickin' me up."

I moved over to Allie and gestured to Paige as she disappeared to answer Kelly's honking car horn in the drive. "What's with her?"

Allie took a sip from her mug, "I don't know, hormones."

I gestured to the commotion in the breakfast nook. "What's with them?"

Allie took another sip, "I don't know, hormones—sounds philosophical, though. I heard something about the underprivileged, something about the man, and several fuck yous."

"Sounds like Karl Marx meets Freud. You get a good night's rest?"

"Ohhh, I slept like a log!"

"You slept well?"

"No, that thing of yours was like a log in my back."

"Oh, sorry. I guess I was just glad to have you home."

She smiled, put down her mug, and locked those gray peepers on me. "Well, maybe when the debate is over and they leave, you could show me how glad."

"Allie, could you come in here, please?" boomed Jennifer in an authoritative, businesslike voice.

"Duty calls," she said, waving her hand for me to leave. "You'd better go. Girl talk, ya know."

I nodded, took a few steps to convince her I was gone, and then doubled back, curious what they were up to. (Hey, I was part of the team too. How could I give them good press if I was out of the loop?) I peered out from behind the cabinets that separated the kitchen from the nook. The three of them sat around the table in their T-shirts, robes, and pajamas, with unkempt hair, looking more like teenagers at a sleepover than powerful superwomen.

Jennifer began by saying, "Allie, Rebecca and I have been talking. The Afghan operation proved how well we could work together and how much more effective we are as a team. But we can't stop there. We need to move to the next level."

"I think that's true," Allie agreed.

"I think we should take what we've done in Scranton and move on, geographically. Maybe go to New York next," continued Jennifer.

"What do you mean, 'what we've done'?" Allie asked.

"Don't you read? Isn't it obvious? Scranton is a boomtown. Everybody wants to be part of it. Organized crime is all but gone. Real estate values are skyrocketing. Just look at this house we're in. This whole neighborhood didn't exist a year ago," Jennifer said, leaning in Allie's direction.

Rebecca chimed in, saying, "And it's all because of us. The cops help people. The city has a budget surplus. We used to have First Friday celebrations; now we celebrate First Every Day. The downtown is alive. Remember when the comedy club was only open on weekends? People used to joke that no one in Scranton laughs on weekdays. Now that place is open every day, featuring some big-name acts. We made that happen."

"First we end fear and crime in New York, then maybe Philly, then the whole country!" Jennifer glowed.

"The three of us, taking on all the evils in the country?" Allie asked suspiciously.

"The fucking world! We have these powers for a reason. Let's use 'em," Jennifer exclaimed.

Rebecca began shaking her head. "See, that's where Jennifer and I disagree. That's why we wanted to talk with you, Allie. Remember, you said you wanted to use our powers to create opportunities for everyone and promote world peace? I believe in cooperation, whereas Jennifer believes in confrontation. She wants us to go head to head with anyone who makes the world a lousy place. I think we should stay here and create things that will make the whole world a better place."

"Things?" asked Allie, folding her legs under her as she sat in the chair.

Rebecca's eyes glowed as if she was holding a winning lottery ticket. "I've been working on some ideas. I've done some computer modeling for some really low-cost energy projects that could make cheap, clean power available to everyone, even in the Third World. We could connect everyone around the globe to the internet, so we would all have the same educational opportunities and the benefits of knowledge. We could jumpstart the entire world economically, philosophically, and educationally! It would be a massive leap in globalization!"

"Do you have any idea how much all that would cost? It sounds like the infrastructure alone would be staggering. Where would we get money like that?" Allie asked.

Rebecca glanced over at Jennifer, who folded her arms and huffed. "Jennifer could get us started. She's just being a ...she's just being difficult." Rebecca turned her laptop toward Allie (and me) and rotated a 3D model on the screen. "We start with a fluid disk generator. It looks like a wind turbine, but the gear reducer and generator are replaced by these magnetic disks. The result is that it will turn even in a slow wind while current turbines would be standing still. You can make them any size you want, put them anywhere, and cheaply." Before I'd made much sense of the first image, Rebecca flashed more of them across her laptop, growing more excited as she spoke. "Here: cheap printed solar cells that are 50 percent efficient, as compared to 20 percent efficient, which is what you get with the most expensive cells on the market today. You could wrap these puppies around anything. And how about broadcast power? Imagine electrical power all around you, just like Wi-Fi is now. Can you imagine driving an electric car that never needs to recharge? It would take in the power it needs to run from the air, just like your laptop takes in Wi-Fi! We build this all here in Scranton!"

Jennifer stood incredulously with her hands on her hips. "You do know my money is in oil, right? Why would I want to support things that will put me out of business?"

Rebecca leaned strongly toward Jennifer. "Oil is just the way you make money. You have no attachment to it. What does it matter if you make money on oil or on selling kumquats as long as you make money? You'll get your investment back and then some. Then we use that money to do more!"

"I don't know, Jenny, I kind of like it," Allie mused.

"You would!" Jennifer shot back.

Allie stood and stepped toward Jennifer. "It makes sense. Rather than fight all that riffraff in New York or wherever…you know, the mob almost killed me. What we did in Afghanistan was good for morale, but it did nothing to stop terrorism. The only way to make a hopeless suicide bomber value his life and others is to offer him a future. Only the terrorists can stop being terrorists. No matter how many we arrest, there will always be more, until the roots that spawn them are gone. That's why I don't think confrontation works,

Jenny. You get rid of one bad guy, and up pops another. Why don't we try building things to make everyone's life better right here in Scranton? No one will get us here. That would create even more jobs in Scranton. Scranton becomes our shining model to the world. Rebecca, you're the engineer. Jennifer, you're the moneybags. And me, I'm the ...what?"

"The only one of us that's getting laid," Jennifer said in a snide tone.

Allie smiled and let out a short laugh."What, am I supposed to feel guilty?"

From behind the cabinets, I smiled at Allie's comment and Jennifer's jealousy...of me, of course. I had to hope none of them heard my little chuckle.

Rebecca entered the fray. "What's so special about him anyway?"

"We're in love," Allie said.

"Love?" challenged Jennifer.

"He's a good guy and all...I just don't get it," Rebecca said, shaking her head.

"Oh yeah?" Allie chuckled. "I do."

"Someone who loves you *and* sex? You're disgusting!" Jennifer said turning away from Allie.

"No, really?" Rebecca said. "I broke my fiancé. He still won't talk to me."

Jennifer raised her hand. "Broke about forty...maybe sixty.... Then there was last month."

Allie laughed. "I broke one. That was enough."

"When you two do it, he keeps it up for you? You don't break him?" asked Rebecca in disbelief.

"Just about every night. You ever orgasm for an hour? It's just soooo exhausting," Allie said with a hand to her forehead, feigning weariness.

Jennifer and Rebecca stared at Allie and, at the same time, blinked.

"You ever melt into the warmth of your partner and merge together like you were a single pool of consciousness?" said Allie, looking back and forth between them.

Jennifer and Rebecca looked at each other. "You're messin' with us, right?" Rebecca asked after a moment.

"How does he do that for you?" asked Jennifer seriously.

"Yeah, you could at least share the secret with us," Rebecca said.

"Or maybe you could share him," Jennifer added.

I had to cover my mouth to prevent them from hearing me snort.

Allie shook her head. "I don't know, and I'm not asking. And no, I'm not sharing. All I know is, I'm on a wave and I'm ridin' it," she said, making a scooping, wave-like motion with her hand.

Rebecca shook her head. "Yeah, I'll bet you're ridin' it."

Jennifer decided to change the subject, which was clearly frustrating her. "Well, it looks like I'm outvoted, then. We try Rebecca's plan. I'll get an LLC set up and fund the bank account. I can get you one of my procurement people and an assistant to help you get a prototype built. We have a 3D printer in the R&D department. You'll have to hire your own engineering staff to clean up behind you and try to keep up. There's space in my…the company's building on the eighth floor that you can start in."

"I'd like Allie to work with me, run the office, and make sure things get done," added Rebecca.

"Sure, you may need me to fly out and get coffee," Allie joked.

"Or fly a wind turbine to Uganda. With our powers, this whole thing could happen super fast. We could give this all to everyone."

"Give? Did you say give!" Jennifer said in dismay. "I'm a freakin' businesswoman. I don't give!"

Both Rebecca and Allie laughed. "You are such a bitch!" Rebecca said.

"I'm just being real," said Jennifer pacing. "I don't do half-assed. If we're gonna change the world, it's gonna take a lot more than hour-long orgasms," Jennifer added, pointing at Allie.

"I don't know. They work for me," Allie said. I still couldn't see her face, but I could hear the smile in her voice.

"Hey, I just thought of something," Rebecca said. "What about Dr. Jones? We haven't heard a word from that little bastard. If we go off doing this, we're going to make ourselves vulnerable. Who's got our back? He's supposed to be helping us."

"Actually, maybe he can help us with the tech. He's supposed to be a some kind of scientific genius," Allie added.

"Yeah, right. What about the things he's done that weren't so genius?" Rebecca fired back.

"I'll get Logan to talk with him, see where he's at," said Allie.

"Don't tell Logan what we're planning—that way, we won't have to worry about him telling Jones," Jennifer instructed Allie, who saluted sarcastically.

Rebecca stopped for a second, thinking. "We need to know what that little bastard's up to."

From behind the cabinet I smiled, then quickly beat feet when the women got up to leave.

EIGHT

What That Little Bastard's Up To

LOGAN

"Hey, dude, the girls asked me to find out how it's going with you. Any progress on the Super Born research?" I asked Jones when I corralled him in his apartment.

"What? Do I look like someone who gives a shit what they want?" he answered in a monotone as he sat slouched on his couch with his feet up, watching TV. On the big screen was a reality show about housewives living in Miami. He wore a T-shirt that said *E=MC... Who the F__k Cares* and was covered with stains and crumbs—the attire of a disillusioned geek. His hair was two or three days past a shower, and he seemed to have developed a small beer belly. He just lay there, zombie-like, picking peanuts out of a can that sat on his stomach and launching them indifferently at his semiopen mouth. Most of the nuts bounced off his nose or face and onto his shirt or the sofa.

"What is wrong with you, man?"

"Wait, wait—April is about to confront Amanda about the pool boy!"

"What?"

"Yes, my friend, I have been watching this TV marathon. April found out that Amanda's sister had the Cuban pool boy, Estefan, clean her pipes, and Amanda knew about it but couldn't tell April because of her husband selling the illegal bonds to April's sister's ex-boyfriend. You know, the one with Mob connections from the real estate deal that went bad—April's brother lost all the money and couldn't pay the drug dealer back."

"What do I care about illegal bonds? Wait, those were illegal?"

"Oh yes, but April is married to Anthony, the banker who holds Christine's mortgage and could ruin the condo deal. Also, I haven't seen his first two wives since the first season. I think he might have done away with them."

"The whereabouts of his wives? That's the great mystery?"

"This I need to see. Also, what kind of salmon they will have at the dinner with the neighbors, who currently—"

"Okay, okay! Enough! I understand that you're going through a hard time these days, what with not being able to get laid anymore. But you've got to pull it together here." I reached for the remote, but he held it away from me. I lunged for it, snatched it away from him, and turned off the set. Jones didn't seem to react. But then his hand slipped into a crack between the cushions of the couch, and he turned the TV back on with a second remote. I turned the set back off, and he quickly clicked it back on. We volleyed back and forth with the dueling remotes for a few seconds before I went after the second remote and plucked it from his hand. "Come on now, man! This is too much. Just look at yourself. Are you gonna just fall apart just because you lost a little female companionship?"

"No, I am falling apart because I lost a lot of female companionship, a lot lot…lot," he said, beginning to blubber at the sight of a lace bra under a nearby chair.

I bent down and got in his face. "This isn't the Jones I know. Remember when you had superwomen under your command? Remember when you tried to kill me, the B.I.B., and Jennifer? Hell, you had Rebecca tied up in energy bands."

"Yes, yes, the good ol' days," Jones said, smiling and slowly nodding. But when he caught sight of the bra again, his head dropped. "But I am not that man anymore."

"That's a good thing. Otherwise, I'd have to kick you square in the nuts right now. This gives you have a chance to be a better Jones."

Jones leaned back on the sofa and interlaced his hands behind his head."Let me think, what kind of Jones is better than someone with superwomen under his control, who scores like a pinball machine, with a big, growing…trust fund? Hmmmm, let me think."

"You, the you right here!"

Jones looked at me incredulously. "What are you, on crack?"

"That evil stuff is not you!"

"It's not?"

"No, you are a scientist. You're a frickin' genius. Who else could come up with a way to control women who are strong enough to tear a man in half?"

Jones thought for a moment and then feebly pointed a finger at himself. "Me?"

"That's right, you! Who else could put together the epsilon radiation contamination with all the things that happened here and in Russia, calculate the peak of the occurrence to coincide with the Super Bowl halftime that year, and then go out and find the women to prove his theory? Along the way betraying his best friend and causing a couple deaths, but hey, you can't make a salad without breaking a few eggs."

"Salad?"

"Ok, maybe not a salad, but something with eggs in it. And the guy who did all that stuff was you! Now you have the chance to help these women change the world for the better. Believe me, they have big plans, and they want you to be part of it!"

Jones again feebly pointed at himself.

"Yes, you. Alone, you were each powerful, but you were fumbling in the dark. Working together, you'll be like the power of the sun focused in a laser beam."

Jones began to tap his finger to his lips, "Ouch, that would be an incredible number of joules and could warp the space-time continuum."

"I was just trying to show you that together, you and these women can do anything."

Jones sat up, and a few peanuts rolled off his shirt. "If it were a plasma laser and we had sufficient megavoltage to counteract the Doppler effect of multiphase frequencies of photon variance…"

I grabbed him by the shoulders. "Hey, forget the laser-beam analogy. Focus, focus."

Jones' distant gaze seemed to return to the present.

"You okay?"

"You know, my friend, you are right. I am a genius, and with this very important, very big project, whatever it is, the entire world will know!" he said, standing up and releasing a shower of peanuts to the ground. "And maybe now Mom will stop hounding me."

"That's the spirit! Come on. You go clean up, I'll take you to lunch, your treat, and we'll figure this whole thing out."

"Yes. Who your daddy is! I am the man!"

"You're the man! Who's the man? You are!"

Jones' chest puffed out, and he strode proudly across the room to the hall on his way to the bathroom. Unfortunately, his march was halted by the sight of a fluorescent pink dildo on top of a stack of books in the hall. He stopped for a second.

"Forget it! You're the man!" My encouragement got him moving again, but in the distance, I heard him whimper.

I sat amongst the peanuts on the sofa and turned on the TV. Almost immediately, the reality program was interrupted by a news broadcast. Dramatic music played over the network logo before a news anchor, whose tight face showed her love for plastic surgery, appeared in the center of the screen.

"Good afternoon. We've received news today of a terrorist attack in Ottawa, Canada. A man and a woman wearing suicide bomber vests entered the Parliament Hill building while both the Senate and Commons were in session. The female bomber detonated her vest in the building's lobby while the male bomber managed to enter the Commons chambers before detonating. Numerous injuries are reported, including several elected officials and members of the Canadian Mounted Police. There is no information at this time concerning the bombers themselves."

I shook my head. *What a crazy world*, I thought. *Somebody should stop all this.*

* * *

My damage-control lunch seemed to get Jones back on track. After joking and talking with me, he seemed like the same old Jones I had met months ago. By the end, he was revealing ideas concerning the Super Born based on blood tests he had begun conducting on his other Super Born. All seemed to be going well until we returned to his apartment.

As Jones stopped at the door and fumbled for his key, his eyes fixed on the knocker. He stared for a moment and then jumped, dropping his keys. "Did you see that?"

"Yeah, it looked like you dropped your keys."

"There it is again!"

"What are you talking about?"

Jones turned to me with wide eyes. "I saw Demetri's face right there on the door!"

"Demetri, your dead colleague? The one who got Spinderella-ed to death?"

"The very same! Huh, now it's gone," he said, cautiously running his hand over the door. Then he turned to me. "Did you see the door?"

I looked blankly the door. "It could use a little paint."

"Don't you be joking with me. There is some really weird shit going on," Jones said, picking up the keys. He checked the door again and then finally opened it. We had only taken a few steps inside when we heard the jingling of keys coming from the living room. Jones and I looked at each other, and then Jones leaned into me. "It could be dangerous. Perhaps you should go first."

I shook my head, trying to act cool and unaffected. I took two steps toward the living room and then pulled Jones ahead of me. The entire living room was filled with gray clouds of smoke, but we could hear the jingling and see a bit of shadowy movement in the corner.

"Who's there? I must be warning you I have my friend with me...black-belt friend...ex Marine-type guy. Who's there?" Jones asked, squeaking a bit.

"You knew me as Demetri," bellowed a voice in the corner in a thick Russian accent.

"Dead Demetri? Speak words of comfort to me, Demetri!"

"I have none to give."

Jones began to lose it. "What do you want? Am I going to be visited by more ghosts? It's not even Christmas. You're dead, dead as doornail!"

The shadowy shape slowly moved toward us from the far corner of the room accompanied by the metallic jingling. "You doubt your own eyes?"

"Things affect them. You could be a blot of mustard or a bad chili fry!"

We heard a cough in the corner and then another, followed by the sound of windows sliding open. Then there was a horrible, rasping cough. The room began to clear, and we could finally see a figure in the corner. "Damn Russian cigarettes. They'll be the death of me," said Demetri.

Jones' fear drained out of him. "Demetri! I thought you were dead!"

Demetri took a deep breath, still coughing a bit, and then straightened up and smiled. "As you can see, I exaggerated...a little. I needed to be dead for a while, so I planted those emails myself. None of my dear friends bothered to come to my funeral—which, not coincidentally, featured a closed casket. Technology—everyone believes in it more than their own eyes. I noticed you, Dr. Jones, were among those who did not attend."

Jones turned sheepish and looked down at his feet."What can I say? It was Two-for-Tuesday at the Banshee—but I did mourn." Then he looked up. "I did mourn you, Demetri, for days!"

Demetri smirked a crooked smile. "How deeply I am touched. Believe me, you find out who your true friends are when you're dead. Who is this ex-Marine black-belt friend of yours?" Demetri paced up close and sized me up with emotionless eyes. I couldn't tell if he was friendly or a rattlesnake ready to strike.

"Oh, this is Logan. He is working with me on the Super Born project."

"Indeed? We are calling these female freaks of nature Super Born now? I see your attitude has changed a bit in my absence."

"Well, you were tough to reach when you were dead," said Jones timidly. Then he paused and looked up at him with a new energy. "Demetri, a lot has happened since we last spoke."

"So I have heard," Demetri said, slowly pacing away from me back toward the corner with a large set of keys jingling as they hung from his belt. "So I have heard." He thought for a moment and then paced back to stand in front of Jones. "A lot has changed for me as well. I would love to discuss it with you in detail." Then he turned to me. His gaze felt like a hand pushing me out the door. "In private."

Jones took a deep breath and put his hands on his hips. "Oh, yes, well, whatever you want to discuss, you can talk about in front of Logan. We are like partners."

Demetri paced slowly in front of me with his hands clasped behind his back like a professor. "Indeed, you should know how much I hate partners, Dr. Jones." He stared at me intently with a frosty gaze. "Oh, I understand now. You are no Marine or black belt. You are *him*."

"Him?" I asked, almost laughing. "Oh, that's right I'm him. I'm the guy. Naturally, you would have heard about my website. Perhaps you've read some of my articles. I'm flattered they reached you in Russia, especially with you being dead and all."

"No," he said with a quick, dismissive wave of his hand. "Your lack of knowledge is obvious." He stepped up close to me, standing nearly chest to chest. "You are him…the guy who tames these bitches with your…special connection to them, shall we say."

I stood as tall as I could and leaned toward him. "I don't know where you get your information, but no one tames the Super Born."

Demetri stared at me with his dead eyes and raised the corner of his crooked smile before turning and pacing toward Jones."How disappointing that you don't understand. Jones, I thought you said he was your partner. He doesn't seem to know anything. He is the one who unlocks the passions of those freaks? Don't make me laugh," he said, coldly staring at me. "Let me guess, you think you are in love. She connects with you on so many levels," he said sarcastically and chuckled. "That's how they work, you idiot."

My right fist clenched, and my feet slipped into a fighter's stance. Luckily for him (and my fist), he turned and jingled back toward the corner of the room.

"You will learn soon. She will show her true colors. Tell me, how many have they killed so far? Have you lost track? I know I have. My Super Born are like children. If I didn't take away their toys, they'd end up killing everyone around them. Soon you will learn they are just tools. Left without direction, they will inevitably turn on themselves and their own flaws will destroy them. The sooner you learn that, the less painful it will be."

I had to admit that Demetri's statement made me think of the red energy storm that Jennifer had turned against herself the other night. I remembered her frightened face when her own memories smashed her against the wall.

Demetri walked to the corner and then stopped, pulled a pen out of his pocket, and used it to pluck a red pair of panties out from under an end table. He held it up to Jones. "Was this what you were doing on Two-for-Tuesday?"

Jones smiled, embarrassed. "She was Ladies' Night at the Banshee. Maria, or Heather, or something."

"Ah, now I see how your judgment may have been—clouded, shall we say. Obviously, you can't function without me." He dropped the pen with its pair of panties to the floor and then turned and stamped out his last cigarette, which was still smoldering among the others on a crowded plate he was using as an ashtray. Then he picked up his jacket and headed for the door.

"Demetri? Where are you going? We have so much to discuss," Jones said, chasing after him.

"I agree. I will be in touch."

"Where can I reach you?"

Demetri stopped and turned back to Jones, cocking his head. "Did you forget? I'm dead, Dr. Jones. I will contact you, you and you alone." With a flourish he opened the door and was gone.

I shook my head. "You never told me Demetri was an—"

"A very complicated man? Yes, he can be a bit—heavy at times, but the man is a genius with algorithms, and you should just see the way he plays bocce ball. We might be best advised to take what he says seriously."

"That crock of BS? Listen Jonesy, for your own health, you better not talk to that guy again."

"Or what, they're going to kill me? Just listen to yourself! Don't you see? You sound like you're under their power, just like what he was saying. The Super Born are dangerous."

I sent a stare burning at Jones. "No, he's dangerous!" I said, pointing at the door. "It doesn't bother you that he just shows up and lets himself in? What was he doing here? He probably was digging though all your files, all your research."

Jones glanced around the room and at his laptop on the desk. "My porn collection?"

"Everything!" That comment made Jones swallow hard. "Something isn't right about him."

"Maybe you just feel that way because he seems to hate you intensely for some reason."

"You noticed that too?"

Jones grabbed his can of peanuts and began throwing them into his mouth, catching one after the other from amazing angles. "Ah, things were so much easier before. Everything was so clear."

"Screw before. That's your problem: you're living in the past. I like the right now."

"Easy for you to say. You're *the guy*."

I put my arm around Jones' shoulder then gave him a pat on the back. "Okay, you can be *the guy* too, if it makes you feel better."

"That would make us *those guys*. Sounds too much like a Broadway show."

"Whatever," I said, turning to leave. "You need to get your head on straight. The girls will want to see a report from you soon."

"There it is again. You're *the guy*. They're *the girls*. What am I?"

"Dead meat if you see that clown again," I said pointing at the door.

"Oh, thank you ever so much for the reassurance," Jones said as I exited. Then I popped my head back through the door and pointed a finger at him.

"I know," Jones said before I could speak, "dead meat."

As I closed the door and began to walk down the hall, I heard him yelling after me, "Why am I dead meat? Can't I be sick meat still in hope of redemption?"

I ignored his whining, hoping that my tough love would snap him out of his funk. I had bigger fish to fry, or grill, or maybe sauté in a little garlic butter. Meeting Demetri had unnerved me. It was a warm day for fall, but I felt a shiver as I walked down the hall. I wanted to believe he was just Jones' crony, maybe just an eccentric old professor type with a splash of nasty and a ton of bitter. But an uneasy feeling kept me from fully embracing that idea or even giving it a mild grandma hug. I could imagine no way that his presence could bring good news and plenty of ways it could bring bad. "Screw him. I'm *the guy!*" I reassured myself.

My shivering became worse when I recalled Demetri calling the Super Born dangerous. Then I remembered Jennifer with that energy cloud of her own creation drifting over her bed—the same one that sent her flying into the wall. Images of Carmine Camino's shocked face appeared in my thoughts as Rebecca slowly dissolved him into oblivion. I couldn't help thinking about Jennifer as a teen slamming a baseball bat into those thugs' faces and then torching her own house while still in it. All that was normal—right? Right?

Then I thought of Allie. What secrets was she carrying around?

NINE

Lowe LLC Is Born

ALLIE

I saw my daughter head off to school, called in sick to my job at the phone company, and headed off to the offices on the eighth floor of Jennifer's building. Today would be the first day of our new venture to make Scranton a larger dot on the map and improve conditions for people around the world. I wanted to see if there really was a place for me in the new company before I gave ol' prune face news of my early retirement.

Security directed me to room 807B, the new home of our little venture. When I arrived I found the large glass-walled room filled with flashing computers, buzzing printers, and huge plotters drawing on large pieces of paper. I was super impressed with the sense of activity but amazed to find no people present. I stopped in the doorway and looked around, wondering if I was in the wrong place. Just then Rebecca dropped a wall of wide paper she was inspecting from one of the plotters, revealing her tiny form and frantic face in the center of the room. When she caught sight of me, she gave me a huge, welcoming smile. The cavalry had arrived.

"Thank God you're here!" she called out in the sea of noise.

It took me a few seconds to wade through the maze of desks and cubicles to reach her. "So, how's it going?"

"Hell if I know. I've got circuit diagrams over here and dimensional drawings over there. Bills of materials and spec sheets are pouring out everywhere. I need help!"

"What can I do?" I asked, putting my stuff down on a nearby desk.

Rebecca studied the plotter printout of an electronic circuit before her. "See this number, the prefix in front of the number? I think that relates to an assembly, some part of the machine. So all the parts for this do-hicky should all have the same prefix."

"We need to organize these by the prefix?"

"I think so."

"You think so? Didn't you design all this?"

Rebecca turned to face me, frustrated. "You wanna help or be a smart ass? I design by thinking of the thing I see in my mind, and the machines break it down for me. I'm not an engineer or a programmer. I knew it would be a big project—I just didn't think it'd all come out at once. I hope the digital files are more organized than this mess."

I glanced around the room at all the drawings and technology, and it made me wonder. "Does all this mean you can make me a high-tech bat suit?" I saw all the circuits and parts being drawn on the frantically flashing computer screens and imagined me standing invulnerable on top of a building like Batman in a movie, a world of gadgets at my disposal. *I could show everyone what a real female superhero could do, not that Hollywood fluff*, I thought.

Rebecca thought for a moment and smiled. "Yeahhhh, I don't see why not!" Then she shifted back to the space and time around her. "Once we get through all this. Where to start?"

A deep voice interrupted our puzzlement. "Is this where they're interviewing for the engineer job?" Beside us stood a tall, heavily built black man dressed in a suit and wearing black-framed glasses. He looked to be in his early thirties.

"Crap, I thought I'd be ready to interview by now," Rebecca said out loud, his presence clearly adding to her frustration.

I leapt in, as Rebecca seemed unable to deal with it. "Yeah, this is the right place."

He handed me his resume. "I'm Alex, Alex Harper."

"Allie," I said shaking his hand and looking at the Greek written on his resume.

"I went to NYU in NYC for my BSEE, but my masters is from MIT."

"OMG!" I blurted, not knowing what else to say.

Alex looked at the circuit diagram the plotter had printed out of the corner of his eye. "Man, that is brilliant. Who's your lead engineer?"

Brilliant seemed to wake Rebecca up. "You understand this circuit?"

Alex nodded. "Sure, we tried to do something like this at my last job, but we could never figure out how to eliminate the feedback or the capacitor drain. Now that I see what you did, it seems so damn simple." Alex looked at all the flashing computer screens in amazement. "How long have you been working on this project?

Rebecca put down her papers and focused on Alex. "Actually, I designed it last night. This is just the computers trying to catch up."

Alex gave her a disbelieving look. "You're joking, right? This is what, six months of your team working? Maybe eight. How many engineers in your team, anyway?" he said, looking around at all the empty desks.

I pointed a finger dramatically at Rebecca, myself, and then Alex. "Three. Welcome to the team."

Alex chuckled in disbelief.

Rebecca rubbed her hands together. "Maybe you can start by telling me what these circuits do so we can start organizing this crap."

Alex chuckled again and then stepped back a little. "Riiiiight," he said slowly, waiting to be told she was joking.

"No, she's serious," I said. "You can pick whichever desk you want. Your pay will be double what you made at your last job, and we only work twenty-four hours a day. Hope you're not married or have any family, hobbies, small pets you're fond of, or a personal life of any kind." I was half joking.

Still, that's when it finally seemed to hit Alex that we were serious. A smile came to his face as excitement suddenly undermined his MIT manners. He slapped his hands together. "All right, let's do this!"

Just then Jennifer marched into 807B and over to us in a frustrated rush. "You didn't tell me this was going to happen! You're monopolizing my computer and tying up the whole network!"

"So?" Rebecca shot back.

"That thing is the latest frigging supercomputer, and you've tied up its queue for the entire day!" She shook her mobile phone at us. "Everyone's bitching at me."

"Don't get your panties in a twist. It should be freed up by Friday," Rebecca consoled her. "Then you can go back to looking for oil or whatever."

"Friday!" exclaimed Jennifer.

"She said Friday. Cut her some slack," I said.

Alex seemed to have heard them, because he slapped his hands together again with excitement. "Are you telling me your designs have tied up the queue of a Cray XC for an entire week?" he asked.

"That's exactly what I'm complaining about! At least he understands," answered Jennifer.

"It might be done late Thursday," Rebecca said without a bit of remorse.

Alex began looking left and right to find a place to start working.

"Calm down, Jenny," I said. "This is what we discussed. It's happening. You should be glad."

"Glad? Do I look glad?" Then, finally, she seemed to notice Alex. "Who's he? He doesn't work for me."

"He does now," chimed in Rebecca.

"He's our new engineer," I added.

"Engineer?" questioned Jenny.

"We have to have one in the company," I said.

"One? What do you mean one? We have Rebecca," Jennifer said.

Rebecca and I looked at each other, smiled, and then Rebecca pulled me away to begin helping her organize the output of the printers.

"What do you mean, one!" said Jennifer chasing after us. Then in panic she turned back to Alex, pulled a stapled stack of papers out of her bag, and handed it to him. "Confidentiality/noncompete agreement. Everybody has to sign one before they can see anything we do here."

Alex studied the thick stack of paper for a moment and then looked up at Jennifer. "What, is this where I promise you my firstborn?"

"And your left nut. Just sign it." She whipped out a pen as if it was a sword.

Alex looked around at the activity in the room and then signed the document without reading a word.

"Great. The company thanks you," Jennifer said before stuffing the agreement into her bag and scurrying after Rebecca and me.

Just as Jennifer caught up to us twenty feet down the aisle in the cavernous open room, a young man and woman stepped through the door with computer bags over their shoulders. They were imports to the project from Jennifer's procurement staff. Josh was a thin man in a nice suit but with hip hair and manners, and Iesha was a compact black woman in a stylish, professional suit.

"Good morning, Ms. Lowe," Josh greeted her.

"Ah, good morning Josh, Iesha," Jennifer said, trying to seem composed.

"Wow, it looks like you've got quite a project going on here. Just how many products will we be doing the purchasing for?" Josh asked her.

"I honestly don't know, Josh. You will have to ask the designer." Jennifer pointed at Rebecca.

"Twenty-four products, fifty thousand components and services, I would imagine," Rebecca estimated calmly.

"Holy…" mumbled Iesha, obviously involuntarily.

I tapped Josh on the shoulder. "And you get to source and buy each and every one, as well as source all the subcontractors."

"Where will my team set up?" Josh said, seeming overwhelmed.

"Wherever you'd like," I said. "But window seats are fifty bucks extra."

Josh looked confused, so Jennifer soothed his concerns. "She's joking. Over there is good."

"And how many will I have in my procurement team?" Josh asked.

I pointed dramatically at him and then Iesha. "Two. I count two."

Josh's smile drained away, and he stopped taking his bag off of his shoulder. "Well, how many months will we have to source all this?"

Rebecca flashed by on her way toward Alex. "We don't have months here. We have days."

I looked into Josh's stunned face and gave him some advice. "That's right, but if you don't sleep or maintain anything approaching a life, those days can be twice as long." His face was still frozen, so I decided he needed encouragement. "How does tripling your normal completion bonus sound?"

"Hell yeah," Iesha said in a barely audible tone while pumping her fist. She slapped Josh on the back. "Come on. You always claim to be a workaholic. Let's kick some butt!"

Josh paused for a moment and then seemed to get caught up in the swirling excitement of the atmosphere around him. "Yeah, let's buy shit and build it!"

I caught up to Rebecca and Alex in the corner of the room where the 3D printer was located. Rebecca was standing with her hands on her hips watching as the machine deliberately printed an elongated disk-like shape that had curved contours in its middle. Alex sat at the nearby computer clicking through screens.

"This won't do," Rebecca said, shaking her head. "We need more 3D printers."

"From this backlog it looks like about ten…at least," Alex agreed.

Suddenly Jennifer was marching at all of us like a charging Roman legend with her mobile phone in hand, but Rebecca attacked first. "Jenny, we need more printers ASAP. It's really slowing us down."

"More? More!" she said, frustrated, looking around at the growing chaos around us. "Is that the only word you know? How many more?"

Rebecca looked at Alex. "Alex says ten, but twelve would be better."

Jennifer bent over as dramatically over as she could in her tight skirt, put her hand behind her, and then straightened up. "Nope, guess I can't pull them out of my ass! Just where am I supposed to get ten ASAP?"

"Very funny. But you're right, it will take too long to get them ordered and delivered," Rebecca reasoned. "Allie, call the manufacturer and ask if they have any time available we could buy on their demo machines."

"Buy! What am I buying now?" exclaimed Jennifer.

"Then ask them if any of their customers have free production time we could rent on underused machines," Rebecca instructed me. I nodded before setting to work.

"Rent!" exclaimed Jennifer holding her hand up. "Hold on!"

Rebecca strode up and got in her face. "Remember, this is what you agreed to. Don't stress me out more than I already am."

"Stress? You want my stress? Well, how about this," Jennifer said, pointing her phone at Rebecca. "What's this press release thing, huh? Who did that?" You could tell someone used to control was getting frustrated by the self-directed chaos happening around her.

"I don't know anything about a press release," Rebecca said, shaking her head. "I wouldn't know what to say or how to do it."

We shared a long moment of looking at one another. "Don't look at me," Alex joked. "I don't even have a left nut anymore."

Both women turned to look at me. "Allie?" Rebecca asked.

I put on an innocent face. "I thought we needed something to show us what kind of market there is, so I asked Logan to put a press release together based on what Rebecca told me this generator could do. That is what he does, you know. He's got lots of media contacts. And he does know how to summarize all the technical stuff into language that people can actually understand."

"Yeah, Jennifer, what's the problem?" Rebecca shrugged.

Jennifer sighed, glanced at the ceiling, then cocked her head and attacked. "The problem is we've been getting calls all morning from around the globe. There are fifteen customers and twelve distributors who want price lists, brochures, and spec sheets. Oh, and they all want to know what our booth number will be at the World Industrial Expo next month." Jennifer shook her phone at Allie in exasperation. "We don't even have a copy of what the release says! Other than those minor details, I don't see a single thing wrong."

My phone beeped with a new text arriving. It was a copy of the release from Logan. I proudly held my phone up to Jennifer. "Not to worry, here's a copy. Want one?" I taunted Jennifer.

"May I?" Jennifer asked sarcastically. Her phone rang just as someone called her name from across the room. "Ahhh, melting terrorists was so much easier." Then she stormed away.

Alex looked at Rebecca with a questioning look. "Melting who? Who are you guys melting?"

"Oh, just the last engineer we hired…I'm joking. And she's joking too…sort of," I reassured him. Then when an email popped up on my screen, I clapped my hands together. "All right, Rebecca, I just found a company with three printers totally idle. We can have 'em for a song! You a singer, Alex?"

"You guys are nuts!" he said, but I could tell he was totally amused.

I gave Alex a friendly slap on the back, "Hey," I said, "at least we've got ours!"

TEN

Hard at Work

LOGAN

It was three thirty a.m. when I heard Allie slink into the dark bedroom, get undressed, and slide under the sheets as if I was asleep—right, fat chance. Even in the dark I could tell she was staring at the ceiling, wide eyed, with adrenaline pumping through her veins. It was like lying next to a fully charged, sparking electric cable. I rolled over and lay on my side facing her.

"So? How'd it go?"

"Oh Logan, it was great! Just great."

"You save the world yet?"

"Don't laugh. This is going to be amazing. Besides, there are a lot of ways to save the world."

Allie sighed and huffed as if she was weighing the excitement she felt against her need for rest. She turned to spoon me, and I put my hands on her shoulders, which felt like iron, and gave her a deep massage.

"Ohhh, that feels great. I'll give you just a year to stop doing that."

I couldn't help it. Listening to her sigh and feeling the warm firmness of her muscles made me slip down and kiss her neck, but the usual silver glow was nowhere to be seen on her skin.

"Logan, not now. I'm, like, all wired."

My massage became halfhearted, and then I stopped completely as I rolled back onto my side of the bed.

Allied sighed and flipped over to face me. "I'm sorry. I know with all these things going on, one after the other, we haven't had much time together." Then she dropped back onto her back. "But that's still what I want…us. I promise I'll make it up to you. How about we spend a couple days alone on that little island in the Pacific you like?"

"Sure," I mumbled but not very convincingly.

"I know something we can do together! Why don't you come to work with me tomorrow? They loved your press release. We got, like, a gazillion calls. Jennifer can't handle marketing along with everything else. You could be our VP of marketing."

"Yeah, we could say hi in the halls, pass notes, and everything."

"Come on. You could really help. At least it's something we can do together."

I flipped over and ran one hand over her cheek. "I know one thing we could do together right now." Then I started a kiss that drifted down from her mouth to her neck and down along her chest, accompanied by the beginnings of a molten silver glow.

"Logan, I need to get some rest, and there's only three hours before I have to get back to work."

My eager fingers made her sigh and then moan deeply. Then my lips sliding down her belly made her take some deep breaths. "Well, I am one of the bosses. Maybe I could be a little late." She moaned. Then my tongue made her shiver. "Four hours, but that's it," she purred. "Maybe four and a halfffffff," she said as we became engulfed in a molten silver glow.

* * *

Needless to say, Allie and I were fashionably late the next morning when we arrived at 807B. Allie stopped in the hall and stared as if she was in the wrong place.

"What's wrong?" I asked, backtracking to her.

"Holy…the place is full. When I left last night, there were maybe fifteen employees."

I looked around at the room full of people, ringing phones, conversations, and flashing computers. Almost every desk was occupied, as was the hallway. Thank god Jennifer owned the entire building and we had room to expand. People sat in chairs, some filling out job applications while others tapped away on laptops. I put the number at more like fifty.

"I swear, Logan, I don't know who most of these people are."

I took hold of her hand. "Don't worry, it's cool. Show me were my desk is."

Allie led me down the main aisle. All along the way, makeshift handwritten signs had been posted describing the work function of the area: *Procurement, Patents, Engineering,* and *Design.* We found an empty desk near the area where Rebecca and Allie worked. Allie wrote out a sign that said *Marketing* and taped it to the wall. As a joke, I took the marker and added *VP* after *Marketing* and then wrote a sign saying *International Trade Division* and taped it to a chair beside my desk.

Jennifer and Rebecca strode up to us purposefully. "There you are!" Jennifer greeted Allie. Then she saw me. "What's he doing here?"

"Your new VP of marketing. Remember all those annoying calls for info? They're his problem now," answered Allie.

Rebecca considered me. "That's a great idea, Allie. I just finished all the specs for the first product, the fluid disk generator," she said, plopping a two-inch-thick stack of papers in my hands. Then Rebecca grabbed Allie's hand and pulled her away. "Boy, do I have a load for you to do." The two of them disappeared down the row of cubicles.

There was an awkward silence between Jennifer and me. Her body rocked, and her lips threatened to move but then stopped. I could feel tension in the air. Finally, she said, "Yeah…I'll send the marketing calls over to you. We have a marketing meeting planned for one thirty over in the conference room."

"Well then, it's lucky I'm here."

"Does it make sense to you that we can actually build this thing? And that anyone will want it?" Jennifer asked. I was surprised at how insecure she suddenly seemed.

I held up the stack Rebecca had handed me. "If this thing works, you guys can change the world, in more ways than one."

Jennifer smiled. My reassurance seemed to have to plugged the hole in her sense of security. "Then just be sure you don't screw it up," she said, back to her cocky self. With that she walked off, but slowly. I couldn't help but think that was for my benefit.

I sighed, took a deep breath, and looked over the office. All the people were buzzing around frantically; I just felt like I was late for a nap. Halfway through a yawn, I spotted a familiar face. I had invited Dr. Jones, with a twisted wrist, to come help the project. And amazingly, there he was, joking and laughing with the engineer, Alex, whom Allie had told me about. They were standing over a computer screen that was drawing a housing that contained numerous parts when I interrupted their little party. "You guys seem to be having fun. Maybe you should try to get some work done."

"Oh, Logan, my friend, we are getting so much work done. When you told me I had better show up and help, you didn't mention what a hoot it would be. We've been consolidating circuits and touching up the cowlings all morning! I bet we've cut…what would you say, Alex, two weeks off the production time?"

Alex turned from typing at his work station, revealing a smiling face full of energy. "At least! Man, what you can do with spatial integration! That algorithm you came up with for the contour smoothing, it still busts me up!" Both Alex and Jones had to cover their mouths to contain their laughter.

"Greaaaaat," I said.

Just then Rebecca stormed toward Jones. She slowed when she saw me. "What's *he* doing here?"

"Saving you a fortune," said Alex, still smiling.

"I asked Jones to help. He is a freakin' genius," I said.

Jones nodded. "Thank you, my man. Rebecca, I am familiar with the prototyping and building of electronic devices."

"Yeah, I remember your devices quite clearly," she said, holding up her wrists, which still bore scars.

Jones offered her a fake smile. "I am sure I can help you here. I'm telling you this."

Alex fairly glowed. "Rebecca, this guy is on fire. Just look at the improvements he made to the frequency polarity circuit. It's a work of art."

Rebecca seethed for a moment but then seemed to get ahold of herself. "Just remember, Jones, this is *my* art you're working on."

"Yes, yes, of course," Jones reassured her before turning back to Alex. "Didn't you say the rectifier hierarchy had a bipolar relationship with the depth of input?"

"Not that she told me!" Alex said, and then he and Jones burst into laughter. This appeared to be a private engineering joke of some sort.

Rebecca threw me a threatening look for having invited Jones to be part of her project. She looked at them with distain then left in a huff.

I returned to my desk and began skimming through the specs for the first product I would sell, certain that Jones would explain what the heck it all meant sometime later. When the phone rang, I grabbed it with a smile in my voice. "Marketing, this is Logan."

ELEVEN

Out with the Old

ALLIE

Years of habit made me sulk my way into the old prune's office to give her the news that my career at the company was over. Inside, I was jubilant, ready to tell her to take that job and shove it, but outside, I still felt the years I'd spent under her intimidation, needing the job and my paltry check. I promised myself that I would keep calm and just get through this. I crept up to her desk with a wrapped gift in my hand (something I'd wanted to give her for years) and sat down in the chair in front of her as she sat tapping her pen on the desk. Was she nervous? Or was that maybe just a pre-rigor mortis muscle reflex?

"Did I say you could sit?" she bellowed. Apparently, it was her month of the month.

I stood up awkwardly. "Sorry."

"Sit!" she commanded, so I sat back down again. My calm was starting to slip into irritation.

"What are you wasting my time with this morning?"

I took a breath to regain my composure. "I've come to tell you that I'll be leaving the company. I'm here to give you my resignation."

Her eyes were wide, and she was more animated than I'd ever seen. "We won't take you back, you know! Once you are gone, there will be no weaseling your way back in after you fall flat on your face."

"I understand," I said resisting the desire to smack her in the face.

She leaned toward me, peering at me over the tops of her glasses. "I hear they're hiring people of your caliber in the food services industry. You might be able to get fries with that," the old prune said, smiling at her own joke. I'm certain she expected that I would cave in to her as I had always done in the past. Instead, I just sat there, waiting for her to finish. She stared at me for a long moment before continuing. "So, are you certain you want to make this tragic error in judgment? After all, you are due an increase in your pay in just another twenty-three months. After this, I won't be able to save your butt anymore, as I have for so many years."

"And I won't save yours. I'm quite certain I want to leave," I said forcefully. My patience was gone.

"Then," she said digging through her calendar, "your last day will be October twenty-seventh. At four p.m. that day, I will have security lead you out of the building…forever."

Finally, I'd had it. "No, you won't! My last day is today. I'm leaving this very instant!"

The ol' prune was taken aback. "What on earth? I never…"

"You have *never*, and that's probably your problem!"

She huffed, her hand to her chest, and then huffed again.

"Oh, and I brought you a little going-away gift to thank you for everything you've done for me over the years," I said, leaving the wrapped box on her desk. "Have a nice day," I added before turning to leave.

She yelled after me. "I wouldn't be expecting my last paycheck if I were you! You have not followed the required termination procedure!"

"Yeah, yeah, I wouldn't expect anything less."

I breathed a giant sigh of relief as I marched away from the glass walls of her office. Then I slowed as I remembered the gift I had left her. I knew the curiosity would kill her, and I was right. Out of the corner of my eye I saw her pull the gift box to her and open the lid, and I heard her muffled scream as the spring-loaded cream pie flew out of the box and into her face.

TWELVE

The Brain Is Such a Scary Place

IYLA

Dr. Jones was exactly where Demetri had said he would be. "You will find him drinking at the bar called the Banshee, on what they call Ladies' Night." he'd said, and though I didn't really think I was refined enough to be considered a lady, I went there anyway. He sat at the bar silhouetted by a large TV screen. The bar was loud and humid, filled to standing room only. It was difficult just making my way through the crowd, and the room smelled like riding on a bus in Siberia with goats. Occasionally, someone would push me, so I would be forced to push them right back. I came up behind Jones and stood off to the side behind a skinny young man seated next to him.

All the thoughts and conversations screaming into my head made it difficult to channel the thoughts of any one particular person, so I had to get as close to the young man as I could. Our shoulders touched, which helped me make contact with his mind. I felt a change like a door shutting, and I was able to close out everyone's mind but his. In the recesses of his thoughts, I felt emotions for someone named Sarah, so I planted an urgent compulsion into his mind: *You need to call Sarah right now*! In a flash the young man had his phone out. He looked frantically from side to side for a quiet corner, and then he finished his drink, threw some bills on the bar, and hurried outside.

Before I could drop into the now empty chair, a burly, bearded man tried to cut me off. I pushed him away with both hands. "It's ladies' night, asshole. Don't you know a lady when you are seeing one?"

He stared right through me. "I don't see shit," he said, blocking my way to the chair.

I looked at the blond beside him who was eyeing my chair, channeled his mind for a second, and then said, "Does Mary know about her?" Then I said to the blond, "Do you know about Mary?"

"Who's Mary?" the blond exclaimed.

"Nobody," the burly man said, shooting me a look that could kill, taking the blond's hand, and pulling her away.

"Who the fuck's Mary?" I could hear her ask angrily as she punched the man in the arm repeatedly and they disappeared into the crowd.

I sat down next to Jones, the chaos of everyone's thoughts bombarding me once more. I couldn't connect with Jones, but I did channel the bartender as he passed. I convinced him I had already ordered three shots of Stolichnaya vodka, my favorite brand, though mother always said it tasted like piss. Well, I guess she would know. I also assured the bartender that I had paid for them in advance, including an outrageous tip for his services, leading him to believe I might have more than cash to offer. He returned with the drinks and smiled. I gave him a flirty smile to keep his hopes alive and the drinks coming. I downed the first shot. I could feel Jones looking me over from the corner of his eye, so I turned to him. "What is it they say? Why don't you take a picture, lasts longer."

He stammered, the poor fool. "I was just marveling at that awesome tattoo you have over your arm. The curves and colors are amazing."

But he wasn't looking at my tattoo, he was looking at my breasts. I could feel his eyeballs all over them. So I gave a little smile and sat up straight. "Yesss, they are quite amazing."

Finally, his eyes moved over to my tattoos. "Those roses on your arm are beautiful."

"Don't forget the thorns."

"Ah yes, I see them now. Ouch!" Jones said, pretending to have been pricked by one. "What is that word there buried in those vines?"

"Mother."

"You are close to your mother?"

I sipped the Stolichnaya. "Not in the least."

"Then why…"

"You know what they say, keep your friends close and your enemies closer. Mother dear I keep the closest."

"Ah, I see," he said, but of course he didn't.

"I am Iyla," I said, offering him my hand. He shook it, and in a flash I was into his brain.

It was an awesome, cavernous place. There were flashes of energy, numbers, symbols, images, binary codes, pictures, and videos everywhere I looked, and none of them lasted for more than a brief second. It would take me forever to find the information Demetri wanted. If I was going to get anywhere with Jones, I would have to find a way to bring up the information I needed by calling it into his conscious thoughts.

"I am Dr. Jones," he said proudly.

"Is that supposed to mean something to me?"

He looked confused. I guess that wasn't the reaction he normally received. "Well, my full name is Dr. Rashid Patel Jones…PhD."

"Let's stick with Dr. Jones, shall we? You work in a hospital?"

"No, I am a professor and researcher at the university. Perhaps you've seen me on TV or read one of my articles."

"No, I have not had the pleasure," I said, trying to imitate the way Valeria used the word, hoping to get the same effect she had on the customs agent days before. I picked up my second shot and held it to my mouth, trying to look mysterious, like my mother in an old Russian movie. "What do you write your articles about, Dr. Jones?"

"I am the foremost authority on the B.I.B. and all of the Super Born. You know, those women who guard this town? I have met them all personally, you know. In fact, I saw them just this morning."

Take me now, little man, I am so impressed was apparently the reaction he expected, but he would not get it from me. Instead, I began taking in images from his brain of the faces of the women, a crowded office, and dozens of people. "Really? I think you are telling me lies just so you can—how do you say? Be wearing my pants."

"No, no. It's all quite true. They were all there this morning."

"And exactly where were all these Super Born women?"

Jones thought for a second. "I'm not at liberty to say, but you can trust me—I spoke with all of them today."

Images of the office and memories of him walking into the building flashed through my mind. Finally, I saw the sign and address on the building as he entered. "I think you are trying to pull the wool over my ears, Dr. Jones. Okay, so how many of these women are there? You like them better than me?" I asked, taking hold of his hand again. He was intimidated at first, but then he imagined me falling for him. He imagined pinning me to a wall with our clenched hands, me screaming with excitement, so he tightened his grip as well.

"I never release my sources," he said, smiling. I received images of three women followed by four others. The final four were dimmer than the others for some reason and made him feel sad for a moment.

I downed my second shot and held his eye while I swallowed. I watched his Adam's apple jump up and down as his eyes widened. "So," I said, moving in closer to him. I put my elbow on the bar and my chin in my hand. "You spend your time with these Super Born, women who could crush your little walnuts like that," I said, snapping my fingers. "Aren't you afraid?"

Dr. Jones swallowed hard. "Well, actually, I am quite concerned they may hurt me someday."

"So what is to keep them from doing that?" I snapped my fingers again. "Or taking over the world? It makes me scared just thinking about it."

"Well, I did have a way to keep them in line. It worked very well too."

"Oh? Tell me, Dr. Jones, how could you control these powerful women?" That question caused a flurry of activity in his mind that moved so fast I couldn't take it all in. I saw three women standing around him with lights beaming out of their eyes. I saw a lab, injections, unconscious women, circuit diagrams, a tube-like machine, and lights flashing like lightning. I felt the women's pain, sensed their feelings of confusion and sadness, and heard their anguished screams. Suddenly, I was afraid. No, in fact, I felt as terrified as those women had been. The connection to Dr. Jones left me cold. I let go of his hand and jumped out of my chair.

"I have to go," I said, downing my last shot. My whole body was shaking.

"Why, what is wrong?" Jones got out of his chair and reached his hand out after me. "Don't tell me you saw some tall guy!"

"No tall guy."

"I was too intense, wasn't I? I'm sorry. Let's start over."

We played cat and mouses, and you were the mouse, Dr. Jones, is what I wanted to say. But he looked at me with sad eyes, which made me feel sorry for him. "By the way, the answer is, I'm not wearing any."

"What was the question?"

I smiled and cocked my head. "You were wondering what kind of underwear I have on. You think maybe black satin. But no." I spun to leave but then turned back to him. "You're a nice man, so I'll give you a tip. Skinny woman behind you with long dark hair and big glasses, she is thinking you are cute. But I warn you, she has five-date rule, lives with mother, and is hard to climax. If you can handle all that…go for it, big boy."

THIRTEEN

If I Can Make It There…

JENNIFER

New York. Maybe Rebecca and Allie were content to help the world progress, but I had a different idea of how to use my God-given powers. I was certain we could end crime, make everyone feel secure, and bring even greater prosperity for everyone, just as we had done in Scranton. After all, Scranton had turned from a backwater to a boomtown thanks to us. What could we do with a city that was already vibrant, like New York? I had come here to find out—and to prove my approach to the girls. Once they saw what I could do here, they would have to agree.

I drifted through Times Square, watching the gigantic video screens that covered the walls of entire buildings flash images of models selling clothes and sexy underwear, and promoting theatrical events. I couldn't help but imagine my image on the screen as I catwalked beside the square, twenty stories tall. Then I imagined myself on every one of the dozens of huge screens around me. Soon this place would be mine. I took in a deep breath and smiled.

But not tonight—tonight I was here just to test the waters. I stood in the square feeling the thousands of heartbeats and chaotic minds around me. They flowed wildly, seemingly out of all control, but like the molecules within those minds and hearts, I knew, they moved according to an intricate order. I stood and watched, feeling that I was the only stable observer to this ocean of motion and emotion. Over and over people tried to stuff brochures in my hand, but I pulled my hand away. People dressed as human-sized cartoon characters offered to take pictures with me for a price but didn't act much like their characters when I refused. Every now and again a man would pass carrying on a full conversation with himself. Around us the enormous, towering video screens flashed, making night as bright as day. It was a city of chaos you couldn't escape, no matter where you went. This was a place that needed me to give it direction.

One block off the square, with its raging human torrent, I found a loud, crowded pub that in comparison felt calm—O'Brien's, an Irish bar, full of dark wood and green. The air buzzed with conversations, hopes, and laughter. The younger crowd was full of energy and optimism, which made the place feel like one big hookup—my kind of place.

I slipped through the crowded mass of tables and humanity, getting jostled, poked, and blocked the whole way to the bar. The bartenders moved back and forth without taking note of me, which was a new and strange experience for me. I raised my arm to flag one down, but he flashed right by. I even opened my light fall jacket, to no avail. Finally, a thin, dark-haired, goateed young man seated at the bar took note of me. In my peripheral vision I could sense his eyes lingering on me. Then he turned, raised his hand, and yelled, "Tony! Tony! Can we get this lady a drink?" Far down the bar a bartender held up one finger as if to tell the man "wait a minute." Then he wiped his hands on a towel and came over to us.

"Yeah, Michael, what ya need?" Tony asked.

Michael turned and presented his open hands at me, my cue to order.

"How about a double thirty-year scotch on the rocks," I told Tony.

"You got it," Tony said before hurrying away.

Michael yelled after Tony, "And don't try giving her the twenty-nine-year-old crap!" Then he turned back to me. "Strong drink for a lady. You must have had one whale of a day."

"You have no idea."

"That scotch must be older than you."

"As a matter of fact, that scotch is younger than me but not as potent."

Michael smiled, and we both felt the awkwardness. Finally, he held up one finger, seemed ready to speak, but then stalled.

"What? What's a girl like me doing in a place like this? Do I come here often? What's my sign?" Then, when he chuckled and didn't say anything, I crossed one foot over the other. "Ohhhh, I get it. You want to know where I got these shoes."

Michael laughed, shook his head, and put his hands up in defense. "No, no, nothing like that...but those are great shoes. Jimmy Choos, right?"

"Hell! I should have known you played for that team!"

"No, I just did some fashion photography—you know, to pay the bills. Excuse me," Michael said, sliding over and tapping the small Latino man on the bar stool next to him. The way they exchanged a short, light conversation told me he knew the man. The Latino stood up, looked me over, and then moved behind another friend farther down the bar. Michael invited me to sit in the newly vacant seat with a sweeping gesture, an invitation I accepted.

"Wow, all this just to see my shoes? And they said chivalry was dead."

"What can I say? There are still some of us real men. Besides, those shoes deserve a seat."

I grabbed my drink as soon as it arrived and halved it in a flash. "You're not still looking at my shoes, are you, Michael? Don't fool yourself. It's the feet in them that make these shoes great."

Michael smiled in a way that made it clear he'd been checking out more than my shoes. "Isn't that the truth." Finally, he put out his hand. "I'm Michael Boyer."

I shook his hand and gave it a squeeze greater than his. He responded by crunching my hand even harder. We played that game back and forth for a few seconds until I got bored. *I can rip your arm off, little man*, I thought. "Jennifer. My name's Jennifer, but most people call me Jennifer."

"Well, I'll just call you Jennifer, then."

"Wait. You're not *the* Michael Boyer, are you?" I asked.

"Well, yeah—you've heard of me?" Michael asked, flattered.

"Nope."

"Funny," he said after a moment. "You some kind of…"

"What? What do I look like to you? Be careful now," I said, leaning in toward him and keeping my glass close to my lips.

"I don't know. You're definitely hot, but you're not the model type."

"Oh? Why the hell not?"

"You've got a lot more going on than just your looks. From the clothes, I'd say you have plenty of the bucks floating around—Wall Street, maybe a lawyer. You do something, I'd say, with a lot of power. There's, like, this dynamic aura around you."

I rested my chin on my palm and planted my elbow on the bar. "Not bad. I may have to spare you. And what do you do, Michael?"

"I'm a journalist."

"Really?"

"Well, you know, citizen journalist," he said, lifting a small video recorder out of his pocket. "Photo journalism at NYU, and I freelance some. I did have a piece that trended number ten in all of New York for a while."

In a flash, I began to connect the dots. Here I was meeting a journalist in a bar, the same way Allie had met Logan. Allie met Logan at O'Malley's. I was meeting Michael at O'Brien's. That seemed too similar to be a coincidence. Suddenly, I imagined Logan's face on Michael, and I imagined him with Michael's level of interest in me. My brain dared to toy with the possibility that Michael could be my Logan, the one man who could connect with me, satisfy me, chronicle me to the world. Before my intellect could tell me how stupid that was, hope had sent my heart racing.

I downed the rest of my drink and gestured for him to do the same. "Come on, drink up. You're gonna need it," I said, standing up.

Michael grinned. "Why? Where're we going?"

I took hold of his lapel. "I wanna show you something."

"I don't know. Women who drink scotch that's older than they are scare me," he said.

I had started to leave but then returned and moved in close. "Are you really gonna give me a line like that with that rock you've had in your pants for the last ten minutes?"

Michael jolted back as if I'd punched him. "Rock? I like to think of it more as a sculpture."

"Then bring your camera, your tablet, and your sculpture. Have I got a story for you."

* * *

"Twelve? We're only trending twelve?" I exclaimed.

"No, now, twenty-two." Michael shook his head and sat back in his chair at O'Brien's, which was now half empty and quieter than before. "Sorry. I thought it was pretty amazing, and that outfit you had on—how did you do that stuff? I guess we just picked the wrong day. Who knew they'd land another plane in the East River, the president would be at the UN, and the Yankees would fire their manager all on the same day?"

"Yankees? The friggin' Yankees?"

"Yeah, that's number three." Then Michael mopped his forehead with his fingers. "Maybe I'm just a lousy writer."

"What about the video?" I said, grabbing his laptop and turning it to face me. I hit play and watched again as I stood in Times Square in my red leather outfit and mask with a cone of crimson energy glowing around me. The cone and flashes of red lightning from my fingers drained the energy out of every car in the square. Then I shot lightning up to the tallest video screen in the square and projected my image a hundred and fifty feet high. There was a brilliant flash, brighter than any of the video screens, and I was gone. "How can that be twenty-two?" I said spinning the laptop back to Michael.

"Forty-three now and dropping like a stone. I don't get it." Michael logged into his social media accounts and began to read, his face souring as I sat and pouted.

"What? What is it?" I asked. He seemed to get more depressed the more he read.

"Here's why," he said, looking at an internet media feed on his computer. "It seems everyone thought that it was a hoax of some kind. Just a light show and some fancy video, a little CGI. They were entertained, but it pissed them off that we blocked traffic all the way around the square to get the footage. This is a tough town to impress. Everybody's seen it all before."

"So I was just another freak at the square?"

Michael smiled and raised his eye brows. "Hottest freak I ever saw."

I bent at the waist and leaned into him. "Oh, that makes me feel sooo much better." Then I straightened myself and turned away from him. "Tell me, does someone have to get hurt for people to pay attention in this town? I lit up the lights on the square. Maybe they'll notice if I turn the lights off."

"Maybe. You wouldn't do that, though, right?" He seemed to get frustrated when I didn't answer. "Look, why don't we just go back to my place and come up with a plan for tomorrow?"

I shook my head. I enjoyed my banter with Michael, and like a giggly teenager, I still sort of hoped he would be my prince. But my failure to impress New York had left me cold. "I don't think so."

"Why?" he asked.

"'Cause if we do the first half of that, we won't be doing the second," I said.

"What the hell does that mean?"

I made no attempt to explain that if we went back to his place, there would be no tomorrow, at least for him. I felt my optimism slowly dripping out, then took a good look at Michael. He was just a man, like all the others. Yet the possibility that he was my Logan left me feeling a strange exhilaration like none of them had. Michael created a vulnerable sense of fear in my stomach that even an army of killers hadn't. This feeling of being out of control was unsettling. Maybe there was a way to salvage something out of the night. "Did you say your place is near here?"

"A short subway ride, but close."

"Tell me, Michael, you like to play games?"

"Sure. What kind of games?" he said with a knowing smile.

"Maybe Monopoly or some *rad* video games," I said suggestively, screwing with him again. I waited until the anticipation drained out of his face before I moved in close and put my hands on his lapels, whispering, "No, I mean rough ones. You ever been tied up, Michael?"

"Check please!" Michael called to the bartender

FOURTEEN

Ms. Suit's Watching My Pimple

LOGAN

Have you ever been standing in a line when a guy somewhere in front of you breaks wind or been on a plane and smelled all hell drifting toward you, though none of the cowards in your vicinity will fess up or even offer so much as an apologetic glance? That's how I felt sitting across from my contact with the FBI, Ed Baker, at lunch in a little two-star downtown restaurant. Ed had changed a bit since my last memory of him, which involved him avoiding his portion of our bar tab. Today he was clean-shaven, with an expensive gray suit trying to cover the belly he was developing. Instead of chopped and wild, his blond hair was short and styled. It seemed things had looked up for Ed after the girls handed over their group of terrorists to him and given him a taste of promotability. I studied him, trying to determine if the air bagel had come from his freshly pressed butt. The other two possible perps were an FBI, stuffed-shirt, middle-aged fatso who seemed more interested in the basket of bread than our conversation and a thirtyish black woman I'd never met who sat regally dressed in an expensive gray suit, a medium-length straight wig, and expensive designer glasses. The smell was emanating from one of them, but I couldn't tell which. The foul air made it hard to concentrate on what they were saying. The woman's smug smile and that subtle butt wiggle a moment earlier made me suspect her, although the stuffed shirt was also a good bet.

After the Super Born had turned over their terrorist haul from Afghanistan, Ed and his bosses had come out smelling like roses—in contrast to the current atmosphere at this table. When he'd asked me to lunch, I'd assumed it was for a belated thank you. But when I saw the other two accompanying him, I knew better. That, and one of them cutting the cheese, set a tense mood at our lonely table in the corner.

"So, who're your buddies, Ed? Do I need a lawyer?" I laughed but no one else did, which caused me immediate concern.

"Sorry. This is Mike McKenzie, my section chief, and this is Ms. Johnson," began Ed. "We wanted to meet with you today to thank you for your help on the turnover of those terrorists. And we'd like to discuss how we might continue to work together in the future." Ed was a dick whose head I'd had to keep from falling into the porcelain throne on occasion. It was strange to hear him speak with such formality to his ol' buddy. That and the fact that he'd failed to tell me Ms. Johnson's title set the hairs on the back of my neck into "escape-now" mode.

"Cooperation? Shouldn't you at least buy me dinner first?" I looked from face to face, finding not even a hint of a chuckle or wrinkle of a smile. "What, I don't even get a dinner? How about a tube of lube—at least."

Ms. Johnson apparently didn't share my highly developed sense of humor and ended the pretense. "We know that you are in contact with the women who apprehended those killers we call the Scranton Fifty. We think those women could be of significant aid to our national security and want to open a dialogue with them. We need you to help us do that. Simple."

I leaned back and laughed. Her face made me think that this was not the reaction she had expected. "You guys are just a little too late," I said, holding my finger and thumb infinitesimally close together. "I sold the website. My webmaster quit, and I couldn't do it anymore. That was my only source of information on and contact with them, so I'm afraid I'm permanently out of the loop. I've moved on. I'll be glad to help you however I can, but as far as the Super Born are concerned, that ship has sailed."

"Just exactly how did they contact you to help arrange the turnover of the Scranton Fifty?" asked Ms. Johnson, leaning in toward me.

"We checked your phone records. The only call we found was you calling me," injected Ed.

Ms. Johnson continued the attack. "No texts, nothing. Just how do you communicate with them?"

I lifted my hands. "It was all though the website. You'd have to ask the new owners about that." I turned to Ed angrily. "Ed, I have to say, you are really a lousy date. You treat all your sources like this?"

"Logan, we don't want this to be a battle. We just expect your cooperation," Ed said with a hint of an apology in his voice.

"It is a matter of national security. We are within our rights to demand your cooperation," Ms. Johnson said in a threatening tone.

"Let me guess, you're not with the FBI, are you, Ms. Johnson?" No one attempted an answer.

Ed leaned in toward me."You don't want to know who she's with. But she can bring all varieties of hell down on you, Logan."

I chuckled. "All varieties of hell? Ed you forget I dated the Nelson twins…for a year!"

Ms. Johnson still didn't get my humor."Your phone records, your emails, your tax records, even the pimple on your ass is gonna be right on my computer," Ms. Johnson said while burning me with her eyes.

"I must say, Ms. Johnson, that's pretty kinky."

She continued, missing the joke. "Not just you but everyone around you, everyone you've ever known—even people you've just thought about knowing."

"Just tell us how the superwomen contact you, Logan!" Ed said, losing his cool.

I slid back my chair a few inches and shook my head, trying to keep calm. I looked at the three of them in their expensive suits and recalled the mayor and Mob boss Carmine Camino's shiny attire, feeling the same type of pressure they'd applied. "I already told you, man. And hey, isn't one of you supposed to be the good cop? How can you do good cop/bad cop when one of you is a vicious fed and the other is an ungrateful ex-friend? I did my bit to help national security, but that's all I got. If those women ever contact me again, you'll be the first to know. In fact, I'll just write the information in marker on my ass for Ms. Johnson, right next to the pimple. If you'll excuse me," I said, pushing my chair back farther and rising. Ed stood up and put out a hand to stop me, but then Ms. Johnson gave him a subtle nod. He backed off. But as I walked out of the dump, he came after me. Apparently, he'd changed his mind.

He stopped me in the restaurant lobby. "Logan, this is serious. You don't know what's going on."

"No, Ed *you* don't. And thanks for the grilling in there. You know, I did my best to help you. You got your fat promotion and that silk tie, didn't ya? Now you turn on me like an ungrateful snake."

"Hey, man. I am sorry. We just got off on the wrong foot. Coming down hot and heavy wasn't my idea."

"Gee, let me guess whose idea it was…little Ms. Stomping Boot in the Versace suit?"

Ed's eyes blurred for a moment. "Ver-what? How do you even know that shit?"

"You ever take a woman shopping, Ed? Never mind, you'll learn." I tried to calm down and sell him on my sincerity. "Listen, I'm trying to get my life together. I'll help you all I can, but I can't give you the connection you expect. The website's gone. I'm not mixed up with those women anymore. What the hell do they need me for? Do I look superwomen-friend-worthy?" I said, laughing. "I've got a real job and a house now. I've even got a girl

who's moved in with me, and she's got a daughter and a Versace suit. Can you believe that? And the topper is…I like it."

Ed looked at his feet for a long moment. In my body-language-to-English dictionary, that meant I was reaching him. He nodded silently and then looked up at me. "Yeah, I know. She checked out, and so did her daughter. Who'd ever think you'd end up with a normal lady like that…and quite a looker. Congrats, man."

"You checked them out?"

"Ohhhh, yeah," said Ed lecherously.

"You fuck!"

"Hey," Ed said, holding up his hands, "it's a new world. Privacy is a thing of the past. Besides, you should be happy."

"Happy you're checking out my girl?"

"Happy because everything you said checked out before you said it." Ed gave me a tap on the shoulder. "Listen, I know you'll do your best. Heck, I owe you one already. I'll do my best to keep Ms. Suit off your back if you'll shake on helping me find these women if and when you can." Ed held out his hand.

Reluctantly, I shook it. "And you have to assure me you're done checking out my girl and her daughter."

Ed kept hold of my hand and nodded. "Sure. You got yourself a deal." Then, after I flashed him a wary smile and turned to leave, he added, "Logan, you might want to warn your girlfriend…"

I turned to him slowly with my heart jumping into my throat. *What does he know?* "What?"

"Her car payment—it's five days overdue," Ed said, smiling.

"Thanks for the tip," I said with a fake smile of my own. I pushed through the front doors of the restaurant into the wondrously sunny fall day I'd been missing. My instinctive reaction was to reach for my phone and warn Allie. But when I looked around and saw the cars, vans, and people standing nearby, I imagined everyone with earpieces, pulling out surveillance equipment, ready to record my every move. Maybe my phone was already bugged. Looking from face to face, there was no way to say who worked for Ed and who didn't. Even the old lady and the kid with the skateboard looked a little suspect to me. Probably going for my phone was exactly what they hoped I would do. So I lowered the hand that was reaching for my phone and used it to get the key to my car. Overhelmed by the feeling that Big Brother was watching, I started the car engulfed with a new vision of the world.

* * *

After I reached the office, I tried to play it cool, taking care not to draw suspicion to the girls by immediately running to them, just in case Ed had eyes here. I returned a pile of calls, having to actually cool down potential customers anxious for information about our product release. These products would sell themselves as long as they did what Rebecca said they would.

After an hour or so, I sought Allie out in the aisle outside her cubicle, handed her a file of papers, and whispered, "Conference room, ten minutes."

I found Rebecca in the design area anxious, shaking her head, and complaining to a female staffer. "No, you are not going to do that! We aren't moving fast enough as it is."

"Rebecca, can I talk with you?"

"If you haven't noticed, Logan, I am a bit bussssyyyy."

"It's *important*," I said.

Her attitude changed as she took the hint.

"Conference room, five minutes?"

She looked at her watch and the computer screen in front of her and then sighed. "Sure."

"Where's Jennifer? I can't seem to find her."

"Last I heard, she was tied up in New York City."

* * *

The girls stepped into the room within seconds of one another, and I closed the door behind them.

"What's so important, Logan? I've got a simulation running," Rebecca said, obviously irritated.

"Are there any bugs here, at the company?" I asked, reluctant to speak freely.

"You mean besides the one on your phone?"

"There's a bug on my phone? Why didn't you tell me?"

Rebecca waved her hand. "Don't sweat it! I made it broadcast static."

I spun my head around the room. "Are there bugs in here?"

"If there were, they would talk to me. The rest of the company is clean."

"Bugs? Who would be bugging us?" Allie said.

I leaned my hands on the conference room table. "Well, I just had a meet and greet with Ed Baker and his Hitler SS friends. They tried to put the squeeze on me to introduce them to the Super Born."

"Crap," Allie said.

"Worse, they've been checking me out and Allie and even Paige."

"Paige!" exclaimed Allie. "What the hell for?"

"They wanna know how I got in touch with you when I arranged for the turnover of the terrorists. They want you to help out with national security missions."

"Fat chance," Rebecca said, seeming unaffected by the news.

I looked at each of them in the face. "So no more group meetings at the house, no more Super Born talk over landlines or mobiles. We have to assume we're being watched and can't give them anything unusual," I told them.

Rebecca seemed as if she was just barely tolerating this conversation. "Fine, I'll work up some encrypted internet-based phones for us to use. Give them normal, day-to-day talk on our regular phones."

"We need to let Jenny know about this before she does something stupid," added Allie.

Rebecca typed something into her tablet and then, a moment later, showed us a video of Jennifer at Times Square. "I think we might be too late about the stupid part."

"What do you mean?" asked Allie.

Rebecca pointed at the screen. "That."

Just then a knock came on the door, and a woman entered with several file folders. She had black hair with red streaks and a tattoo covering her arm. She sheepishly approached Rebecca. "Sorry to be bothering you. But we need your signature on these patent applications and the courier is already here waiting—like a big stupid."

Rebecca took the papers and flashed through them, impatiently scrawling her signature. "There you go."

"Thanks again, sorry to have interrupted." With that she turned and was gone.

"Somebody new?" I asked.

Allie filled me in. "Yeah, that's Iyla Stevenson. She started yesterday—really good too. She seems to know what I need even before I tell her. Why, you checkin' her out?"

I gestured toward the place where Iyla had just stood. "Please, with you around?" It was tough dealing with a superwoman with super insecurities. "There are just so many new people around here, it's hard to keep track."

"Yeah, I'll bet something's hard."

I pointed at Allie. "Steak—filet mignon, USDA prime." Then I pointed out the door at Iyla. "Meat loaf."

"So? You like meat loaf."

Rebecca seemed impatient. "So we're done here? New phones tomorrow, I'll plant some anonymous emails on the BIB.org website to make it look like we contacted you through it, and I'll get in touch with Jennifer, somehow," she said, standing up to leave.

"You're not worried?" I asked.

"Looogan, can't you see what's going on?" she said, gesturing in a big circle with her arms. "I've got bigger fish to fry."

"How about sauté, a little olive oil and some garlic," Allie said slipping away on a Super Born hunger tangent.

"The FBI or NSA or whoever has ahold of our ass, and you've got bigger fish to fry? Really?" I asked. "What's bigger than that?"

Rebecca came back and slapped her things down on the conference table, getting in my face. "To you, apparently nothing. But to me and the *big* picture—look, I've got Alex over at that old factory complex Jennifer owns meeting with the industrial engineering firm in order to get the assembly lines designed, ordered, and installed as quick as possible. I don't have to tell you that means permits, money, construction, and big bucks, millions of dollars. We need to think way, way ahead. I have a product stream of twenty-two products now that we need to integrate."

"And my bat suit!" chimed in Allie.

Rebecca held up a finger. "Right, I did promise you that. I've already got some great ideas for that. So now that makes twenty-three products. How fast can we have them ready? I've got a staff that is now taking over the seventh floor too. Next week we move everybody over to the factory complex. I've got feet on the ground in three locations in Africa just to get our footprint started there. Do they have any capabilities there, or do we have to build the components here in Scranton and ship them? See, I've got a bit on my mind."

"Africa? Friggin' Africa?"

Allie joined in. "Yeah, we're going there first. That's where we'll get the most bang for the buck. The whole continent is full of natural resources, but their economies are underdeveloped. It's hunger central and a big center for terrorism. If you want change, that's the place to start. Can you imagine the plains of Africa growing food like the Midwestern United States? What hunger?" Allie snapped her fingers. "Rebecca's got me working on the conversion of farm equipment to electric motors so they can be powered by our generators and her new batteries. It's pretty exciting."

Rebecca picked up where Allie left off, saying, "That's right, you haven't heard the plan yet. I sent you an email just a few minutes ago. We're going to license the products to other manufacturers in the developed nations so we can leverage our capital by letting them use theirs. Registering, licensing, and getting governmental approvals will take a while in the developed nations, but we can move right along in the Third World. So we'll use Jenny's capital there. A few greased palms will go a long way fast there."

Rebecca drew closer to me. "I installed a server connection and our software on your laptop so you can work from home. You'll need it to deal with the time difference with Africa, though. I sent you a list of the contacts to start with and a list of the various aid organizations and volunteers that are already set up to distribute aid on the continent. You can connect with them to magnify our reach. You can also use them to help determine the best location for the pilot installation of the generator, the satellite internet, and agricultural programs." Then she moved in even closer and pointed a finger at me. "In the meantime, I need you and Allie to keep the FBI off my ass. Okay? Are we good?" And with that she picked up her things and walked toward the door.

"Okay, I'll handle it. Got my frying pan right here. Bring on those friggin' fish," I conceded.

"Fry 'em up!" Allie said.

I saluted Rebecca as she shuffled out the door. Now I was informed but no less concerned about Ed and Ms. Suit.

Allie shook her head. "We just better be careful. I can't believe they would check out Paige," she said.

"It's okay, they didn't find anything suspicious…but they did warn me that your car payment is late."

Allie shook her head. "Again? I've got to get better system…or maybe just more money."

"Ed also wondered what a normal woman like you"—Allie let out the contents of her lungs in a massive, whooshing laugh as I said this—"was doing with a guy like me."

"You know, I've been wondering that same thing," she said. She scooted past me, laughing. I reached out but was only able to catch a fleeting squeeze of her butt.

I followed Allie to her cubicle, thinking she'd want to talk. I arrived only a few seconds behind her, ready to chat, but instead found her already focused on work. She was stooped over at her desk, reading something on her computer screen, seemingly oblivious to my presence. (Can you imagine?) I stood awkwardly for a moment, tapping some papers against my hand. I even tried clearing my throat, but Allie's intense relationship with her computer continued, making me a bit jealous.

I couldn't help but take note of the curve of her hip under her tight skirt, which hugged her form down to her calf. I was imagining her naked and sprawled over her desk, waiting for me to ravish her—you know, the usual—when I heard a muffled laugh at the entry to her cubicle behind me. I turned to see Iyla Stevenson with her hand over her mouth.

"Something funny?" I asked.

"Sorry," Iyla stammered. "I was just thinking about this funny cat video I just saw on my phone. You two want to see?"

"No," I answered.

"No thanks," Allie said. "Those for me?"

"These are the hard copies of today's patent applications. You asked me to bring them to you for the master files."

"That was just fifteen minutes ago. You've got them already?" said Allie with an amazed look on her face. "How did your last boss ever let you go?"

"I think I let him go, actually," Iyla said with a smile. She placed the large stack on the corner of Allie's desk and then turned to leave, favoring me with a knowing smile, as if the two of us now shared a secret. Her look seemed so suggestive that I had to check to make certain my fly was shut.

I turned back to Allie but found her already engrossed in her work. "I guess I should go." But I just stood there, still a bit lost in my fantasy. Before I could make my exit, Allie turned around and caught my look.

She smiled, clearly entertained by my predicament. "You thinking about the one with me on the desk again? Maybe you should go home and take a cold shower."

"You wanna join me?"

She stood up and stepped close to me. "When I get home, I'm gonna come after you like a wild animal."

Her comment got my blood flowing instantly. But with her commitment to the project, I had no idea when she actually would get home—it could be tonight or even tomorrow.

Our moment was interrupted as the entire office, including Allie, erupted by saying, "Pizza!" The deliverymen had arrived, their arms stacked with pizza boxes, and soon they were surrounded by an army of employees with grabby hands. Rebecca and Allie were at the front of the line.

"Pizza break!" yelled Rebecca. "Did you bring plates and forks? Which one is the vegetarian?" she badgered the deliverymen.

One of the young men handed her a box.

"And how many pepperoni? You guys screwed it up yesterday," Rebecca complained.

The man shuffled through the boxes and held out one. "Just one, I guess."

There was a sudden outcry from the employees along the general lines of, "There's just one pepperoni!" With that battle cry the employees mobbed the two deliverymen, who desperately tried to hold their ground against the eager ocean of hands assaulting them.

Pizza Break was a company routine, soon to be tradition, as was Donut Break, Brunch, and Second Lunch. (Oh, and the Midnight

Buffett was to die for.) They were all billed as perks for working long hours for the fledgling company, but I knew they were just a way to hide the sort of eating that would otherwise expose three Super Born women's appetites. I'll bet you couldn't work here without gaining fifteen pounds. In my case it was five, but I'd only been here a week.

I made my way back to my desk with two dripping slabs of sausage double cheese in hand—that's right, like a real man, with no sissy napkin. I folded one piece in half like a taco and took a messy bite, grease dripping all over my fingers and maybe the floor—probably the floor—okay, definitely the floor. But I didn't care, 'cause I was the VP of marketing and a real man, a real hungry, manly man. As I munched I dreamt of when Allie would get home and come at me *like a wild animal*, though I realized all that would most likely await me was that cold shower—a cold but manly shower.

FIFTEEN

Chinese Movie Night

LOGAN

I staggered home around seven p.m., leaving Allie, Rebecca, and half of the staff still buzzing around the office, pushing the project forward like a thousand ants carrying a piece of bread uphill. I had a few hours to kill until the time difference would kick in so I could make my calls to Africa. I felt myself begin to chill and a smile come to my face when I saw Paige in the kitchen.

"Hey, Tiger, how's it goin'? I brought that Chinese you like from Wang Woo or Fuk Yoo's or whatever it's called." I held up two brown bags, hoping to make her happy. But I should have known from all my recent experience with women that doing what you think will make them happy and making them happy were often two different things. When she kept digging in the refrigerator and ignored me, I walked up to her. "Don't you want some? I even got you two…one egg roll and this very special brown paper bag."

"I'm having a salad," she said dryly, pulling the lettuce out of the crisper.

I shook the bag in her face. "Fuk Yoo."

She gave me a disgusted look and rolled her eyes. "What does Mom see in you anyway? You're like a child." She began viciously chopping at some lettuce, but I caught her glancing at my food when I took the containers out of the bag and opened them.

All my experience living with these women in their native habitat—what was it now, three whole months?—told me to press on despite the uncalled for but obvious rejection. "Suit yourself," I said, dramatically folding the brown paper bag in front of her. "Paper—brown paper. Could have been yours, but no."

I took two bowls from the cupboard and set two forks beside them. When I placed two napkins beside them, I made a long, sustained *dun dun dun duuuuuuun* sound. She began to waver, fumbling with her salad ingredients. Then I scooped spoonful after spoonful of her favorite, General Tsao's chicken, from the container into the bowls, picked them both up, and said, "Doesn't that smell good? Man, am I ever hungry."

As I'd hoped, she turned and grabbed one of the bowls. We wrestled for it for a moment before I let her have it. She almost smiled for a quick second but then returned to her cold demeanor, removed the fork from the bowl, threw it in the sink as if it (and I) were filth, and replaced it with a pair of chopsticks from a drawer. In a flash she shuffled out of the room, down the hall, and into the TV room.

I followed, paced slowly into the room, and sat next to her on the sofa. But I learned the war was far from over. She slid down the sofa away from me without taking her eyes off of the TV. Paige began digging her chopsticks into the bowl, shoveling the food into her mouth.

"Tiger, I know it's been hard on you the last few days with your mother working crazy hours and now me too. We haven't had time for you."

"Oh, really? I hadn't even noticed you were gone," she said, sarcastically chewing away.

"What your mother is working on is really important, and she loves it. It won't be like this forever."

"I've got no problem with either of you being gone. I'm glad the queen is so happy. Okay?" *The queen* was what she called her mother sometimes.

"Well, then, what's wrong? Why have you been giving the cold shoulder the last few days?"

"Really? You're gonna go with *that*—really?"

I put my arms up, as if clueless—okay, not as if. "Let me have it," I said, sticking out my chin for her to hit. "Right on the ol' kisser."

Paige did a good job ignoring me and staring at the TV for a long while. Then I could see her face begin to quiver and tears forming in the corners of her eyes. She tried hard to continue being cold, but when she lifted a large chunk of chicken from her bowl and it fell from the chopsticks, her head dropped too and she began to whimper. Finally, she turned to me and said angrily, "I saw you. I saw you leave her room."

"Who?" Man, am I quick.

"Jennifer, I heard her—*sounds*, and then I saw you sneak out of her room."

"Is that what this is all about?" I was relieved now, knowing this was all a misunderstanding, though I realized the hard part would be convincing her of that. "Nothing happened. Thanks, by the way, for thinking I could make a woman scream like that—in a good way, you know what I mean—but no way did I sneak out of her room. That was a very upright, honorable walk."

Paige snarled her lips and rocked her head."Very funny, but you can't joke your way out of this. Don't worry, I didn't tell Mom—yet." Paige stared ahead for a moment then looked over at me with her lips tight. "I've seen the way Jennifer looks at you like a piece of meat when your back's turned."

There was a good meat joke there, but I had to let it slide. "This is all a misunderstanding. Let's go back over what happened that night. I checked on you. You were asleep in this very room. A few minutes later, I heard Jennifer screaming. I went to her room, and she was having a nightmare. I stayed with her until she calmed down and then walked out of her room in a very not-sneaky way. That was it," I said, making a long horizontal line with my hand. From her look and silence, I could tell she still wasn't buying it. "Look, you were asleep. What woke you up?"

Paige sniffled. "She screamed, I guess."

"Right, that's what I heard too. I walked to her room and calmed her down by just being there. She made herself scream—it was horrible how scared she was."

Paige shook her head. "Jennifer, scared? Fat chance. She's tough, like the B.I.B."

"You didn't see her like I did, shaking and frightened like a little girl."

Paige bit her lip."Really?"

"Ohhhh, yeah."

"What could scare her that bad?"

I took a deep breath, recalling the image of the energy storm throwing Jennifer against the wall, the image of Jennifer as a child standing alone in her burning house. "She had something really horrible happen to her when she was a child. She was reliving it in her nightmare."

"How do you know?"

"She told me. That's what I did in her room—I listened. That was it. I swear," I said raising my hand.

Paige shook her head."You didn't…"

"Paige, I love your mother. I heard Jennifer scream, and thought I should help. What would you expect me do? Listen to her screaming and just stand there and eat a piece of toast?"

Paige hesitated.

"Okay, don't answer that."

Finally, she began to smile.

"With all this stuff going on at work, the long hours, and this chaos at home, you know what I miss most?" I asked.

Paige raised her eyes and thought a bit before concluding, "Your sanity? Drinking? Having a life?"

"Very funny. No, it's movie night with you. We haven't watched a movie we could laugh at in a long time. What do you say we find some horrible piece of crap and watch it together?"

Paige opened her eyes and mouth with excitement. "How about one of those old black-and-white sci-fi films? Those are so bad they're good," Paige said, moving in closer to me.

I worked the remote till I found the right screen and selected a movie to play. "Here's a classic, *Creature from the Black Lagoon*. Just wait till you see this senseless cinema. You can be the voice of the damsel in distress, and I'll be the ever-clean hero."

"I get to be the monster!"

"Girlfriend, you are the monster!"

Instantly, we were back to being "peas and carrots," as they say. But then Paige asked, "Where'd you put my egg roll?"

Oops. "What eggggg roooo?" I struggled to say with my mouth full.

* * *

For two hours of a raucous-laugh-fest movie night, Paige and I made up fake dialogue to go with the lousy film. By the time the creature sank lifelessly into the black lagoon (probably due to the excessive weight of his vinyl costume), our Chinese food was ancient Asian history and Paige and I were fine.

When she wandered off to bed, I made about twenty contacts in Dubai, Cairo, and Lagos to get the ball rolling on facilities, dealers, and aid agencies in Africa. Despite the international accents of all those involved, I was happy to hear everyone spoke English. Man, was I smooth on the phone, I had to admit as I finally set aside my mobile phone, put up my feet, and munched a piece of victory toast in the great room. It was late now and without the phone call adrenaline, I knew I would soon be crashing. Somehow, I did find enough energy to stagger to the bedroom, get undressed, and climb into bed.

An hour later, I woke up to Allie doing her version of the stagger-in-get-undressed routine. She rolled over next to me, a silent lump. In a foggy tone I asked, "What happened to coming at me like you were a wild animal?"

Allie weakly ran her nails over my chest. "Roar. Happy?"

A few minutes later she was snoring in my ear.

SIXTEEN

We Give Birth

LOGAN

The Super Born's Africa project progressed with amazing speed, quicker than anyone had imagined. In fact, things moved so fast that no one, not even Rebecca, could keep up with it. It had begun evolving on its own, much like any life form would. All three Super Born and me were chasing after it as if it were a rock we had foolishly allowed to roll downhill ahead of us. Soon it was impossible to catch. It wore on all of us.

Rebecca seemed constantly on the verge of exhaustion. Her commitment to the project made her anxious and impatient. Fast was not fast enough. She saw what could be and wanted it now. Much like a runner who sets too fast a pace early in a race, she was nearly spent already. It showed in her sunken eyes, her graying skin, and her restlessness, which no longer seemed to have any real energy behind it.

Jennifer was more used to stress, I suppose. While frustrated at dealing with a living, growing project that was out of her control, she still managed to keep her focus. Even paying the astronomical bills Rebecca approved without a moment's hesitation didn't seem to faze her. This was all the more odd due to the fact that she did not seem to share the confidence in or commitment to the project that the rest of us did. She was not making sarcastic comments or complaining, even when approving commitments to spend millions of dollars. Of course, she took little breaks and getaways to keep her sanity that the rest of us didn't and maybe should have. For days at a time she would suddenly be unavailable, then reappear seeming refreshed. Allie and Rebecca made sarcastic sexual innuendos about her sudden disappearances, but with the limited time Allie and I were having together, I didn't find them funny.

Watching Allie work and seeing her commitment made her seem even more of an amazing woman to me, but at the same time, everything she was doing took her away from me. It was like finding the greatest beer ever brewed and then learning the only bar that carried it was closing, if not forever, then for the foreseeable future.

Don't get me wrong, I felt a profound feeling of accomplishment with my role in the project. It was unlike anything I had been a part of before (although those two weeks as a barista came close to saving the world. Without my giving people their caffeine fix every morning, who knows what could have happened.) Before long I was managing a network of customers, distributors, aid agencies, marketing groups, nonprofits, for-profits, bleeding hearts, greedy bastards, and religious, environmental, and medical aid groups that literally spanned the globe. We were all lining up to work together. Maybe there is more than one way to change the world.

Allie showed signs of exhaustion, but she seemed able to power through it better than the rest of us. While most of us were spent by the time the Midnight Buffet rolled around, Allie seemed to catch her second wind. The only one who came close to keeping up with her was her new right arm, Iyla Stevenson, who had become like Allie's shadow. Everyone joked about their relationship—while I lay alone in bed at night, I didn't find that one funny either. Of course, what I lost in terms of time with Allie, I gained with Paige. Movie night seemed to turn into every night.

The only sore spot in everyone's mind was Rebecca's insistence on ramping up production and committing to delivery times without anyone having seen a working prototype. She insisted that the first fluid disk generator would come off the assembly line, work perfectly, and ship to the customer immediately. In fact, everything hinged on it.

Our plant in Scranton was filling with manufacturing equipment, including robots that were waiting quietly to move the partially assembled units from one area of the plant to another. People were being hired and trained to build a product that didn't exist. Orders for raw materials, components, and subassemblies were ordered with set delivery dates, leaving no room for reworking the design. Thousands of computers, satellite communications equipment, custom-modified farm equipment, medical equipment, and educational tools had been ordered and were soon to be delivered, all based on the first unit working as Rebecca imagined it. This was going on not only in Scranton but in two other plants in Cairo and Lagos, which weren't far behind. Cutting out the prototyping phase would save us months or even years, but the risks of failure were immense.

With her fortune resting in the balance, Jennifer was amazingly calm. You could tell she cringed at the amount of her money at risk, yet she stood like a pillar facing the coming storm. Whenever her tension and frustration neared their boiling point, she would disappear for a few days and return calm, sometimes even smiling for a day. Something kept her from putting on the brakes on the spiral of spending. On several occasions I meant to ask her why she didn't do just that, but instead ended up just going on with my life.

* * *

JENNIFER

The windows were just beginning to show the gray of the coming dawn when I climbed out of Michael's ransacked bed. As I shuffled around the bed, the boards of the rough floor creaked, and I feared

I would wake him. I bent down over Michael. I watched the slow, slumbering breaths lift his nearly hairless chest for a while, and it made me smile. That is, until I noticed the scratches my nails had left in his arms and the cuff that still bound his hands to the bed frame. It had taken a concerted effort, as usual, to control myself enough to be with him all night without hurting him. I looked at his contented face and compared it to the anguish I had left other men feeling and was proud of myself.

I paused, debating what could happen if I freed his arms. Before Michael, I'd never undone the cuffs once I had them locked and my partner safely restrained. Still I made him wear them, and I was certain the novelty was wearing thin. Despite my affection for him and the seedlings of trust, caverns appeared in my mind that I had never known before. Trust, affection, and vulnerability were frightening unknowns. Visions of Michael and the words he'd spoken hours ago smiled in my mind. He surrendered a caring and sweetness in his unbridled desire for me that I had never known before. That allowed me to push my concerns aside, rub my hand over his cheek, and begin freeing his hand.

"No, not again," he mumbled into his pillow, semi-conscious. Then his eyes slowly blinked open. "Okay, one more, but that's it."

"You wish," I said.

Michael took his free hand and ran it over my cheek. "I do wish."

I reached over him, freed his other hand, and he buried his face in my breasts. "Don't you ever get enough?" I said, pulling away. "Anyway, that thing of yours is dead. I killed it. I have sculpted your sculpture."

He sat up. "You did. That was amazing…hey, I'm sorry that you couldn't…I mean, that I didn't, again…you know."

"Not to worry," I said.

"I did try really hard for a longggg time," he said, running his hand over my thigh.

"I know you did," I said, standing up and beginning to fish around for my clothes.

"Was it me? Is there something else I can do?

I stopped fussing with my clothes and looked at him. "Just don't give up on me. We'll figure it out."

"Hey, next time how about you don't tie my hands—or better yet, you let me tie you up? I've already got about four or five fantasies in my head about that. I promise, you'll be a very happy woman. I'll bet you wake up all my neighbors."

"Again?"

"Oh, don't mind those two old hippies. I'll bet they got it on too as soon as they got back to their apartment." Michael rattled the cuff connected to the bedpost. "So," he said, "how about it?"

"Maybe we could try it sometime," I said, already knowing that day would never be.

"Man," Michael said, shaking his head, "I thought I could talk dirty. What, did you just get out of prison?" He laughed.

"Something like that," I said with a smirk, remembering some of the guttermouthed things I'd said. I had to admit that I had no idea what he'd unleashed in me or if it was good or bad. I worried that the depth of my emotions would bring to life one of my nightmares as payback for my sins, hurting me…or him. The thought unsettled me.

I finished dressing and then gave him a peck good-bye, which he turned into a long, passionate kiss, with his hands beginning to roam my body again. I was instantly nervous, almost frantic. With the restraints off, the world suddenly got complicated. The caverns flashed panic in my mind, so I backed away and tried to smile to disguise my sudden fear.

Michael shook his head. "You know this isn't fair. You just show up whenever—I never know when or how. Then you give me the time of my life, and *poof*, you disappear again. I don't even know your last name?"

"It's Goddess."

"That's what I mean. Like, what's all the mystery?"

"Me."

Michael just shook his head. It was clear he was getting nowhere with me.

"What? You're complaining now? I didn't hear complaints last night."

"Last night—man, you are a wildcat. Hey, can you at least put your number in my phone? It's over there on the table. Then I'll feel better. Please, please?" he said, putting his hands together like a beggar. "I'm only gonna ask you a thousand more times before I give up."

I tried to cover my nervousness with a smile as I grabbed the phone and went into his contact list. "Ah, I see, Brenna, oh, and Carly. And here's Hermione. Is anyone really named Hermione anymore?"

Michael sat up against the headboard and grinned. "What can I say?"

"What, I'm not enough for you? You have to do it with Harry Potter characters too? I'm not gonna find Professor McGonagall in here, am I?"

"Oh, yeah, Minerva—big time freak. Ooh man, the threesome we had with the Sorting Hat," said Michael, shaking his fingers as if they were on fire.

"Maybe I should delete them."

"Maybe you should," Michael said seriously. "Except McGonagall," he added, smiling.

"Let me see if there's a Jennifer in here already…nope, just a Jenna. That's pretty close though, isn't it?"

"Not even close. She's a delete. Let's make plenty of room for you." He put his hands behind his head and rested against the headboard. The sight of his bare chest and tight stomach drew me right back into bed with him, but I restrained the pounding, feverish urge to go at him the way I had with all the men before him, not holding back. But then it would be over.

I took a breath—resolving, once again, to control myself—and then moved my thumbs over the keyboard. "There, Jennifer," I said, putting his phone down, my fingers shaking. I hoped he wouldn't notice.

Michael gave a relieved smile. "Great. I'm gonna call you as soon as I regain my strength and get this smile surgically removed from my face."

"Aren't you gonna work today?"

"Please. You've got my brain spinning. How am I supposed to think about anything else?" Michael sighed and his smile disappeared. " I've never met anyone like you, Jennifer."

"You can say that again," I said, trying to make light of his sincere comment, though there were knots in my stomach and my mind was reeling. When he got up to give me another good-bye kiss, half of me wanted to flee. The other half stared at his muscles moving, feeling the desire to run up and pin him back to the bed.

Instead, I rushed to the door as fast as I could. "See ya."

When I closed the door behind me, I stood in the hall for a moment, debating whether or not I should go back in. In the end, I didn't, and I hated myself for it. I heard him begin joyfully singing the song "Maria" from *West Side Story*, replacing Maria with my name. It made me smile, until I was hit with the realization that I hadn't put my number in his phone. He would have to be content with Jenna.

* * *

LOGAN

It was a cloudy and cold late afternoon in April when we rolled out the first fluid disk generator. Like everything else the Super Born did, it happened on short notice and several days earlier than we had been planning. I struggled to notify all of the customers, distributors, government officials, and other dignitaries I thought should be present. There was no time for fanfare or elaborate preparations, so we all crowded around outside the loading dock area of the plant—no grandstands for VIPs, no decorations, no wild light show. Employees stood together, smiling and excited as high school students with a team in the state finals. Those we'd invited to join us intermixed with the employees—I mingled, greeted, and smiled, in between nervous belches from my growling, acidic stomach. The mayor and his entourage were front and center in the crowd, having ridden the skyrocketing economic boom in Scranton into a campaign for the governor's office—the local news these days was dominated by his smiling face. I had invited Dr. Jones despite the objections of Rebecca. He stayed in the mayor's wake, sucking up all the attention he could siphon from the cameras.

I was handling it all well until I caught a glimpse of Ed Baker, Mr. FBI, with Ms. Suit beside him. They hadn't been invited but somehow had entered with the mayor's party. Ed looked at me and waved while Ms. Suit just stared at me through her designer glasses. Suddenly, I had a sense of déjà vu, remembering how I'd felt the night of the Searchlight Event, the disastrous night the mayor had tried to coax Allie into joining forces with him and instead destroyed half the city. The sense of panic hit me like a burning shot of adrenaline. I turned left then right before bumping into Jennifer.

"So, is this piece of crap going to actually work today?" she asked. When I stammered to answer, she continued, "What, are you getting sick?"

"I'm okay…Allie and Rebecca ran diagnostics about a half hour ago. They say we're ready." I turned to notice her expensive suit, the effort she'd put into bringing fullness and waves to her hair, and the uncharacteristic glow to her face.

"What?" she asked taking note of my stare.

"Nothing," I said looking away. "Don't worry, Rebecca knows what she's doing."

"I hope they're right. They just took it off the production line yesterday and tested it this morning. Seem a little rushed to you?" Jennifer asked, giving me an uncertain look. Despite it not being a warm day, she fanned herself with one of our brochures.

"You know Rebecca, Ms. Impatient."

"Ms. Financial Disaster is more like it. God, the money," she said, hiding her face behind the brochure for a moment.

I leaned in close to her and lowered my voice. "To top that, the FBI is here, and so is that Homeland Security agent I was telling you about."

"Really? Where?" said Jennifer. "Show me!"

"They're over there, behind the mayor."

"Is she the one staring at us?"

"That's her," I confirmed.

"Cocky lil' bitch. Should we be worried?"

"I don't think so, but I can't seem to convince my stomach of that."

Jennifer waved at Ed and Ms. Suit, causing them to avert their gazes.

That was when the massive doors of the assembly building began to slide open and one of the sort of vehicles they use to tow airplanes pulled the generator out into the parking lot. Technicians ran long electrical cables out and connected them to the wheeled tower that supported the generator some fifty feet in the air (this being the smallest model in our product line). Hydraulic jacks swung out like insect legs from the base of the tower to stabilize it to the ground.

With Jennifer preferring the shadows, Allie finding it hard to hold her lunch when forced to speak in public, and Rebecca too mentally active to stay on point, it fell to me or Alex Harper to turn the switch. With my nervousness should the generator fail, I found it easier to contemplate the joy of nothingness rather than be present in the moment. So, considering his infatuation with the product, I had Alex do it.

As Alex approached the control mechanism at the base of the generator, I scanned up the gleaming silver tower, up to the fan blades that looked like a standard wind turbine with three long, sweeping blades. The blades dwarfed the generator, which sat atop the tower enclosed in a sleek, curved silver housing. I watched Rebecca whisper some last-minute instructions to Alex before she scurried off into the assembly building to join Allie and Iyla.

"Ladies and gentlemen, may I present the FDG 1.0 one-megawatt power system," said Alex through a handheld microphone.

When Alex turned to start the generator on a nearby control screen, the wind seemed lethargic. I could barely feel the breeze on my face. How could it run with so little wind? I started going through the reasons I could give customers as to why the generator wasn't generating. My concerns made me barely realize that Jennifer had taken hold of my hand and was squeezing the living crap out of my fingers.

I held my breath. The massive blades of the generator jerked as they were unlocked but then turned only so slightly.

"Oh God, no," Jennifer whispered and squeezed my hand tighter. Believe me, when a Super Born squeezes, she squeezes.

We all stood silent for a moment while the generator stood lifeless. Then came the humming sound of electric actuators extending a second set of shorter, curved blades between each larger blade. They came together, forming something like a blower wheel in the hub of the turbine. The large blades began to creep slowly into a steady spin, one painful revolution after another.

"Come on, you son of a bitch," I whispered.

"Move, you goddamn money pit!" Jennifer added in a low tone.

The blades seemed to pause for a second, and I could feel my heart stop. Then the revolutions picked up pace until they became constant and regular, although slow. After a time, the second set of small blades retracted back into the propeller hub, and the large blades spun faster. The crowd began to cheer. One by one, the exterior and interior lights of the neighboring buildings came on, and soon the entire complex glowed brightly, powered by the generator. A giant video screen—my idea, thank you—came to life with a live feed of the spinning generator followed by a promotional video. Dramatic music flooded through a speaker system—everything powered by the generator.

Jennifer freed my hand, put her fingers in the corners of her mouth, and whistled loudly. In the assembly building, I saw Allie, Iyla, and Rebecca holding hands and jumping together like cheerleaders. The mayor quickly reviewed his notes for his speech (I'm sure to take credit for what we had done). Alex monitored his control screen to measure the generator's output, stopping periodically to pump his fist with excitement.

Now that everything was wonderful, it was my turn. I walked up to the control panel under the giant whooshing blades and took hold of the microphone. I felt like someone doing their first stand-up comedy routine and resisted saying, "I just flew in from Cleveland, and boy, are my arms tired." Instead I smiled like someone had just bought me a round of drinks, held my arm up, and said, "The FDG 1.0!" The crowd cheered louder. "Delivered as promised, ahead of schedule, performing as predicted, and currently generating"—I glanced at the control screen—"357,000 watts of clean power right here or anywhere on the planet! At one quarter the cost of fossil fuels or any current alternative energy system." Dramatic pause. "The power to light the world!"

Within seconds, I was surrounded by people interested in buying the unit or licensing the technology. I lost track of all the Super Born amid the chaos and shouted conversations of those surrounding me and demanding my attention. Just like that, I was the man again.

* * *

An hour later things began to settle down, and the crowd faded away, leaving my schedule, order book, and contact list full and my energy level depleted. I walked into the assembly building, looking for Allie, when Ed Baker appeared, leaning against a steel beam by the door of the cavernous building.

"Looks like you caught yourself a hot one," Ed began.

"Are we talking about my girlfriend or something else?"

"Relax, I'm not watching her…much." Ed pointed out at the spinning turbine. " What a great job you stumbled onto here, all this amazing technology. Really super tech, wouldn't you say?"

"Ed, I told you, if I hear from them, you'll be the first to know."

Ed nodded. "Yeah, I remember you saying that." Then he moved in close to me. "But the trouble is, buckeroo, we haven't heard from you. I can only hold Ms. Johnson off for so long. And now you're here doing things way over your pay grade. I don't remember you being that lucky."

"And I don't remember you being such a prick."

Suddenly I felt arms around my neck and the weight of a delightful body on my back. "Was that awesome or what!" Allie declared. "Did you see that sucker light up the whole plant?" Then she saw Ed and dropped off my back, her smile fading.

"Allie, this is Ed Baker, the guy who's been telling you when your car payment is overdue."

Allie gave Ed a suspicious glance. "Oh. Gee, thanks, Ed—don't know how my credit rating ever made it without you."

"You should explain to your buddy here just how valuable I can be," Ed said, slapping me on the shoulder. "Well, Logan, I gotta get going. Just keep in mind what we talked about. Remember which side your bread is buttered on," he said as he turned to leave.

"The top, right, Ed?"

"The tip-top," answered Ed, pointing up to the sky without turning around.

"Are we in trouble?" Allie asked as she wrapped her arms around my arm, watching Ed fade into the distance.

"Not hardly."

"You want me to fold him in quarters, dribble him like a basketball, or fly him out and dump him in the ocean?"

"I didn't know you were so devious."

Allie turned to face me,"You have no idea. Just leave the toilet seat up once—once," Allie said, holding up one finger as a joke. (I hoped.)

Still, I had to wonder if she had ever dribbled anyone. The thought drifted around in my mind for a while. It didn't leave me until she looked up and disarmed me with a sensuous look.

As we walked through the glowing vastness of the plant accompanied by the echoes of our steps, we passed dozens of unassembled generators, towers, and blades that would soon be shipped all over the world. At the far end of the building, robots were busy transporting assemblies while welding sparks flew and employees studied computer screens. A large four-wheeled platform robot leisurely hummed by us, transporting the nacelle of a generator to the shipping dock, and Allie waved to it as if it were a fellow employee.

"What a day! We should celebrate, don't you think?" she said.

"What did you have in mind?"

"How about I get you home and naked and let you have your way with every inch of my body?" When I grinned she added, "If we cut through the testing department, we'll get to your car faster."

Instead of turning into the testing area, I found an unused office open to our immediate left. I took hold of her hand, led her in, and closed the door. "No, actually, I think this way might be faster."

SEVENTEEN

New York, New York, Ever Do It on a Torch?

ALLIE

I could feel the calm cloud of endorphins carrying me off to the first good night's sleep I'd had in weeks. My head slid onto Logan's chest and nestled into his warmth like I belonged there. I floated on the tantric breeze as if hovering over a field of fragrant wild-flowers—or was that the smell of freshly baked chocolate-chip cookies? Either way, it was great. I surrendered to the sensation and ran my hand over the firm muscles of Logan's chest, feeling at peace and certain that life didn't get much better than this. *Wait, are there chocolate chips in the cupboard? And flour, did I remember to get that at the grocery store?* I could feel the tension draining out of my muscles like cool waters trickling into a rocky pool glisten-ing in the sun. *Crap, I forgot to pick up Paige's homecoming dress.* Logan's hand drifted gently over my back, making me feel alive. I curled into him more deeply and released any concerns I had about my life.

Just as I began to feel myself drifting into a contented sleep, the phone rang on my nightstand. The little bastard wouldn't stop, and the cheery ring tone—"Happy," which I'd thought was so cute—assaulted my ears. I resisted but felt myself climbing back out of joy and into the present, so I grabbed the phone and answered it with an irritated, "What?" On the other end, I heard Jennifer's frantic voice, and I knew my little trip to contentment was over. But God, those cookies smelled good.

* * *

LOGAN

The seismic event occurred at 4:47 a.m. just off the New York/New Jersey coast and sent a tsunami on a beeline to New York Harbor. With the close proximity of the event to the coast and the late hour, most New York residents were blissfully unaware of the impending danger. Worse yet, with the high speed at which the tsunami traveled, authorities had little time to warn them.

When Allie set Jennifer and me down on Liberty Island, it was nearly dawn. The harbor before us had already been completely drained of water, having been sucked out to sea to feed the monstrous surge that was coming. The Statue of Liberty stood behind us with her torch raised in defiance of the onslaught that was bearing down on her.

On the shoreline the city was sluggishly beginning to respond. Horns sounded from the disaster warning system and from ships and boats that now lay listing helplessly in centuries' worth of deposited mud like beached whales. Rather than escape or panic, many of those who were outdoors at the time came to see the spectacle of warships, ferries, and oceanliners resting at the bottom of the harbor forsaken by the sea. The emptiness of it made it hard to comprehend the vast volume of the ocean's water that was shooting toward them like a missile.

Jennifer stood in her red Super Born attire, staring out to sea with a look of determination on her windblown face. Allie seemed more concerned.

I looked in amazement at the empty harbor and all the muck and debris that had been revealed. "I thought you guys were kidding. Jennifer, how did you know this was happening?"

"Rebecca was giving me an update on expenditures in Africa and then suddenly said her network showed a massive energy spike outside New York. Then she went back to discussing the Lagos build out like nothing had happened. I asked her what she meant by that whole energy spike thing, and she said 'massive explosion or something.' When I called my source in New York, he said disaster alarms were going off but he didn't know why. From the look of that harbor, a tsunami is a safe bet. It'll be here soon."

"Are you sure you want to be here?" Allie asked me.

She had told me what was happening, and I had insisted, without giving it much thought—as was my general policy—on coming along to chronicle the event. It all sounded very cool at the time, but now, facing the black, vast ocean coming to smash the city—cool? Not so much.

"Why should I worry? You're…gonna stop it," I said uncertainly. "You two know what to do, right?"

There was a pause—way too long of a pause, if you ask me—before Jennifer and Allie both turned to me, saying simultaneously, "No."

Then Allie added, shaking her head, "Haven't a clue. I should get you farther inland. Come on."

"No way!" (What? Who said that?) "How am I going to see what happens unless I'm here…with you?"

Allie looked around us for a safer location.

"You're a moron, Logan," Jennifer editorialized. "Get him the hell out of here."

"Wait, help me get up there," I said, pointing to the torch of the statue behind us.

Allie shook her head. "I don't know. I doubt she can withstand the surge. Maybe back there on top of one of those tall buildings."

I looked at the massive statue and cringed at the thought of Lady Liberty being toppled by a wall of water. I looked up at her weathered, resolute face and suddenly felt the same. "No, I'm going up there!" I said, beginning to hike toward the statue. "I won't be able to see what's happening if I'm anywhere else."

"Suit yourself," said Jennifer indifferently. "Been nice knowin' ya. Allie, you think it will be hard to get another VP of marketing?"

"Shouldn't be that hard, there was that guy from New York…oh yeah, he'll probably be dead too," Allie said, piling on.

"Funny, really hilarious! You gonna zip me up there, or do I have to climb?"

"It's your funeral," Jennifer said. "If they find your body."

"Come on," said Allie, hooking her arm under my shoulders. In a flash she lifted me up to the top of statue and dropped me off behind the railing just below the glowing gold torch.

"You're coming back to get me, right?" I asked, leering over the rail.

Allie was preparing to fly then stopped, looked up into the sky, and turned back to me. I could tell she was worried."I hope I can. I want to wake Paige up for school in a few hours. I want to get the first donut at work. I've got some unfinished business with you too. But I have to do this."

"I know," I said, giving her a kiss. We both wanted to say more: I saw all the thoughts in her mind flashing across her face. I guess mine did as well. There was a long pause before we heard Allie's phone ringing. It was Jennifer calling from the base of the statue.

Allie hesitated and then dropped down in a whoosh to join her. I leaned over the railing and watched as they spoke for a moment before flying off toward the mouth of the harbor into the distant light of the coming dawn.

I dug around in my bag for my video camera and my infrared binoculars. Using the latter, I located the tiny images of the Super Born past the narrows in the outer harbor. Jennifer had gotten dropped off in the muck to stand alone facing the goliath of the dark and merciless ocean. Lacking Allie's ability to fly, there was no way for her to escape, as far as I could see. It was a do-or-die plan the two women had concocted. I watched Allie fly off toward the incoming surge, climb up into the air, and then dive down into the water; she was trying to use her speed and power to create massive countercurrents in the blackness under the sea's surface. Everywhere she dove, a vast whirlpool soon appeared spinning out to sea.

Of all the thoughts running through my mind, the only one I spoke was, "Holy shit!"

In the distance, I saw a red glow surrounding Jennifer that grew into a giant ball and then slammed into the ground before disappearing. She did it again and again in a rhythmic pattern. A few seconds later, I began to feel the statue shaking beneath my feet in the same pattern but time delayed. She had used this seismic pounding to free oil from underground shale to make herself rich and was now using it to create her own tsunami, which would shoot out to sea and collide into the incoming one and thereby counteract it. I watched the coming and going of her far-off red glow while I braced myself with one hand on the hopping statue beneath my feet. From the shore I began to hear the distant murmur of panic.

Where the hell is Allie? I scanned my binoculars across the horizon until I saw a speck of a figure shoot out of the water, climb into the sky, and then plunge back into the sea. She spun in the water, creating a giant whirlpool that spiraled out to sea. When it collided with the oncoming tsunami underwater, a giant waterspout would shoot into the air. This time "holy shit" didn't seem to be an adequate response. My jaw dropped. I was speechless.

Out to sea, just beyond where Allie dove and plunged, water that had been calm suddenly bristled with peaks of massive waves that shot into the air and then collapsed. The tsunami and Jennifer's countertsunami were colliding beneath the surface, sending up towering waves. The peaks began to appear closer and closer to Allie, the shore, and…me.

Jennifer began to increase the pace of her pattern, and the statue beneath my feet entered into constant, vibrating motion. Allie's climbs and plunges also accelerated to a hyperdelirious rate as she came in closer to shore. Water began to flow under Jennifer's feet and the peaking waves marking where the tsunamis met moved in toward her. Allie flew out of the ocean for the last time and then hovered over Jennifer.

* * *

ALLIE

"We gotta go! It's still coming!" I told Jennifer breathlessly.

"You go."

"We slowed it down, but it's still coming," I said, dropping down to grab her.

"You go. They'll need you when it hits."

"There's no use in you staying here. Come on!" I said, grabbing her, but then I felt her burning heat, which forced me away.

"Get the hell out of here! I've got one more idea. If it doesn't work, you came come back and get me."

"Yeah, right," I said, pointing at the wall of water rising up out of the sea as the tsunami began to roar into the shallower water toward shore.

"Get the fuck out of here, you stupid bitch!" Jennifer raised her arm, and a glowing beam of red light and heat enveloped me, causing me to shoot up into the air. I screamed and almost lost control of myself. Then she projected a beam of light from her hands, creating a wall from Breezy Point to Sandy Hook, a massive, curved wall protecting the entrance to the harbor. (Waters from the shorelines outside the wall hadn't been pulled back into the sea, so it seemed the tsunami we were fighting was somehow focused on New York.) Flashes of steam formed instantly wherever the water hit Jenny's wall and tried to climb it. The pounding waves and hissing of the steam sounded like a thousand titans battling for their lives. The water was held back, but some waves broke over the wall and ran themselves out, spreading in toward the harbor. The surge climbed the wall, and more and more water scaled it and ended up at Jennifer's feet. Soon her knees where covered as steam rose violently all around her. I dropped down in the air, preparing to scoop her up.

"Nooooo!" she screamed. I could barely hear her. "Noooo!"

The crashing waves overflowed the wall and rapidly raised the water level across the entire harbor to Jennifer's chest. But after that brief breakthrough, the water level out in the ocean slowly began to drop down the wall, which was holding it at bay. I screamed with joy as I watched and then turned to see Jennifer defiantly shoulder deep in water.

"You can't get me, you motherfucker! You can't get me!" she screamed with her arms still up, projecting the red wall. As the waterline dropped farther down behind her wall, she struggled to stand upright in the swirling current around her. She looked up at me impatiently. "You can get me out of here! Now would be nice!"

I dropped into the cold, frothy water behind her until I could get my hands under her arms. Then I lifted her out of the sea without affecting the energy wall...much.

"Can't you keep me steady? This is really hard from here!" Jennifer whined.

"I'll do my best. I was made to fly, not keep your fat ass steady. We *are* hovering over the ocean, you know!"

"Really? I hadn't noticed! Hold still!"

From then on Jennifer controlled a shorter version of her energy wall while I held her in the air. She regulated the height of the wall to allow water back into the harbor at a controlled rate and then raised the wall again when a second, smaller tsunami wave appeared. By eight o'clock the harbor was a harbor again. Ships and boats floated amidst the debris the ocean had stirred up and given New York as gifts. There was some damage to docks and ships, some flooding, but the harbor had been saved from most of the ocean's frightful assault.

Soon TV-station helicopters that had come out to film the disaster found us and hovered nearby.

"We better go," I said.

"No, not yet," answered Jennifer. "Otherwise, they'll never know what we did," she said, before turning off the wall and releasing the water to surge back and forth and find its own level.

Suddenly, two black helicopters appeared and shot in toward us. A tall black woman in an expensive suit sat in the front seat. Two armed men were leaning out of the doorway behind her.

"Crap!" Jennifer exclaimed.

"What?"

Before she could answer, Ms. Suit's voice came out of a loudspeaker. "I am Agent Johnson with Homeland Security. Would you two please accompany us?" There was a pause as she realized we would not be cooperating. "Okay, this is not a request. I am authorized to open fire on you if you do not comply." She gestured to the two riflemen, who nodded. One fired a few rounds into the air.

"It's up to you," Ms. Suit said dryly.

I looked at Jennifer, and we shared a nod of our own. With that, I jetted off toward Scranton, and the gunmen from both black helicopters opened fire on us while the TV helicopters rolled tape.

"Stop it! You idiots," Ms. Suit screamed, apparently unaware she was still talking into the loudspeaker. "What part of 'we're bluffing' didn't you understand? You could have hit the people we want on our side!" Then she paused, studied the gunmen, and shook her head. "You morons couldn't hit anything anyway."

With the helicopter now a distant speck, I slowed.

"Can you believe they found us?" Jennifer asked from under my arm.

"Can you believe they shot at us? Some thanks."

"Not *at* us."

"What do you mean?" Then I felt the sticky warmth of Jennifer's blood beneath my fingers. "Jenny!"

"I don't think it's too bad," she said just before slumping into unconsciousness.

* * *

LOGAN

I raised my fist in the air and yelled as I watched the women who'd tamed the waves approach. I had a big smile on my face, until I saw them shoot by and disappear into the west. I had seen the helicopters and heard the gunfire but had no idea what had transpired. Nobody would shoot at a hero…right? Still, one of the black helicopters seemed to make a feeble attempt at chasing after them.

"Guys?" I mumbled to the disappearing speck in the distance. I tried to reach Allie on our encrypted satellite phone but got no answer. I circled the torch platform looking for a maintenance door I could use to climb down the statue's arm, but found it locked. I looked back at the western sky. "Guys?"

EIGHTEEN

High and Dry…God, I Hate Being Sober

ALLIE

Jennifer had told us about the doctor she kept on retainer, the one who charged enough to have just a few patients, make house calls, and not ask any questions, no matter who the patient was. She'd given us his number and encouraged Rebecca and me to use him, but neither of us had seen the point—until now. Jennifer had turned a large pantry area of her penthouse into an exam/procedure room containing a bed, exam table, medical monitoring equipment, and medical supplies. That's where I took her. I thought it best to pull off her bloodied red outfit, hide it, get her under a sheet, and keep pressure on a towel I had placed over the wound. She didn't move, though I could see her still breathing—but the blood, oh, the blood.

I did take a break to run to Jenny's closet to find a shirt and some jeans. I slipped out of my black costume and into her clothes.

I'd called the doctor en route explaining the urgency, so he and his nurse arrived just a few minutes later. He stormed in, and the emergency-room experience Jennifer had told me about appeared to kick in.

"Anything I can do?" I asked.

"Get out," he said. The nurse ushered me into the hall. I heard their voices, and then the beeping of a heart monitor. Thank God she was still alive.

A nervous, pacing sixty minutes later, the door cracked open. I took that as a hint that I could come in. There lay Jennifer propped up in the bed with a heart monitor and an IV attached to her. The nurse was injecting a drug into her IV.

I looked into the doctor's eyes. "She okay?"

"Lucky girl. Lucky you got her here so fast, and lucky it wasn't an inch higher. Bullet went clean through. You should feel lucky too that you weren't standing next to her."

"Yeah, good thing." I turned my head to Jennifer. "Will she make it?"

"Sure, I'll make it," said a groggy Jennifer, struggling to open her eyes. "Make what?"

I looked back at the doctor, and he smiled and nodded. "Emily will stay here while I get someone who can remain here round the clock. What she needs now is blood and rest. The blood part will be expensive."

Jenny waved her hand weakly, barely lifting it off the sheet. "Do I look like money is real important to me right now?"

The doctor nodded. "I'll see to it."

"Thanks, Doctor," I said, moving to Jennifer's side.

"Well, how do I look?" she asked me.

"You look like shit on toast...maybe with a little jelly."

"Well, it's probably because I am really exhausted."

"I know. Battling billions of tons of water and a gunshot wound takes a lot out of a girl, even you." I moved up beside her and took her hand. "Don't worry. I'll stay with you a while."

"Oh? Aren't you forgetting something?" she asked with half-open eyes, making a tortured attempt to laugh.

"Logan!"

I ran into the laundry room next door where I had stashed my things, closed the door, and let Jennifer's clothes fall off my body while I searched for my stuff, including the satellite phone Rebecca had given me. I rang Logan as I searched for my black outfit.

"Hello?" he answered dryly.

"Logan!"

"He's in a meeting right now. Can you call back later?" he said with the sound of the wind whistling in the phone.

"Very funny!"

"No, you know what's funny? You leaving me to rot up here!"

"I'm sorry, but I had my hands full."

"Me too. You wouldn't believe how much there is to do on top of a friggin' torch!"

"Logan, your FBI friend and that woman—they shot Jennifer."

For a long second all I heard was the whistling of the wind. "What?"

"I had to get her to a doctor as fast as I could. She was bleeding really bad."

"Is she all right?"

"Doc says she'll be okay. She's conscious and talking, so that's good...to a point."

"Well, that settles it."

"What?"

"Ed Baker is definitely off my Christmas card list. And if he shoots anybody else I know, he's unfriended, for sure."

"I'll unfriend the little bastard, and that woman in the suit. They're dead meat."

"I love it when you talk rough. So, what are you wearing?"

"At this moment, nothing."

Logan was quiet for a moment and when he returned his voice was lower and his speech slower. "Tell me, have you ever done it on a torch?"

"Is that all you ever think about?"

"When it comes to you, yes," he said.

"As a matter of fact, I *have* done it on a torch."

"What? Really? With who?"

"Plenty of times. It's great." If there was one way to shut Logan up, it was to make him wonder. "Listen, I'll get there as quick as I can. It may be tricky in daylight. Scranton is no problem—everybody loves to see me flying around, but—"

"Especially if you're not wearing anything."

"You wish. But New York will be tough. Those people may be still looking for me. I can do without seeing that helicopter again."

"Wouldn't want you getting shot saving my ass."

"Well then maybe I'll just stay here. Who says I'm saving your ass?"

"Someone has to. I'm stuck on a friggin' torch!"

"Lay low. I'll be there soon."

"Be careful. The harbor is a mess. Never saw water opaque gray before. But it's crawling with activity on the shore, helicopters flying every which way. Only good thing is, the tsunami cancelled the statue tours, so nobody's out here—except me! I'll be easy to find. I'm the guy on the friggin' torch!"

"See you soon." I clicked off the phone, found my black outfit, and began putting it on, only to find two holes in the cape just below where it met the shoulder. I paused for a moment, realizing how close I had come to being in that bed next to Jenny. I sighed and paced a few steps. All the feelings I had experienced when Carmine Camino's bomb had almost killed me came roaring back—the pain, the struggle to breathe, feeling the life flow out of my body, and worst of all, almost leaving Paige alone. Then I imagined that black helicopter flying in at me, them shooting me or maybe Logan. I had to push it all back down. There would have to be time for feelings later.

* * *

LOGAN

I sat slouching with my back against the torch, trying to get as small physically and mentally as I could without a half dozen beers.

Below, I saw tugboats pursuing ships that had broken away from their moorings and begun to drift through the harbor, scurrying people, and police cars, whose sirens I could hear even up here. I thought, *This is what happens after we avoid being hit by a tsunami? What kind of mess would we be in if it had hit?*

That was when my satellite phone rang, and I grabbed it in excitement. "Hello?"

"Logan? Where is everybody? I can't reach Jenny, and Allie won't answer. Are you with them?" It was Rebecca, who sounded overwrought.

"Welllll," I began, trying to figure out whether to give her the long version or the short one. "You've heard about New York?"

"Don't tell me they're involved in that disaster!"

Again I paused, debating long or short. *Let's go short.* "Jennifer's been shot." Too short?

"What!"

"She and Allie came to New York to stop the tsunami, and that Fed woman in the suit shot Jenny. Jenny's back in Scranton, and she's okay, but I guess it was really serious."

"That's insane! Why would the Feds shoot Jenny?"

"Haven't a clue. I haven't really got the whole story yet."

"Where is she? And where are you?"

"Sort of trapped, at the moment. Long story. Let's just say we'll talk to you when we get back."

"So when's that?"

"Talk to you soooooooon," I said to Rebecca as Allie suddenly dropped down out of the sky, landing hard on the metal platform next to me. She took hold of me and then immediately rocketed straight up into the sky.

NINETEEN

You Vant to Party?

IYLA

The apartment where Demetri, Valeria, and I stayed was small and old, just a main room, a dirty kitchen, and two bedrooms. But it was fine with me. No one knew me here, so it was like a clean start…another clean start. And I liked working for Allie. She was a good woman and treated me like I was somebody, not some freak, like back home in Russia. Suddenly, I had a little peace in my life; every day was like a sunny picnic, like I was eating cheesesburgers in the park.

Every night like clocks work, Demetri was always there to greet me with a warm, welcoming grab at the documents I had brought him. With a grumpy sound that wasn't Russian or English, the sweetheart man ran off with them to his desk like a squirrel with a nut. Every day at work, I made one copy of any important papers Allie had requested for her and one for me, and at the end of the day, I brought them for the crazy squirrel to see. Today, he was rifling through the copies of the patent applications I had stolen for him. He lifted one page up in the air with his right hand while he ran his eyes over next sheet, and then he pushed back his chair and stood up, yelling like a madman.

"No, no, this is not what I want! There must be something else!"

I looked at the stack of papers I had given him so far. It stood like a little mountain next to the desk. "This is everything. I've done as you asked."

"It can't be!" He started coughing like his lung was coming out. I hated when he bent over and couldn't stop coughing like that. It made me feel like coughing too. Finally he stood up straight, lit a cigarette, and sucked the death out of it. He paced away. Squirrel was angry now. "This is just energy device. There is nothing about controlling the Super Born. There are no weapons here."

"It *is* energy machines. I see them at work every day! They want to light up the world, bring power, food, and education to everyone so the world is not so terrible a place. What is wrong with this?"

Demetri paced as he spoke. "It's a lie. Look at history. No one has power like they do and does not use it to control others." He put his arms behind his back like a schoolteacher. "What about Dr. Jones? He's working on this, correct? Dr. Jones is up to something. I know him."

"He is there, but he is not in control."

Demetri came at me, pointing a bony finger in my face. "The hell he's not! See? He has fooled you too. Jones told me how close he was to a control device months ago. It is here somewhere," he said, throwing the latest documents across the room. Then he lit a second cigarette even before the first was finished.

"Why don't you just light the whole pack at once? It will save you time and get you to your grave sooner," I said, taking a seat on the sofa.

Demetri waved off my concern and then paused, paced a bit more, and puffed his cigarette. It seemed to calm him and allow him to think better. "When you were in Jones' mind, you said you saw Jones controlling the women. They screamed with pain and fear, then beams of light came out of their eyes. And you saw a metal tube with coils around it?"

"Yes, it scared me so bad, I had to leave. I could feel burning pain everywhere, like being roasted in a fire. It was awful."

Demetri put his hand to his chin and looked up at the ceiling. "See! The secret *is* in his head. Maybe you have done all you can, little one. Maybe we just need to try something different."

"Demetri, you know I will do whatever you ask."

"No, not you. Valeria."

I stepped back, mad like a hive of bees hit by a stick. "Valeria! You don't need that cow! Leave her at the strip club. She brings home good money."

Demetri's only reaction was the thin smile that rose on his face. He moved in close until he was standing over me where I sat on the sofa. "No, pet, you have done everything I asked. Jones is controlling these women and their plans. Somewhere there is a focusing device to control their powers. I know it because I know him."

I had to laugh. "I know him too. I've been in his brain, you know? He is a strange little man but not in control. Not like you, Demetri," I said, stroking his thigh. "Besides, don't you remember what Valeria did to that poor man in Kiev?"

"I remember. Unfortunate, but she did get the information we sold the Chinese."

"But, Jones is your friend, yes?"

"Friend? I have no friends."

"You have me, Demetri."

"Yes, I do have you." He began stroking my hair. "You have done everything I asked. You always do." He looked down at me with sudden calm, and then he smiled. I love it when he is happy with me. It makes me feel like a safe little girl.

"I try," I said, wrapping my arms around his waist and putting my head on his belly. "Demetri, I have done as I promised. It's time for you to do as you promised."

Demetri patted my head. "A promise is a promise," he said, reaching into his shirt pocket and pulling out a glowing blue lozenge.

I giggled. "Yes, Demetri." He slipped the candy into my open, eager mouth, and within seconds I could feel the candy running through my body. I fell back on the sofa and felt the surge of his reward take over, making me feel as if I was floating on a cloud of ecstasy. The room seemed to glow, and time slowed—every heartbeat seemed to take forever. I was in a world with no cares, and every touch, every sensation, dominated my mind. I surrendered to it like breathing. When I had my candy, my powers went away, and I no longer felt the pressure of all the thoughts and feelings around me trying to climb into my head, like spiders trying to crawl through every crack. It was peace. I raised my arms like I could touch the stars. It was glorious.

Thoughts I had stolen from Logan and Allie floated by like clouds, and I grabbed them. I felt his desire for her and her acceptance of him as strongly as they did. Their emotions and pure sexual energy took me over.

"How are you feeling, my little Iyla?" Demetri asked.

I just laughed like a wicked little girl and began running my hands over the sofa like its cheap material was luxurious. I slid my fingers into my jeans and moaned with exhilaration when the fiery wave of sensation rushed there to greet them. Logan and Allie's feelings took me to a place I could never have found alone. I let my mind drift into their world. I imagined the energy of their lovemaking and the molten glow as they touched one another. I replayed their sounds and words, and it drove me to glow with my own fire. Each thought of them together increased my excitement.

When Demetri dropped the zipper of his pants, he came out already long and firm. "Little one, you do me first, then you can finish your party."

"Then you watch me?" I said, smiling, boiling with sexual energy. I took firm hold of Demetri with my hand.

"Like always," Demetri struggled to answer with the force of my approach.

In a flash, he was Logan and I was Allie. I went at him wildly while keeping my fingers busy in my jeans. Logan and Allie's sensuousness surrounded me, and I wanted it. I suppose it was too much for poor Demetri, because it wasn't long before he moaned and dropped to his knees, drained. I laughed at him like a crazy woman and then fell onto my back, like splashing into a warm pool of joy. Thoughts of Logan were on me, in me, and all around me, breathing love and desire into my body, just like he did to Allie. Somehow I could forget that I wasn't her, and his desire wasn't for me.

Demetri took deep breaths and watched me for long time, exhausted but aroused. I could hear his heavy breathing, and it excited me. When he began giving me dirty sexual commands, his breathing became so quick and shallow I thought he would pass out. I hoped he would pass out. I hoped I was being so sensuous with my own body that it would kill him dead. Suddenly I felt like I was soaring into the heavens and poor old Demetri was struggling to rise up after me like a bird with a broken wing.

That was when Valeria burst through the front door. The big stupid began searching through Demetri's jacket and desk. "I vant to party!"

"Valeria," Demetri moaned.

In an instant Valeria was on him. "Where is it, Demetri? I vant my share!" Then she smiled, pushed Demetri over onto his back, and straddled him. "You give Valeria her candy, and I do that thing you like."

"No, I'm too tired," he moaned unconvincingly.

She took hold of his little man, which proved to be the quickest route to changing his mind. "Where is it?"

"In my pocket. In my pocket." For a man in control, he had no control, and I suppose he knew it.

Demetri's hand shook as he took the candy out of his pocket and made the inside of Valeria's mouth glow with it.

Valeria savored the candy for a moment, rolling it around in her mouth before a very satisfied swallow, as if it were the last bite of an expensive dinner. "You don't seem too tired to me," Valeria said before going at Demetri with her mouth and hands like a starving woman eating pizza for the first time. Demetri moaned and rolled on the floor like a man trying to escape but not actually wanting to get away. He began crying out to a god he didn't believe in and then screamed weakly and slumped into pile.

Valeria immediately stood up and raised her eyes to the ceiling with a big smile on her face, like a cat that had just eaten a little bird. "Don't try party without Valeria! No party until Valeria is here." She straightened out her long, messy hair and then closed her eyes. When she opened them again, she had changed. I could see the candy taking her away. I watched the fire in her eyes go away, disappearing like a train leaving the station. As she paced around the room, her movements turned from those of a clumsy big stupid to those of a gliding cat. I swear, there was a blue aura surrounding her boarish self. Valeria smiled like she had just told a joke, as if her idiot brain could think of one. She stopped, let her clothes drop off her like falling water, and took a deep breath. She held out her arms like she was free for the first time and turned to Demetri. "Watch, old man." Then she moved toward me like a lioness. "Valeria is here. Now party can begin."

TWENTY

Tsunami or Salami. You Choose.

LOGAN

Allie, Dr. Jones, Rebecca, and I sat watching the panel TV on the wall of the conference room at our new offices at the plant. The more times we watched the video of Allie, Jennifer, and the helicopters hovering over New York Harbor, the more disbelief we felt and the more enraged Rebecca grew. As we watched the gunfire erupt once again, while Allie and Jennifer made their escape, it proved too much for Rebecca.

"This is wrong, wrong, wrong on so many levels!" Rebecca said, pacing and throwing her arms around in a highly animated but klutzy way. "You could have been killed! You are endangering everything!"

"Rebecca, we saved thousands of lives and prevented suffering," Allie said.

"Now Jenny's in a hospital bed, they just missed hitting Allie, and Logan got stuck on a torch. You guys took a big chance. If something had happened to you, everything we've done would have been lost. I can't run this by myself."

"We're right here, Rebecca. Nothing was lost, and what Jenny and Allie did was amazing," I said, joining the fight.

"Let me try to understand," Dr. Jones said, facing Rebecca.

"You are mad because they used their powers to save the world because you would rather they use their powers to save the world?"

Rebecca stopped pacing at stared at Jones. "What are you talking about?"

"Well, that is what you are saying. Or are you mad because they helped people their way, not your way?" Jones asked.

Rebecca shook her arms in the air. "I am mad because they almost died!"

Jones shrugged. "This is life. The more alive you are, the more chances you take. There is unknown risk in everything. Who would think a six-volt charge of nonpolarized current to a parabolic transducer would control brain waves?"

Allie and I had welcomed Jones' argument at first, but at that point we were forced to look at each other and simultaneously mouth, "What?"

"In mice…of course. Theoretically." Luckily Jones returned to earth and continued, "They risked their own well-being to save people they did not even know. They had a free choice to watch or take the risk of being involved. What could be more heroic than that? And did you catch the hit count on the internet? We even got playtime in all the major TV markets. With this little video, the world will know our power," he said, raising his fist, his eyes wide.

We all stared at him.

After a moment Jones looked from side to side at our unamused faces and slowly lowered his fist and hid it behind his other hand. Finally he seemed to realize he was not in control anymore.

"So, you think good TV ratings justify this kind of risk?" Rebecca said.

Jones nodded.

"Rebecca, it was a mess, but it all worked out. So what's the problem?" I asked.

"So? You'll do it again! Maybe they'll catch you this time. Did you ever wonder how Ms. Suit just happened to be there?"

Allie and I hadn't considered that—well, I hadn't considered that. "Yeah, I wonder what tipped her off."

"I'll tip her off. Wonder if she'd like the helicopter dropped on her head," Allie vented.

"Or maybe a good beer truck full of Miner's Lite," I added. "You haven't dropped a beer truck for a while." Allie gave me a nonencouraging stare.

Rebecca shook her head. "You're still missing the point. You can't keep taking chances. She was one step ahead of you. She'll keep doing it until she finds us and ruins everything. Whatever happened to us laying low?"

As she spoke, Jones kept creeping closer to the TV screen, which was now replaying a video map of the course of the tsunami. He paused the video and ran his hands over the screen adoringly, as if it were alive.

I watched his odd behavior for a minute, unable to contain my curiosity. "You stand too close to the microwave again?" He just continued to finger the screen in sweeping arcs, seeming deep in thought. "Jonesy?"

Finally, he looked over at me and smiled. "Yes?"

While Rebecca and Allie continued their debate, I pulled Jones aside and wrapped my arm around his shoulders. "I know you haven't gotten any for a long, long…long time, but, man, you gotta pull yourself together."

"What are you talking about, my friend?"

"What am I talking about? You were just running your hands over the TV screen like it was a woman's ass! That's what I mean."

"No, no. There was no ass rubbing going on…believe me, I can assure you of that."

"Then what's the deal?"

Jones pointed at the TV. "There are no grinding plates."

I put both my hands on his shoulders. "This is worse than I thought. Now you're talking about plates? I get the woman's ass thing.

I get the grinding part, but dinner plates? You want me to get you a burger or something?"

"No, there are no asses or dinner involved. I think the plates should be grinding," he said, gesturing with his hands, colliding over and over.

I patted his back. "I know, I know. I'd like to be doing some grinding myself, if you know what I mean."

"No, the friction is what makes for the eruption!"

"Amen, to that brother. No need to preach to the choir. I hear ya. But…"

"That's what makes the earth move," he exclaimed, shaking his arms.

"Sure, if you do it right. I can see that happening…moved the earth a few times myself."

"Then the waves can't be contained anymore, and they explode out of control," said Jones flipping his hands into the air.

Now he was getting personal. "Hey, I haven't had that problem for a long time. With that one chick and her squirrelly voice, I think I just wanted to get it over with as fast as possible."

"No, no you are pointing the miss…missing the point!" Now he had his hands on my shoulders. "There was a tsunami in New York the other day, right?"

"Duh, I was there!"

"Tsunamis originate from geologic shifting of the plates in the earth's crust where the plates overlap."

"If you say so."

Jones held up his arms in victory. "Well, there can be no eruption and no grinding without plates!"

"Christ, back to the plates again," I said throwing my hands up in the air. I took a breath then put my hand on Jones' shoulder, "Uh huh, no grinding or eruptions, I get it. You're lonely."

"I am not lonely…well, much, okay. I'm lonely, but that is not germane to my point."

"German? You're, like, Indian, dude."

Jones was clearly frustrated now. "Get the sexes thing out of your freaking head!" He moved back to the TV and the frozen image of the map, which showed with an X the origin of the seismic activity that had created the tsunami. "Here is where the tsunami originated, right?" I nodded. "Well, there are no geologic plates overlapping here. There is no grinding, no eruptions to make the earth move and release that kind of massive energy."

"Oh, that kind of…I'm with ya," I said, though I wasn't quite yet.

"Good, then look at the location. It was as if New York was targeted," Jones said, making a funnel with his hands and directing it at New York Harbor.

Allie had apparently been listening to Jones, because she suddenly joined in. "So it wasn't an act of God. It was some kind of act of terror?"

"Yeah, an act of terror," I joined in, trying to catch up.

"Is that possible?" Allie asked, studying the map.

"With a device of sufficient megaton range buried in the appropriate geologic formation and channeled by submarine structure formations, allowing for current and tidal disruptions…."

"Is it possible?" I interrupted.

"Child's play," Jones answered with a smile "It would have to be a sick little genius child with an A-bomb, but yes, it's very doable."

"Who would do such a thing?" Allie asked in amazement.

"Yeah, why not just set a bomb off in Times Square?" I asked.

Jones gave me a frustrated look, as if I were an idiot. "Do you have any idea how hard it would be to get a bomb or any type of high-tech explosive device into this country?"

I shook my head.

"Well, I do, and believe me, it is not easy. Even in pieces, it's a nearly impossible task. But lowering it from a boat in international waters… sheer genius."

By then we were all gathered around the TV again. Rebecca slipped into the group with her arms crossed defensively. "You did say Ms. Suit was already there waiting for you."

"With bells on," I added.

"Maybe she knew what was about to happen. Why else would she be there?" asked Rebecca, looking anxious.

"Holy crap," Allie said, putting her hand to her forehead. "What are we up against?"

"Goddamn it! I don't need this shit!" yelled Rebecca before storming out of the room. Allie followed after her.

I watched Jones as he stared up at the video screen, deep in thought. "Or it could be an act of God," he added.

"Really? It could have been an act of God?" I asked, hoping for a less sinister explanation.

Jones thought for a moment, then shook his head. "That would be a big fat noooooooooo."

* * *

I searched for Allie in every open doorway I passed, trying to catch up with her. When I checked out the employee lunchroom, my eyes were drawn to Iyla, Allie's assistant, huddled over a brown bag and soda. She sat in a back corner at a table alone but, strangely enough, seemed to be trying hard to hold back a smile and laughter as she stared down at her food. Then I heard a woman at a table nearby delivering the punch line of a story. It was as if Iyla knew the punch line before the woman had spoken. It seemed curious, but I didn't make much of it until I turned to leave and it happened again. As the people nearby talked, I watched Iyla's lips move like she was speaking to herself, and then she smiled several beats before the table nearby exploded with laughter. Once again, it seemed like she knew what the people around her were going to say before they said it.

Iyla noticed me watching her, and her eyes instantly ballooned. She stared at me as if frightened, and then her lips moved as if she was saying something to herself. In a flash, she gathered her things and fled out the side door. I suppose that's just the effect I have on women…okay, not every woman…a couple—okay, Christie O'Connell looked at me like that in second grade, but I was wearing my sister's hand-me-down shorts. (Don't ask.)

I finally ran into Allie in the hall and tried to keep up with her frantic pace. "Rebecca okay?"

"Not good."

A graying middle-aged man in an expensive suit whom I hadn't seen before walked past us. As he did, I saw him shake his head and heard him say, "Fuck. Goddamn it," under his breath.

"Who's that?" I asked Allie.

"The new CEO Rebecca wanted us to hire. This place was getting to be too much for her to handle."

"He seems happy," I said

"Yeah, only his second day. Wait till you see him next week. And I'm the one who offered him the job."

"What kind of pressure did you use to force him to take it?"

"Well, he told me how much money he wanted, and I said okay."

"You conniving bitch."

"I know," said Allie chuckling.

"So what's his problem?"

"From what I gather, we don't run this company the way he's used to running a company—plus, he thinks we're growing too fast. So he's a teeny bit stressed."

Another man in a shirt and tie slowly staggered toward us, staring at papers and shaking his head. I pointed my thumb at him and gave Allie a quizzical look.

"New CFO, not having a good day either," she explained.

"Call me crazy, but it looks like they're not all that happy."

"Huh, what gave it away? I think doing things at hyperspeed and doing nothing by the book makes them a tad uncomfortable. Once they've had Pizza Break and the Midnight Buffet a couple times, they'll be fine. Everybody is."

We reached her cubicle and stopped so abruptly she caught me glancing down her shirt. "Really?" she exclaimed. She thought for a moment, moved in close to me, and whispered sensuously, "Really?"

"Not being with you is driving me crazy."

Allie smiled, moved up against me, and brought those gray peepers to bear on me.

From behind us the voice of Alex boomed, "Excuse me, Allie, Rebecca needs you right away."

She turned her head toward him. "Okay, be there in a minute." Then she turned back to me and hit me with those eyes and pouting lips. "When I get home I'm…"

"Gonna come at you like a wild animal," we said in unison, both knowing that it wouldn't happen.

When she turned to follow Alex, I added, "Try not snoring in my ear."

"Then don't take all the covers," she said, walking away backward.

TWENTY-ONE

I'm a Dad, Paige Is Sad

LOGAN

I got home early, planning to offer to take Paige out to Charley's for a daughter/stepdad dinner—okay, maybe not stepdad, but mother's-boyfriend guy. It was my way of helping to make up for her absentee parental figures of late. I imagined walking in, finding her hard at work on her homework, jubilant at the prospect of liberation, and excited to share a jovial dinner with dear old me.

I came in to find her looking both nervous and a bit disheveled, watching TV. I should have put things together—the extra-large pizza box, the two plastic cups on the coffee table, the pointless TV show she was intent on watching. Was there really a program about what a privileged celebrity family of unattractive, unaccomplished women do on a Tuesday? And hadn't she always said she hated that show?

She shot me a glance, said, "Oh, hi," and then quickly looked away. "What are you doing home so early?"

"I came to whisk you off to Charley's for a fun night with... *me*. I see you already got a pizza, though."

"Yeah, couldn't wait," she said with a fake smile before returning to the TV.

I looked at the pointless TV show and noticed that the remote was not tightly locked in Paige's fingers the way it usually was. There was an unusual smell drifting its way into my nose—or was that numerous smells? Paige's music system was on nearby, but no music was playing.

What was I thinking? No problem here.

A boy's jacket lay across a chair—maybe she'd borrowed it from someone? I flashed a look at Paige, and she smiled back at me limply. I spent a moment investigating nothing in particular in a corner of the room and then turned back to see Paige looking over her shoulder behind the sofa. Nothing suspicious going on, I concluded.

I flipped open the box on the table, pizza being one of my best buds, and saw that 90 percent of the massive pizza had already been eaten. "Boy, you must have been one hungry lil' mofo."

Paige patted her stomach. "You know me. Go ahead, have a piece."

The clues finally began drifting into my head like small twittering birds collecting on a bird feeder. All that other stuff could be a coincidence, but the pizza? That's where I had her. "Okay, what's going on? You never offer me a slice without a battle!"

"Nothum," she said with her mouth full of a fresh bite of pizza.

"Nothum, hey?"

"What, you don't trust me?"

"Where is he?"

She coughed up her last bite. "Who?"

"The guy who ate the pizza and drank out of that cup! I'll bet he'd like to see my collection of ninja swords. Let me just get one. I've haven't seriously cut anybody in days."

With that the head of a tall, unshaven young man slowly rose out from between the wall and the sofa wearing the same limp smile Paige had given me. Paige dropped her head into her hands and shook it in disbelief.

"Logan, this is Rick."

"Prick? That's an unusual name. Is it Swedish?"

Paige shook her head some more. "It's Rick. Rick."

"Rick, Ricky, the Rickster, would you mind if I call you Vladimir?

Would you like to see my ninja sword collection? Just got a new sharp one. Or maybe you'd rather run off and see what's going on at your house?" Rick climbed over the sofa in a spritely fashion, waved to Paige, and then hightailed it for the door.

"See ya, Nick!" I shouted after him.

"I'm sorry. I didn't think you guys would be home." Paige was apologizing but not too convincingly.

"Yeah, I can see that. What were you thinking? After that incident last month with 'all tongue' Tommy, your mom will go apeshit. Remember the rules? No boys without her being here, no booze, no drugs, no sex. I guess you probably only broke three out of four."

Paige lowered her head, but then in an instant lifted it again, like an attacking wolf. "Well, what am I supposed to do? You don't come home till late, and I never see the queen. It's like I don't even have a mother anymore."

"What your mother is doing—"

"Is really important! I heard! Working at an energy company—ooh!," she said, shaking her hands as if awed. "Well, you let me know when she drops a beer truck on the mayor or arrests fifty terrorists like the B.I.B. Then I'll think she's doing something important!"

I fought a twinge of emotion that wanted to fire back and tell her that it was her mother that had done all those B.I.B. things, but I controlled it. Instead I rubbed my fingers down my goatee. "Regardless of what you think, now we have a problem. What am I gonna tell her? You got anything else you want to tell me?"

Paige stared at her feet. "No."

"Well, this is awkward," I said, dropping onto the sofa beside her. When I did, I heard a little *ooof* from behind us. I looked at Paige, who tried to act unaffected.

"I didn't hear anything," she said, clearing her throat.

I studied Paige's face for a second and then peeked over the sofa to find another teenage boy and girl packed between the sofa and the wall. The boy tried to smile and waved to me. My first thought was to wonder how the hell they'd all managed to fit back there. Had teenagers become so much more nimble since my day, when we hid in closets? I thought about it for a second and then took another look just to be sure. (Even though I hadn't been drinking since I met Jones at the Banshee, I did have a history of seeing things that, shall we say, weren't really there.)

"Well, things just got a little more awkward."

Paige stood up, looked to the ceiling, and then took a defensive pose with her arms crossed.

Slowly, one by one, the teenagers rose, acting skittish and uncertain as to what I might do.

"Oh, were you guys looking for the door? It used to be back there, but now it's this way," I said, pointing toward the front door. But when they beat feet, I called after them, "Sure you won't stay for pizza?" I heard them exit through the front door—and then heard another group from somewhere else in the house scurry out the back door, letting it slam behind them. I paced out to the kitchen to see if anyone was hiding in there when my eyes caught sight of two pizza boxes covering an empty bottle of Jack Daniels in the trash, which Paige must have planned on taking out to the curb before I got home. I poked through the boxes, grabbed the bottle with two fingers, and strutted back to Paige with the smoking gun.

"Quite a party, huh? You wanna explain?"

Paige's face teemed with things she wanted to say, but then she just turned her back on me.

"Calm down. I was your age once…I think. I get the frustration. I get feeling alone. I just don't get how you guys ate all that pizza."

Paige seemed to find that a little funny, at least. "There were just three…extra large. We didn't do any drugs. I promise."

"Just a bottle of Jack. No one considered having sex, I'll wager."

When she didn't answer I continued, "Hey, I already told you I was your age once. How old are you, anyway?"

She turned back to me. "Okay, everyone knows Jamie's a slut, and Prick…Rick was tryin' for third base."

"Third base? He didn't score, right? I mean, no squeeze bunt or sacrifice fly?"

"Noooo."

"What's important is that you're okay, no one got hurt. No one did get hurt, right?"

"Right."

"You know this was wrong, right?"

"What happened to you were my age once?" she countered.

My arms guided her down to the sofa beside me. "What you did is, like, totally normal. It's what kids need to do to find themselves, to grow up. The way you did it is the problem."

"You mean, alone and without any adult supervision," she said sarcastically.

"No, I mean doing something that you know your mother wouldn't approve of behind her back in her own house. How's she going to trust you now?"

"Oh, so if I get slammed at Kelly's house, it's fine?"

"No, because she trusts that you won't. Me too—I know what a great kid you are. I'm sure you'll make the right decision, once you get used to making your own decisions. Just don't let being mad at us force you to make a lousy choice…like this."

"So when are you gonna tell her?" Paige asked, dejected.

"I don't know. See, you've put me in a bad situation too. If I don't tell her and you do it again, it's me she won't trust. If I tell her what happened, she'll blame it on herself—I know her. She'll choose you over her job, and she'll sacrifice something she loves to be here for you. If you haven't noticed, she's sacrificed herself for you since the day you were born. Don't you think she deserves to do things for herself now that you're getting older?"

Paige lowered her head. "Sorry to be such a drag on her life."

"No way. It's a choice she would make over and over again with no regrets. I'm just asking you to let her fly."

Paige let out a disbelieving laugh. "Fly? I can't imagine my mother doing any kind of flying. She's, like, rooted."

"You might be surprised about that," I said, imagining flying with Allie over New York. "Maybe she's rooted because of you. Maybe it's time you let her know you're cool, and she can tear up some roots. This thing you did tonight will make her think she has to clamp down."

Paige was silent for a moment and then looked up at me. "You think I'm cool? Like I can handle myself?"

"Yes. In fact, I think you're ready to leave the nest, like a junior B.I.B."

Paige smiled and laughed. "I'm not that cool."

"Well, you only let Prick get to third base. Bet he was hoping for a homer."

"Eww no, Nick…Rick was out when he tried to steal third, big time."

"Okay, then," I said, holding out my hand. "I won't tell her anything. You won't pull a stunt like this again, you'll start cutting your mom loose so she can try her wings while you try yours, and you'll clean up all of this garbage. And don't put it in our trash. Your mother will find it for sure—made that mistake my junior year."

Paige smiled the minimum necessary to be considered a smile. "Okay," she said and shook my hand.

"And I get the last slice of pizza," I said, grabbing for the box.

"In your dreams, loser," she said, tearing the box away from me. We laughed, tussling for it, until the box flew open and the last piece dropped onto the carpet.

"Five second rule!" I yelled, and we began battling again, back to being peas and carrots. (I think I'm the carrots.)

TWENTY-TWO

Forlorn Again

LOGAN

The Special Products Division of Lowe LLC was growing like a benevolent virus. We had moved out of 807B and into offices in some renovated buildings at the manufacturing facility. The plant was a Rust-Belt-era industrial complex Jennifer's real estate company had bought for a song (and dance) during Scranton's hard times. Now over 450 people worked there and the number never stopped growing. The combination of people and robots was creating a steady stream of massive fluid disk generator towers that filled a steady line of semi trucks each day. High up on the ridge of North Mountain outside of town, ten of the giants spun, satisfying the plant's massive appetite for electricity.

The plant's employees were just the tip of growth in Scranton. Fueled by the construction boom, the hiring of many of the subcontractors for Lowe LLC, and the growth in all the support services (stores, restaurants, entertainment, and apartments) for the new population, Scranton's boom continued.

In Africa the story was similar. Although the plants there had started from vacant lots, they had begun or were nearing production readiness. The first trial units had been delivered to a Nigerian farming cooperative made up of small landowners that had bonded together and been chosen by Rebecca personally. She'd ended up greasing a number of palms in Lagos in order to get expedited approvals and permits. They had been sent three generators and accompanying electric farming equipment and had been given agricultural training from onsite consultants in conjunction with an aid agency already in place. The aid agency prospered and drew more funding, bolstered by the vast amount of resources Lowe LLC had provided. Other aid organizations slipped in to run the school and medical center that were part of the generator package. The cooperative was given the equipment at no charge up-front with the stipulation that a percentage of the cooperative's output would stay in the local market; another percentage would pay a long-term, low-cost lease for the equipment; and a final percentage of each year's harvest would go to a hunger aid agency appointed by Lowe LLC.

The triangle of plants in Lagos, Cairo, and Dubai was preparing to change the face of the entire continent. With Rebecca's insistence that as many raw materials as possible come from local suppliers, the three plants pulled a long train of subcontractor growth behind them. The Lagos plant was small but was already in production. The Cairo plant was in start-up. But it was in Dubai where things were in hyperdrive.

I had personally negotiated the agreements with the licensees in Dubai that were bringing in a billion dollars into Lowe LLC in fees. Man, I was a tough wheeler-dealer. I walked into our Scranton boardroom, a lone Lowe employee prepared to do battle with Dubai's finest billionaires, prepared to lie, bluff, schmooze, and arm twist to get the deals signed—that is, if my wit, charm, and dazzling white teeth failed. It was around ten o'clock, and I was right on time-ish. I had a Lowe LLC coffee mug in one hand and the contracts in the other, beaming with a radiant confidence that would let these guys know they were already defeated, ready to bend to my will.

"Good morning, gentlemen. After all the emails and phone calls, it's great to finally meet you. I hope your plant tour assured you of the viability of our technology."

One of the four Arab men dressed in suits that made mine look like a T-shirt—a torn one from an old rock group—answered. "Yes, we were quite impressed."

With a cocky smile—and without another word—I let the contracts drop on the table in front of them while I coolly reached for a donut from the box they had somehow ignored on the nearby table buffet. Before I could turn back to them and wipe the powdered sugar off my face, I found them eagerly flipping the pages, making hurried conversation among themselves. They pointed at certain paragraphs, appearing to argue with one another, but when they found the signature page, they both signed with a smile. One of them shook my nondonut hand and said, "You will have the wire transfer from our bank within an hour."

I thanked them, suavely wiped the powder off my mouth, and watched them leave with their copy of the contracts. *I let you off easy,* I said to myself as they exited. I sat down at the head of the table, sipped my coffee, and put my feet up for a well-deserved rest. A few minutes later, I left but then returned to collect the box of donuts. If the Arabs weren't interested in them, I couldn't let them go to waste. I was sure they'd be stale before my meeting with the Chinese at three.

* * *

After the meeting with the Chinese licensee, which lasted nearly eleven grueling minutes, I was strutting my way down the hall with signed contracts in hand. I also carried a bag of fruit and lo mein they had left untouched on their buffet. (Crap, was that a spot of sweet-and-sour sauce on the contract?) I whistled on past the new CEO. "Afternoon, Craig. How's it going? Just signed up the Chinese order," I said, proudly holding up the contracts.

The CEO slowed and looked at me for a second and then continued on his way, shaking his head. A moment later, I heard him say, "Fuck! That's more goddamned work for me! Take the job with the little start-up company—my ass! I used to have a family, goddamn it." *Some people just don't know a good time when they see it.*

For me, I felt useful for once, maybe even a little happy, but that couldn't fill that pining cavern in my chest where Allie should have been. She'd become like a drug; okay, she'd been my drug ever since I saw those eyes, but now, like an addict without a recent fix, withdrawal seemed to be setting in.

I thought back to the times before Lowe LLC entered her life, when we sat arm in arm on the sofa watching TV, or made dinner together, or simply flew to Fiji for a weekend of wild sex on the beach like normal people. Those days seemed like faded memories, years and years old. Now, I was pining again, while Paige had begun to revolt. *Maybe I should drag Allie away just to recharge our batteries.* I was sure she could use some time away as well, and the company could do without us for one night.

Yeah, I am so effing right about this. I lifted my phone out of my pocket and dialed the limo service I had used back in my B.I.B.-authority celebrity days. I ordered a limo to pick Allie and me up at work at seven p.m., specifying that it have a chilled bottle of champagne and a rose waiting inside, and drive us to Maison Neuf restaurant for a magical night alone. I was told it was romantic and expensive. It had to be good—after all, it was French. I texted Paige the plan. She responded with a text that she already had plans for a drug-filled orgy at Kelly's house, so not to worry. I responded with *Joke. Right?* J L. She came back with *Duh. Hope you and the queen have a good time.* She should like that. *It is French, right?* Paige's reassurance made me smile. Then I began searching for Allie.

When I reached the conference room, I found everybody gathered around the large-screen TV. Jennifer was finally back from her convalescence. Allie, Rebecca, Alex, and Jones were all eagerly watching the news. I came in ready to give them a smile and the news about the Chinese deal when I heard Allie say, "Oh my God!" as she put her hand over her mouth.

"Is that where our people are?" Jennifer asked.

Rebecca shook her head. "Really close."

As they continued to watch the video, which appeared to be of some disaster in Lagos, Alex pointed at the screen. "Look, right there, that's our plant!"

I silently joined them as the news report told of the terrorist gas attack in Lagos, Nigeria, and its rapidly rising death toll, currently estimated at 20,000. The local government was unable to deal with the scope of the calamity, as numerous officials were victims of it. Most of the footage on the news had come from mobile phones, and it showed victims who appeared to be sleeping on the streets and sidewalks. Cars and trucks had crashed into each other at weird angles or into buildings and poles. Yellow vans blocked the streets, their drivers either slumped over the wheel or sprawled out of the door. Background wailing and cries filled the sound tracks. Then there was footage of those running from the holocaust site, clearly terrified of the gas. With no one claiming credit for the devastation, there was no answer to the monstrous question of why. There among the carnage we could see our plant, with workers dressed in their light-blue Lowe company overalls "sleeping" in the streets and parking lot.

"No wonder they didn't return my call," Allie said solemnly. "There's no one left to answer. They just went…offline."

Rebecca was in shock, staring at the TV with her palms over her cheeks. "What about Ima and Omotayo?"

Jennifer was blunt. "Gone. They're all gone. Can't you see?"

Tears began to slide down Rebecca's cheeks.

"Who would do this?" Allie asked.

"Who, indeed?" asked Jones.

"And here we are with our thumbs up our asses, doing nothing!" Jennifer said "Our people are dead, and our plant will be a ghost town for months, until they unravel this mess."

Allie suddenly seemed hit by panic. "What about the cooperative? Are they okay? Rebecca, it's nighttime there. You have any phone numbers?"

Rebecca didn't seem to be able to bring herself to move, so Jennifer added, "Try an email. There should be someone at the power room." Allie tapped on her tablet for a while and then stared at it, waiting for a response.

I slid on over to stand next to Jones, speaking in low tones. "What do you make of this, Doc?"

"Could be terrorism. There is a lot of unrest in that area."

"Orrrr?"

"Or it could be an industrial accident that happened to hit close to our plant."

"Orrrr?"

"Or…someone might not like what we are doing there."

"That's sort of what I'm thinking."

Then Allie jumped. "I got through! The folks at the cooperative heard about Lagos, but they're okay!"

"For how long, though?" Jennifer asked.

"We should go there now," Rebecca said, suddenly revived.

"Yep," agreed Allie.

Jennifer said, "I'd love to kick whoever did this right in the—"

"Does your plane have the range for Lagos?" Rebecca interrupted her.

"If hers doesn't, mine does," Allie said.

Jennifer pulled out her phone and barked orders to her crew at the airport as the three of them hurried toward the door. I held up my arm, but my protest went unnoticed. "Fuck," I mumbled to myself as they disappeared, leaving me to envision an empty limo and wilted rose in my future.

Jones patted me on the back. "It will all be fine," he said in a comforting tone. "I know what it is like to be forlorn on the prairie and abandoned by the Super Born. You'll learn to live without…like me…every night…alone…forlorn…"

"Okay, I get it!

"Not anymore."

My face wilted.

TWENTY-THREE

Africa. Are You Ready for the New World?

ALLIE

It wasn't until we were wheels up and climbing in Jennifer's gleaming silver jet that I sat back, dropped my head into the plush beige leather headrest of my seat, and took a calming breath. Like someone had opened a door, I suddenly dropped my singleminded focus on the events in Nigeria, and the picture of the rest of my world appeared. It felt like the first chance I'd had to relax in weeks. Weeks in which I'd pretty much left Logan and Paige to their own devices. And now here I was, jetting off halfway around the world. My God, there had to be more to my life than this.

Not giving it two seconds of thought, I had left Paige and Logan behind without a word to either of them. That was so un-me it felt frightening. Who was I? What had I become? Instantly, the weight of guilt fell like an iron collar around my neck. I had to wonder where I was headed and what path I was on. Then images of Paige, angry and resenting me for not being there, began to flood in. I thought of all of the love, support, and comfort that Logan had given me—a first for any boyfriend in my life—which I chose to repay with this. I felt my heart begin to pound in my neck. I wanted to leap out of my chair and make Jennifer turn the plane around. Most of all, I wanted to see Paige smiling in her homecoming dress, hear Logan make one of his off-the-wall sexual comments, and fall asleep with his comforting arm wrapped around me. I shot out of my seat and almost bumped into Rebecca approaching from behind.

"Whoa, you almost got me. Here, thought you could use this," she said, handing me a bottle of Miner's while holding her own in the other hand.

"I…" I said, stammering.

Then Jennifer clicked a remote, and the large satellite TV came to life with more scenes from Nigeria. The three of us crept closer and watched. The aerial view of the devastated area appeared, followed by video footage of workers in white plastic hazmat suits taking samples from the streets near body bags containing victims of the gas.

"You two still think we should just worry about Scranton?" Jennifer asked as she munched a spoonful of butter-pecan ice cream from a frosty half gallon.

"Bastards," said Rebecca in a low tone. "Those were our people."

They both looked at me, but I said nothing, just took a long sip of my Miner's and returned to my seat. I stared out the window and marveled at the clouds below. It was weird to notice the beauty of the world while you contemplated doing something violent and horrible in it.

Then I heard Jennifer exclaim, "My God! You have got to be fucking kidding me!"

When I looked up, I saw a banner on the screen saying, *Ms. Latisha Johnson, US Antiterrorism Task Force* below the image of Ms. Suit. Beside that it said, *Live from Lagos.*

"I just wanted to assure the people of Nigeria that they are not alone in this struggle and that the full weight and support of the United States of America is behind them. I am here to aid Nigerian authorities in the investigation of this crime and help direct them to the parties that perpetrated this tragedy," Ms. Suit said while we stared.

"That bitch is making my side ache," Jennifer said, rubbing her ribs where the Suit's bullet had hit.

"Doesn't anybody see this? She's already there!" exclaimed Rebecca. "Maybe not for long," I added.

* * *

When the jet landed in Lagos, my body told me it was the middle of the night, but my eyes were telling me it was a bright, sunny morning. It was a good thing we landed when we did, because Jennifer and Rebecca had resorted to rock-paper-scissors over a bag of chips and then all-out arm wrestling over the yogurt in the refrigerator. (I didn't tell them about the two bags of pretzels in my pocket that soon wouldn't be there.) As we deplaned, Jennifer looked at the overfilled trash bin in the cabin and commented how we needed a larger one for the return flight.

As I swayed my way down the jet's stairs, I saw Jennifer on the tarmac speaking to two men. They were both wearing the latest sunglasses and the latest automatic weapon over their shoulders, and they were built like two brick houses. "No one, you understand, no one gets on that plane," she said. They nodded.

"Except maybe a competent housekeeping crew," I added as I walked by.

"Is there a place we can stop and get something to eat?" Rebecca asked as we boarded a white helicopter with our bags for the commute to the cooperative. The pilot started the engine, and the blades began to whirl, filling the cabin with noise.

"What are you bitching about? You got the bag of chips," Jennifer complained as she climbed in front next to the pilot. "I still don't think scissors cut rock."

"You just don't know how to play," Rebecca replied as she tightened her seat belt in the back beside me.

"Here," I said, tossing Rebecca a bag of pretzels, which she attacked.

"You bitch!" Jennifer was joking, but not really, so I tossed her my other bag.

"Happy? Can we go now?" I said as the noise grew louder and everyone put on their headsets.

Jennifer turned to the Nigerian pilot and instructed him to take off. In a second, we were on our way. As we skimmed over Lagos, the pilot pointed to the area of the accident below and the crowds of people and vehicles surrounding it. We all remained silent as we passed and then left the devastation behind. I felt as if I was deserting our Nigerian employees all over again. But there was no turning back time, and there were others who could still benefit from our help.

Then, like night and day, the city ended, and we were in open country. The whole time I looked out the window, I imagined how I could fly rings around this eggbeater. "Mind if I stretch my legs?" I said, unbuckling my belt.

Rebecca put her hand on my shoulder. "We stay together! We're stronger that way." She gestured with her thumb toward the pilot as if to say, *He doesn't know you fly.*

"And that bitch in the suit is out there somewhere," said Jennifer over her microphone.

The pilot tried not to act as if he was hearing all this, but his curled smile was a dead giveaway.

I sighed and buckled my belt. "You guys are no fun."

Jennifer turned in her seat and looked at me. "We're not here for fun."

* * *

We banked to the east as we overflew the cooperative, which had appeared out of a desolate, rolling plain. The three slowly spinning generators we had installed formed a line that marked a ridge at the edge of the village. Already you could see the rows of fields plowed and being plowed by tractors that seemed tiny from this distance. You could barely see the simple dirt road that had once had marked the village. It had been widened, and fingers of new roads had been added to accommodate the traffic to the fields, barns, garages, grazing livestock, generators, school, and medical center. All sorts of buildings, both temporary and permanent, were sprouting in a helter-skelter way. There were tents alongside mobile homes alongside permanent homes beside businesses. The simple one-horse village was being transformed, and the dust had yet to settle. Active people of all sizes, shapes, and ages were everywhere.

We landed and were greeted by the young man and woman who were our Nigerian employees in charge of the cooperative project. They gave us a quick tour of the project and then, seeing we were exhausted, directed us to a large white tent that would serve as our communal lodgings. As we got near the tent, something caught the attention of Rebecca's nose, and she suddenly veered left. "Is that bread?"

I ignored her and flipped open the flap of the tent, flopped onto my semicomfortable cot, pulled out my tablet, and started a videoconference with Paige and Logan. Thanks to Rebecca's satellite feeds, the Wi-Fi was amazing, even in this remote location.

* * *

The hustling of people and sounds of equipment running outside the thin cloth of the tent awoke me early the next morning. I tried hitting the snooze button on my brain; I needed to be better rested before I could face the day. Instead, I swiped some strands of hair out of my eyes and found that I was the only one still in bed. The bright sun overpowered my eyes as I staggered to the door of the tent and looked out on a world of activity.

I hadn't taken two steps before Rebecca came by and grabbed my arm. "Come on, you gotta see this."

She pulled me to a small building nearby that contained a kitchen and tables. Rebecca pulled me to one laden with food and cups. "Coffee! Freshly brewed coffee. Isn't it amazing? Two months ago, there was nothing here, now we have all this food and power, not to mention the internet. It's like we moved this place forward fifty years in two months! This morning I ate goat! And you gotta try these things." She nearly glowed as she popped a doughy bite of something into her mouth.

I took a cup of coffee and a handful of the doughy bites and stepped to the window. "Where's Jenny?"

Rebecca appeared over my shoulder. "Out there," she said, gesturing to a small hill in the distance beyond the generators. "Been there all night. Aren't those generators amazing? Look at those puppies turn. You know, the tractors have had zero maintenance so far. Each charge is lasting three hours longer than we estimated. The school is gonna open in a week. The network is already up and running. And have you tried the Wi-Fi? It's terrific, better transfer rates than at home. Isn't that great?"

"If we can keep Ms. Suit from turning this into a desert."

"Yeah, right," Rebecca said, sobering up a little.

In the distance, I saw Jennifer get into a small electric jeep and begin driving toward us.

"Here comes trouble," I said as I took a sip of coffee. But when I turned, I found I was talking to no one, as Rebecca had gone out into the village like a child on Christmas morning to check out all the gifts Lowe LLC's technology had brought to the cooperative.

Jennifer pulled up and stopped abruptly outside the window, and I joined her in the street. "You still wanna fly?" she asked.

"What are you talking about?"

"I can hold down the fort here. You and Rebecca should check out Cairo. I know Ms. Suit hit us in Lagos, so it makes sense that she'll be after us here or in Cairo next. Dubai has their own security force, so they should be okay. Leave me the chopper, check it out, and come back. Then we can go back to Lagos and find Ms. Suit, if she's still there. Rebecca won't give you a hard time—she's like a kid in a candy store, seeing all her machines finally working. "

I looked around at the village, imagining the horrible scenes at the plant in Lagos, reluctant to leave these people to a similar fate.

"I've got this," Jennifer reassured me. "Believe me. You go—now."

"Okay," I said, trying to smile. "Maybe it will shut Rebecca up."

"Yeah, she's just a little too bubbly."

"It's annoying, right? I thought it was just me."

Just then, Rebecca approached with her arms in the air. "Six megawatts! Do you believe it? They have enough power to sell the excess! The ROI is gonna be twice what we thought!"

I gave Jennifer a look, and she sent it right back.

Rebecca noticed our silence and glanced back and forth between our frozen faces. "What? Why aren't you happy? I just told youuuuuuu," she cried out with surprise as I took hold of her and we shot into the sky, headed for Cairo.

* * *

Everything seemed fine in Cairo. The plant was fully staffed and in testing, ready to start production. Rebecca had insisted on a young but mixed-gender staff in an effort to give hope to the new generation and to create opportunities for women that weren't always available. The factory had been built with a local partner to help disguise the foreign ownership. But with the local name or without, the equal-opportunity employment had sent shock waves through the local community. The plant donated power and internet services to the surrounding community to help allay any concerns from religious conservatives.

After inspecting the plant and interviewing our limited security staff, Rebecca and I found ourselves in the office portion of the complex. Rebecca was reviewing production schedules with the managers as I sipped tea in a relaxed mode. I was on my phone with Jennifer to see if all was well when I heard a racket outside. I told Jennifer to wait a minute at the same moment she was telling me to wait a minute. As I put down my phone, there came the sound of a loud explosion near the entrance to the plant. I ran to the window to see the gate destroyed and our security men running in terror. Then I watched heavily armed men with their faces wrapped in black cloth emerge from the normal traffic on the street and charge the building. Automatic weapons fired into the building, and I could hear the employees screaming. The plant turned to chaos.

I ran to the door but was stopped by Rebecca's hand on my shoulder. "Wait, let me take care of this," she said with a stony calmness. "That bitch in the suit and her hit men aren't gonna stop us." I stood there thinking of the faces of those we'd lost in Nigeria and imagining another set of faces in the building around me. But this time I was here and ready to help. My adrenaline said, "Let's go." I decided to give Rebecca a minute, but just one.

Rebecca closed her eyes and stood for a moment as the bullets continued to hit the building. I heard another explosion and got ready to move.

"Wait!" she repeated.

So I stood nervously and waited.

From outside I heard a long string of small explosions go off in a ring around the building. When I looked out the window, I saw the black-hooded attackers quickly disappearing, one by one, in the black clouds created by the explosions. When the smoke was gone, so were they. Then I realized Rebecca was using her power with machines to pop the pins of the grenades clipped to the belts of the attackers, sending them into instant martyrdom with their own equipment. I watched a rocket-propelled grenade that had been launched at the office where we stood suddenly disappear in flash, with no sign left of it or the man firing it. As the ammunition in their guns began to explode, the attackers threw off their weapons and ran. Suddenly, the attack had turned into a rout, as Rebecca was using their own weapons to repulse them.

I couldn't contain myself any longer. I rushed out of the office, passed the retreating ex-gunmen, and cut them off. Their faces all bore the same expression of shock when I appeared

before them. They stopped and tried to run before I bid them good night with a quick fist to the

skull. I quickly shot from street to street around the plant, stopping more than a dozen more men so that none would escape to tell the tale.

The employees had been watching the gunmen retreat and now poured out of the building in pursuit as well, men and women alike. Neighbors in the buildings surrounding the plant, knowing its value to the community and the hopes it represented for the future, also turned on what was left of the attackers, tripping them and joining the plant's employees in surrounding the gunmen with fists, kicks, and rocks.

Within minutes it was over. The employees dressed in the light-blue Lowe company overalls howled in victory, raising the attackers' weapons over their heads and smashing them to the ground. They celebrated in the streets outside the plant for a while and then began filing back into the plant to continue their shift.

When I returned to the building, I smiled when I found Rebecca already studying the plant's proposed production schedule. "Rebecca," I said, amazed at her lack of reaction.

"What?" she huffed, breathing heavily but otherwise showing no sign that she had just been the life half of a life-or-death battle.

"Rebecca!"

"What? I'm busy here." Then she turned back to me. "We're doing the right thing. We are." Then she returned to her paperwork. Suddenly a group of office workers surrounded her, cheering, and raised her up on their shoulders. I had no idea what they were chanting, but it sounded good. I found my phone on the desk and checked to see if Jenny was still holding, but she was gone.

* * *

JENNIFER

I had given up holding on the phone for Allie and drifted into the dusty street, downing a bottle of water in the heat, when I heard a familiar sound. In the distant western sky I saw the shape of a black helicopter whirling its way toward me. Passing nearby was Adetayo, the site manager for Lowe LLC. He was directing several construction men toward the medical center.

"Adetayo, you expecting anyone today?" I asked, pointing at the oncoming helicopter.

He thought for a moment and then queried the other men, who shook their heads no. Adetayo replied, "No one. No deliveries. No guests."

"Thanks," I answered as he continued on his way. I stepped into the middle of the road and stood with my hands on my hips, staring that the intruder. As I watched, a second helicopter appeared from behind the silhouette of the first, and then a third, and finally a fourth—together, they created a staggered line attack formation. I knew immediately they were not friendlies, but I hesitated to drop them from the sky without knowing who the helicopters contained and what their intentions were.

The answer came soon enough, as small puffs of smoke from the first helicopter turned into explosions on the street around me. A truckload of building material exploded no more than a hundred feet from its delivery point and two hundred feet from me. Another empty jeep flew into the air, and then two more explosions hit empty ground. There were screams and panic all around.

After the smoke from the explosions drifted by, I raised my arm and sent a hot crimson beam at the lead helicopter, hoping Ms. Suit was in it, just as she had been in New York. The beam missed, but then I adjusted my aim. When the next beam hit, the exterior of the 'copter—including its frame, engine, weapons, and all the metal parts—suddenly began melting, dripping from the sky, while the nonmetallic parts—its fuel and unsuspecting occupants—burnt up in a flash of fire that rose into a black pillar of smoke. The rest of the 'copters began a quick, panicked bank to the right, turning broadside to me. *Great, now you're that much easier to hit*, I thought as I sent another beam after the second chopper in line. Its course turned it right into the beam, producing another molten waterfall and cloud of smoke. The others completed their turns and began hightailing it away.

There was an open-topped jeep nearby. I got in and floored the accelerator, making the electric motor spin and whine until I was traveling at full speed toward the disappearing 'copters. As the jeep flew over bumps and dips in the dirt road, it seemed determined to eject me from my seat. When I reached a smooth patch of road, I raised my arm, igniting another crimson beam from my hand that eventually landed a solid hit. Poof! I bounced down the road awaiting another opportunity to deal them some of my fire, and then the final 'copter turned and came back at me firing long-range rockets. I charged at it, joining the high-speed game of chicken with a smile rising on my face. With the road getting worse and it becoming difficult to stay in the jeep, I brought the vehicle to an abrupt halt and waited. The rockets from the 'copter came closer—two hundred feet, one hundred feet, fifty feet—sending out shrapnel that webbed my windshield with cracks. I took my time, enjoying the challenge before I raised my arm again, sending a searing flash into the 'copter. A moment later it was nothing more than a shower of molten metal, flames, and a fluffy black cloud. *It's a new world. And guess who's not in it*, I said to myself before returning to the cooperative.

When I stopped near my tent, I had to pause and take several deep breaths before my body wanted to get out of the jeep. The exertion of hanging onto the jeep and downing the choppers was catching up with me, I guess. By then a small group of people had surrounded the jeep to welcome me as I got out. Adetayo was first to greet me with a shocked but happy smile.

"I have never seen anything like that! How did you do it?"

"You should see me when I really get mad."

He reached out to pat me on the shoulder but stopped short, just staring at my left arm as the smile drained from his face. I looked at my arm and saw the trickle of blood flowing from the shrapnel that had lodged itself in my triceps. "God, you must have some monstrous mosquitos in this country," I joked.

"This is no insect," Adetayo said in earnest.

I patted him on the shoulder with the hand of my other arm. "It's a joke. Don't mind this little scratch. Is everyone okay in the village?"

Adetayo lowerd his head. "No, the driver of the truck is gone, I am afraid. Two other men have wounds. Everyone else is frightened but well. Let me get the doctor for you."

"No, have them see to the others first. Did anyone else get a look at what happened?"

"The three of us, I think," he said, pointing to the two men with him. "Everyone else was hiding."

"We need to keep it that way. No news of this can get out," I instructed him. Adetayo nodded. "We will take care of the wounded men and, of course, help the family of the truck driver. But we must try to keep the authorities out of this. Understand?"

"We'll tell no one," Adetayo said, looking at the other men.

"You swear? Lives may depend on that."

"I would love to tell everyone what I just saw, but I won't. We have come so far so fast thanks to you. We wouldn't dream of doing anything to endanger all you have done. Do we all agree?" Adetayo said to the men around him, who all nodded their heads in agreement.

"Good," I said, taking out my phone for a selfie of my wounded arm. I texted it to Allie and Rebecca, saying, *I had an interesting morning.*

In a flash Allie texted back a picture of the parking lot of the plant in Cairo, which was pockmarked with craters and bodies. *Me too!*

"What are you doing?" asked Adetayo.

"Gloating. Makes a great tat, don't you think?" I said, showing him my arm. "They shot their shot, and I'm still here." I raised my face to the cloudless sky and shouted, "I'm still here!"

TWENTY-FOUR

Jones Breaks the News

LOGAN

I was supposed to meet Dr. Jones at eight o'clock at O'Malley's, so I felt good when I got there before nine. I saw Jones hunched over the bar with his head down and two RFDs sneaking up behind him. (The men of Scranton with reduced functionality disorder tended to cluster in various bars about town, playing childish games.) When I approached Jones, they struck. One pushed against his back while the other pulled the barstool out from under his butt, sending him to the floor with a thud as they giggled and escaped.

Jones struggled to stand, holding his hands out in front of him, aghast at having touched O'Malley's floor. "Morons!" he yelled after the RFDs.

"Poopyhead!" one yelled back. They giggled some more and melted into the crowd in the back room.

"I see you're busy making new friends," I said, handing him some napkins from behind the bar.

"Assholes," he muttered, wiping his hands. Then he yelled to the RFDs, "For your information, I am Dr. Rashid Patel Jones, PhD!"

Someone in the back room calmly replied, "Dickhead."

"Why on earth did we decide to meet here?" Jones said. He recovered his stool and settled back down at the bar.

"I don't know, Dr. Poopyhead. You called me. What's up?"

"Before I tell you, you may want a drink," he said. (Don't you hate it when people try to prepare you for bad news?)

Just then the stout old barkeep appeared. "Well, well, if it ain't me ol' buddy. I ain't seen you since…I can't say when!" I couldn't say how long it had been either. O'Malley's had always been the place where Jones and I met; it was also the place where I had first seen Allie. In fact, we'd had our first date here. (As the clientele were generally RFDs, it was a good place to come if you wanted to disappear.) The barkeep and I didn't quite have a friendship—more like an understanding. I knew as long as he was on the receiving end of my cash, he would be borderline civil to me.

"Good to see you, my good man," I said.

"Well, it's good that you're good, and I'm good too, thank you very much. What can I get you on this good evening? As I recall it, you enjoy our good ol'-fashioned chili fries."

"How good of you to offer—but what good is a snack when you have such a good cellar of good libations?"

"I got those and a smack upside the head. Now, what the hell do you want?"

"Your finest Miner's Lite…in a dirty glass."

"Only kind I have," he said. The barkeep turned away to pull a pint off the tap. Then he handed it to me, greedily grabbing a bill from me. "Won't be needing any change, I imagine."

"Would you give it to me if I did?"

He stuffed the bill in his pocket and smiled for a second. "So, what do you think of the new place?"

Jones and I looked around and then at each other. After a quiet moment I said, "I see a new Miner's sign over there."

"Yeah," Jones added, "and I think someone tried to clean the urinal."

"No, no, my bigscreen!" said the barkeep, clearly offended.

Again Jones and I scanned the room and then turned to each other with quizzical looks.

"Over here," said the barkeep, pointing to a TV about the size of a small computer monitor mounted behind the bar. "And it's HD."

Jones squinted behind his glasses. I leaned my head forward. "Is that golf or baseball?"

"Football, you ninny!" replied the barkeep. Then he handed me a new menu. "See, O'Malley's Sports Bar and Grill. With all these new people comin' inta town, I figure I can branch out and not have to depend on those assholes anymore," he said, pointing to the RFDs in the back room. "All this new money comin' in, gonna get me a big bite of that pie! Sports bar, that's what everybody wants. Got a new sign comin' too. Then I'll be rakin' it in, hand over fist."

Jones studied the new menu. "What is a *hangaburger*? Doesn't sound like something you would like to be eating…voluntarily. And who spells sports *S-P-P-O-R-T-E-S*?"

The barkeep angrily grabbed the menu and scanned it until he found the misspellings. He turned, and as he went through the kitchen door, I could hear him say, "Millie! You told me you could fuckin' spell!"

I stared at the TV. "That's not a football game, is it?" I found a remote beside the beer taps just across the bar and changed channels. Up came the news network with live scenes from the London disaster. "You heard about this?" I asked Jones.

"Horrible. All these terrorist attacks in such a short time. First New York, then Lagos, and now England. What is the world coming to?"

"The world is on fire, my friend," I declared as the announcer recapped the day's events.

In his sober voice, the news anchor spoke as video footage played from earlier in the day. "It was 12:33 p.m. in London when the attack occurred. According to eyewitnesses and security videos, the drone approached at a low altitude, appearing out of the clouds to fire two missiles at the iconic Big Ben clock tower from point-blank range. The two missiles struck almost simultaneously, blowing out the northeast corner of the tower halfway up. The top of Big Ben collapsed under its own weight, taking much of the support column down with it, which landed in Bridge Street. The drone then proceeded to the east before exploding over the English Channel." As the newscaster spoke, video footage of the scene, pictures of the tower days before, and an animation of the drone's course over the Channel appeared. "There are conflicting reports as to whether the drone self-destructed or was the victim of the Royal Air Force, which has yet to make a statement. At the scene now live we have Amanda Miles."

"Thank you, Roger," Amanda started. "The news here at the scene is grim indeed at this moment. Authorities have moved the known death toll up to fifteen. With scores of individuals unaccounted for at this hour, that number is expected to rise. Along with those who've lost their lives comes a shattering of pride at the loss of the tower, which has stood as a symbol of strength for the entire nation. In a few short seconds, a small drone accomplished what the entire German Air Force could not during all of World War II. Live from the scene of the strike—where workers are in for a long night—I am Amanda Miles."

I turned down the volume and looked at Jones. "Holy crap."

"I don't believe holy is the word. This crap is of the smelly variety."

I stroked my goatee. "You think the girls are in danger?"

"Funny you should mention that."

"What? What is it, Ms. Suit?" Jones said nothing, just sat and looked at his half-empty beer. So, naturally I panicked. "I haven't heard from them. You think they're okay?"

Jones waffled as the barkeep stormed out of the kitchen and grabbed the remote out of my hand. "Here now, that is serious equipment for adults only. Where's my friggin' football? Go, Manchester!" he said when he found the right channel. Then he squinted at the screen. "Wait a tick. That's not Manchester! Why are they all wearing helmets and shoulder pads? Millie! This big screen ain't workin'! Can't get me Manchester!"

Jones gave me a sickly attempt at a smile. "Remember when you said the Super Born only kept me around so I could give them more information about themselves?"

I nodded. "Yeah, if you don't come up with something soon, I think you're going to have Rebecca on your ass. And not in a good way."

"You remember those blood tests we did on the three of them? I do have some…information."

"They'll be glad to hear that."

"Maybe not so glad."

The look on his face and his reluctance to speak worried me. "Am I gonna have to beat it out of ya?" I asked, threatening him with a fist.

"It's not good news."

I pushed my fist closer to his face. "Come on, you little weasel!"

He stared at me. "The fourth blood test shows serious signs of senescence of certain markers in their hemoglobin as compared to the first test, especially in Rebecca." He cringed, clearly expecting a violent reaction.

I just looked at him blankly. "Did you really say blah blah blah, especially in Rebecca?"

"No, you asshole, they're dying!"

I chuckled. "Yeah, right. Plenty of people have tried to kill them and failed!"

"You wanna listen or act like a tough guy? They're aging—and fast. Their hypermetabolism is burning them up."

"Tell that to the tsunami they smacked back into the sea," I said, laughing. I took a long drink of my beer. "You ever been with someone who has two-hour orgasms? Allie is a dynamo. I'm reading every posted sex tip I can find on the internet just to keep up with her. Dying, my ass!"

Jones sighed and stared at the bar for a long moment before he raised his head, but he couldn't look at me. "Rebecca is the worst. I calculate that she has aged ten years in the last six months. I believe there is a link between how much they use their powers and how quickly their blood declines. Rebecca is the one who has used her powers the most. She is literally trading her life for this project of theirs."

I huffed a dubious laugh before the concern started to set in and adrenaline began pumping into my blood. I stood up and paced around Jones. I thought for a moment and then came back at him with, "So? Big deal. Their powers burn out, and they become normal people again. There's plenty of great stuff about Allie besides her powers. In fact, it might be better if she were normal. Hey, I could finally win at arm wrestling—maybe. I can live with a normal orgasm…I think. No more flights to Fiji for weekends, though. But she'd still be the same woman, right?"

"Would you just listen? Here is my point." Jones held his hand out at chest level. "And you are down here," he said, dropping his hand toward the floor. "You're not getting it. It's not their powers that will burn out, it's them."

I laughed in disbelief. "Yeah, right."

Jones pushed me back into my seat. Then he looked around for anyone listening and spoke in a low tone. "You remember the other Super Born who have died?"

I thought for a moment, and it finally clicked. There was a Super Born, Allyson, who Rebecca told me had died, and Jones had seen two other Super Born die while he was trying to train them. "Yeah, I remember."

"Well!" said Jones, holding out his open palms.

"Well, what?"

"This explains everything. They didn't die from accidents or from my experiments. Their very own powers burned them out, like the little rockets you made as a kid."

"What little rockets I made as a kid?"

"Remember how you would pack ammonium perchlorate into a cylinder then ignite it with a direct-current power source to send the little rocket on a parabolic trajectory, which lasted until the fuel was consumed and it fell back to earth?"

I blinked…twice. "No."

"Didn't you ever watch your friends make rockets?"

I blinked again. That was telling him.

"Are you kidding me? You never sent an ant up in a rocket, your own little astronaut in your own little space program?"

"You had your own space program?"

Jones gave a faraway look. "Actually, yes. One time my friend Rodney and I sent a whole crew of two ants and a firefly to a thousand feet and returned them safely to Earth. We opened up the reentry capsule…"

"Capsule?"

"And all three were alive and well. They ran off before we could do a full medical workup, though, ungrateful little bastards." Then Jones seemed to return to Earth himself. "But that is not the point." He paced for a few moments, staring at his feet, and then lifted his hands and turned back to me. "Okay, how about fireworks on the Fourth of July, the all-American Fourth of July?" I nodded. "The firework looks like an innocent device, but once it is ignited, it soars into the sky with amazing power, defying gravity, doing things ordinary people can't, just like the Super Born."

"Right."

"But what happens when the fuel is gone? An explosion, and nothing is left but the memory of the beauty of their flight."

"So…Allie is a firework?"

"Soaring into the sky."

"But soon, she'll explode and then…nothing?"

Jones was first relieved that I understood and then lowered his head, sad that I understood. "I am afraid so."

"This is just a theory, right? You could be wrong."

"When has that ever happened?" Jones laughed then thought for a moment. "I mean, it's possible."

Then denial kicked in. I stood up and laughed, then pointed a finger at Jones' face. "You, my friend, are an asshole. The girls will be fine, all of them." When he failed to respond, I continued, "Man, you scared the crap out of me there for a minute."

"Is that what that smell was?"

"Well, your theory stinks too. You should see how strong they are. Allie is amazing."

"They deserve to know," Jones said soberly.

The denial wore off. "Then you tell 'em! You tell 'em to give up everything they love. You tell 'em not to use their powers or they'll explode like a firework! You tell Paige her mother ain't comin' home! You tell Allie good-bye!" I said, feeling the corners of my eyes glistening. I put one hand to the back of my head and ran it down over my hair. "I spent all this effort and emotional energy just to find her, and now you tell me she'll be gone before I know it? How can that be fair?"

Jones put his hand on my shoulder. "It is not over yet. Perhaps there is a serum. Perhaps with enough research we can prolong their lives. Maybe they can learn how to ration their strength."

"I'm not listening anymore," I said, swiping off his hand and pointing a finger in Jones' face. "They're fine, you're an idiot, and that's it!" I started to storm away but then turned back to him. "Goddamn it! Why don't you try doing some research that makes sense for a change?" Jones looked at me with a sympathic expression but didn't say a word. That's when it hit me that Jones was never wrong about matters of science.

I couldn't look at him a second longer, so I slumped out of O'Malley's.

TWENTY-FIVE

Shamil Wants a Sandwich

IYLA

I was in the kitchen but not so much cooking as looking at the food Demetri had spread on the counter. He wanted a sandwich, but there was no meat, no cheese. What did he expect me to do? If he hadn't blocked me from reading his mind, maybe I would know. "What do you want me to make? What do you think I am, a mind reader?" I shouted at him in Russian as he sat in the living room, as always, shuffling his papers like a squirrel with nuts.

"Find something. Look in the refrigerator. Do I have to think for you too?" he asked, frustrated. Clearly, he didn't get the 'mind reader' joke.

Then I heard a key turn in the front door, and I knew Valeria was home. "Oh great, Valeria is here. I'm sure she brings home some bullshit. Maybe you can have a bullshit sandwich."

"Ahh," Demetri said, waving to me, "stop your childish fighting."

When I looked up, Valeria had come into the room, but she was being pushed by two men in black suits holding handguns. A third man came in behind them with a sick smile and a large black design tattooed on his face. This worried me a bit, but it wasn't until Demetri jumped to his feet, scared like a rabbit, that I knew something was wrong.

"Evening, Demetri," said the dark-suited man who with the tattoo. He was a short man, and he was wringing his black-gloved hands like a kid picking out a cupcake.

"Shamil! What are you doing here?" Demetri said, slowly stepping away from them.

"We've met Valeria, haven't we, boys?" Shamil said, looking over at the other two men. "Quite a show she puts on at that club." Then he looked at me. "Which one is this, the one who sees the future or the one who reads minds?" he said, giving me a good look over. "She's not the one who stabbed Alexsei and caused me all that trouble in Moscow, is she?"

"No," said Demetri.

Shamil looked me over again. "Alexsei still walks with a limp. Are you sure that's not her?"

"She is no one, just a cook," said Demetri.

Shamil looked at Valeria and stroked her bruised neck. "Who is she?" he asked Valeria.

"No one, just stupid ugly nobody," Valeria answered bitterly. "Just look at her. You think *that* has powers? Give me a break."

Shamil stepped slowly over to the opening of the kitchen and gave me icy stare. "You are right. Demetri, your other girls are beautiful," he said, looking over and smiling at Valeria. Then he turned back to me. "But this one is not so thin, not so attractive. And her clothes are a mess."

As I channeled his mind, I felt the sear of his dislike for me. He already knew who I was, so I felt no need to hide. "Hey, Pig Man, you want a sandwich?" I said, angrily stabbing the point of the knife into the cutting board just as I had put one into Alexsei's thigh.

Shamil looked at me with disdain and then turned around and closed in on Demetri. "Wasn't easy to find you this time. You're not trying to get away from us again, are you?"

"No, never, Shamil. I am just following a lead."

"Ah, a lead," he said, looking at his men and smiling lightly. Then he turned back to Demetri with anger. "The Lion is not happy. These American women make us look like fools. We need that information! We need it now! These Super Born are the only thing standing in our way. The world is ours except when they are around. You promised us control, but you don't give us control! You asked for the drugs for your women, so we made you your 'candy' at great expense. You ask for money, we give you money. You ask for help with your 'condition,' we give you treatment. So? Where is the device you promised?" he said, holding out his open hands. "Where is it?" He gestured toward the men, and one of them pinned Valeria's arms back while the other put the vise of his arm around her neck.

"I don't have it yet. But I know where it is. I need Valeria to get it. You can't hurt her, or it will be lost!" pleaded Demetri.

"Now you are sounding a little better. When?" barked Shamil.

"Soon, very soon!"

"Good. Also, I have something for you, Demetri—your next treatment." He pulled a small case out of his coat pocket. When Demetri greedily reached for it, he pulled it away. "After…after you give us what we need. No more treatments until you do. Understand?"

Demetri lowered his head, humbled, and said softly, "Yes."

"What did you say?" questioned Shamil.

"Yes, I understand," Demetri answered like a defeated man.

"Good," Shamil said, walking back to Valeria and gesturing for the men to let her go. "And I have something for your girls. But they can have it right now." He reached into his pocket and lifted out two glowing blue lozenges.

As he approached, Valeria eagerly grabbed one from his hand and popped it into her mouth. Then he came to me and held out his hand. I hated the little man, but the glow of the candy made me take it like a big stupid, just like Valeria. I held it for a second, trying to fight my desire to become free. Then I swallowed it and felt the warm surge shoot through my body from head to toe like bright sunshine. I watched the room begin to glow and drift as the spiders of everyone else's thoughts crawled out of my head. It was wonderful to be alone and drift like a cloud.

Shamil smirked, then stepped toward Demetri holding out one arm and pointing it back at me. "So, she's just a cook? Then why does she want candy? Candy would probably kill a woman who's not…special." He stopped close to Demetri and got in his face. "Demetri, I don't like it when you lie to me. She's that same troublemaking bitch from Moscow, and you try to hide her!" Shamil laughed as if he were disgusted. He moved in front of Valeria and studied her face, made stupid and happy with candy. The two men eagerly grabbed her and began tearing at her clothes—she barely protested. Shamil took off his jacket as he walked toward me. "I think I will have that sandwich now."

My fingers tried to grip the knife on the breadboard but then slid off the handle as my strength and will slowly gave way to the candy. With one swipe of his arm, Shamil sent the knife and breadboard flying across the kitchen. I could watch him approach and feel his hand take hold of my throat, but I was powerless to control the events around me. I watched the evil glow in his eyes at the same time I felt my mind drifting away from my body, as if it were all a movie I was watching. He pushed me against the stove, ripped open my vest, and dropped my pants to my ankles. From a hate powerful and deep within me, I gathered the strength to overcome the candy for an instant and spit into Shamil's face. Fire shot out of his eyes as his fist crashed into my face and sent me to the floor.

"Alexsei sends you his regards," Shamil said as he got down on his knees over me.

TWENTY-SIX

Life Isn't Any Easier with Super Powers

ALLIE

We left Cairo the next morning, after a brief ceremony marking the completion of the first fluid disk unit that was destined to be part of a group that would provide power to the plant and the neighboring homes and buildings. While the local partners of the plant handled the Egyptian authorities' investigation of the previous day's attack, Rebecca soaked in the admiration and the buffet. Meanwhile, I stood back, out of the limelight. I looked at the smiling faces and worried about what would happen to them when we were gone. The memory of our people in Lagos was never far from my mind. But unlike the images of Lagos, our Cairo employees, dressed in the same blue Lowe coveralls, were alive, well, and excited about their jobs.

Eventually I got antsy to see how Jennifer was doing and decided to drag Rebecca away from her fans. As I approached her at the buffet, she turned and said as she munched, "I'm eating lentils! What's a lentil? Not a bug is it? And lamb!"

"We gotta go. Jenny's waiting."

Rebecca said her quick good-byes as I pulled her out the door. "I wonder if they'll have any of those doughy things when we get back?"

"Probably," I said as I hooked my arm around her. A moment later, we shot into the sun.

* * *

After we landed outside our tent at the cooperative, Rebecca and I had to search to find any signs of the helicopter attack. Where we were expecting devastation, we found things much as we had left them. Jenny had moved the damaged vehicles into a barn and filled the craters the missiles had made. As Jenny approached with a bandage over her arm, I gestured with open palms, "Where's…"

"What attack, right?" she answered, smiling. "Sounds like you had a rough time in Cairo."

"They'll think twice before hitting us again. None of them survived, slimy bastards," Rebecca said.

"Yeah, with 100 percent casualties and no one alive to report on our defenses, it'll be a while before those pricks come back," Jennifer said with a sadistic glow.

Their comments seemed so hardened and callous that I had to marvel at what different women we had become. In my mind Rebecca still seemed sweet and frail, yet she had sent so many to meet their maker. "How's your arm?" I asked, pointing at Jenny's bandage.

"It's cool. Compared to New York, it's just a scratch—should be a unique-looking scar, though. You know how guys dig chicks with scars."

"Is that true?" asked Rebecca innocently.

"Not as far as I've ever heard," I answered.

"So, what does Logan like?" Jennifer poked.

"Well, it isn't scars!"

"Wellll? What's it like with him?" queried Jennifer.

"I don't know."

Rebecca put her hands on her hips and stared at me. "You never share anything! You'd think the only one of us who's getting some would share a little," Rebecca complained.

"Yeah, does he make you, you know, happy down there?" Jennifer probed.

"He makes me happy everywhere!" I blurted.

"That was cruel," Rebecca said.

"Yeah, you could at least complain about something, like everyone else," Jennifer added.

"Well, there is one thing that bothers me…"

"What?" asked Rebecca, intrigued.

"He gets off on pleasuring me and sometimes it can really be exhausting. He just won't stop."

Jennifer turned away. "Bitch."

"That's enough sharing for me," Rebecca said.

I clapped my hands. "Great, so can we get back to business?"

"Fine," said Rebecca, "let me check the net for any signs of Ms. Suit."

"I'll bet she's a little pissed right now," Jennifer said with a chuckle. "She's about four helicopters light." She lifted a silver necklace out of her shirt and held it up for us to see—it was a simple chain with a small blob of melted metal mounted on it. "Here's one of 'em. Biggest piece I could find. Did I tell you how those suckers melted?"

"About five times," Rebecca said.

I shook my head. "No, I think it was six." Then I took a step toward Jennifer. "You into trophies now? Little ghoulish, don't you think?"

Jennifer held her gaze on me for a long moment then smirked. "I've got plenty of room on this chain for more."

"I hope there aren't any more," I said, following Rebecca into our tent.

"Where're you going?" Jennifer asked.

"I'm going to video conference Paige and Logan."

"I hate people with lives," Jennifer said as she turned to leave.

Rebecca stuck her head back out of the tent and asked Jennifer, "They got any of those doughy things over there?"

Jennifer began to run. "If there are, you'll have to beat me to 'em!"

* * *

I felt sweaty, dusty, and gross, but a shower would have to wait till I saw Paige and Logan again. I dropped onto my cot, adjusted some pillows, and flipped open my laptop. Paige was in school, but I was able to catch up with Logan. Though his face dominated the screen, I could see that he was at the office. His hair was unkempt, and he looked tired. I fought a spontaneous desire to reach through the screen and wrap my arms around him. "Hey, babes, how you doin'?"

"I'm doin'. Lonely, depressed, hopelessly missing you…almost poked myself in the eye with my toothbrush this morning 'cause I couldn't see through my tears, but other than that and suicidal thoughts, I'm good."

"Sounds like it."

"Okay, I won't sugarcoat it anymore…I wish you were here. There, I said it. Are you all right?"

"You hear anything about us in the news?"

"Oh no. What happened?"

"We had problems in Nigeria *and* Cairo. I'll tell you about it later. We handled it, and we're fine. We're goin' after Ms. Suit, but then I'll be home. How's Paige?"

"Paige who?"

"Don't mess with me."

"She's good. The doctor says there won't be any permanent damage…other than her eye and leg…but he was able to save the baby."

"Very funny. She okay?"

"Let me get some coffee in her to sober her up, and I'll ask…once the boys leave…anyway, you know Paige. She's fine."

"Can't you ever be serious?"

"Not without you here."

"What's wrong? That almost sounded sincere, and you look like shit."

"Thank you. You don't think I roll out of bed and look like this, do you?," he said, pretending to fluff his hair.

"No, I can tell by your eyes, like you're drained." I studied the screen for a moment then pulled back and crossed my arms. "What was her name?"

"You know, I'd didn't catch her name…something with a letter in it."

"Like *slut*?"

"That was it!" Logan laughed, paused, but then looked serious again.

"It wasn't Iyla, was it? I think she has eyes for you."

"Ms. Meatloaf? No way." He paused and rubbed his fingers over his goatee. "You think she does, really?"

"Maybe you should go for it. At least she's there…unlike some people."

"No effin way! I was thinking about *you* last night, a lot."

"You rub it, thinkin' about me?"

"Please! Don't be crude," he said, acting offended. Then he grinned. "Twice—man, were you good."

"The one with me on your desk or the one on the beach?"

"The desk. You know me, I'm a workaholic."

"I'll make it up to you when I get back."

"I know, you're gonna come at me like…" he began, then we both said, "a wild animal."

The banter made Logan smile for a minute, but then I could see it drain out of him, forcing me to ask, "Seriously now, you don't look right. Is something bothering you?"

Logan looked away and then mopped his face. "I'm fine. It's just early, and I haven't had my coffee."

I checked the time. "It's, like, ten o'clock there."

"I didn't sleep too well. You know, lot goin' on at work and all the bosses are gone for some reason," Logan tried to smile then just turned his head.

"Bullshit. You can't fool me."

He pushed up a smile. "I have so far. Look, I'm fine, so stop the nagging."

"Nagging? You haven't even seen nagging!"

"Let's keep it that way." Then he looked down and back up. "Hey, Alex is calling. I gotta go. Call me later if you want. Love you."

"Love you too. Tell Paige I'll try calling later. Bye."

"Ah bent toe."

I chuckled. "You mean *à bientôt?*"

"That's the one."

"Byeeee."

He put up a good act, but I could tell something was wrong. And it obviously wasn't just the stress from work. I'd been ignoring him, and now this. He couldn't even look at me. Was I losing him? I felt guilty for leaving him and Paige. I felt guilty for abandoning the people in Lagos. I worried about the people I had left behind in Cairo and hoped they would be okay. I was concerned about our little African project. (Were we really helping these people or putting them at risk?) I was concerned about Ms. Suit. I was concerned about Jennifer and Rebecca, each of whom seemed to be trending in different directions. Blah, blah, blah. Life isn't any easier with super powers. In fact, sometimes it super sucks.

TWENTY-SEVEN

Inside Jones' Head

LOGAN

Work was just blah on a stick without Allie and the other Super Born around, leaving me free to obsess over Dr. Jones' latest theory. That was the last thing I wanted to be doing, so I decided to leave work early. (I did wait till Pizza Break was over—I'm not a complete idiot.) My plan was to surprise Paige and Kelly as they got home from school and offer to take them out to dinner at Charley's, but when I got home, Paige was just finishing a video call with Allie.

"Bye, Mom. See you soon," Paige said before clicking off the video and turning to Kelly. "She looks like crap."

Kelly made a disgusted face. "Yuck, dust and greasy hair. Don't they shower over there?"

"It's, like, ponytail city."

"And what's with the khaki everything?" said Kelly, shaking her head.

"I just could not do khaki every day—oh, hi, Logan," Paige said, finally deciding to acknowledge my presence.

"You girls up for dinner at Charley's?"

* * *

The girls had a good time at Charley's, in part because they seemed to know just about every diner in the restaurant. (Apparently, their friends dragged their parents to Charley's as well.) They chitted and chatted and greeted away while I sat in melancholy silence like Scrooge hunched over a bowl of gruel. Humbug.

When I got the girls home, Paige asked me what was wrong.

Well, your mother's dying, she doesn't know it, and it's killing me, is what was in my brain, but instead I said, "Nothing, just a rough day at work. It was great to see your mom, wasn't it?"

"The queen? I think she needed a shower. Is she ever coming home?"

"Soon," I said soberly, "soon." But I was already tired of being Donny Downer, and I had a thought. "Paige, I'm gonna step out. Got a meeting with somebody from work. You and Kelly be okay?"

"Gee, I don't know. Maybe if you give me a bottle and changed my diaper first."

"Paige!" yelled Kelly from the TV room. "You gotta see what Mandy posted!"

"Go!" Paige said with a wave.

My woes had brought a frosty, bottomless mug of Miner's to mind. In my months with Allie, Miner's had virtually disappeared from my thoughts and liver. But now seemed like a great time to get reacquainted with my old friend. As it was Wednesday, I headed for ladies' night at The Banshee. I wagered that Jones would be there, which meant I wouldn't have to drink alone.

* * *

The Banshee proved to be full of a mob celebrating Scranton's Third Wednesday Bash. (yesterday having been the Third Tuesday Bash). In pre-Super Born Scranton, they just celebrated the first Friday of each month. Now the once-lonely downtown was alive and crawling with revelers almost every night of the week. The Banshee was standing room only, with patrons silhouetted by the flashing lights of a dozen bigscreen TVs. I took note of the beautiful images on their screens and mentally compared it to the tiny screen at O'Malley's. These big babies were exactly what the barkeep needed to draw in a crowd. I thought about suggesting it to the old sod, then decided nay.

The row of tables along the front windows of the Banshee was fully occupied and loud. The maze of booths was packed with laughter, smiles, and booze, as was the aisle between the booths. The bar was two or three deep with customers standing or waiting to place orders. Scranton was happy and alive, and The Banshee was cashing in.

I weaved through the crowd, taking elbows in the ribs and splashes of beer on my sleeves, until I found Jones staring up at the TV with a Miner's in his hand

"Remember when this place looked like a funeral parlor?" I asked as I slipped into the open space behind him.

"Logan, my friend! Pull up a…" he said, looking around at the full bar around us. "Stand. Pull up a stand right there."

"How's ladies' night treating you?"

"About as good as Allie being in Africa is treating you, I suppose. We are now brothers forlorn on the praire."

"I'll drink to that…if I can get to the bar."

"Allow me," he said, signaling the bartender, who blatantly ignored him. "Mark, the barkeep, is a friend of mine. We go way back," Jones said, waving at the bartender again as he flashed by. "Mark, Marky, my man," he called on the man's third pass. Having failed, Jones just gave me a cutesy smile.

I saw a small opening at the end of the bar where the waitresses went to place drink orders and decided fishing might be better there. "Be right back," I said as I began wiggling through the crowd. As I stood waiting at the waitress' station, I noticed a familiar face at the opposite end of the bar. It was Iyla, Ms. Meatloaf herself, sitting in a booth near the hallway to the restrooms looking nervously between the woman next to her and Jones. *That's really odd*, I thought. Then I remembered maybe she knew him from work.

Iyla leaned over her table to talk to her companion, a tall, gorgeous blond. Anyone familiar with the best Russian smut would recognize the round face, defined cheekbones, and strong nose of a classic Russian beauty. (Not to say that I am such a person, of course.) Plus it sure sounded like they were speaking Russian. I remembered Allie telling me that Iyla was Russian and wondered where were they all coming from. *Russia*, I promptly replied to myself. And it didn't take more than a man with a pulse to notice the exceptional rack on Iyla's companion. The beauty turned her attention to Jones with a focused look, like an artillery battery taking aim. Damn, what did he have that I didn't, and what color panties would Jones soon be collecting? Not that I wanted her tentacles sliming around me, but geesh, I'm right over here! Open your eyes! Could Jones be back on the panty trail despite having been marked?

Then the blond stood—I watched, amazed, as she walked up to Jones and hit him with a smile and conversation, much like a fisherman setting her hook and beginning to wind in her reel.

Sometimes I'm as slow as the process of getting a drink in a busy bar, so it took a while, watching her sliding her hands over Jones' shoulders and laughing at his silly banter, for it to hit me: the Russian thing, the Olga Settchuoff thing. What an idiot I am! This invasion of Russians was no accident. They were all Super Born, the product of Russia's flirtation with epsilon radiation. But why were Iyla and this beauty here? Were they working together? And what did they want with Jones?

The answer came like a wrecking ball in the face when I saw a tall, dark man emerge from the bathroom hallway and begin talking to Iyla. Holy squirrel nuts! It was Demetri, the man I'd warned Jones about ever seeing again. Iyla was with him, this beauty was with him, he was with him, and they all were after Jones. Or was Jones with them? Had Jones turned? The possibilities bounced around inside my head like a tennis ball on speed. Every way I spun it, it came out bad. A waitress had finally asked if she could get me anything when I panicked and started fighting my way back to Jones.

"Your shoulders are sooo big and strong. But you are tight like drum. Let me rub for you. Doesn't that feel bettttter?" the beauty said digging both hands into Jones' shoulders and neck. The way she said the word *better* would have made a eunuch climax. In fact, a couple of them nearby probably did.

"Oh yes, indeed," moaned Jones. His right foot bicycled slightly, like a dog whose belly has been rubbed in just the right spot.

I was only a few feet away but had to fight my way through the crowd. It seemed like they were attacking Jones, and I was the calvary charging, at a snail's pace, over the hill, bugle blowing, sword drawn.

"Ooh, I love a man with a big brain. Makes me melt like little girl," she said, beginning to run her hands through Jones' hair. "You like to spank little girl?"

When her fingers locked on Jones' head, I saw him straighten up and his eyes roll back in his head. Either Jones really liked the idea of spanking her or something was seriously wrong. I finally pushed my way through the final few feet, emerged from the crowd, and drove the beauty away from Jones with my shoulder. When her hands pulled away from his head, I saw blue sparks shoot from them as they disconnected.

Instantly, the cat turned on me, showing her claws. "Get away! This is none of your business!"

"I know what you're doing. Take your friends and get out!" I said, pointing to Iyla and Demetri, who appeared stunned by my appearance. Everyone around us in the bar gave us quizzical looks but then just went on with their lives.

"Why don't you ask him what he vants?" the blond barked. "Maybe is you who should leave!"

With Jones being my only hope to counter Allie's firework condition, there was no one more valuable to me than him. I couldn't let them have him. Jones reached for Iyla's companion, looking like a puppy, but I grabbed hold of his arm and dragged him away. Something about his vacant stare made me wonder if I was too late. Iyla, Demetri, and the vamp started after me. I heard Demetri yell to Iyla, "Get Logan! You convince him!" Iyla fought her way through the crowd like a battering ram, but I was long gone—or so they thought.

I ducked behind a dumpster in the alleyway beside the bar with a subdued Jones at my side while the two women ran up and down the sidewalk looking for clues as to which way we'd gone. I hoped the dumpster would keep them from seeing us and that the bar crowd in the street would disguise our thoughts from Iyla's I-know-what-you're-going-to-say-before-you-say-it Super Born mind. Eventually, they circled around Demetri, who stood just inside the opening to the alley. I peered out at them from behind the dumpster.

Iyla held out her arms and panted. "No sign of them."

"Valeria, did you get anything?" Demetri asked. He sounded near panic.

Valeria closed her eyes. Suddenly she smiled and gave a quick laugh.

"What is it?" asked Demetri.

"He does have device," she answered.

"Yes. A control device?" Demetri asked excited.

She kept her eyes closed as she spoke. "It is long cylinder that he has, but I shouldn't tell you where he usually puts it."

"Ahhh!" said Demetri swinging his hand in frustration.

Valeria kept her eyes closed. "There is more. He has metal cylinder too."

"Yes, with batteries I bet," added Iyla.

"No, there are tubes winding off of it and digital panel," continued Valeria.

Demetri was immediately relieved. "That sounds like it! That is what he described to me, an epsilon radiation gun. Do you have the plans?"

"I have something, maybe just a fragment. I will have to download everything I got from his head into your computer to see what is really there," Valeria said, shaking her head.

"Valeria and I will get back and download," Demetri said. "Iyla, you look for Jones so we can finish with him if the downloaded plans are not complete. The Lion will want a report, and I know Shamil is near. We have to hurry."

"Did you see Jones' face?" Iyla asked. "Are you sure you didn't drain him? It looked horrible."

"What concern is it of you, ugly stupid! At least I get information," stated Valeria with pride.

"I don't hurt people for no good reason."

"Maybe you should try, is fun."

Iyla stared at her with disdain. "I am Iyla, daughter of Olga Settchuoff! I deserve your respect."

Valeria laughed. "Some has-been old lady? Why should I respect her—or you?"

"My mother is a hero of the Russian people. Everyone loves her, and I am her daughter!"

"From what Demetri tells me, she lives on a farm with pigs now!"

"Pigs? Funny, with your nose, I'd have guessed they were your relatives."

"Yes, your mother lives with pigs. Now at least you know who your father was!"

Iyla's bitter eyes burned deeply into Valeria.

"What, are you trying to get into my mind, you cow? Not working, is it? I don't know why Demetri keeps you around. Is it pity, or are you just a good whore?" Valeria asked.

Iyla's face burned red as she swung her arm back to hit Valeria. Before she could, Demetri moved in to block her. With one broad blow, he struck Iyla's face with the back of his hand and sent her staggering back on her heels. "Enough. Come, Valeria," he said and then turned back to Iyla. "Do your job! Valeria will have candy tonight, but none for you." Then he lifted a 9 mm out of his jacket pocket and placed it in Iyla's hand. "Here is the gun I took from you in Berlin after that disaster with the Israelis. Like your mother once told me, sometimes the crudest weapon is the best tool. Use this or your mind—whatever you have to do. Just find Logan and Jones and keep them here in case we need them. Call me when you have them." With that they turned and left. As they walked away, I heard Valeria say to Demetri, "You don't need her. Let me finish her, so you don't have to."

Iyla huffed and puffed her frustration for a minute and then walked down the street to the left of the alley. Jones and I waited for a while and then started to creep out from behind the dumpster. Jones felt like Jell-O and didn't utter a sound. Out of the corner of my eye, I saw the red highlights of Iyla's hair coming back around the corner, and we ducked back behind the dumpster. Iyla reached the middle of the alley and stopped, looking right at the spot where we were hiding. She stayed there for long moment and then slowly continued across the alley. A minute later, when I thought the coast was clear, I led Jones out from our hiding place, but when I looked up, there was Iyla's face peeking around the corner of the building. Our eyes met and held each other's for a long moment before she disappeared.

* * *

IYLA

I felt sick. I couldn't breathe. I only could walk a block down the street before I stopped to lean against a building. My chest moved up and down, but I got no air. My mind was like the inside of a beehive. Thoughts of people walking by buzzed into my head and flew around, and Valeria's and Demetri's words hurt even more than the sting of where Demetri had slapped me. He had never hit me before. I always did my best to do as he please. Yet he hit me. My Demetri hit me.

Then that pig-nosed bitch insulted me and my mother. I'd spent my whole life in my mother's shadow. Everyone knows Olga—she is a myth that no one can reach, especially her daughter. Yet Valeria laughs. Big stupid laughs at a hero of the Russian people. Worst of all, now she is with Demetri. They walk together. She has candy tonight but not me.

I need candy right now. I need to get all this noise out of my head. The thoughts of a hundred people passing by made me feel like my head would explode. I heard them worry about their girl-friends, their problems at work, and getting somewhere on time. I heard hundreds of hearts beating, their stomachs gurgling, and I listened to phone conversations. I saw Valeria's ugly face and felt her hate. I could see Demetri and felt his hand across my face. *Get out! Get out of my head!* I felt like I would faint.

And me, why didn't I get into Logan's mind and make him stay so Valeria could come and finish stealing Jones' brain? Why didn't I do this and run to Demetri? Maybe then he would give me candy. Maybe then he would love me again.

Why was I standing here? Why was I waiting?

Then I thought of Logan. Remembering the way he looked at me created a small spot of calm in my head. He knew I was with Demetri and we were hurting Jones, yet he didn't run from me. Did he trust me? He was not the one hitting me. There was no sign of hate in his eyes. Reading his mind, I found nothing but thoughts of protecting the woman he loved and saving his friend.

I thought about Logan with Allie and the way she treated me. They were good people. I wished Logan would look at me the way he looked at Allie. I wished I was the center of his thoughts the way she was. Maybe someday a man would want me that way.

Suddenly, I felt calm. The air came back into my lungs. *I am Iyla, daughter of Olga Settchuoff.*

TWENTY-EIGHT

Jones Reboots

LOGAN

Where to go to hide? Iyla worked with Jones at Lowe LLC, and Demetri had been to Jones' apartment, so together, they knew where Jones worked and lived. They probably knew where I lived too. What a terrible time for the girls to be gone.

What was I thinking? When you need to disappear, there's only one place to go. I took a good look around for anyone who might be following us and then opened the door of my car and stuffed Jones inside. He fell against the door as I tried to close it, so I pushed him back inside and slammed the door.

Soon the new, glowing sign of "Omalley's Sports Bar (and Grille)" loomed through my windshield, and I parked on the street right outside the door. I came around the side of the car to collect Jones and made a great, saving catch as he tumbled out the door when I opened it. I sighed with relief as I pulled him inside the two sets of doors and into the bar. Though as I did, I noticed Jones' head turn slightly from side to side like a defective robot. When I planted him in a booth, his head dropped onto the table. I propped him up so his head leaned against the back of the booth.

The barkeep came and looked us over. "I'm not even going to ask what kind of crazy shite this is. But if he dies in here, it's not on me."

"No one's dying," I said. "How about a Miner's and some privacy?"

"Officer, I didn't see anything," he said as he walked away.

"Ice cream, Mommy, I want some ice cream," Jones said, suddenly perking up, but then his head dropped down onto the table again. I slid into the booth beside him, shaking my head at what my life had become. There sat the great hope I had for saving Allie crying to his mommy for ice cream. *I am fucked.*

Suddenly, Jones lifted off the table and crossed his arms over his face, yelling, "Penguins! Penguins!" As quickly as they had opened, his eyes closed, his head dropped to the side, and he fell back in the booth.

The barkeep arrived with my Miner's. He looked at Jones apprehensively. "He all right?"

I shook my head and sipped the Miner's. "No, not at all."

Jones raised his head and looked at a spot on the table before him with half-open eyes. "Who made the chicken?"

"What chicken?" asked the barkeep.

Jones pointed at an invisible plate before him. "That chicken."

"What are you, daft? There's nothing there!"

Then Jones' eyes closed. The barkeep gave me a questioning look, and I just shrugged.

"I don't know what he's on," the barkeep said, "but you didn't buy it 'ere." He took a step away, but then returned, leaning in closely. "Got any more?"

I shook my head.

"Pity," he said before turning to leave. But I grabbed his arm.

"It is essential that you bring me one of these every fifteen minutes," I said, tapping my Miner's on the table. "Lives are at stake. Can I count on you?"

The barkeep shook his head. "Now I know why I always collect from you when I deliver. You're as crazy as those loons back there," he said, pointing to the RFDs in the back room. He held out his palm for payment.

I paid him, plus tip. "Remember, every fifteen minutes!" I shouted after him. I watched him ignore me then downed a long pull from the beer.

Jones suddenly screamed in terror, his eyes wide open. He looked over his shoulder. Then his panic turned to anger. "Mom! Are you following me again?" Then his eyes closed and he slumped back in his seat. I just sat back and stared.

I pulled out my phone to call Allie, but realized it would be the middle of the night in Nigeria. So I tapped out a text—*Call me when you can call. Love u*—and hit send before I noticed the auto correct revision of the text: *Call me camel. Love zoo.* Then I texted Paige to tell her I was tied up, and she texted back, *Logan who?* I set down my phone, wondering how my night could get anymore dysfunctional. I stood up, drifted around the bar, and took a super long drink from my Miner's. Was fifteen minutes up yet? 'Cause I needed another.

With the sound of scurrying feet and gunshots in the back room, it was clear that the RFDs had started a round of the antler game. It had become a tradition for them: one RFD fired a rifle loaded with blanks at the other RFDs, who scurried around the back room wearing leather helmets with antlers protruding from their sides in a mock deer hunt. The chaos in the bar reminded me of the chaos in my life, and I took another drink. I glanced over to find Jones on top of the table of the booth, pointing under it. "Captain, I've found the tunnel. This way to freedom!" he said before slumping into a pile on the tabletop.

I drifted back to the booth, slid Jones' foot out of the way so I could put down my Miner's, sat down, and sighed.

I looked at him calmly, as if this was the way I spent every night. I downed what was left of my Miner's and held up the empty bottle to summon another. The barkeep came with two bottles and held out his hand. "Thought I'd save a trip."

"Thanks," I said throwing cash at him.

The barkeep moved in close. "Just in case, for the right price, I've got a friend with a bag and a shovel."

"Good to know," I said as he left. I leaned back in the booth and started to feel the alcohol chilling my mind and slowing my body as I watched Jones sucking his thumb. What to do? What to do? I needed to hold down the fort until the girls arrived. I looked about me at my formidable defenses: Jones busily thrusting his pelvis into an invisible woman, saying, "Who your daddy is!"; the old barkeep ready to throw us out at any moment; a flock of RFDs scurrying about; and then there was me—wonderful, marvelous me! The pit I was in just seemed to be getting deeper, and I felt like I was being buried alive, one shovelful at a time.

Suddenly Jones climbed off the table and tapped me on the shoulder. "Are these files indexed or sequential?" he asked.

"Indexed," I guessed.

"Okay, thanks," he said. Once more, his eyes closed and his head fell back against the booth.

Then a theory hit me. (Maybe my brain worked better after a drink!) Slowly, Jones was progressing. He had become more and more animated, his actions more mature since he'd stated his childish need for ice cream. Maybe he was simply rebooting. While a computer takes a minute to do so, maybe a person takes longer. *I've got time*, I thought as I relaxed and took a sip of my Miner's.

Jones awoke again and held his arms up in surrender. "No, officer, I was framed. I swear the strontium 90 and palladium catalyst aren't mine! I have no idea who put them there." Then he fell face-first onto the table.

Well, I thought, *I have time*. After ten minutes, watching Jones reboot was getting a bit boring, so I paced to the bar and squinted at the big screen. "That the news?" I asked the barkeep, who stood on the other side of the bar.

"Nooo, it's one of those bleedin' singing shows—*Who's Got the Best Voice and Biggest Ass*, I think."

To our left, the head of a RFD slowly rose until it was over the top of the bar. It hung there for a moment, expressionless, and then it slowly dropped back down again.

"Got any chips?" I asked, causing the barkeep to put out his hand without taking his eyes off the tiny TV. I handed him money. He reached under the bar and threw a bag at me while continuing to watch TV.

"What about my change?"

"Your what? Sorry, didn't hear ya."

Then, to our right, the head of the same RFD slowly appeared and then drifted down below the bar. Neither the barkeep nor I felt compelled to comment on that.

"Oh man, if it's fat ass they want, that one on the left is the winner!" I pointed at the TV and munched my chips.

"That's not the show. I just put in a video of my wife, you idiot!"

"Sorry."

"Quiet. Try not to speak. I don't come in your livin' room, eat your food, drink your beer, and talk, now do I?"

I was ready to protest with the whole "but this is a bar" argument when I spotted Jones running around, hopping up and down, and hitting his invisible horse with an invisible crop. "This way, men!" he said. "They can take our lives, but they can't take our beer!" He extended one of my empty beer bottles in his hand out before him like a sword. Behind him a jumbled group of six RFDs ran, charging with him. "Hooza!" shouted Jones. "Hooza!" The RFDs joined in, each with a slightly different, butchered variation of the word.

The barkeep just looked at Jones in amazement. "Sweet Mary, Joseph, and me aching balls."

I calmly munched some chips. "Hey, at least he's up to running—*and* he's making friends!"

Someone started the jukebox, and when I turned back to Jones, he was leading everyone in a lively version of the Chicken Dance. It proved so contagious that RFDs from all over the bar joined in, as did the barkeep and his wife Millie, who burst out through the swinging doors of the kitchen dancing. I smiled and downed my Miner's, licking the lip of the bottle the way Allie used to. Jones was going to be just fine…I hoped.

TWENTY-NINE

Iyla Is Free

IYLA

It was late when I returned to the apartment. I came through the door silently to find everything dark and quiet. No one was in the living room or kitchen, so I crept toward the bedrooms. When I heard Demetri wheezing, I thought he might be having one of his attacks and needed my help. I gently pushed on the door to find him naked on top of Valeria, gasping from the exertion of driving into her. She was in a candy cloud, drifting somewhere. Finally, the creak of the door made Demetri realize someone was there. He stared in my direction for a moment before he recognized me.

"Iyla!" he said, climbing off Valeria with effort to stand at the end of the bed—and I mean, standing at the end of the bed. "This isn't what it looks like."

"Really? 'Cause it looks like you are fucking a pig."

"We're just having a party…to celebrate. Join us! There is candy on the nightstand. We found it, little one. The download has the complete plans from Jones' head. We have it all! I have a meeting with Shamil tomorrow. Then we will all be rich. You can have the beach house you always talked about. You can have all the candy you want. You'll never have to be stressed with all those people getting into your head ever again!"

I paced back and forth a little. My silence worried Demetri. I could tell by his uncertain face.

"What is the problem? This?" he said, pointing to Valeria, who writhed on the bed with her hands drifting over her stomach and between her legs. She moaned, not seeming to notice that Demetri was gone. "You are still my favorite. It is just a party, nothing more."

"Funny, 'cause it seemed to me like you were fucking her brains out. No wonder she has none left."

"No! We wanted to celebrate the download. You were not here. What could I do?"

"Wait for me."

"I didn't know where you were!"

"That is funny too, 'cause I knew where you would be. And there you were." I shook my head. "You disgust me."

"Forget this! We have everything we want. We can start again!"

"Again and again and again. Right, Demteri? Tell me, how do I have a beach house and all this money when Shamil has the control device? He controls me, her," I said, pointing at Valeria, "and all of us. We are not free. You are, not us."

"It won't be like that. I'll make sure of it. Take the candy."

"Don't you see they want to burn the world down? They will burn us too. That treatment they promised you is a lie."

Valeria called for him in a candy fog: "Demetri, come back to bed."

I paced. Remembering the past and anticipating the future made tears begin to form—in a moment, they were rolling down my face. "No, you need to know what the worst part is, Demetri," I said, pointing a quaking finger at him. "I thought I was your favorite. I thought you really cared for me. You made me feel safe."

"That's true. All true, and it can be again," Demetri said, holding out his arms. When I didn't buy what he was selling, his attitude changed. "Come on, you little bitch. You are nothing without me! Take the candy and join the party!"

"Or what, you hit me again?"

"What? I never hit you!"

His lie brought my tears to an abrupt halt. It was then I realized everything with Demetri was a lie. I was nothing to him. I turned to face him. "I am sorry, Demetri, but I can't let them have the control device."

"What? This is crazy. After all be have been through together?"

"There was good, yes, but mostly bad. The worst part is, you broke my heart. Now, I break yours," I said coldly. With that, I raised my right arm, pointing the 9 mm in my gloved hand at him, and sent a double tap into his chest. Demetri fell back onto the bed with a shocked look plastered on his face. I moved to him and put the barrel of the gun between his eyes. "Here is the treatment Shamil promised you. Same as he would give you once you gave him what he wants. There is no money, no freedom from them. Only this," I said—and fired.

I stepped around the bed to where Valeria lay sensuously wiggling and moaning in her own oblivion. Suddenly I understood how weak and vulnerable the candy made us. There was no way I could leave her here. Even with Demetri gone, if I took the plans for the control device with me, she would simply steal them again from Jones. But this time she would give them directly to Shamil. I put the gun in her hand, put my hand over hers, put the gun to her head, and squeezed her finger on trigger. She jolted and then didn't gyrate anymore. Which reminded me of something Mother used to always say: "Bad things happen—just make sure they happen to someone else."

Now there was only one place left where the control device lived— in Jones' head. Perhaps I would have to deal with him too.

I circled back around the bed to the nightstand and put the bag containing four glowing candy lozenges in my pocket. I dug through Demetri's clothes on the floor, took most of his cash out of his wallet, left his credit cards, took out his key ring, and opened the black metal box he kept in the nightstand. I dug through papers to find my passport, Valeria's passport, and more cash. I stuffed everything in my pocket. Then I went to my bedroom, put some of my clothes in a bag, put some of Valeria's clothes in the bag, and then went to the living room. I found Demetri's computer, with plans for the control device still on the screen. My first thought was to smash the stupid thing to tiny, tiny bits—was this device worth so much pain? But then I decided to unplug the laptop, close it, and put it in my bag. Iyla was in control now.

When I closed the door to leave the apartment, I had already forgotten what I'd left behind.

THIRTY

Allie on the Way

ALLIE

Was that a wrinkle? It wasn't there yesterday. "Yuck," I said as I stared blankly at the bathroom mirror. I was trying to rise and shine this morning, but this wrinkle wasn't helping. A few days without her arsenal of cosmetics could sure change a girl. I tried to straighten out the tangled mess of my hair, deciding to go ponytail, when I found gray hair poking between my fingers. Not one little hair either but three or four. I shook them off my fingers as if they were a virus. "Eew."

"Ms. Suit's gone!" yelled Rebecca, barging into the communal bathroom at the cooperative.

"What?"

"I found a manifest for a private flight from Lagos to New York. She's gone."

"You tell Jenny?"

"Yeah, she's getting the pilot off his ass. We should be able to leave in a half hour."

"Not a moment too soon."

"I don't know, I like it here," Rebecca said, popping a doughy bit into her mouth. "Everything is working so well. There's all this positive energy. Did I tell you about the power curve on the generators being way better than we estimated?"

"Twice."

Rebecca looked at me with a hurt expression, "Okay. Helicopter will be ready soon. You better get moving," she said. She turned to leave and then turned back to me. "You okay? You look like crap."

"Thanks."

Then she ran off like a happy little nymph in the woods.

I looked in the mirror one more time then waved my hand at it in disgust. I'd gone back to my tent to pack when I found Logan's text: *Call me camel. Love zoo. Lord, he's been drinking again*, I thought as I started to dial home. Then I stopped, realizing it was the middle of the night in Scranton. This time change made things impossible. *Okay, camel. Glad you enjoyed the zoo. Did Paige go with you? Leaving today. Be home soon.* ☺ I texted. Then I sent, *On way home. See you soon. You have fun at the zoo?* to Paige. I hurried to pack my bag with a sudden burst of excitement at the thought of home.

* * *

LOGAN

It was pushing three a.m. when Jones finally became coherent. He sat in the dark booth at O'Malley's sweating profusely, with his elbows on the table and his head in his hands, moaning and groaning about his life. "My aching head," he said. "Why is it always me?"

I sat across from him. "How you feeling?"

"You don't have to yell!" He cringed at the sound of his own voice.

I whispered, "Is the headache any better after those pills from the barkeep?"

We both thought about that statement for a second and then looked at each other. "Those were headache pills…right?" Jones asked.

I whispered a reassurance: "Oh, yeah. I'm sure." I looked over at the barkeep, who sat in a booth across the bar canoodling with

Millie—horny old fart. Those pills were aspirin, probably. I hoped.

"Can I get you anything, coffee, water?" I asked.

"How about a gun?" Jones moaned.

"Your memory coming back?"

Jones looked up at me with bleary eyes. "Why do I keep remembering a chicken?"

I decided to have a little fun with him. "Oh, I didn't tell you about that. All I can say is that when that chicken left here, she had a big smile on her face."

Jones swallowed hard, not sure what to believe in his sorry state.

"You had quite the night. Your dance routine even got Martin and Millie out on the dance floor and then into the booth at the back, if you know what I mean," I said, pointing a thumb at them. "I doubted you when you said you could have a career as a stand-up comedian, but not after tonight. You were smoking, especially in your second set…you need an agent?"

Jones was lost. His normally quick brain couldn't keep up with me. I was lovin' it.

"Why am I sweating like a thunderstorm?"

I gave him a disbelieving look. "Don't be so modest."

"What?"

"Michael Jackson had nothing on you." I began counting on my fingers. "Chicken Dance twice, the dance from "Thriller," and *Swan Lake*…how did you manage to throw *and* catch yourself? That was epic, dude."

"Really?" said Jones with a hesitant smile.

"Damn straight."

The last RFD in the place walked up to us and stopped. He had a beer in his hand and wore a leather pilot's helmet outfitted with antlers. Around his neck he wore a Broadway-director-style scarf over his T-shirt. He stopped and introduced himself. "Robert, Robert Symthe the Third, of the Exeter Symthes. Let me shake your hand," he said, offering Jones his hand and causing Jones and me to look at each other in surprise. "Your Macbeth soliloquy was the finest performance I have seen since Olivier. Tears, you literally brought me to tears." Then he handed Jones his card. "I doubt a talent like you would consider us, but if you would, we are opening the new Scranton Performing Arts Center with *Hamlet* in two months. I would appreciate it if you would honor us by playing the lead. I hear that President Cobb and the first lady are friends of the mayor, and they will all attend the opening. No doubt your performance would seduce the ghost of Shakespeare himself to attend as well. Please say you will consider it."

Jones took the card and humbly said, "I will, surely. Thank you."

"Do. Please, do," Robert said, giving us a bow and then turning to leave in as slow and dignified a manner as can be accomplished with antlers on one's head. Then suddenly he began to hop and hoot like a cartoon character and tripped over a chair. Robert straightened himself up and then continued his slow walk to the front door, before running through it yelling, "He's considering it! The idiot's considering it!"

"What the bleep was that?" I asked.

"No idea. Never seen an RFD like that," Jones was forced to admit.

"Was he just messing with us?"

"Maybe. Maybe something else," Jones said reflectively. "You know, I do remember having coherent conversations with several of the RFDs tonight. At least, I think I did."

"Remember, you were talkin' to a chicken too."

The barkeep slid over to us. "I couldn't help but notice you two assholes are still 'ere."

"A guy with antlers just walks by and trips over a chair, and we're the a-holes?" I objected.

"As I was saying," the barkeep said, gesturing with his thumb at Millie. "Mind giving a bloke a little privacy?" When I just sipped on a cup of coffee and looked up at him he added, "You wanna move your bleedin' ass right now?" Then he walked over to Millie, moving as if his overweight frame were that of a Hollywood star on the red carpet.

"Oh, isn't that sweet," I said, looking over at Millie's smiling face. "Do you?" I asked Jones, "want to move your bleedin' ass?"

"I believe I do," answered Jones, looking around at his back side.

"Great. Where the hell are we going?"

Jones looked puzzled."What's the problem? I'll just go home."

"Ahhhh," I said as I smacked my palm into Jones' forehead, "wrong answer. They'll just get you for good this time."

"Who?"

"The people who did this to you...the people who gave you the headache!" Jones just stared at me blankly. "Look, you remember Demetri, your buddy?" Jones nodded. "Well, your buddy and two Russian superwomen tried to corral you tonight and drain your brain. They were after something inside your head. I had to pull you away or you'd be in produce section of the nearest grocery store. I told you Demetri was up to no good. He couldn't find what he wanted in your apartment, so now he's after it in your head."

Jones raised an eyebrow and chuckled. "Drain my brain?" Then an ache in his head made him wince and put his hand over his temple.

"Call it what you want, but that blond had her hands on your head, and when she let go, you just went away for a while. They could be anywhere out there, waiting for us."

The barkeep cleared his throat loudly from across the room.

I began helping Jones out of the booth. "Let's go. I'll get you a room somewhere. You'll have to lay low for a while."

Jones continued to rub his forehead. "Maybe you are right. This sounds like I had a really shitty night."

"Look who just caught up!"

The barkeep ran up to us as we neared the door and spoke to Jones. "Hey, you ever consider doin' your act for a living? I could use an entertainer like you to spark up the old sports bar. That Chicken Dance thing got everyone moving and buying beers. Here's my number. Give me a call." The barkeep gave Jones his number before tiptoeing excitedly back to Millie.

Jones gave me a puzzled look. "My act?"

"Never mind," I said as I pushed him out the door. After we got in the car and I slammed my door, I was hit with the realization that it was the middle of the night. Soooo, it was morning in Africa! I rang Allie to catch her up on the situation with Jones and Demetri but instead got her voice mail. *Really? Really?* I thought before texting her: *CALL ME!!!* ☹

Suddenly Jones was lucid. "She may be on her way back and out of the range of cell towers—or she left the co-op and is beyond their Wi-Fi connection."

"Oh, yeah? Well, this whole long-distance relationship thing sucks. Save the world! How about someone saving me for a change, huh?"

"Yes, how about it?" said Jones, rubbing his aching forehead.

THIRTY-ONE

Swelling Problems

ALLIE

"Satellite's up!" yelled Rebecca from behind the high-backed desk chair. The jet was 30,000 feet over the Atlantic on our way back to Scranton.

"Great," Jennifer said, grabbing the remote and turning on the wide-screen TV. She turned to walk back to her seat, and I heard a popping sound. Both hands went to her knee. "What the heck was that?"

"I never heard bones creak like that before, Grandma," Rebecca said.

"God, how could I hurt my knee just walking?" Jennifer hobbled back to her seat, plopped into it, and picked up her bowl of spaghetti.

"Hey, Rebecca, did you know she has spaghetti?" I asked as I pulled out my tablet to call Logan.

Rebecca turned in her chair toward Jenny with a sub in her hand and a bite still in her mouth. "Hey! Where'd you get that?"

"Snooze ya lose," said Jenny, setting up her laptop on the table between a row of facing reclining leather chairs.

I sniffed the air like a food voyeur, receiving gratification from just the smells, then took my tablet into the bedroom at the back of the plane for some privacy.

"Oooh, a little cybersex!" Jenny called after me.

"Yeah, can we watch?" Rebecca added with her mouth half full.

"No," I said firmly, slamming the door shut. But their comments gave me an idea, so I slipped my bra off under my shirt and unbuttoned it. Logan deserved a little reward for all his patience.

"Hi, babes," he said appearing more tired than excited on my screen.

"Hey to you too. You at work?" I asked.

"No, I was feeling too well to go in."

"Great," I said opening my shirt.

"Wow, it is *good* to see you."

"Miss me?" I said, lying on my side on the bed, my elbow bent, my head resting in my hand.

Logan stared, lost for words, and then finally said, "Is it getting warm in here?"

"I don't know about there, but it's awfully hot over here."

"Allie, I've got a lot to tell you…" he said. He was trying to resist me, which just fortified my determination.

"I'm sure you do," I said, running my hand over my breast and then down to my belt. "I've got a lot to tell you too. Where should I start?" I said, undoing my belt and pants and slipping my hand beneath my underwear. I moaned a bit just to see his face implode, then stopped and put my hand up over my chest. "Wait, I can't do this."

"You can't? Why not?"

"I'm being self-centered, just thinking about me. You said you had a lot to tell me."

"It can wait. Really, it's nothing."

"You sure?" I said.

"Positive."

"I don't know. This looks a little one sided at the moment," I said coyly.

"What?"

"The shirt, off…and the pants…now get back in the camera…there you go. Oh, you *are* glad to see me." I could see his face turning red, but the excitement was making him grow. "You are very glad indeed," I said, shimmying out of my jeans to join him naked on the screen. He tried desperately to hide his hard-on but every angle he turned clearly made him feel more exposed than the last. Finally he sat in his desk chair, intently watching me. Logan had a way of looking at me that made me feel like a piece of art.

"You are so beautiful," he said. "I've missed you so much."

"I can see that. I've been missing you too."

Then he began slowly rubbing his entire length and breathing heavily.

"Oh, it looks like you've got quite a swelling problem going on."

"Yeah, I do…you think you can help me with it?"

"I'll try. Does this help?" I asked flirtatiously as I slipped my hand between my thighs, arched my fingers, and gave him a pleasured moan.

"I think that's making it worse," he said.

"Oh, you want the swelling to go *down*?"

"Not just yet," he said, his eyes closing.

That was when Jenny slammed on the thin door with her fist. "Allie, we need you out here."

"I'm a little busy in here!" I complained.

"It's important, or I wouldn't be here bothering you!"

I dropped my head and sighed.

"What? What was that?" Logan asked. "What?" He repeated as I stood up to get dressed and disappeared from his computer screen.

I tugged on my jeans and threw my shirt over my shoulders, trying to think of what to say to him. Finally, I dipped my head back in front of the camera. "I swear I will call you back later."

Bam, bam, bam came Jennifer's pounding on the door. "Now! Put your pants back on and get out here! It's happening."

"I swear I'll call you back. Something's happening, and I have to go."

"What?"

"I'm sorry," I said as I disconnected from the video conference. I opened the door and went out into the cabin with my shirt buttoned unevenly. "What's so goddamn important?"

Jenny led me over to Rebecca, who was sitting before the desk with earphones on, feverishly typing on her computer as multiple screens flashed. Then she opened up another laptop, and that screen flashed like cars on a race track. Jenny gestured at Rebecca. "This."

Rebecca glanced up at me and then returned to work. "I was tracking cell traffic trying to find Ms. Suit. Got something interesting on a call out of New York. Turns out it was her, and she was making a call to this building in Chechnya."

"So?"

"The *so* is that there are encrypted signals coming out of that same building. When I translate the signals, I get this," Rebecca said, clicking some keys and sending four small windows to appear on her second laptop. They were images of clouds and aerial views of cities with GPS information as well as speed and altitude.

"What is that?"

Jenny couldn't resist joining in. "Drones. They're goddamn drones."

"Where are they going?" I asked.

Rebecca pointed to each of the four small windows. "According to the GPS readings, this one is headed for New York, this one Washington, this one Berlin, and this one Vienna."

"Who's the pilot?"

Jenny looked at Rebecca—they laughed and looked at me. "Who do you think?" said Jenny. Then she pointed to the computer screen with the satellite map of the building in Chechnya. "And that's her little hive."

As Rebecca stared at the screen, she became still, and I watched her eyes turn to black. Suddenly one of the images on the screens began to spin, and Rebecca started to laugh. "I'm in! Wooo hooo!" Then the image in the second window began to wave as if the drone was dipping its wings, then the third, and finally the fourth.

Jenny laughed. "I'll bet they're shitting their pants right now!"

"All I need to do is find the circuits to arm the missiles and set off the detonators."

"Blow those mothers up!" said Jenny smiling.

One of the four drone screens showed an aerial view of a city, visible through the clearing clouds—you could see the monuments of Washington, DC, and in the distance, the White House. Rebecca slammed the keyboard with authority, and the image of Washington turned to snow. "Splash one," she said and coughed loudly. She laughed, and it turned into a cough again as the second drone image disappeared.

"That's two!" said Jenny, excited. "Kill 'em, kill 'em all!" With one hand she rubbed the molten metal medallion trophy on her necklace she had recovered from the battle at the co-op.

With two more quick strokes, the image from the drone flying over Berlin went dark, as did the final drone's video feed. Rebecca leaped to her feet and hugged Jenny in celebration. They hopped and laughed together like high school cheerleaders. Jenny lifted her hand to her head like a pretend phone. "Hello? This is Ms. Suit. Where are my drones?" she joked.

"I don't know. Maybe in pieces," Rebecca answered. Then Rebecca's laughter turned into a cough and then another, until she began to wheeze.

Jenny's face turned to panic. "What's wrong?"

I stepped in and took hold of Rebecca, examining her face for clues. I sat her down in her desk chair.

"What is it?" asked Jenny.

"Rebecca, can you talk?" I asked, looking into her eyes—they seemed double in size.

"Can't...can't breathe," she wheezed.

"Just relax," I said, rubbing her arm. "Try to take deep breaths." She tried, but her chest seemed stiff and rigid. I took her pulse, and it was racing. "Come on, let's breathe," I said, breathing deeply, slowly myself. Inhalation by inhalation, her lungs seemed to gain flexibility. As she recovered, I watched her eyes blink black and then back to normal to their own rhythm. After a few minutes, she slumped back in her chair and began to relax.

"What happened to me?" Rebecca asked.

I shook my head. "Don't know. Why don't you go lie down in the back? Just rest," I said, helping her up. I checked her pulse again and then helped her to the back of the plane. She seemed to get steadier with each step.

"Man, that was weird," she said, trying to laugh.

I moved my computer from the corner of the bed and got her to lie down. "I'll check on you in a bit. Call if you need anything."

"Thanks. I feel like a dope."

"Don't worry. We're here for you. Show me a deep breath."

Rebecca took in a deep breath, held it, and let it out. "See, all better."

I smiled and closed the door. I expected Jenny to be all over me with questions, but instead found her standing in front of the TV. "She's resting," I said but became curious when I didn't get a response. "Jenny?"

She pointed at the screen at a news network broadcast.

The male anchor was reporting with a sober face, "The first drone struck the Israeli Knesset building, firing two missiles before crashing into the building itself. Nearly simultaneous drone attacks hit the Palais Bourbon in Paris, the Kremlin in Moscow, and an undisclosed building in Beijing. Reports at this time are still sketchy, so we will update you as we receive new information.

"Joining us now is Robert Outlander, a consultant to the US and European Union on drone technology. Good afternoon, Robert."

"Good afternoon, Michael," said Robert, whose image appeared side by side with the anchor's. He was a studious-looking, bearded man.

"Michael, the question on everyone's mind is how these drones could penetrate protected air space and deliver these devastating attacks without detection."

Robert nodded. "Exactly. Well, there is little to go on at this time, as there has not yet been a thorough investigation, but it is certainly possible that these drones may be using offshoots of the same stealth technology that existed on the United States stealth drone that was captured by the Iranians some years ago. This might explain their radar-evading abilities."

"Yes, but could a terrorist organization build high-tech drones like this?" asked Michael.

Robert lifted his hands and interlocked his fingers. "Think of it this way. They're like the kamikaze aircrafts the Japanese used in World War II in that they are intended for one mission only. They only have to run a few hours, not years and years, as more sophisticated Western drones are made to. Therefore, they can be cheaply made. So the answer to your question is yes, they have the stolen technology and can build expendable weapons like this at a relatively reasonable cost."

Jenny looked at me with a blank face. "There were eight. We only got four."

I mopped my face, folded my arms, and paced. "Well, at least we stopped half of this disaster. What do we do now?"

Jenny remained silent, but I could see she was angry. "Is Rebecca okay?"

"She's better, but I don't understand what happened. She ever tell you about having any health problems?"

"She's been under a lot of stress with the company. That's all I know."

I sat down, and Jenny sat down across the aisle from me.

"Why don't you get back to your call with Logan?" she asked me. "Sounded pretty good, from what I heard."

"Stop it."

"Look, your shirt is on crooked."

"So?"

"That was some swelling problem was he having," Jenny said, shaking her head.

"You were *watching*?"

"Rebecca had it on video until she found Ms. Suit calling Chechnya." Jenny grinned ear to ear. "Boy, was he ever happy to see you. Looked great on wide-screen."

"Damn internet!"

THIRTY-TWO

The Tale of Fireworks

ALLIE

Dinner was really awkward. Sure, Logan had been great and greeted me at the airport with a rose and hug. But when he, Paige, and I went to a welcome-home dinner at Charley's, the silence set in. The three of us were a nearly mute island in the midst of a dinner rush. Logan was not being his usual happy-go-lucky self, and I could tell he was holding something back. (Who knew what had crawled up his ass.) And Paige was trying to be cool but holding onto some frustration or resentment toward me. The worst of it was that normally the silly banter between us always allowed me to sneak in a couple extra appetizers without being overly obvious. With everyone diverted by eating, talking, and laughing, it was harder for Paige or the people in the restaurant to keep track. But this silence was cramping my style.

"You should see what we're doing in Africa. There was a dirt road, and now it's a bustling town with a clinic, a school, farms, and hundreds of people," I said, trying to relieve the guilt I was feeling for having abandoning them.

Logan mumbled something like, "Great," and Paige munched a spring roll, mumbling "Uh huh." It felt good to have my audience so riveted by my story.

"The best part is, next month there will be five more just like it starting up, then twenty more after that. Even with the problems at Lagos, with Cairo and Dubai starting up, we should still be able to stay on schedule."

Logan mumbled "Sure," and Paige, again, mumbled "Uh huh."

I stared at their blank faces, tempted to tell them about battling killers in Cairo, melting helicopters in Nigeria, and splashing terrorist drones. The words were on the tip of my tongue, but then I reverted to plan B. "So, what's up? I feel about as welcomed as a raging zit on school picture day."

Logan sipped his drink and murmured, "Who?" Paige took hold of an imaginary zit on her face and pretended to pop it. "There ya go, Mom."

"Anybody else gonna talk?"

"Soooo, you gonna be home for a while, or is Africa your new thing?" asked Paige.

My mind swirled. I wanted to tell her no, but then I realized that my life had become international and there were horrible people spreading lighter fluid across the world. How could I make a promise to her that I couldn't keep? I wanted my family back, but how could I abandon the multitudes that needed me? How could I let the terrorists torch the world when I had the power to help bring it peace?

"Well, things are really busy right now, but I promise I will try to be home. In fact, I'm gonna shorten the hours I'm at work. We have a great staff now."

"You gonna eat that?" Logan asked, reaching for my barbecued-chicken-strip appetizer.

"Yeah!" I said, pulling the plate away from him.

"I don't care if you go do your thing," Paige said, trying to sound indifferent. "I just wanted to know."

"Honey, I know I've been away too much lately," I started but then stopped to fill my mouth with a full chicken strip. When I'd chewed and swallowed, I went on, "Believe me, when you see what we've done, you'll know it was worth it. In fact, you were a part of making it happen."

"I'm supposed to be…proud?" Paige asked sarcastically.

I gave Paige a serious look then nodded my head, "Yeah, your mom helped do all this, and I couldn't do it without your support." Paige winced a bit at that. I was frustrated and leaned back in my chair. "Tell you what, next time I have to go to Africa, I'll take you two along. You can see for yourself." As soon as I said the words, though, I regretted them, remembering the rocket-propelled grenade that had been leveled at my head in Cairo.

"That would be cool," Paige said, softening.

"And the company has a super cool jet. It's, like, this glossy silver color. You should see it: bigscreen TV, packed refrigerator. It even has a bedroom."

"Really?" asked Paige, smiling now.

"And the people we're working with are great."

"Any lions or cheetahs?" Paige asked.

I thought about the killers running at me through the gate in Cairo. "Yeah, some really wild, vicious animals." I turned to Logan. "What about you, Mr. Talkative?"

* * *

LOGAN

You should see what we're doing in Africa, blah, blah, blah. Allie seemed so proud of what she was doing and totally unaware of the fact that she was a rapidly burning firework that wouldn't even last to see the next the Fourth of July. I looked at her across the table with the same focused fascination I always felt. Despite her being a superwoman, my instinctive reaction had always been to wrap my arms around her and protect her from a world of worries, like she was a child instead of someone who could kick me into the next county. Now I knew I couldn't even do that. How could I tell her our days together were numbered? Maybe Jones was wrong. Of course he was. *Look at her, so vibrant and full of life.* Her gray eyes glistened like the day we met. (*And just look at those knockers.* Those perky girls weren't going anywhere soon.) I wanted to be alone with her but instead felt the frustration of having to be patient and deal with the moment in silence. I had to be the strong one.

It was tough to feel the static in the air between her and Paige. I had done my best to be there for Paige while Allie was gone, but watching movies, having dinner, and engaging in silly chatter couldn't make up for not having a mom there. Allie's promise to be home more was meant for Paige, but it perked up my ears as well. The only thing I couldn't understand was why she kept trying to steal *my* chicken appetizer. I had offered to buy her one. I reached out my hand in protest.

Paige tapped me on the arm in warning. "When she gets like this, I would keep my hands away from her mouth if I were you."

"Thanks for the tip," I said, dropping my protest. I reached for one of her spring rolls, but she pulled her plate away and slapped me on the hand.

"*Et tu*, Paige?" I said as she stuffed a roll in her mouth and smiled.

When Allie finally pulled her plate closer, I decided I'd better get another appetizer for myself the next time the waiter appeared. Where was that guy anyway? Paige wanted bread and Allie more water.

What, now Allie was taking us to Africa? *Lions? People screaming while they swing from vine to vine in loincloths? And no Miner's Lite? No thanks. But maybe I should go.* It would make them both happy, and who knew how long the two of them would have together.

Screw that. We'll go to Africa for years and years. Everything will be fine. It always is. Just wake up, and it's a new day.

"What about you, Mr. Talkative?" she asked, raising the hairs on my arm.

Was she really hitting me with that sarcastic crap when here I just wanted to protect her from the truth? "Mr. Talkative is just fine. Anybody seen that waiter?" Paige pointed him out, and I raised my arm. "Hey, my man!" I said. He turned away and began taking another order.

"No, I mean, you up for the next trip to Africa?" Allie asked. "Wouldn't you like to see what we've helped build? We're changing the world. It's amazing." Allie popped the last bit of my appetizer into her mouth.

"Sure, especially if that's the only way I get to see you."

"Amen to that, brother," added Paige.

"What, you two ganging up on me now?"

"Yes," we both said simultaneously.

"I'm hearing that, loud and clear. That ours?" she said as our food was delivered.

I watched them both attack their chicken pasta. I watched them smile at one another. I saw my family, happy and together. The feeling was like no other satisfaction I'd ever felt—and I'd made love to a superwoman. But I couldn't shake the feeling that I was watching the exploding glow of a beautiful firework. The best I'd ever see. In a moment it would be gone.

* * *

ALLIE

Paige came and pounded on my bedroom door. "Can you keep it down in there? I can hear you all the way at the end of the hall...and I've got my headphones on!" She stomped a few steps away before turning and clomping right back to the door. "Maybe you two should get a room...in some other building!" Then she plodded away, sounding like a disgusted elephant.

Logan and I just laughed. I fell back onto the pile of pillows on the bed with my arms falling limply over my head against the headboard. I smiled like a lottery winner and stared at the ceiling. "We've had great, but that was amazing," I said. "I think I had three, and that's not counting those miniorgasms along the way…how do you do that?" I asked, turning to curl onto his shoulder.

"I have to do a lot of research when you're not around—hours and hours of research, mostly on the Indian Kama Sutra and Cleopatra's sexual secrets."

I tapped him on the shoulder in fun but he winced (guess I was a little too strong). "I'm the one trying to keep up with you. You were like, errrrr, an animal coming after me for real, like…ahhhh, it was amazing." I looked up at his face, and even in the dark, I could see the glistening of a tear on his face. I caught a deep breath and lifted my head up for a closer look. "Are you crying?"

"Sweating. You got me all hot and heavy. Just some manly sweat—it takes a lot of energy to be a Greek god."

"Eye sweat? That's a new one."

"My eyes, my back, and you don't want to know about my butt."

"You're right about that," I said, wiping the "eye sweat" from his cheeks. "But I'll take care of this for you." I curled back onto his shoulder. "What got you going like that?"

"I love you, Allie."

That made me smile. I gave him a long kiss, but when I pulled away I could see tears rolling down his face again. "Boy, you are really sweating," I said, wiping his cheeks again. "You miss me that much?"

"What can I say? You inspire me."

"Really? Let's see how much," I said rubbing my hand over his belly, making it quiver and glow like molten silver. Then I slid my hand between his legs. "Oooh, you seem to have that swelling problem starting again…oh, and it's getting worse…oh my, when's it gonna stop? That must be really painful. Does this help?" I teased as he began taking deep, heaving breaths. I kissed his chest. "I'm gonna go after you like a wild animal," I said, kissing my way down his chest as I clawed my nails into his sides. "Roaaaaaar."

THIRTY-THREE

I Get My Suit

ALLIE

Rebecca opened the door to a small storage closet in the R&D lab. "Well," she said, "what do you think?" She saw my unimpressed face and then turned to peer into the gloomy room and sigh. She fruitlessly flicked the light switch over and over. "Damn. Here, help me pull it out." She stepped into the shadows and struggled with a large display that she could barely move. I took hold of Rebecca's arm and led her out of the closet, then with two fingers flicked the life-sized-display out of the closet and into the lab.

"Man, I gotta get in better shape." Rebecca appeared taken aback for a second but then got her bearings. "Well, what do you think?" she asked, proudly gesturing to the display the way a showroom model would.

There stood a female mannequin on a pedestal wearing a gleaming black leather version of my B.I.B. bodysuit, complete with boots, mask, and cape. At first glance I thought it was merely a new version of the tattered, overused costume I already had, but when I looked closer and ran my hand over the material, I realized there was a texture to it. There was something other than the mannequin's form supporting the suit from inside. The cape was not free-flowing cloth but made up of many panels of a self-supporting, semirigid material. I ran my fingers over the side of the bodysuit and the cape. "What is this?" I asked.

"This is so friggin' cool! Remember that laser scan we did of you? Well, this suit is laser measured for you to fit into…plus or minus 2 percent, in case you have a few extra pieces of pizza one day."

"It feels like leather but also like something else."

"Bet your ass there is! The exterior *is* leather."

"Cause it's aerodynamic or something?"

"No, silly, cause it's cool! That texture you feel is a radar-reflective coating. Underneath that is some banging tech. Well, the layer beneath the leather is a flexible ceramic than will stop a knife. Under that is even more sass: a network of small explosive panels. You ever hear of reactive armor?"

"Back up. Explosive what?"

Rebecca waved my concerns away with her hand. "Don't get your panties in a bunch. They're charges that blow outward. If someone tries to shoot you, the bullet will ignite the reactive armor, blowing a charge away from your body that will neutralize the incoming force of the bullet. It's better than heavy body armor 'cause you won't lose any flexibility and the force of the bullet won't knock you on your ass. Inside of that you get a comfort layer that conducts body heat and moisture out through vents in the armpits and inner thighs. The cape is a semirigid, flexible ceramic that automatically interlocks in varying configurations based on wind pressure to give you the ability to glide, hover, and maneuver. You should be able to turn like a mofo. I'm guessing about a 162.37 percent improvement in aerodynamics."

".37?"

"Give or take a few thousandths."

"Oh, of course," I said, rolling my eyes. "How about this?" I asked, lifting the mannequin's left arm, which bore a wide bracelet.

"Oh, cool, cool, and cooler!" Rebecca said, excitedly unclicking and lifting the cover of the bracelet, pointing as she continued to speak. "GPS, COMM, internet, night vision, altitude…wash, rinse, spin, delicates…everything you need to be globally connected, along with totally redundant systems and battery packs recharged by solar-sensitive materials in the cape. You can see everything on this heads-up eyepiece display that folds out of the awesome-looking heated mask…sorry, I got a little carried away," she said, becoming more subdued.

"What, there's no button to order pizza?"

Rebecca put her finger to her lips. "Could be if you want. I would just make a loop to the COMM circuit…"

"Hey! I'm joking!" I said tapping her on the shoulder. Then I thought about it. "Although, really—would it be hard to add that?" I asked, rubbing my finger on my chin. "Oh, just forget it. Do we know this thing works?"

Rebecca put her hands on her hips and looked at me with disdain. "Pleassssse. Did the generators work? Did the new batteries outperform their power curves?"

"Sorry, I'd just like to be certain. It's my ass in there."

"Doubters. I'm surrounded by doubters!" Rebecca sighed, lifted her tablet, and displayed a video of the mannequin being shot by a handgun from a few feet away. Small panels of the suit exploded on what appeared to be contact, but the force meter measuring the impact on the mannequin only moved slightly. "This is only good against small-arms fire. You get hit by a heavy-caliber gun, it's adios, muchacha. I've fine-tuned the charges since this crude test, of course."

"Of course," I said, watching the mannequin. Then she showed me a flight simulation in which the cape changed its configuration based on various wind speeds—a side window showed the information on the eyepiece display, including course, distance, and speed. "Holy…" I mumbled.

"What? Something missing?"

"Think my fat ass will fit in there?" I said, running my hands over the suit in admiration.

"Well, I could modify the posterior…"

"Could you just shut up? When do I get to try it out?"

"Tonight sounds good."

"Wait till Logan gets a load of me in this."

Rebecca grinned. "Oh! Schwinggggggg!"

* * *

The elevator to the roof was a bit tight with Rebecca, Jennifer, Logan, me, and the suit in it. We all stared up at the floor indicator as if it were of some great entertainment value—all of us except for the suit, which seemed deep in its own thoughts (contemplating its fear of heights, perhaps?). Rebecca impatiently bebopped to some unknown tune, trying to compete with the elevator's bland music.

Jennifer was excited. "If this sucker works, I'm getting one too."

"It will work just fine!" insisted Rebecca. "Just pick your color."

Logan stood beside me with his arm around the suit's waist like he was supporting a drooping, drunken bud. He whispered in my ear, "Did you ask her about adding those special features we discussed?" I elbowed him in the stomach and sent him a step back, into the wall.

"We don't need any special features," I answered, smiling, remembering the night before.

"Please you two. I just had dinner," Jennifer complained.

The elevator dinged cheerfully, and we stepped out into a hallway on the top floor, where Rebecca slid her identity badge through a reader to unlock the door to the roof. When she opened the door, a warm, breezy summer's night air flowed in. We all walked silently to the roof's edge, and Logan and I looked over it and then back at each other. "Piece of cake," he said in encouragement.

"Well," said Rebecca, holding out her arms. When I began trying to open up the suit and step inside, she continued, saying, "No, it's not going to work with those clothes on. Laser scan, plus or minus 2 percent, remember?"

"I'll take care of that for you," Logan said. He moved up close and slowly unbuttoned my shirt, slipped it off, and caught it on his arm. I always enjoyed when Logan undressed me; it was intimate and exciting. We kept close eye contact and both smiled as he began working on my slacks and shoes. Soon we were no longer aware of why we were on the rooftop. Logan and I could feel the steam rising between us, and unfortunately, everyone else could too.

"Pleassssse!" said Jennifer, walking away in disgust. "You're horny toads. We get it."

"Really, Allie? Can't you two control yourselves…ever?" Rebecca asked. "Ever?"

I sighed, sorry but not, and slipped into the suit, which sucked me in like a magnet grabbing a piece of iron. It fit so perfectly that I felt free in it. I raised the zipper and looked up at Rebecca. "There."

"How does it fit?" Rebecca asked, looking it over and powering up the control bracelet.

"Super," I said, smiling and flexing my arms and legs. I did twists, squats, and stretches. The suit moved with me, feeling more like another layer of skin than clunky armor.

"Great, now that's getting him excited," complained Jennifer, surveying Logan's hypnotized gaze. "Does he really have to be here? Yoko destroyed the Beatles, you know!"

"Who destroyed who?" Rebecca asked. Her mind was clearly focused on the suit. "Can you two juveniles stop your bickering? We have work to do." Rebecca clicked buttons on the bracelet and then unfolded the eyepiece from my mask and centered it over my right eye. "Everything look good? You remember what I said about the night vision, NAV, and COMM systems?"

"Roger," I answered with a salute.

"Who the hell is Roger? Are you guys all insane?" Rebecca asked. "Allie, take a short trip over to Route 81 and then come back. And no hotdogging until we check the systems out."

I saluted again. "Wait a minute. You said the suit would work. Why are you so worried all of a sudden?"

"Can't you ever just listen to anyone? Short trip. No hotdog-ging. Go!"

I bent my knees and shot into the air, spiraling up to take in the glow of the town below me. That view never seemed to get old. Soon the rooftop of our building was a small speck behind me. I flipped on the night vision in my eyepiece, and the city took on an eerie green glow, as if it were daylight. As I slowed, the cape clicked, and the panels moved like falling dominos, unfolding into a wing to provide extra lift. When I accelerated into a dive or climb, it folded back into a delta shape. Flying had been fun before, but now it was nearly effortless.

"Come back, you're too far away," commanded Rebecca over the COMM system.

Yeah, right.

Below me, I noticed the string of well-lit bars filled with well-lit people and dove until I was merely twenty feet above Adams Avenue. I flashed down the road and then turned for another pass, which was greeted by cheers and catcalls from those in the streets enjoying the Second Tuesday bash. A couple RFDs shot blanks up at me as I flashed by. It was good to remind the people of Scranton that we were still here for them.

Then I did an exhilarating, high-gravity climb that sent my heart down into my feet. I laughed with delight, taking notice of the eye-piece screen as the numbers for position and air speed blinked at me. If I focused on a building, a "distance to target" readout appeared. I had instant access to my location, course, and any information in my network. As I changed speeds or dove, the suit was one with me, and it effortlessly amplified every move I made. Until now, I had been feeling my powers grow steadily, increasing my confidence. But now, with this technology to supplement me, I felt like I was ready to take a quantum leap in capability. I felt unstoppable.

"Allie, goddamn it! Quit the hotdogging, you….you hot dog!" Rebecca yelled in my ear.

"Someone told me the suit would work. And it does. Boy, it sure does. You should be happy," I answered.

"I'll be happy when you bring it back in one piece…Allie? Allie!"

* * *

LOGAN

I smiled to see how free, powerful, and excited Allie was. I sensed her joy, and it made me happy. I listened to Rebecca pleading for her to return, knowing the rebel in Allie would cause her to come back when she was good and ready.

Then, from the dark pits of my mind rose the nasty realization that every minute out there flying could be shortening her life by many more. I swallowed hard and took a deep breath. Maybe I should tell her, but how?

Just then, a gust of wind grabbed me, and I shot up into the sky under Allie's arm. "Holllly shiiiiit," I struggled to say against the g-force, while I heard Jennifer scream from below, "Goddamn it, that's enough!"

THIRTY-FOUR

Life Depends on It

IYLA

It was lonely in the tiny hotel room…what am I saying? *I* was lonely in this tiny hotel room of this new Scranton hotel. I'm sure other people had been in this room and been happy, laughed, been drunk, and merrily made love in here. But none of those experiences were mine. Iyla, daughter of Olga Settchuoff—what a joke. Russia was gone. Demetri was gone. I missed neither of them, but now I felt as if I had become pointless. I sat on the edge of the bed and popped the last bite of my all-beef-patties-special-sauce-lettuce *cheesesburger* into my mouth. I rolled up its wrapper and tossed it into the pile surrounding (but not in) the trash basket. I sipped my last noisy slurp of Coke and stared out the window at a starlit sky. It was lovely. But in my head, I was empty and, how you say, blah, blah, blah.

Spiders of people's thoughts from the rooms around me trickled through my brain. I had ignored them most of the night, but now they were crawling through the crevices and cracks. Little kids in the room below fought over control of the TV remote while their mother tried to take a relaxing bath and their father worried about his business. A couple in the room next door were both thinking of sex. She was excited but had become suddenly apprehensive. He debated making a move but then decided to pour another round of drinks.

"Try some romance, you horny fucks," I mumbled, giving them a little free and worthless advice. He decided to give her a sweet kiss on the neck; she hoped he would tear off her clothes and attack her like Daniel used to do, whoever Daniel was. The world was a sewer filled with fears, doubts, and anxieties—I waded through it, polluting my brain. Sometimes I lost track of where I began and it ended. I looked at the little bag of candy I had taken from Demetri sitting on the nightstand. As the kids fought, the couple bungled their sexual encounter, and the thoughts of people outside in the street began to wear on me, an escape with candy started to look attractive. But then I remembered Valeria, her stupid self, defenseless from that drug. I didn't want that to be me. So I decided to fill a small glass with vodka from the bottle on the desk. I downed it like a good Russian and then poured another. It wasn't candy, but it helped me cope.

I drifted over to the small table by the window where Demetri's computer sat looking at me, saying, *Why don't we do something together? I am a smart machine, and you are a glorious, intelligent, beautiful woman.* What could I say? The computer was right. So I started looking at the files Demetri had stolen from Jones' head. I highlighted them and prepared to hit delete; I didn't want that garbage in the world. But then I thought, what if I needed it for trade, to save my life? What if Shamil found me? So I kept the garbage.

But then I saw file after file about the Lion. I saw dozens of email accounts Demetri had used to talk with this person. There were no emails, but there were coded messages in the Drafts folder. Apparently, Demetri and the Lion had access to the same email accounts and communicated in these "drafts" rather than sending emails over the internet for the American secret police to see. If I could read them, maybe I could find the Lion. Maybe someone would kill the Lion before the Lion killed me. I was sure many people would love to do the job, 'cause the Lion had many enemies: dozens of governments and the ghosts of thousands of his victims cried out for his head. Demetri was afraid of the Lion, but not Iyla Settchuoff, and now I had a sword. Too bad the Lion had no heart I could put it through—a bullet to his head or drone strike exploding his car would have to do. He wanted to control all the Super Born, me included. I could never live like that, under someone's control. One or the other of us would have to die. My vote was for it to be him.

Now I needed someone to decode the files, but who was there I could trust? My life depended on picking the right person. The thought just made me feel that much more alone. I was surrounded by a darkness that crawled after me wherever I went. I drifted in it and waited.

Anxiety overpowered me. Panic sent a surge of adrenaline into my blood. I couldn't sit still, so I stood up just to move. I sipped my glass of vodka and stared out into the hopeless night, feeling like no matter where I moved, it would be there with me. Vodka was good, but it could only do so much…I sipped more anyway.

Suddenly I stepped back, almost spilling my glass, as a black shape flew by my window and then up into the sky. A moment later it flashed by again in the other direction. I followed it with my gaze as long as I could as it rose into the star-lit sky and disappeared into the darkness. Allie? I knew she was one of us special women, but I never knew she could fly! Why couldn't that be my power instead of dealing with all these little minds and their little problems and their stupid little everythings? It was like a curse. But flying, that was a different thing. My feet would never touch the ground if that was me. Allie must be special in more ways than one for her to ever leave the sky. What could be worth seeing back on the ground? *Good lord, she must have a life!*

Maybe one day I too could have a life, leave behind the darkness and creepy crawlers that assaulted my peace. Maybe then I could walk on the beach and hear only the waves. Maybe one day someone sincere like Logan would look at me and smile, would want to pin me to my desk and let me steal all the food from his plate. I could be a wonderful mother like Allie. (After all, my mother had taught me all the things not to do. Doing the opposite seemed like it would be easy.)

But first things first. Before I could do all that, I needed to survive and find a way to defeat the Lion. I needed more vodka.

THIRTY-FIVE

Of Fireworks and RFDs

LOGAN

Jones was such an ass. He called at the height of Allie and Rebecca's postflight jubilation and told me that he needed to see me urgently. I was getting hugged and hugged and hugged again by an excited Allie. Even in her suit this was a good thing, and if she was thrilled, then I was thrilled. Happy wife, happy life; excited wife, get lucky in life, if you know what I mean—not that she was my wife, get my drift. I tried to explain to Jones, but he just said, "Okay, see you soon," and hung up—the heartless bastard.

When I tore myself away from Allie, she and Rebecca were still laughing and making sweeping hand gestures across the sky. Jennifer sat alone, nursing a knee that she had somehow hurt by doing nothing. As I walked to the rooftop elevator, I looked back several times to watch Allie glow.

When I got down to the street, I fought through the crowds and a conga line marching down Penn Avenue, heading toward O'Malley's "Sports Bar." People I passed on the street were still glancing up at the sky, hoping for the B.I.B. to reappear over the street. Those who had seen her flash by were still talking about how cool she looked. I wanted to stop and tell them, "You have no idea…that's my girl, and she's cooler than you can imagine." But when I walked by the inevitable idiot who made a comment about the B.I.B.'s sexual appeal, I had to grab him by the lapels. He just stared at me and asked, "What?" I took a breath, let him go, and walked away.

As I opened the door of O'Malley's, I could hear him call from behind, "Hey, what's your problem, man? It's not like you're getting any of that."

I stopped and took a couple steps back toward him. "*That* is what allows idiots like you to have a good life. *That* is what's made this town great."

"I can think of one thing she could do that would make my life great," he said as his friends around him chuckled.

My blood was boiling, and I began to scan him, trying to figure out where my first punch should land, when a young woman wearing a B.I.B. necklace and her hulking boyfriend slipped between us. The woman squared off in front of the guy.

"Want the B.I.B.to do something like this?" she said, giving him a swift kick in the nuts. The crowd around him groaned as he doubled over. "That make your life great? That woman saves the fucking town, and you wanna make your little sexist jokes?"

The man waved his hand and tried straightening up to tell her he'd had enough when she stepped aside and her boyfriend stepped in, landing an uppercut that sent the man flying onto his back. The woman and her boyfriend raised their arms in victory, and the crowd exploded into a cheer.

I smiled, blew on my fist like a smoking six-shooter, and turned to go inside O'Malley's. When I opened the inner door, I was immediately assaulted by a wall of Irish music. Across the bar were two lines of RFDs and others making a brave but fruitless attempt at Irish dancing. Millie was not bad. Her long skirt flew about her rounding form. She was endeavoring to teach Jones the basics while her husband and the RFDs stomped their feet, spun in mysterious circles, or simply fell to the floor. Most of the RFDs wore the official costume of RFDs: a T-shirt, jeans, and an antler helmet. But surprisingly, many were better dressed than usual. I couldn't help but notice that one was wearing the same shirt and pants I was, stylish chap, while a couple wore nice shirts and sports jackets.

Luckily for me, the song soon ended. The exhausted, perspiring dancers high fived each other in celebration, or tried to, and then they drifted around the bar.

I approached a smiling, sweaty Jones. "You just missed our big number," he panted with his arm still around Millie.

The barkeep flashed by, escorting Millie away. "Wanker," he mumbled. "Keep your mitts off."

"Looks like you're having quite a time," I told Jones.

He held out his arms. "What can I say? These are my people!" he shouted. The RFDs cheered back at him.

I wrapped my arm around his shoulders to try to bring him back to earth, and we sat in a booth. "So, what did you want to tell me that was so important? Allie's having a really good night, so, you know, I might be having a really good night too, if you know what I mean."

"Oh, no! You can't be doing that! Haven't you told her about what I said? "

"Well, it may have slipped my mind in between her first two screaming orgasms…what, you didn't mean sex too, did you?"

"Especially!" Jones said, agitated. "The way you two go at it!"

"Wait, what do you mean, the way we go at it?"

"Never mind! I asked you to come here so we could plan how to help them, and here you haven't even told them!"

"I was getting to it…it's hard. In fact, it's incredibly hard for even me to think about it," I said.

"Ignore it, and it will just go away, huh?"

"Pretty much."

"So, tell me, my friend, how is that theory working for you?"

"It's probably not working at all."

"Good, then let's try science, shall we?" said Jones, rubbing his hands together. "I can't start working without fresh blood samples, so let's get those. Because you haven't told them the truth, tell them it's just a routine test." He stopped, appearing to reconsider that. "But you have to tell them! And they have to slow down in using their powers. They won't do that unless they know how serious this is."

I paused, unable to deal with what I knew had to be done. "All right. I'll tell 'em…but not a word from you!"

"Deal," said Jones before turning to catch a glimpse of Millie smiling at him. He looked at me. "You don't think…"

"Nayyyyy."

"Anyway," said Jones, glancing back toward Millie. "There was another reason I wanted you to come here tonight."

"What?" I gestured for him to hurry.

"Do you see them?" asked Jones, gesturing around the room with his outstretched arms.

"Just what am I supposed to be looking at?

"The RFDs. Do you see them?"

"Yeah."

"Anything unusual?"

I saw the usual RFDs wearing antlers, holding beer bottles up their eyes like binoculars, and struggling with the bathroom door. I was ready to tell Jones "So what?" when I noticed a few RFDs wearing antlers but tapping away on laptops, mobile phones, and tablets. Some, in addition to scurrying around, were taking self-ies, playing chess, and in the back corner, a table of four was even drinking wine rather than beer. "My God!"

"Yes! Quite amazing, isn't it? That one in the suit just emailed me his dissertation on the future impact of globalization on genetically transmitted diseases."

"What?"

"Yes, quite interesting work."

"What the hell's going on?"

Jones looked from side to side then leaned over the table. "You know how the Super Born are burning through their powers like brilliant rockets? Well, apparently, the RFDs are the slow-cooking variety. You're looking at future senators and presidents."

"Funny, the way they used to act seemed more like most congressmen."

Jones gave me a questioning look. "Yessss." Then he continued, "It may take some time, my friend, but nothing about the Super Born is static, whether they are male or female. There is an evolutionary process underway."

Just then two RFD's walked by with pool cues. The first said, "No, my dear William, the angle of incidence always equals the angle of attack in any geometric progression."

"Oh, so that's why I couldn't sink the eight ball! And stop calling me William; it's Billy Bob."

When they left Jones' face glowed. "Looks like my career is made! There is a lifetime of research over there with the RFDs, not to even mention all the research I still need to do on the women…as long as they last."

"As long as they what?" I asked. "Thanks for your confidence! What ever happened to your looking for a cure? I hope these a-holes aren't going to divert you from that! Besides, what about Olga Settchuoff? She's an old broad, right? Allie can live just as long as her!"

Jones nodded and held up one finger. "You have a good point there."

"Well, if I wear a hat, no one notices," I said, putting my hand over my head.

Jones looked at me, puzzled. "Riiiiight." Then he seemed to shake it off. "You're right about Olga too," said Jones, raising a finger and then sliding it between his lips. "How has she beaten the clock? Aren't the Russian Super Born on the same timetable?" he asked, looking at me like I was the expert.

I shook my head and shrugged. "I was just hoping what worked for Olga might work for Allie."

Jones stood up to pace, studying the floor at his feet. "Too bad Demetri is gone. I'll bet he knew."

"Maybe, but I doubt the bastard would have helped us."

"Did you hear about him, murdered by his lover? Murder-suicide I hear."

"Yeah, I'm broken up about it," I said, glad that Jones had blissfully forgotten Demetri trying to suck his brain. Frankly, I was happy that Demetri was really dead this time and that he'd taken the "brain sucker" with him. But that led me to wonder where Iyla had gone. Was Jones safe?

Jones snapped his fingers in my face. "Hello? Where did you go there?"

"Sorry. I was just thinking about…poor ol' Demetri."

"Yes, quite a loss to science."

"No, all the world lost was a slimeball and his slime-ette." I gestured for Jones to sit down again and leaned in toward him. "Do you remember Iyla, the woman who worked with Allie?"

"Hot little number, tattoos, accent, big…?"

"Yeah."

"Sorry, don't remember her at all."

"Funny, you're a funny man. You should do well in your stand-up career," I said.

"Of course I remember her. In fact, I can't seem to get her out of my mind."

"Well, she hung out with the slimeball. She was, like, part of a Russian Super Born invasion. If you see her again, you'd better run and tell me about it. Okay?"

"Hey, can I even have one girl?" joked Jones.

"I'm serious."

"Isn't she at work?"

"No, she hit the bricks after Demetri tried to suck your brain."

"Suck my what?" Jones asked with a questioning face.

"Forget it. Just stay away from that Russian weasel."

Jones gave me a mock salute. "Will do," he said. "Besides, in Russia, it's not weasel, it's mink."

"I'm fucking serious. She's trying to get something out of you."

"Don't worry, I won't tell her a thing…unless maybe she ties me up and tries to torture me. Think she has her own restraints, or should I bring mine?"

"You wish."

Jones looked longingly past me. "I do wish. Do you know how long it's been?"

I put my hands over my ears and began humming.

Luckily for me, the Chicken Dance song began, and Jones leaped to his feet. He pulled my hands away from my ears and said, "Remember, you've got to tell them. I'll be over for the blood samples tomorrow. Let them know."

"Okay."

"Now, if you'll excuse me, they're playing my song," he said, joining the mob that was beginning to form from every nook and cranny in the bar. Even the RFDs with laptops shut them down and merged into the melee, gyrating like barnyard fowl. Millie ran out of the kitchen dancing as the barkeep shouldered his white towel and did his own, nasty version of the Chicken Dance behind the bar.

THIRTY-SIX

Iyla Joins the Team

LOGAN

The next morning I was full of coffee and conviction, the way I'd been full of beer and conviction the night before. I had to tell Allie about Jones' firework theory. But the night before, when she'd dropped her robe and come to bed, telling her sort of somehow slipped my mind.

I'd tried again that morning (before coffee), but that hadn't worked either. Maybe because I tried to talk to her in the shower, and before I could get a word out, she pinned me against the wall. (What? I couldn't be rude.) So now I was determined to tell her at the office where there was *no* chance of finding her naked—unless...let's just say there was a *remote* chance of finding her naked as long as I kept her away from the office supplies closet...*and* the empty office on the third floor. As long as I did that, there should be no chance of my being distracted. Crap, I forgot about the parking lot...and the rooftop—oh God, and the desktop. Let's just say the chances of finding her naked at the office were slightly less than at home.

After checking her desk (and the office supply closet and empty office on the third floor), I finally found Allie sitting on top of the conference-room table, her legs showing in her short dress. (Okay, maybe she was a little sexy, but at least she wasn't naked.) Standing around her were Rebecca, Jennifer, and…Iyla? I hesitated a moment after entering and then stormed toward them. "What is that weasel doing in here?" I exclaimed, gesturing toward her. Rebecca turned and searched the floor as if there might be a real weasel on the loose.

Iyla turned to Allie, confused. "What is a weasel?"

"A weasel is a little animal—like a mink."

"Oh, he thinks I am a little mink?" said Iyla, clearly flattered.

Allie hopped off the table and came over to intercept me with her arms extended. "Don't worry, Logan. It's okay."

Rebecca ended her search for the weasel, sat down at the conference table, and made the computer begin to flash and blink with page after page of data. "Wow!" she said.

"See! Didn't I tell you!" said Iyla. "I knew Demetri had dirt on them like an insurance policy."

"What's going on?" I asked as I pulled Allie aside. "I told you what she tried to do to Jones," I whispered, gesturing toward Iyla with my head.

"Looks like she decided to switch sides. She's already given us the plans for Jones' Interrupter. Now she's dishing on Ms. Suit. Apparently, Iyla has IP addresses and encryption codes that can help us find her and stop her once and for all."

I looked over at Iyla working with Rebecca. "Really?"

"Looks like it. But she says Ms. Suit's really called the Lion, and she says the Lion's henchmen are in town and after the information on that computer. She came here to help us finish Ms. Suit and bury this Interrupter thing, but she needs our protection."

I was shocked. The simple formula of Demetri equals bad, Iyla with Demetri equals bad seemed to have failed me. Okay, maybe she wasn't a weasel. Maybe, like Jones said, she was a Russian mink. Anyway, she was some kind of furry, rodent-like thing, and I couldn't trust her so easily. Why had I come here, anyway? Oh yeah, the firework thing.

"Was there something you wanted to tell me?" Allie asked prompted by my open mouth and raised finger.

"Well…"

"Can we talk later? I wanna see this."

"Sure.

Allie returned to sit on the table and look over Rebecca's shoulder. I caught a glimpse of her butt swaying as she walked away and wished I hadn't. She smiled when she glanced back and caught me staring.

"Holy…" said Rebecca. She fell back in her seat and pushed a button dramatically. A world map popped up on the computer screen with dozens of lines arcing around the globe but all leading back to one spot. The lines were all different colors, some flashing, some not.

"Is that it? Did you find the bastard?" said Jennifer, excited, over Rebecca's shoulder.

"This isn't the bastard," Rebecca started with a smile. Then she gestured in a big circle over the computer screen with her hand. "This is all the bastards! This is terrorist central." She pointed to a yellow flashing line that started in Scranton and bounced from Cuba to London to Madrid and finally to Chechnya. "That's him, the Lion's local guy who's looking for Iyla and this computer. He's right there and online at this very moment."

Iyla stormed over to the screen. "Where is the bastard? Which buttons do I push to kill him?" she asked, poking at his dot in Scranton on the screen.

"It doesn't work like that," said Rebecca, shaking her head.

"Can't you control-alt-delete that pile of shit for me?" Iyla asked, poking at the keyboard.

Rebecca shook her head again. "No!" she exclaimed.

"Okay then, tell me where is that dot. I have a gun—I can go there right now, kill him, and be back before lunch," Iyla said, grabbing her bag and pulling out a 9 mm. She turned to Rebecca. "What's the address?"

Allie moved over to Iyla and put her hands on her shoulders. "That's not the way we work."

"What? You want to kill him? Here, you can use my gun, but I get to watch him fall."

Allie pushed Iyla's hand with the gun back into her bag. "Not today."

"Tomorrow? How about Wednesday?" asked Iyla.

Allie just shook her head.

I slowly moved up to the conference table, deep in dastardly thought. "Wait a minute. He doesn't know we have this, otherwise he'd be using a different address."

"Yeah, once they know we have the codes, it'll be game over," Jennifer said.

"I'll copy what I can before they figure it out," said Rebecca, typing away.

"Why do they need to figure it out? He's after *this* computer. We give him *this* computer," I said coolly.

All the women turned to look at me. "Are you nuts?" asked Jennifer. "What's wrong with me? Of course—we already know you're nuts."

"I risked everything to get this computer," Iyla interjected. "Now you give it to him? You are a crazy, stupid man!"

"No, I get it!" joined in Allie. "We copy the computer and let Ms. Suit's men have it back without knowing we're monitoring them. They have the computer, so they have no reason to change their addresses and codes. They report their success to Ms. Suit/ Lion, whoever. They light up all the communication lines and talk like teenage BFFs. Then we get them all."

"You're forgetting one little thing," Rebecca said as she continued to copy the files. "The Interrupter plans are in there, and according to Iyla, Demetri already told them they were there."

"So?" I said. "You're the engineer. Screw up the design. Lead them miles off course. Demetri never said the thing worked."

Jennifer nodded and then looked at me in amazement. "You know, I like it. Maybe you aren't as stupid as you seem."

Iyla added her two cents. "I like it too. We can toy with those stupids, learn what we can before the ax falls. But Shamil is mine. I have a score to settle with that bastard."

"Can you do it?" Allie asked Rebecca.

Rebecca tapped some keys. "Already done. I swapped out some generator schematics. Plus, I put a little bug in there. Every time this computer gets turned on, it will send out a GPS signal telling us where it is. So we'll know when they get it and where they are."

"Now we need to let them find it. How do we do that?" Allie asked.

"We rent a room in some fleabag hotel out of town," I proposed, "leave the computer and some clothes, and a suitcase, toothbrush, whatever—put out some wet towels, mess the bed, leave some pizza boxes and trash around. We can put the room in Iyla's name, so they'll be sure to find it. They find the room, get the computer, and then waste their time waiting to catch Iyla there. Instead, we're waiting for them—trap within a trap, presto chango, no more bad guy. Sweet, neat, and complete."

"I'm in," said Jennifer, holding out her hand.

"Me too," said Rebecca, adding her hand to the pile.

"All right," said Iyla, and placing her hand on Rebecca's.

Allie added hers, and then mine went on top.

"Maybe now I can start forgetting the faces of our people in Nigeria," Allie said, looking hopeful.

"Maybe now I can forget...that sandwich Shamil took from me, that bastard," grumbled Iyla.

"All I know is that if we pull this off, no one will be able to question whether we're for real," Jennifer added with a smile. "World on Fire..." She puffed her lips like she was blowing out a birthday cake. "No more."

On the inside I thought about evil Demetri and his woman tearing out Jones' brain and imagined how much more evil the people we were after must be to have killed thousands in Lagos just for show.

* * *

I drove Iyla to a motel outside of town and waited in the car while she checked in alone, carrying the laptop and rolling a suitcase for the security cameras to see. (Since she was using her passport as her ID, the Lion would have no trouble finding her.) Iyla walked along the outside of the pink two-story building, up a staircase, and along the outdoor balcony to the door of her room. I followed with a trash bag full of props we were planning to plant. Iyla carefully opened the door for me, clearly already afraid that the henchmen could have arrived. She rushed me inside, searched the parking lot below for anyone watching, and then closed and latched the door.

"Unpack your clothes, throw 'em around, and mess up the bed," I advised her.

"Please, I know how to make a mess," she said, pulling the blankets off the bed. She piled up all the pillows and then jumped into the bed. "Can you move the TV a little bit this way? I can't see."

I stopped unloading a pizza box and other trash, thinking she was joking. Then her words seemed to echo in my head without her speaking them again. I took a step back and tilted the TV screen toward her in the bed. "That good?"

"Little to the left and down."

"You know you're not really staying here, right?"

"Hey, I know these fools. They have no brain. They are all guns and biceps," she said, smiling. "But Shamil? Sometimes he is shrewd."

I moved into the bathroom while Iyla began carefully, too carefully, placing clothes around the room. I placed half-empty bottles of soap and shampoo in the shower and put toothpaste and a toothbrush on the counter with some mascara. I used tissues to wipe the counter and then placed them in the trash, wet some towels and washcloths and hung them, as if used. Then made certain the toilet seat was down. Believe me, terrorist or no terrorist, *that* was key. Living in the world of estrogen had taught me that one.

I turned suddenly when I felt a presence in the room. I looked over the room with adrenaline running through my veins. Nothing, no one, not even the weasel. I went back to my work, when I heard someone laughing—but not out loud, just in my head. I had a sudden flash of Iyla wearing a thin blue dress.

I crept out of the bathroom to see Iyla laying a thin blue dress over a chair with great care. She turned toward me, held the dress up in front of her, and smiled. Then she put the dress down and began looking for a place to put some slacks before balling them up and tossing them aimlessly over her shoulder.

"Bathroom's done," I said.

Iyla picked up an empty bottle of soda I had placed earlier. "I don't drink this."

"Maybe you had a friend over and they drank it."

Iyla just stared at me, unmoving.

"Okay, okay," I said, grabbing the bottle from her. I pulled a Dr. Pepper bottle out of my bag. "How about this?"

She shook her head, so I grabbed a root beer, which made her nod. "I would drink that on a Tuesday with lunch."

"Great!" I said, checking out the mess we'd made. "Where should we stash the computer? Would you leave it out and use it or hide it somewhere?" Suddenly an image of Demetri and Valeria making love flashed in my head, as if I was walking into the room and finding them together. I watched as Iyla appeared and shot both of them. Then my mind was taken over by an image of Iyla's panicked face as a man with a tattoo on his face ripped at Iyla's clothes then punched her in the face, dropping her to the floor. The images stunned me, as if it was my face that had been hit.

"I would hide it. Maybe just under the mattress," Iyla said, lying down on her side across the bed.

I looked at her for a long moment, knowing something was going on but not knowing what.

"Then again, Shamil thinks with his muscles, especially the one between his legs. So you better put the computer on the table with a big bow and a sign saying 'Here it is, asshole,' so he sees it." Then she rolled onto her belly, put her chin in her hands, and lifted her calves. She smiled flirtatiously. When I failed to react, her face dropped, making her look like a comedian who had just bombed and didn't know why.

Out of nowhere an image of Allie and me in the shower flashed in my head. And it wasn't my fault this time. Suddenly my mind was full of all the sensations I had felt while deep in the clutches of sexual desire that morning. (It was great.)

"So you think I am…weasel, huh? Like a little mink?" Iyla asked.

"I'm sorry. I didn't mean to call you a weasel."

"What? You don't find me attractive?"

"Sure, you're…"

"Like a mink," she said, smiling, as she sent an image into my head of her walking toward me, unbuttoning her vest and dropping it to the floor.

"You're a Super Born, right?" I asked.

"Super, yes! How nice of you to notice."

"No, I mean, you have powers like…the others, right?"

"You mean, can I fly like Allie? Or talk to machines like Rebecca? No, they are way beyond me."

"Allie told you she flies?"

"I saw her the other day flying over the street while people cheered. She is an amazing woman."

"Yes, she is."

Iyla began twirling her hair in her fingers, "I am amazing woman too. And you are an amazing man. I can tell by your heart."

"What did you say your power was?"

"I didn't."

"What were you doing with Demetri? What did he want you do to Dr. Jones?"

Iyla stopped playing with her hair and shook her head. "It was not me. Demetri and that stupid pig-nosed Valeria wanted those plans from Jones. It was Valeria who hurt Jones, not me. You were there. You saw."

"Yeah. Why didn't you tell Demetri where we were hiding? You just let us get away."

Iyla looked past me then smiled sweetly. Her eyes glowed when they returned to look at me. "It was like I say, your heart. You are…sincere. That's the word, yes? Sincere." Then she lowered her eyes for a second. "You know there is one more thing we could do to the bed to make it seem more real," she said before looking up at me wickedly. An uninvited image appeared in my mind of Iyla naked on all fours looking over her shoulder at me with a pleasured look on her face.

I tried to push the image away and acted like I'd never seen it. "How would you know if I'm sincere? We never even spoke two words," I said standing my ground a few feet away.

Her smile drained and she looked away. "I feel it from your eyes."

"More like reading my mind! You playing mind games with me?" When she shook her head in protest, I continued, "Why'd you want me to see those images? Just what are you trying to tell me, huh?"

Iyla's face soured, and she sat up on the bed. "We should go now." She stood and looked around the room with an emotionless face. "Room is perfect."

THIRTY-SEVEN

Hunting a Lion

LOGAN

I was back at the office, whistling my way down the frantic, crowded hallway. I strutted at half the speed of those around me, trying to resurrect my happy-go-lucky self. I hoped the old me could somehow blot out the firework effect afflicting Allie, the computer sitting there waiting for the terrorists to find it, and the monstrous network that was slowly burning the world down—not to mention the pressures of having a real marketing job, a quasi-adopted daughter, and a floundering writing career, whatever those mind games were that Iyla had just played with me, and having absolutely no idea where the weasel went.

In the distance I saw our CEO with a big circle of empty hallway around him as everyone gave him a wide berth. He was talking to himself as he approached.

"Afternoon, Craig. Beautiful day, isn't it?" I bantered. "You see my Brazilian order? Three times what we thought! Great, huh? Just wait till you see next quarter."

He stopped, stared at me for a long moment, shook his head, and began grumbling to himself. I was watching him walk away, giving him a questioning look, when I felt Allie nearly topple me over by just tugging on my arm.

"Come on, you're not going to believe this," she said, pulling me along. We moved at a quick pace to the conference room, where she led me in and then closed and locked the door behind me. Rebecca sat at the conference table, poking at her computer, while Jennifer and Iyla looked on. Her screen mirrored over to the TV on the wall, and we all turned to it.

"Yep, I've checked three times. It's her," said Rebecca.

"Here in Scranton?" questioned Jennifer.

"Has she found us? Is she here after us?" Allie added with a bit of uncertainty in her voice.

"I don't get it. Who?" asked Iyla.

"The freakin' Lion is two miles from here on her network as we speak!" Jennifer said, caught in pure excitement.

Iyla was surprised. "What? The Lion is here, now? That means Shamil is probably at the same place. If the Lion is a woman, then maybe that's why they can't find her. Everyone says the Lion is an evil man with dark hair and a beard and a big knife."

"Not hardly," Allie said with a smile. "What are we gonna do?"

"Instead of getting them all at once, we cut off the head of the snake," said Jennifer.

"We can't let an opportunity like this pass. She's on our turf," I said, adding my two cents.

"Wait," interrupted Rebecca, "that location is a hotel. She's using her phone and her computer, but she's not on the terrorist network that I'm following from Iyla's computer. Could she have another network? Maybe there's more than one." Rebecca shook her head, apparently unsure of what to think.

"Does it really matter? She's right there! Now is our chance!" insisted Jennifer.

Iyla pulled the 9 mm out of her bag, removed the clip to check for ammo, and then slapped it back into the gun. "We should go, now. You can have the Lion, but Shamil is mine. I just hope my bullets aren't too big for his tiny balls."

"A plan would be nice," added Allie. "We don't even know what we're up against. She could have an army."

"That's right," I agreed (and not just because Allie had suggested it). "Rebecca, can you get up a floor plan of the building and match it to the microwave signals?"

Rebecca clicked away, and then a 3D image of the hotel appeared on the TV. We all watched as signals appeared as arcing lines originating from rooms all around the hotel.

"Now filter out all the signals that aren't on the same network as hers. She's got to have a dedicated network, right?" I said.

Rebecca nodded, clicked some more keys, and all the lines disappeared except a dozen or so on the same floor as Ms. Suit and in the lobby and rear entrance.

"Bingo!" I said proudly. "Look, there's maybe a dozen or so signals flickering on and off. And there they are," I said, pointing at the TV screen

Iyla crept up to the TV and then stood before it, studying it. "Which one of you dots is Shamil?" she said, running her fingers over the screen. "You want another sandwich, Shamil? Well, I got one for you right here," she said, lifting her gun.

The rest of us huddled together at the conference table. Personally, I was a bit uncomfortable with Iyla's vengeful attitude.

"We have to assume they're all armed," began Jennifer.

"Is this a kill mission or what?" Allie asked. "Should we try to bring in the authorities? Catch her?"

"From what I saw," I said, "she's blended in with the authorities. We won't be getting any help from them."

"Well, then it is a kill mission?" Allie said reluctantly.

"Yep, all of the bastards!" Jennifer said. She put her hands on Allie's shoulders. "Remember what they did in Lagos, London, New York. Just think about that."

"There are alternatives," I said, beginning to drift a few steps in thought.

"Like?" asked Allie.

"Well, Allie's fast. Rebecca could disable the hotel around them. Maybe we can…incapacitate the worker bees so we can get to the queen. Maybe she's better captured than killed. She'll have tons of intel," I said.

Allie nodded in agreement.

"You don't have superpowers, do you, whiner?" Jennifer said, tapping me on the shoulder.

"No, what he said makes sense," interjected Rebecca. "We can always go to plan B, the kill plan, if they're tougher than we think."

Jennifer lifted her shirt to show the scar on her side. "Do I have to remind you idiots what even an accident can do? I'm not taking a chance again!"

Rebecca explained the plan as she paced. "Allie's got the B.I.B. suit with the armor. After I cut whatever power and mechanicals I can find, she goes in first, through the front, and works her way up while Jennifer goes in through the back. She takes out the two by the rear exit and meets up with Allie on Ms. Suit's floor. We capture and incapacitate first, and if that fails," she said, pointing at Jennifer, "then you can fry 'em…fry 'em all. Sound like a plan?"

"You are forgetting me," Iyla said as she rejoined the group. "I'll go in first with Allie. I can tell her things she can't see, like what is around the next corner. If I find Shamil, it's a kill mission."

"What do you mean, you can tell me things?" Allie asked.

Iyla pointed at herself. "I have powers too. Just listen to your head, and you will know what I mean."

I could tell Allie was puzzled, so I explained, "Allie, I've seen what she can do. Believe me, she can help you. She may not tell you in words, but you'll get the point. It's like a mind game—she reads thoughts and can forward them to you."

"Sounds…creepy," Allie concluded.

Iyla smiled and nodded. "Is creepy."

When Jennifer began to review the plans for the hotel with Rebecca, Iyla watched intently, and Allie pulled me aside into a small office off the conference room. "What kind of mind games are you talking about? What's she trying to do to you?" she said in a tone just above a whisper.

"That's not it."

"Sure?"

"She put some of her memories in my head…like a confession. She wanted me to know that she killed Demetri. It wasn't a murder-suicide with his lover. And she wanted me to know Shamil had beaten and raped her so I would know why she wants him so dead."

"That's it? She wants you to know she's a stone-cold killer?"

"She wants me to realize she's not. I think she wants someone to understand her, to know why she has to do what she does."

"And that's you?" Allie said pointing her hand at me.

I gestured around the room. "I'm as good as anyone."

"That was it?"

"That was it."

"She tells you she killed Demetri and that woman, and we're supposed to feel safe around her?" said Allie holding out her palms.

I took a couple steps, ran my hand through my hair, and returned, "Demetri hit her, betrayed her, was trying to turn over the Interrupter to the Lion. They were planning to control you and the other Super Born and hold you like slaves. She wanted me to know all that so we would know she had no choice. Demetri was a few hours from giving the Lion the Interrupter, and guess what could have happened to all of us then."

Allie stared through me for a long moment. "Okay…but it's still creepy."

"Allie!" We heard the muffled yell from Jennifer and went back into the conference room to find Jennifer and Rebecca highly animated. "They got it!" Jennifer said. "The computer is on the move."

"Yeah," said Rebecca, studying her laptop, "they must have turned it on the minute they got into their car 'cause it's moving right now on the north side of town."

"Now we hope they buy it," I said to Allie.

Rebecca chuckled. "Wait till they try and build that Interrupter! I pity the guy pulling the trigger."

* * *

The plan changed a bit as we all assembled that night in an alley beside Ms. Suit's hotel. I went in first, as an innocent hotel patron, to verify everything was as we had expected. Rebecca was not feeling well, so she dropped out of our assault, promising to do what she could remotely. Jennifer and Allie debated whether or not they should go on without her, but in the end Jennifer convinced Allie that they could handle it alone. So it was just me and maybe the weasel entering the lobby. As I made my way toward the elevators, I casually surveyed the room: two employees at the desk, six random people entering and exiting, one couple giggling on a couch, and two goon-squad-like guys, one on each side of the doorway, sitting in chairs. One was reading a newspaper, and the other sipped from a cup of joe. Each gave me a quick appraisal and then just went on with his life.

I wanted to tell them, "What, I'm not threatening-enough looking to you? I don't look like trouble? You wouldn't know macho if it smacked you across the face…which I may, 'cause I am just like that. You can't stop me. I'm a wild man." Lucky for them I was on a mission. I'd let my girlfriend put out their lights, that's how badass I was.

"Two in lobby. One on each side of door," I mumbled into my COMM as I neared the relative privacy of the area near the elevators.

I came out on the third floor whistling a tune and hittin' it with a slow, cool walk. Almost immediately I ran into another member of the black-suited goon squad. He passed me with a steely stare.

"Evening," I said.

I could see two more, one at the other end of the hall sitting in a chair and the other standing in front of room 305, just as Rebecca's network layout had predicted. The guy in front of 305 seemed more interested in what was going on inside the room than concerned about my presence as I sashayed by. There was a hallway to my left, and I whistled my way down it before ducking into a doorway.

"Three more. One at each end of hall. One at doorway to 305. Two stairways up, two elevators. Hallway empty," I reported.

"Roger," came a mumbled, electronically altered voice I couldn't identify. (Who was this Roger guy everyone was talking about, anyway?) In the background, I heard Allie coordinating with Jennifer and Iyla grumble something about Shamil being hers. Then I heard Allie say, "Let's move."

I peered around a pillar in the hallway so that I could see the goon in the chair in the main hallway. Then I ducked back and checked the time on my phone, wondering how long the girls would take to reach me. I waited a minute and then began to walk back toward the main hallway, planning to serve as a diversion. I reached it just in time to see Allie flash out of the stairway door in her new suit and deliver a hammer fist to the head of the goon in front of me before he could even get halfway out of his chair. Jennifer stood in her red costume at the other end of the hallway. I watched as she lifted another goon with a red beam of light and smashed him first into the right wall of the hallway and then into the left, forming deep cavities in the drywall on both sides. When the red beam went out, he dropped to the floor faster than my mother's career expectations for me. He was gonna feel that in the morning...maybe. The third goon had turned his attention from guarding the door to room 305 toward Jennifer's flashy display. There was something I'd noticed during my time with Allie: The time it took for a goon to almost get his gun out of his holster before she put his lights out was just about a second.

I joined Allie in front of 305 while Jennifer walked slowly toward us like a thoroughbred, and Iyla ran up from the stairway. When we'd all reunited, Iyla was still catching her breath. She panted, "I don't see Shamil." Jennifer put her finger to her lip for quiet. Then she pointed the same finger at herself and Allie before gesturing for Allie to go through the door. Allie nodded. Iyla raised her gun. And I watched.

Allie put her hand on the doorknob and opened it with a loud pop. We all poured into the room behind her, expecting a hail of bullets. Instead, we all surrounded the large bed that dominated the room and stood in amazement.

Apparently, we had caught Ms. Suit in the act. She was on her knees on the bed, her fit, tall body bare, revealing perfectly smooth, flawless, chocolate-colored skin, defined, sweating muscles from her arms down her back, and powerful sprinter's legs. Beneath her on the bed was Ed, my FBI contact, who had made my life so miserable lately. Our entrance made Ms. Suit slowly stop pumping Ed as he tried to turn in panic.

Ms. Suit took a deep, winded breath and looked at us with disdain. "Do you mind if we finish?" she said indignantly.

My thought was that it would be fine if they wanted to finish. I didn't mind the idea of seeing a body that fit in action, but I guess I was the only one. "Ed, you dogggg you."

Jennifer grabbed a robe from the floor than threw it hard against Ms. Suit's chest. "You *are* finished," she said.

Ms. Suit caught the robe and slid off of Ed, whose ship was rapidly sinking. She stood at the end of the bed putting on the robe as Ed slid up against the headboard. "All this time I've been looking for you," she said, "and here you are, coming to me. To what do I owe this honor?" She did not seem as worried as I would have guessed. Her calm made me scan the room and listen for movement in the hallway.

Allie moved in close. "I can't find any honor in you. You proud of all those you've killed? You're no Lion. You're a monster."

"Lion? You think *I'm* the Lion?" Ms. Suit said, surprised.

"If not, why'd you try to kill us in New York?" Jennifer asked getting in Ms. Suit's face.

"Kill you? I was trying to get you to join me!"

"Yeah, well, your goons almost killed Jennifer. Strange way to treat your friends." Allie was on the attack.

Latisha pushed back, stepping right past Jennifer and looking at each of us as she spoke. "You wouldn't join us. We couldn't twist Logan's arm to get him to help us, so I tried to intimidate you. I needed your help! Those idiots weren't supposed to fire, just look tough." Latisha stopped and shook her head. "I still can't believe they hit you. I'm so sorry. That's the last thing I wanted!"

"Explain New York and Lagos," Jennifer said. "You were in both places just when the attacks hit. That's a little too convenient."

"Listen, I have been after the Lion myself. Now he's after me too. I have been right on his trail a dozen times, but it seems like I'm always one step behind him. So where else should I be when attacks happen, trying to stop them?" Latisha paused and looked at our faces. "That's why I needed to get you to work with me. Every time you're there, his attacks fail. So now he's after you too. He's sent his men to Scranton for me. They're here, right now! That's why I'm hiding out here."

Iyla walked up to Ms. Suit, put her gun to her face for a second, and then turned to us. "This is no Lion. This is not even a pussycat." She walked back, dropping her gun arm, dejected.

That was when I noticed Ms. Suit's eyes. They were the same hazel-my-ass gray as all the other Super Born. Not being an eye color that went with her complexion, they gave her a unique, futuristic look, and it was clear now why she had always hidden them behind sunglasses. "Allie, look at her eyes. They look familiar?"

"They're hazel. So what?" Allie replied.

"Hazel, my ass. They're gray just like yours—and hers," I said, pointing at Jennifer, "and hers," I said, pointing at Iyla, "and

Rebecca's. She's a Super Born." I grabbed Ms. Suit's hand, which she quickly pulled away. "She's boiling hot, just like you, and look," I said, pointing to a nearby table stacked to falling with a dirty pile of room-service dishes. "Does that look familiar?"

Allie and Jennifer looked at each other, apparently reluctant to give up their vengeance.

"And," began Iyla, "there is no Shamil here. If the Lion was here, then Shamil would be with him."

Allie moved in close to Ms. Suit. "Then who the fuck are you?"

"Latisha Johnson. I'm on your side."

"You were born in Scranton, right?" I asked. "January 18, 1976, about halftime of the Super Bowl?"

Latisha smiled. "My dad always said the Cowboys kicked a field goal and I started crying. That's how he knew I was a true Steelers fan."

"Just 'cause she's Super Born doesn't mean she's a good person," said Jennifer.

"You're right, just look at you," I joked but only got a sneer from her.

"So what powers do you have?" Allie asked. "Why are you working for the man?"

Latisha moved in front of Allie. "Can you think of a better way to change things fast? I used my powers to advance and gain trust, to become almost indispensable to key people. So now I have access to all the power of the most powerful nation on earth. I can arrest criminals, prosecute them, bring in the military, fly around the world as I need to…hell, I can even call in air strikes and Seal units. You know anyone else who can do that?" Latisha asked. Then she looked at Jennifer. "Can you do that?"

Jennifer looked at Allie, and they both smiled, confident in the powers they had.

"Not bad for a Scranton girl," I commented.

"Damn straight! So can we move on now?" Latisha asked.

Iyla slowly approached Ed and then grabbed hold of his arm and stroked his palm with her fingers.

"What?" asked Ed, pulling away. "She's right. Can we just move on now?"

Iyla stepped back from the bed and then turned and gave me an expressionless stare. Instantly, images popped into my head of Ed and a man with a tattooed face talking in a restaurant, followed by the image of the same tattooed man getting into a SUV full of men.

"We've got to go!" I said, reaching for Allie's arm.

"What?" asked Jennifer.

"Shamil and his men are on their way here!"

"How do you know?" asked Allie.

"Eddy boy here sold her out. Tell me, Latisha, who planned your security here?" I asked.

Latisha gave me a quizzical look. "Well, Ed. I trust him. He always does it. He's my right arm. He would never…" stammered Latisha.

Jennifer caught on fast. "You wanna take a guess why you've always been one step behind the Lion?"

Iyla laughed. "He sells you out. He is like a rat. All he wants is cheeses, doesn't care who gives it to him."

I looked at Ed, remembering the relationship we'd had, feeling sad and disappointed. I shook my head and said soberly, "Eddy boy, you fucked up big this time."

"Ed, tell them," insisted Latisha.

Ed appeared nervous for a moment but then turned cocky. He brushed back his hair with his left hand while his right slid under a pillow. When he pulled it back out, he had a Glock. As he raised it toward Latisha, Iyla raised her gun, but then Jennifer sent a focused beam of red energy into Ed's chest. In a burst he became a thick charcoal cloud that hung over the bed before slowly settling, giving the room a nasty smell. His Glock lay on the bed amid the black-stained sheets.

Latisha lifted her hand over her mouth.

Iyla raised her arms in frustration. "So quick! Why do you have to be so quick? I had him!" she complained to Jennifer.

Jennifer looked at her and smiled sardonically. "You'll just have to get faster, won't you?"

Allie stepped up to Latisha. "You wanna guess who he was going to use that gun on?"

Latisha stammered in shock, "I don't believe it…I…"

"Gotta go!" I yelled.

Latisha began to put on her clothes, but then Allie grabbed her arm. "No time!" Allie said. So Latisha tightened her robe, hurriedly gathered up her clothes, and carried them with her.

Before I left the room, I turned to look at the black soot on the bed that moments ago had been Ed. I felt a brief pang of sorrow. *Ed, what were you thinking, man?* I thought, shaking my head.

Allie ran to the door, opened it, and checked the hall in both directions in a fraction of a second. "Okay, it's clear. There's a stairway across the hall. That's our exit. Everybody ready?" Then she flung the door open and hurried across the hall to open the stairway door, and we all ran through it. Allie closed and locked the door just as two bullets whizzed through it and buried themselves in the stairway.

"Down!" Jennifer yelled as we all heard footsteps coming up from above.

Allie swiftly moved past us down the stairs to the first landing. We heard shoulders pounding against the stairway door above us, and then bullets punctured the door all around the lock. We followed Allie down, and when she turned off the landing to descend the next flight of stairs, her chest erupted as two of her suit's explosive armor tiles stopped two bullets from hitting her chest. At the base of the stairs stood a solidly built gunwoman dressed in black with a black scarf wrapped around her head, her gun leveled at Allie and an amazed look on her face. Allie flashed to the woman, picked her up, and sent her forcefully down over the railing to crash on the concrete floor below.

Iyla hurried down the stairs, raised her gun, and targeted another black-dressed gunman before he suddenly exploded into a black cloud from Jennifer's beam of red energy. Iyla looked up at Jennifer in frustration. "So quick!"

Jennifer simply gestured for Iyla to keep moving. Instead, Iyla waved Jennifer on and then climbed up to the landing to cover our escape, exchanging fire with a gunman coming down from above. We all hurried past the black cloud and then the twisted body of the gunwoman on the next level down. Finally, Allie opened the ground-floor exit door and, in an instant, checked the alleyway outside. She gestured for us to run across the alley to the side street where our two cars were located. Jennifer and Latisha went first, and I followed.

I crossed the alley and then turned back to watch as Allie stuck her head back in the ground-floor exit door and called for Iyla to hurry. Out from behind a dumpster, I saw the shadowy shape of another gunman appear. He leveled his gun at her, and I screamed, "Allie!" before leaping at the gunman, deflecting his aim as two shots went off.

The gunman's first shot made an explosive armor tile over Allie's hip erupt. His second shot ricocheted off the building. I was on the gunman, my weight driving him to the ground. I hit his face over and over like a whirlwind, punch after punch, never giving him a second to recover. All I could feel was the terror of watching him point his gun at Allie. It created an anger so deep and intense within me that there was no controlling it. For a second he struggled and his muscles were tight, resisting my blows, but that was only for a second. I kept up my assault until my fists ached and there was nothing recognizable to punch on his face. Slowly I rose and took some deep breaths, allowing the animal within me to escape.

I was relieved, so I turned and began to follow Jennifer, assuming Allie would be right behind me. When I sensed she wasn't, I turned to see another dark shape appearing from the darkness behind her, lifting a gun toward Allie's head. I yelled for her again and ran toward her across the alleyway.

Iyla's first shot hit the dark shape's shoulder. His gun fell from the limp arm and hand he could no longer control. Her second shot went through his back and ribs, making him howl like a coyote and spin until he fell, his back to the wall. His eyes were wide, and he wheezed, struggling to get air into his punctured lung. Iyla approached slowly with her gun extended.

"You want another sandwich, Shamil?" she said as he panted. "It may be hard for me to hit those tiny balls of yours. But don't worry, I'm a good shot." Then she fired two shots into his groin, doubling him over in pain.

Shamil lifted his head and growled at her like an animal, and she responded by putting a shot into his tattooed forehead.

"Come on, there're police in this town!" said Allie, reaching for her arm. "Good ones."

Iyla turned, took a step, and then turned back and put another shot into Shamil's corpse. She pulled at the trigger three more times, but her ammunition was gone.

"Let's go!" Allie insisted.

"Do I have time to reload?" Iyla asked, reaching into her pocket.

"Noooo!" yelled Allie, taking hold of her and lifting her off the ground.

They sped by me, leaving me alone in the alley as sounds of sirens rose in the distance. "Crap!" I said as the danger of the place finally hit me. As I looked at the black outline of the man I had beaten and the pile that had once been Shamil, I felt the gravity of the night.

The sight made me freeze when I shouldn't have. Luckily, the approaching sirens woke me up, and I ran to my car and started the engine.

THIRTY-EIGHT

The Aftermath

LOGAN

We entered the Lowe LLC offices from a sheltered entrance in the back of the building. We were all subdued, contemplative, and mentally ragged. The girls changed clothes, Latisha finally had time to dress, and I cleaned the blood off my swollen hands. We'd arrived in the office just in time for the Midnight Buffet as the workers who had stayed late began to feast and chat. No one said they were hungry, but I decided a few pieces of pizza wouldn't hurt. *What, no Swedish meatballs tonight?* I thought as I checked out the appetizers.

When Allie opened the conference room door, we found Rebecca slumped over her computer at the main table. We all panicked and moved to her. She lifted her head and looked at us with foggy eyes. "You guys back? I must have zonked out. How'd it go?" Then she caught sight of Latisha. "Holy shit, what's she doing here? Are you all crazy?"

"Don't worry. You've got a lot of catching up to do," Allie said. She went on to tell the tale of the night's events, though it was clear she was exhausted.

We all settled in around the table. I sat down next to Allie with a relieved sigh as she spoke. Iyla sat down on my other side and grabbed a slice of pizza from my plate, munching it as if starving. "There's a whole table of food out there!" I complained, pointing to the buffet.

"Yours looks better," she said through a stuffed mouth.

Then as Allie spoke, her hand slid over to my plate and stole a slice. I looked at each of them, but neither of them looked at me or said a word, so I climbed out of my chair and hit the buffet, determined to fill three plates so we all could eat in peace. When I returned, I put a plate in front of Allie and one in front of Iyla, creating a free zone for mine in the middle. Within seconds both women had pushed their plates aside and begun taking food off my mine without a peep of explanation or thank you. I was just about to complain when Allie's fingers began slowly pulling my plate toward her as she continued speaking with the girls.

So now I was pissed. If they wanted food, I'd be glad to get it for them, but this stealing thing was too much. I went back to the buffet for another plate and returned, sitting away from them, near Latisha. She seemed like a classy broad.

It worked. I sat and enjoyed a rejuvenating half of a turkey club sandwich with my feet up on the table before Jennifer walked by and, in the midst of speaking to the group, nonchalantly grabbed the other half of my sandwich. Upon seeing Jennifer do that, Latisha got the idea, and there went my potato salad.

I dropped my feet off the desk and gave them all a you-have-got-to-be-kidding-me look. "You guys want some snacks? Can I get you anything?" I exclaimed sarcastically.

They all shook their heads and mumbled, "No, we're good."

Except Rebecca, who thought about it and said, "Are there any burger minis out there?"

"You want some?" I said exasperated.

"No, I'll just pick off your plate," she decided, reaching over and grabbing my egg roll. My only egg roll, goddamn it!

* * *

After we updated Rebecca on what had happened, everyone was pretty much done for. The night's events had stirred up our world to the degree that we all needed to digest what had occurred before we could move on. We decided Iyla and Latisha wouldn't be safe on their own, so they went to catch some rest at Jennifer's apartment, leaving Allie and me to ourselves. That was fine with me 'cause I was already crashing. The events of the night were catching up to me, and the realization of what had happened and almost happened was kicking in. I imagined Allie felt the same, as neither of us said two words on the drive home, and I caught her taking heavy breaths and staring out the window periodically.

When we went inside, Allie went right to Paige's room, cracked the door, and looked in on her sleeping form. Allie stood there for a long minute before heading toward the master bathroom.

I paced the great room for a minute, unable to sleep despite feeling spent. When I saw Allie slip into the bedroom, I called after her, "Can I get you anything?" Really, I was saying, *Are you okay? Is anything wrong?* But it didn't matter, as she said nothing in response. From that I knew there was trouble but she wasn't ready to talk about it. So I lowered my head and rubbed my eyebrows with my forefinger and thumb. Then I lowered my butt into a recliner and stared at the ceiling as I heard Allie turn on the water in the shower. I examined the abrasions on my swollen knuckles from pummeling some now faceless man and wondered if he was dead. I had never done anything like that. In fact, the only fight I'd ever had was when I was in second grade, but that girl deserved it. I felt sick inside remembering the bloody mess I'd made of that man, then felt equally sick when I remembered the explosion his shot had made when it hit Allie's suit. There was no winning with these types of thoughts. One action had led to another, and I had no choice but to do what I did. If he could replay the events, he would probably do it again, as would I. So what was the point of thinking?

But some good had come out of the night, hadn't it? The Lion had been hurt, a new alliance with Latisha and Iyla had been forged, and again the Super Born had been tested and proved formidable. And me, I had had my mettle tested and proved in a trial by fire. My heart was where it should be, and that was good. Take that Mom, Uncle Ned, Aunt Alice, my teachers, and just about everyone else. They said I'd never amount to anything. *Well, you a-holes*, I thought, *I like what I've become.*

That realization bolstered my confidence, and I decided I should pass my thoughts on to Allie. I walked to the bedroom and opened the door to the master bath to find her behind the glass walls of the shower sitting against the wall with all her clothes on while the shower beat on her. She shivered with her eyes closed, strands of her blond hair running over her shoulders like rivers.

I paused for a moment, trying to adjust to the sight of her that way. Then I opened the shower, sat down beside her in the luke-warm torrent, and put my arm around her. Allie's tears turned to full blown sobs and her shivers to violent quakes as she put her head on my shoulder and curled up against my chest as tightly as my wet clothes clung to my skin. The shower and her tears mixed until you couldn't tell one from the other. I reached up and turned the knob to warm the water, and there we sat in silence, our clothes plastered to our skin. We stayed that way for a long time, so long that eventually my arm ached, though I kept it locked around her.

Eventually, her shaking calmed, her eyes opened, and I turned off the shower. "I should have died two or three times over tonight," she said. "You don't know what it's like to feel the bullets strike you and know someone you don't even know wants you to die." She shook her head then glanced up at me with a sad smile. "Some, hero, huh? I get into a fight, and I'm blubbering like a little girl. Paige is sleeping in there and has no idea her mother was almost killed," she said, starting to cry again.

I pulled her in tightly. "Being a hero has nothing to do with what you need to do in the heat of battle to survive. That's why soldiers who survive brutal combat and get medals always say, 'I'm not a hero.' It's knowing why you put yourself through it and the ability to do it again tomorrow that makes you a hero."

Allie shook her head subtly. "I don't know." Then she stared off into the distance. "Maybe I should just go back to being normal, forget the superpowers. It's become so damn dangerous. Not just for me but for Paige's sake and yours."

This seemed like a good opportunity to tell her about being a firework. "You know, that might not be a bad idea. You could at least slow down and not use your powers so much. You could keep working on your Africa project, just stay away from the dangerous stuff."

She stared at a blank spot in front of her for a long time and then smiled weakly. "Maybe I will just give it all up. Would you still love me as a normal, well almost normal, woman?"

"Of course I would!" I said, surprised and excited that she would solve the firework problem on her own. "Are you serious?"

Allie paused and looked at the spot again before breaking into a smile—this time a real one. "No, I was just screwing with you. I wanted to hear what you'd say. I just love flying and feeling so powerful. I wake up every day and know I matter. When we make love I feel so…potent. Know what I mean?"

I slammed my eyelids shut then took a breath, "It's an amazing feeling. I get a dose of it just being around you."

"I know, right?"

"But the danger, like you said. Tonight would have been lethal without your suit. You sure you wanna take that chance?"

Allie thought for a second, nodded vigorously, and looked up at me from my chest. "Now that I've experienced this, it's like I'm a different person. I couldn't be me without it anymore…that's what I love about being with you. You want me to be me. I just love that about you." I guess she noticed my blank expression. "That *is* what you want for me, right?"

Crap, I had to agree with her when she put it that way. "Of course. That's what I've always wanted."

"I know," she said, brushing her palm over my cheek and then folding into me. She was quiet for a long moment and then lifted her head to look at me. "I killed that woman, you know? I had no problem squashing the life out of her like a bug," she said, seemingly half in amazement and half in guilt.

I sighed and leaned back against the wall of the shower. "I know how you feel. I couldn't stop hitting the man who shot you. Seeing his gun pointed at you made me just explode. There's no way to feel good about what's happened. The only way to stop this kind of tragedy is if people never allow the greed and violence of people like them to go unchallenged. But as long as it's around, there's you...and me."

She lifted her head and kissed me on the cheek. "I know," she said sweetly and curled back onto my chest. After a minute of peace she raised her head again. "Did you wear those new shoes in here? The ones I just bought you? Look, they're soaked!"

That was when I knew she was okay. And when I kissed her while she was still trying to complain, I knew I was okay. Talk of fireworks and lives to come would have to wait.

THIRTY-NINE

Midnight Buffet

IYLA

Jennifer's apartment was a big place, big like I'd never seen. She marched in like she had just come home from a shopping trip or a night at the movies. Latisha and I moved slowly and drifted around the room—I felt as out of my element as a monkey at an opera. Latisha seemed just as awed as me.

"Make yourself at home," Jennifer said. "The bar is over there, and the kitchen is over there. Help yourself. There're bedrooms and baths down the hall. Iyla, you can be first door on the left, and Latisha, you're on the right. I could use a drink. How about you?" She seemed suddenly full of an energy that escaped me.

"Vodka," I said, putting my bag on a small table by the couch.

Jennifer scurried across the room to the bar and poured vodka into a glass, stopped, then poured in twice as much. Then she slid over and handed it to me. Two swallows later, it was an empty glass. "How about you?" she asked Latisha.

Latisha looked down at her hands, which were shaking. "Maybe some wine…maybe lots of wine."

Jennifer opened the door of a wine chiller the way a model in a commercial would to reveal a large selection of bottles. "You'll have to be more specific."

"A red," Latisha answered. But then when Jennifer gestured to the whole top two shelves, Latisha pointed at the first bottle in the top row. "That one. Give me that one."

Jennifer uncorked the bottle and handed a glass to Latisha before taking a long drink from the opened bottle. "Bacon, man, I just got the taste for some bacon," Jennifer said, veering toward the kitchen. "You guys want some? How do you like your eggs?"

I followed as she began to clang pans out of cupboards. I opened two doors of her big refrigerator, so big it was stupid. Inside it was full of food like I had never seen except in a grocery store. The freezer was full of boxes of ice cream. I grabbed one with *chocolate* in its name.

Jennifer flashed by. "Excuse me," she said, grabbing eggs, bacon, and butter off the shelves.

Latisha came up behind me. "You gonna eat that or melt it with your stare?"

I looked at her as Jennifer flew around the kitchen and bacon began to sizzle on the stove. "In my old apartment, I couldn't even make a sandwich. You ever see so much food like this?" I asked, gesturing to the open refrigerator.

"Yeah, today at lunch." Latisha took a drink from her glass of wine and looked me over for a second. "So, you read minds? Is that how you knew Ed was dirty?" she asked, taking another sip.

I closed the fridge doors and left the ice cream box on the counter while I looked for a spoon. "It didn't take a mind reader to know Ed was a liar, but yes, I read his mind…" Then I smiled big, like I knew a secret. I always know secrets, everybody's secrets. It's like a curse.

"What?"

"Nothing," I said, popping the lid from the carton. I took my first bite of chocolate crunch, which was better than sex.

"You can read my mind right now?" Latisha asked.

"Yes! Take the butter pecan; it's really the one you want. And yes, Jennifer is making enough eggs for all of us. And yes, Ed would have shot you if Shamil didn't, but he honestly thought you were hot…okay?"

Latisha smiled and then took the carton of butter pecan ice cream out of the fridge. "That's amazing," Latisha took a bite of ice cream, thought for a second, then asked, "How hot, exactly?"

"Steaming!" I said, aggravated that her questions were keeping me from my chocolate crunch…what is crunch anyway? Is *good*.

Latisha savored a bite of butter pecan. "I could use someone with your talents."

"You wish," I said, packing in a spoonful. "Iyla works for Iyla. What was Ed, your boyfriend?"

"Booty call."

"What is booty, like little bird?"

Latisha began to shake her behind but then stopped. "Never mind." She seemed thoughtful for a second then looked over at me. "You ever have trouble with men…you know, doin' it?"

"Ed didn't make the choir sing?"

"They didn't even whisper."

"It's big troubles," I said. "I have the same problem. Ice cream is safer, never lets you down." The ice cream melted in my mouth; it tasted so good.

"You Russian?" Latisha asked, licking the back of her spoon.

"You retarded?" I answered. Hadn't I been speaking all night and big-shot government woman can't figure that out? No wonder she can't find Lion.

The clatter of a platter hitting the granite top of the island announced the arrival of our eggs and bacon. "Bon appétit," Jennifer said in a cheery voice as she placed dishes, silverware, and napkins beside it.

I looked at Latisha, who smiled and put down her ice cream like a kid at Christmas who'd just seen a bigger present. She looked at Jennifer. "What, no ham?"

Jennifer shook her head and then turned and placed a plate of steaming ham slices next to the eggs. "Rookie."

FORTY

I Return to My Roots…or Maybe Stems

LOGAN

The next day the girls were already hard at work. Rebecca had opened a link to Latisha's office and transmitted all the encryption protocols, addresses, and tracking data on the Lion's operatives. Immediately, Latisha began coordinating her people and those of numerous nations around the world to get eyes on the Lion's people. They tracked over five hundred targets in thirty nations, preparing for a massive strike aimed at taking the Lion's network down all at once, before they knew they were blown. Based on the information Demetri's computer had provided, Latisha had set things in motion all around the world, putting hundreds of operatives to work in squeezing the Lion's throat. It was a daunting task to organize and choreograph such a massive combination of agencies, countries, time zones, politics, perspectives, personalities, loyalties, and agendas, but Latisha could multitask like no computer ever made. Through voice, computer, text, delegation, and personal contacts, she somehow balanced it all with a focus that would have made a laser beam envious. She was in the system and used it like a director conducting Beethoven's "Ode to Joy."

The girls had decided there was no way the three of them could accomplish a feat like that, so it made immediate sense to use

Latisha's skills and connections for the bulk of the operation. They decided there was one target, however, that they could and must take out themselves, so Rebecca kept the Lion's location off of Latisha's radar. Rebecca watched patiently as his coordinates appeared and disappeared from the network, following his movements, waiting for the chance to strike.

Jennifer accompanied Iyla back to the motel to keep the ruse alive that she had really been staying there. They had no idea if any of Shamil's men had been sent back to wait for her, so Jennifer would cover Iyla's back as she cleaned out the room and checked out of the motel. They returned without incident, demonstrating the disaster that the gunfight at Latisha's hotel had been for the Lion. Survival and not revenge against Iyla was clearly their current priority.

All day long I tried to be of some use to the girls as they scurried around the conference room, frantic to keep up with Latisha's operation. The Lion was in Chechnya and then suddenly further north in Russia, so that was where they needed to be. Planning such a long-range assault in a hostile area was going to be dangerous—well beyond dangerous. Allie seemed to sense it more and more as the day progressed; her comforting reassurances turned to silence whenever I tried to ask her how things were going.

By late afternoon I was sick of it. To hell with feeling like a fifth wheel—I wasn't even feeling round or like a wheel at all, unless a flat counts. I escaped to my desk, looking at the bustle around me and knowing I was so far ahead of the game here that the game couldn't even see my dust. My PR was so overbooked you couldn't even see my P, so to speak. The company's US production was backlogged for twenty-four months. I had interviews scheduled on three business news networks. Bloggers and newspeople were crying for interviews and updates on the African cooperatives. I was so on it that I wanted to get off it. Sure, it was great money, and I got to see Allie flash by once in a while, but I wasn't feeling satisfied. Well, there was Pizza Break, but that was it—and the Midnight Buffet. But other than Allie flashing by, Pizza Break, and the Midnight Buffet, that was *it*. I was fed up with this job and thought maybe the job and I should start seeing other people.

I looked around, wondering if anyone would miss me if I took off. I gave the phone a glance—it was sleeping. My computer was also asleep. Maybe it was my turn to take a little time off. I was out the door.

When I walked into the house, I was excited by the prospect of taking Paige to dinner and maybe a movie, and I thought she would be happy too. I found her coming down the hall from her room.

"I thought I heard you come in," she said. "What are you doing home so early?"

"Well, I thought I'd come home and take my girl to dinner. You wanna hit a movie, knock over some gas stations, hit up a convenient store, maybe?"

Paige laughed. Someone finding me entertaining was wonderful.

"I know, how about we tear up some clubs, buy the city out of drugs?" I joked, expecting a laugh in response.

Instead Allie stuck her head out of our bedroom. "Clubs? Drugs? Are you totally deranged?"

"He was just joking, Mom," said Paige, coming to my defense. "We joke...oh, I forgot, that may not be a term you are familiar with."

"Allie!" I said. "I thought you were tied up at work. I was just kidding, thought I would take her to dinner, that's all."

"Well, you're too late. Mom's taking me shopping and out to eat," explained Paige.

"Yeah, you can come along if you want," Allie offered.

"Shopping? Let me think. My back hurting from hours of shopper's walk and standing like an idiot holding your purse, or a few hours of just me and my recliner. Hmm, tough one."

"Come on, we're going to your fave restaurant, Fuk Yoo's," Paige tempted me.

"No thanks. I had a late lunch at Fuk Mei's. I feel like Fuk Mei all the time these days."

"No," Allie said, "you should come. It'd be nice to have us all together."

Paige held her fingers out in front of my nose as if dangling a carrot. "Fuk Yooooooo."

"Paige!" complained Allie.

"You guys go," I said. "I have things to do."

"Ooooh, things," said Paige.

"Come on, Logan," Allie said unconvincingly. "Let's go."

I bowed deeply and then waved my hand down the hall. "You two ladies have a great time."

Allie looked at me for a moment then sighed. "Okay, Fuk Yoo it is," said Allie. She pecked me on the cheek and headed away.

Paige followed and then turned back to me. "Good luck with your *things*!"

As they walked down the hall, they began to chat, so I knew I had made the right choice. My guess was that the gravity of what Allie was planning to do had hit her and she wanted more time with Paige. So I'd give it to her.

With them gone, me and my things were free to frolic feverishly. I grabbed my laptop and marched to the room down the hall beyond the guest rooms that was my vastly underused office. I sat down in the black leather chair and looked out through the wall of windows into the evening green of trees and grass, thinking, *Hey, this is nice.* I pushed away a thick layer of dust from the desktop with the side of my hand and then blew it off the desk. (I wasn't a neat freak, but I was no pig—at least not anymore.) I opened the laptop, which greeted me like an old friend (minus asking, "Hey, where's that fifty you owe me?"). Suddenly, memories of my glory days with the B.I.B. website, blog posts, and articles came back to me. I was hit by a surge of inspiration. I opened my word processing program and began filling the blank page with black characters: *Super Born—World on Fire. Chapter One.*

* * *

ALLIE

Paige and I came home late with our arms full of packages and our faces full of successful shopping smiles. We burst through the garage door into the hall chatting like two happy little birds and then dropped our haul of bargains in the great room.

"Whoa, just look at this," I marveled as I counted the bags. "You bought a lot of stuff!"

"You mean *you* bought a lot of stuff," countered Paige. "All I did was say okay."

"Well, you must have said okay a lot!"

Paige looked at me squarely, paused, and then smiled, saying, "I did!"

I dug through one of the bags. "Why don't you try on those jeans? We got such a deal on those. These new stores at the Steamtown Mall have the neatest stuff."

Paige began digging in bag after bag, looking for the jeans.

"Try that one," I advised. Paige pulled out a handful of tops, looked at me, and shook her head. "How about that one?" I advised again.

Paige pulled the jeans out of the bag and then ran off to try on the jeans and the tops.

"Logan?" I called. "Come out and see how much money Paige and I saved! Logan?" I drifted across the great room to the main hall and checked for him first in the TV room and then the bedroom. "Logan?"

I spun around and looked back at the dark kitchen. Then I turned to the dim hall that ran to the garage and the back bedrooms on the other side of the great room to find a faint glow coming from Logan's office. *He's never down there*, I thought as I hurried down the corridor with a spark of concern as the memory of Shamil and his men came back to life in my head. "Logan?"

The door was cracked, so I pushed it cautiously open. "Logan?" I found him slumped over the desk beside the faint glow of his laptop. I tiptoed up to the desk and brought the computer to life with the tap of a key to reveal what he was writing. My eyes widened as I read about myself, Jenny, and Rebecca. I brought up page after page, marveling that this was about me. It was a surreal experience. Why would anyone write a book about me?

After a minute Paige appeared in the doorway with her new outfit. "What do you think, Mom?" she said, modeling a bit.

I turned my head and put my finger over my lips for her to be quiet. When she noticed Logan napping, she likewise tiptoed in. "What's going on?" she whispered. I pointed at the screen, and she read a page. She noticed her name and said, "Is that about me? What's that part about you and your friend Jenny?"

Suddenly I realized this was about the Super Born. I even saw the word *B.I.B.* in the text. Paige couldn't read this! I slapped the lid of the laptop down. "We shouldn't be reading this. It's…private."

"I saw my name! Come on, let me see!"

I directed her toward the door. "It's Logan's personal property. Remember when you used to write in a journal? That was your confidential information."

Paige put her hand on her hip confrontationally. "That didn't stop you from reading it, if I recall."

"I'm your mom. That's different."

"On what planet?"

"This one," I pushed her to the doorway. "You have to promise me you won't look at what he's writing. Maybe he'll show it to you someday."

"Why don't we ask him now?" she asked pointing at Logan.

I pointed at Logan with both hands to remind her that he was asleep.

"I know what will wake him up!" Paige said and took off down the hall. She returned a moment later with an egg roll smothered in sweet and sour sauce. With an open palm under it to catch the dripping sauce, she waved it under Logan's nose, softly saying, "Fuk Yooooooo's."

"Paige! Leave him alone."

"Fuk Yooooo's for youuuuuu," she continued.

In one quick movement Logan awoke and snapped a large bite, almost taking in half the egg roll. Paige pulled away. "Jeez!"

He sat up, munching vigorously, and grabbed the egg roll stub from Paige. "Did you bring me anything else?" he asked before finishing it off.

"You really zonked out, huh?" I asked.

"Can I read the thing you wrote?" begged Paige. "Can I? Can I, please, please, please?"

Logan looked at me and hesitated.

I gave him a subtle but emphatic shake of my head and then tried to smile and act innocent. "Yeah, you want to show us what you wrote?" I said, sneaking behind Paige's line of sight. I shook my head violently this time as Paige clasped her hands together to beg.

Finally, Logan got the hint. "No, sorry. It's just something new I'm working on. It's not really ready for the eyes of the world."

"I don't care about the eyes of the world," Paige said. "How about just a peek for your buddy-buddy, me, who brought you a bag of takeout?"

"Yeah, that I paid for," I pointed out.

Logan opened the computer, giving Paige a shot of excitement, and then quickly saved the file and closed the computer.

"You're no fun!" Paige pouted.

"Tiger, I promise I'll show you when it's done," he said. "Promise. Now, where's that takeout?"

"Get it yourself!" she said, turning to leave.

"Hey, that outfit looks great!" he yelled after her.

"Yeah, right. Too late."

After I heard Paige digging through the bags in the great room, I closed in on Logan and said in a low tone, "Are you crazy? You have to be more careful! What the hell are you writing, anyway?"

"The truth. The world should know about you someday," he said with great conviction.

"Yeah, but Paige shouldn't! Not right now, and maybe never."

"You think this Super Born thing is just going to go on like this forever?" he said, giving me a weird look, as if he knew the future.

"Yeah, or maybe everything gets even better."

"And maybe it doesn't!"

I thought for a second then turned to him and pointed at the computer. "You password protect that thing and lock it up. No one can see it." Then I mellowed, realizing how far out of character I had become. I said more softly, "Okay?"

"All right," he said reluctantly.

"You didn't write about *everything*, did you?"

"What do you mean?"

"You know…everything," I hinted again.

"Really, how much can you write in one night? Oh, you mean *everything*." The thought made him crack a little smile. He turned and studied the desktop for a long moment. Then he studied me before grinning and looking back at the desktop. Then, I must confess, I looked at it too.

"Noooo," I said, knowing what was on his mind, but I guess my cheeky little smile gave me away.

He closed in slowly and put his arms around me, his lips to my neck. I fell into his warmth right away but tried to put up a weak defense. "Paige is out there!" (Strike one.) "It's late." (Strike two.) "And I thought you were hungry." (Strike three.)

"I am," he said with a determined look on his face. Logan led me to the desk, leaned me back over it with a kiss until I was flat on my back, pulled off my jeans, got down on his knees, and pulled me to him. In a second there was nothing else on my mind but his touch.

When the door closed, the chair tipped over, and the items on top of the desk crashed to the floor in the office, we could hear Paige down the hall. "Eeeew, not again! Why do I have to have horn dogs for parents?"

FORTY-ONE

The Lion, the President, and Hamlet

LOGAN

The next day the Super Born worked on their plans to deal with the Lion. Allie stayed late at work, and I took Paige on Allie's ticket to see Dr. Jones' debut as Hamlet at the gorgeous modern performing arts center downtown. It was one of the jewels in the crown of Scranton's renaissance. The exterior of the center was composed of contemporary glass and shining metal panels that had gotten press in every architectural journal. The interior was already gaining renown for its acoustic excellence. Sitting in its plush seats, you felt the substantial nature of the place. Just being in the building had the feel of an event.

The curtain opened on the premier of *Hamlet*. Personally, I thought Jones was odd for the role, to say the least. When he first appeared onstage, I could tell from past experience that he'd tipped a few Miner's Lites before the show for courage. I had to wonder if someone had been mocking him by giving him the role. Without the RFD director on the center's board, Robert Symthe, I'm certain he never would have been considered. But for some reason, the artsy-fartsy folks in town loved the Indian lilt he brought to the part. Who knew? I just hoped he didn't break into the Chicken Dance during the first act.

Everyone wanted to take credit for Scranton becoming the hot spot in the nation for economic growth, population growth, safety, budget surpluses, and therefore new budget spending. The mayor and President Cobb were old friends, and with campaign season coming up, the president wanted to attach himself to Scranton's rising star rather than the rest of the sinking nation.

What better place for him to be seen than the palace of Scranton's high culture, the new, world-class performing arts center? The mayor entertained the president and his wife in a side box, which angled out from the mezzanine level with contemporary chrome and glass railings. The vision of him in the box seemed like a modern-day Lincoln at Ford's Theatre, but Jones was hardly John Wilkes Booth—maybe John Wilkes Uncouth, but not Booth.

Throughout the performance, I would find myself ready to chuckle at Jones while those around me were near tears and applauding. There were even a few scattered bravos as the curtain dropped for intermission and the lights came up. I looked over at Paige. "Well, what'd you think of it so far?"

"I thought it was a pile of crap."

"Paige, we're in a classy theater; watch your language."

"Okay, sorry. I thought it was an accumulation of crap."

"Better."

"Do they have, like, pizza or something?" she asked.

"This is an artsy place. I think they have quiche."

"I don't care what it is as long as it has pepperoni."

I ignored her for a moment to look up and take in the beauty of the modernistic theater, and that's when I saw Latisha and Allie appear up on the mezzanine level near the side box. Ahead of them a storm of suited men had appeared in the president's box. Like a vanishing act, when the men disappeared, so did the president, his wife, and the mayor. From other doorways flashed the figures of running men, yet few in the theater seemed to notice; most patrons sat or stood and chatted about the performance.

I blinked twice, and all the men were gone, as were Latisha and Allie.

"Was that Mom?" Paige asked incredulously, following my eyes up to the mezzanine.

"Where?" I said. (Am I smooth as an oiled apple or what?)

"Right there!" She pointed.

"I didn't see anyone who looks like your mother."

"Look, the president's gone," Paige added.

"Guess he wants to beat the bathroom lines," I said.

Paige shook her head. "Yeah, right. Presidents don't pee."

"This one does, big pee-er—a bathroom accident almost lost him New York in the election."

Paige ignored me, and her eyes remained fixed on the mezzanine. "I think that was Mom. What would she be doing here?"

"That blond? Oh, that wasn't your mother. No way. Allie's at work."

"Blond? I thought you didn't see anyone."

"What? Oh, you meant that blond about your mom's height with beautiful long hair, wearing that dress I got her for Christmas? No, that wasn't her. Trust me—I would know Allie in a dark cave."

"Like your bedroom? Dark *noisy* cave?" Paige asked. "I'm gonna call her." She pulled out her phone and started to dial.

"Oh, I wouldn't do that!" I said, grabbing for the phone but missing. Man, was she quick.

* * *

ALLIE

I answered on the third ring as Secret Service agents hustled a group of four of the Lion's men and women out of the theater behind me. They were dressed as volunteer ushers wearing bright-red jackets. After helping seat people in the theater, they had rendezvoused in the hall outside the president's box. Thanks to Rebecca's intel, Latisha and the Secret Service were waiting for them and nabbed them before they could retrieve the weapons and vests full of explosives that others had stashed for them in a storage closet.

"Hello," I answered and turned into the wall for as much privacy as I could get. I knew it was Paige, and I knew she would keep calling if I didn't answer.

"Mom? Where are you?" she asked.

"You know…at work. It's crazy here right now; can I call you back?"

"Mom, I just saw you in the theater. I'm here with Logan, and we just saw you!"

"That's crazy. I wish I could have been there, but I'm working. Here, you wanna talk to Jennifer? She'll tell you," I said, grabbing Jennifer, who stood nearby. "Here, Jenny, tell Paige about the super boring inventory problem we're having."

Jennifer gave me a questioning look and then took the phone. "Super boring. Hi, kid, how have you been?"

"Is Mom there with you at work?"

"Yep, yep-per-ony. We are here…at work…working," Jennifer said.

"Okay, thanks, Jenny. How you doing? Going to any shows in NYC anytime soon?"

"Yeah, in fact your Mom and I are taking off really soon for a really big show."

"Cool, which one?"

"Oh, your mom wants to talk with you," said Jennifer, bailing.

"So," I said, "you satisfied? I'm at work. You wanna hear about…"

"The five new co-ops that are starting next week in Africa? You already told me," Paige interrupted.

"Yeah, but did I tell you all the generators are coming from the new Cairo plant?"

"You're right, that is boring. Sorry, I must have been mistaken. That lady sure looked like you."

"Wow, then she must have been gorgeous!" I said, and Paige laughed. "You guys having fun?"

"It's intermission. The president just left. That friend of Logan's is a really terrible actor. But it's cool to be here."

"Good. Well, I'll see you at home later."

No sooner had I hung up than Latisha and a group of suited men came over to me. She pointed at a tablet she held while speaking on her COMM and directing agents to check other rooms in the hallway with flashing gestures of her hand. They were trying to evaluate Rebecca's information to determine if there were any further threats to the president. "Are we clear?" she asked me. "Rebecca said six. We got four."

"Six, right Rebecca?" I said into my COMM.

"Yes, six, definitely six. Did you check the alley? I show two were supposed to be back there," Rebecca answered in my ear.

I looked up at Latisha. "Back alley?"

"Team seven, any action there?" Latisha said into her headset. After a moment she looked up at me. "Got 'em. Two in the back alley. One's down."

Just then a group of Secret Service operatives hustled out of a room off the hall talking on their COMMs and leading the president and his wife out of the building now that the exit was secured. As they walked the president seemed surprised and angry. He said to the chief of his security team, "Tom, you said this was a safe place to make an appearance. Now Latisha had to save your ass again. And I've got my wife here, goddamn it!"

"Sir, there was nothing on the threat radar," answered Tom.

The president nervously ran his hand through his full head of gray hair. "Then, Tom, I suggest you get Latisha's radar. Plus, I had to suffer through that awful play. Is that guy playing Hamlet for real? Ah, there she is," said the president, stopping the group beside Latisha. "Nice work, Lattie," he said, patting Latisha on the back. "Guess I owe you another one."

Latisha held back a smile in trying to remain professional. "Just doing my job. We got 'em before they were ready, and we got 'em all."

"Good work," said the president, giving Tom a quick, critical glance. He turned back to Latisha. "Do you know where these bastards live?" he asked.

"Yes, Mr. President, I do," Latisha answered, glancing over at Jenny and me.

"Then let's take the gloves off. Kill 'em. Kill 'em all!" said the president before he and his party took off at a rapid pace.

The Secret Service seemed to disappear as uniformed police began appearing in the hallway. Against the wall stood the mayor—he looked apprehensively down the hall in each direction, wringing his hands, and then drifted sheepishly back to his seat. The show must go on.

Latisha turned to Jenny and me, smiling a little. "Operation Lion's Den just got the green light. You ready?"

I took a deep breath as Jennifer burst out with excitement, "Am I!" We all turned and began walking out at a quick pace down the hall to the main stairway.

"Lattie?" I asked Latisha. "Lattie?"

"What, the President of the United States doesn't have a pet name for you too?" Latisha said, smiling.

"No, *Lattie*. The only name they have for me is the B.I.B.," I said.

"Yeah, the Bitch in Black," chuckled Jennifer.

"No," said Latisha, pretending to think about it. She shook her head. "Doesn't seem to have the same ring to it."

"Not hardly," I told her as we headed down the main stairway into the lobby.

* * *

LOGAN

We, like the rest of the country, were unaware of the reasons for the president's sudden departure from the theater. Ignorance is bliss, I guess, until it turns around and bites you in the ass. When the curtain dropped on *Hamlet*, Paige and I left to attend the opening-night celebration for the actors and crew. The festivities were being held at (where else?) O'Malley's. We entered to see Jones receiving a tearful hug from Robert Symthe, the RFD who had directed the production.

"Incredible, incredible, my good fellow. What else can I say?" Symthe said, struggling to speak through tears of joy. Finally, he let go of the beaming Jones and drifted away with a group of RFDs.

The barkeep walked by them on his way to me, shaking his head. I could tell he was put off by the blubbering of Symthe. "Hogwash, now I'm serving artsy-fartsy hogwash…well, a buck's a buck." Then he turned his attention to Paige, giving her an evil-eyed look over. "She over twenty-one?"

"Turned twenty-one yesterday," I lied.

"Good enough for me," he said and then turned back to Paige. "Wanna beer?"

"One for me," I started. "She'll have—"

"Pink 'tini with a twist," Paige said nonchalantly.

"Soda, she'll have a soda," I corrected. "Your finest." The barkeep nodded and drifted away.

"You're no fun," complained Paige.

"What's this 'tini shit?"

"Jenny made some for her and Mom when she was over one night. It looked cool. Besides, that's what you get for dragging me to a bar! Where is that phone number for the child services people?" she said, pulling out her phone.

Just then two men entered the bar guiding two dollies loaded with large, thin boxes, which appeared to be eight big-screen TVs. They looked around for help, which I provided. "Great, you guys install too?"

"Just deliver," said one young man unfolding a paper.

The barkeep came over with my beer and Paige's soda in hand. "What's all this, now?"

"You can't have a sports bar without big-screen TVs…everywhere," I said, gesturing across the wall.

"I already got one," the barkeep said, gesturing toward the puny screen above the bar. The deliveryman squinted in the TV's general direction.

"When you put these smart TVs up and get a bunch of games going on them, then you'll have a real sports bar…and maybe a couple customers."

"Smart TV? You know how much they cost? I can only afford stupid TV."

"Yes, I know what they cost 'cause I bought you these," I said. "This is what you want, believe me."

"You bought me these? You bought me these bleedin' TVs?" The barkeep walked toward me with a joyful face and open arms. I was expecting a hug of gratitude. Instead he handed me the beer and soda and walked right by to the deliveryman. "Let's put these babies in the back room for now. Do you have the mounting brackets or does *he* have to buy those separately?" he added as he led them away.

I stood in amazement at the barkeep's lack of thanks while Paige tried to pull the beer out of my hand. I jerked it away, handed her the soda instead, and shook the spilled beer off my fingers.

"You've got a lot of weird friends…he was a friend, right?" Paige said, sipping on the soda. "I suppose you wouldn't have given him those TVs if he wasn't. Hey, I could use a new TV."

A large group of people finished congratulating Jones and moved away. He spotted me and came over with a giant smile. "My friend, my friend, I am so glad you could come. Did you love the performance or what?"

"Great," I said, "Best Hamlet I've ever seen." (I hadn't seen any others.)

"It was…amazing," Paige added before hurriedly sucking on her soda.

"Thank you, thank you. Isn't this cast party great?" he said, gesturing about the room.

I nodded. "Quite a night for you, I'll bet."

"Yes," said Jones before putting his arm around me and pulling me aside. "It's good that you came. I've been meaning to speak with you. The blood tests are in. We need to talk to the girls."

"Blood tests?"

"By the way, how did they take the news? They weren't very happy, I'd imagine."

I gestured with my finger across my throat to tell Jones to shut up. "Ix-nay on the ews-nay," I whispered to Jones, pointing a thumb at Paige.

"What? You didn't tell them?"

"Ix-nay!"

"What variety of language is that? Is Allie doing okay? She must have been devastated."

"What's he talking about?" asked Paige with concern.

I saw a booth emptying, so I pointed at it. "Paige, you wanna grab that booth so we have somewhere to sit? I'll be right there." Paige hesitated a moment then reluctantly walked to the booth.

I turned to Jones. "Who doesn't know what ix-nay means! I'm gonna tell 'em. I've just been waiting for the right time."

"So, you're just letting them burn themselves out?" Then Jones thought for a moment. "Ix-nay, isn't that Icelandic?"

"Swedish. Look, I'll tell them…soon. You just can't talk about it in front of Paige."

Jones put his hand over his mouth and his eyes went wide. "That was Paige? Holy mother of crap! I'm sorry!"

"Me too." I said shaking my head and running my palm over my goatee. "I'll tell them soon, I promise. Then you can tell them about the tests."

"Not soon, now!"

"To tell them or not to tell them, that is the question," I said.

"What?" said Jones.

"Though this be madness, yet there is method in't," I said.

"What?"

"Didn't you just perform that play? Forget it. I'll call you."

"Yeah, when you're sober," said Jones, looking at my bottle of beer and then smugly walking away.

I slinked into the booth across from Paige with my head down.

"What was that guy talkin' about? What kind of tests?"

"It's nothing. They're just checking your mom for some research program he's running. Nothing to worry about."

"Nothing? Nothing, hey?" Paige leaned across the table. "Why would she be devastated over nothing?"

"She was hoping to be in the research program, but they found out from her blood test that she can't—no biggie," I said, my nose growing. "And don't tell her she got rejected. It'll hurt her feelings." And then, before Paige could respond, I added, "Let's blow this popsicle stand," rising out of the booth.

"What? Now we're leaving?"

We had taken one step toward the door when the barkeep dramatically jumped out from behind the bar, pulling Millie along. "Let's dance!" he yelled as the music for the Chicken Dance poured loudly out from the speakers. Nearly everyone in the bar joined in, creating a crowd at the front of the bar.

Paige smiled and grabbed my hand. "Let's dance!" she said, joining in. "Come on, we have to!" she declared upon seeing my reluctance. "Come on, you stick in the mud. I know you can do the Chicken Dance. You've got the scrawny legs for it!"

I stood like an unmovable rock for…at least every bit of five seconds and then took Paige's hand. "Let's boogie!" And did those chickens ever dance.

FORTY-TWO

The Hand-Off

LOGAN

The next day the conference room at Lowe LLC looked more like a war room at a military command post than a center of business operations. Rebecca had added numerous video screens to the walls and surrounded her seat at the table with plentiful computers and communications lines. The LED lights of a dozen or more modems and routers blinked frantically, and a line of servers stood against the wall with tentacles of cables flowing out of them over the floor to the table and video screens.

Amongst the electronic jungle sat Rebecca with a headset on and a console in front of her connected to a battery of phone lines. Jennifer stared up at a video screen as Iyla pointed to a location on the map it displayed.

Allie had let me in and then bolted the door. "We're getting ready to go," she said soberly with her arms folded in lieu of a greeting.

"Where?" I asked.

"You really wanna know?" she said.

"Of course. Maybe I can help. I've saved your butt more than once, you know."

Allie turned her back to me and took a few steps away. "You're not going this time."

"Why? Is this some superwoman macho bullshit?"

Allie looked around the room at the other Super Born, who seemed to have noticed the rising tension between us, and then put her hand on my back and led me to the small office connected to the conference room. She closed the door behind us. "Just trust me, okay? You shouldn't go," she said. Her face had begun to soften a bit. In fact, she was almost in tears.

My anger chilled a bit at the sight. "What's going on?"

"You need to be here," she said, folding her arms again and beginning to pace. "I need you here for…Paige, okay?"

"Why, she got a big date?"

Allie stopped pacing and turned back to me. "Logan, what if I don't come back? What would happen?"

"But you are coming back, so what's the problem?"

She went to the door and then turned to me. "Wait here, I'll be right back," Allie said and then went through the door. She returned a few seconds later with a folded piece of paper. "Here," she said, handing the paper to me.

"What's this? You divorcing me already? We're not even married! You can't have my coffee pot. I won't stand for it." When I got no reaction, I decided to add, "If this is about the car payment, I promise the check's in the mail…for sure by next week."

"Not funny. I'm making you Paige's legal guardian if something happens to me. She likes you, and I don't want my sisters fighting over her. Lori's got her own kids, and Janis is trying, still trying, to get it together."

I looked from side to side then leaned in toward Allie. "You've got another sister? Is she like you?"

"Logannnn," she said, irritated.

"Okay, I get it. I wouldn't want Paige exposed to Lori's meat loaf any more than you would."

She ignored me. "It's already filed. That's your copy."

Suddenly (it was about time), the serious nature of the conversation hit me. I moved in and wrapped my arms around her. "Just how dangerous is this?"

"I'd say it's a ten on a scale of one to five."

"Is that all? You forget, I've eaten meals you've cooked."

"You're lucky to eat meals I cook."

"You can't stop me. I laugh in the face of danger. Like, if that was danger's face," I said, holding out my open hand, "I'd laugh right at it, ha." I was trying to lighten her mood, but it wasn't working…well…at all.

Allie pulled away from me, folded her arms again, and resumed pacing. "Latisha and her people will launch simultaneous attacks on the bulk of the network while Jennifer, Iyla, and I go after the Lion himself. We have to fly thousands of miles into Russian airspace and then get in and out before anyone knows we're there. He has a complex in southern Russia. Looks like an innocent little farm. We've got satellite pictures of the outside, but we have no idea what'll be inside. The man who's setting the world on fire—you think he'll have a couple of friends protecting him? It'll be like the fight at the hotel with Shamil and his men but much worse. Still wanna go?"

"What? Is that all? You should be back by dinnertime."

"Come on Logan, this is serious."

I patted her on the shoulder. "You're right, if that's all there is to it, you don't even need my help."

"You're hopeless. Take the damn paper, just in case," she said.

"I'd still like to be there to protect your butt. It's a tough job, *but* someone has to do it."

"Logan, I'm trying to tell you that I'm freakin' scared! Okay?" she said, frustrated.

"Sorry," I said, trying to pull her back to me. "I know you're worried. I also know you have to do this. You'll be fine, like always. I have confidence in you. I'm just trying to joke because I don't wanna deal with you being out there without me. I know it's ridiculous, but I feel I can somehow protect you."

"It's not ridiculous…comical, but not ridiculous." Then, when she saw my hurt-puppy look, she added, "Now I'm joking. I know you've been there for me. If you hadn't stopped Shamil's man in the alley, who knows what could have happened." Allie looked down at her feet and folded her arms. "You know, part of me thinks this is crazy." Then she looked up at me. "Why am I taking a chance like this? And then there is part of me that's drawn to these powers like a moth to a light. Every day I can do more and more and more. If I can do these things, then it would be a shame to not use them to make the world better, right? Even with the risks."

The "more and more" part hit me right between the eyes, reminding me of my conversation with Jones. "Allie…"

"What?"

I shook my head. "This timing sucks."

"What are you talking about?"

"There's something I have to tell you. I've been putting it off."

She smiled, not knowing I was about to hit her with a baseball bat. "I know what this is, so you can just tell me."

"Jones…Jones says that you and the other girls are burning yourselves out like fireworks. The more you use your powers, the faster you burn out. If you wanna be around for Paige, it's not the Lion you need to worry about, it's using your powers."

She stared at me blankly. "What?" Allie shook her head and gave a huff for feeling foolish. "I thought you were gonna tell me how much you loved me."

"I'm sorry I didn't tell you earlier. You just seemed so happy with what you were doing. I couldn't bring myself to worry you."

She pushed me away. "What the fuck are you talking about?"

"Blood tests. He did blood tests, and they show that you all are aging really fast. With your metabolism, the more you use your powers, the faster you age. But it's still just a theory, and even if it's true, he's looking for a way around it. Till then, it'd probably be best for you to not use your powers so much."

"You wait till I'm headed off into the battle of my life to tell me this?" she said with her arms out, pumping them as she spoke. "Well, it doesn't matter. The Lion is done, and I'm going to do whatever I have to!"

I ran my fingers over my goatee. "I know you will. I know. Just maybe cool it when it's over. Just for a while."

She began pacing. "How certain is that little bastard?"

"Very."

"Just what am I supposed to tell them?" she asked, pointing in the direction of Rebecca and the others.

"They should know there's a price for using their powers. They won't go on forever. You're using yourselves up like a tank of gas."

"That's crazy!"

"Jones said Rebecca has aged the most of all of you—like, ten years in six months."

Allie paced nervously, shaking her head occasionally. "Now you tell me. So, we're getting old really fast?"

"Using your powers is like stepping on the gas pedal in a car: it makes you move, but it sucks the life out of you."

Allie stopped in her tracks and stared at me in disbelief. "Gee, thanks for dropping this bomb, Logan—as if I didn't have enough insanity going on in my head right now."

"I'm really sorry I didn't tell you sooner. But I love you so much, I guess I was hoping Jones was wrong. Maybe he is."

"Maybe?" Allie tightened her fist and swung it at the ground. "I don't need this right now."

"Maybe Jones is wrong. You look fine. You feel fine, right?"

Allie opened her mouth to speak but then fell silent. She stayed quiet for a moment in thought and then said, "I do, but now that you bring it up, Rebecca has been sick. It started on the way back from Africa after she downed those drones."

I stared at her and took a couple deep breaths as I felt my heart sinking. "You think he's right?"

"I don't know, could be. I just can't think about it right now," she said. She sighed and looked at her feet. When she looked up at me again, I could see the resolve in her face. "We have someone out there who has killed thousands of people and terrorized a dozen governments and who is trying to stop us from giving people in Africa a global opportunity. We have to finish the job."

"No, you don't! You have Latisha. Have her call in the Marines or air strikes. Let the professional soldiers do their job."

Allie shook her head, giving me a disbelieving look. "The US military attacking in Russia? I don't think so. And what if he gets away? He's prepared for traditional law enforcement and military. He's been evading them for years. He's not ready for us. Every time we've been up against him, he's lost big. It has to be us."

I corralled her in my arms again. "You're right. I know you're right, but I love you, Allie—you, not your powers. I don't care if you ever fly again. It wouldn't matter to me. I just want you. Doesn't that count for anything?"

She paused. (Way too long, if you ask me.) Then she smiled. "Of course it does. And I love you too, because you let me be me. You want me to be me. And right now *this* is me."

That was a whole lot of me's. I was trapped, caught in my own words. (Damn, why am I such a great guy?) "Okay, but when it's done, you all slow down till we figure this out. Right?"

Allie put her hand up to her mouth and said something that sounded like she was in agreement without truly being audible. I should have asked her to repeat it, but as is the way of my people, I didn't follow through.

Allie spun and got in my face. "You talk to Jones and tell him to get his facts ready. And they better be good," she said, pointing a finger at me. "I've got three jumpy superwomen out there, and now I have to give them something else to worry about." Allie opened the door. "This kind of information is not exactly what we wanted to hear."

"Well, this kind of information is why you kept Jones alive," I countered.

She thought about it for a moment and then walked out the door, mumbling to herself, "Crap."

I stood in the office for a long moment in thought, staring at the paper Allie had given me. For a brief second I imagined what it would feel like if I ever had to use it, and it shook me to my core. I sighed and then mumbled the same thing to myself.

FORTY-THREE

I Take a Hit Before the Hit

LOGAN

Allie was all business. There was no tearful good-bye, no hug, no intimacy at all. She was just a worried woman who was pissed at me and focused on the job ahead.

Allie, Jennifer, and Iyla left almost immediately in the company jet, flying to an airport in Kars, Turkey, so they could time their assault on the Lion to match Latisha's simultaneous hits on his other operatives. From Turkey Allie would carry the other two into Russia, flying low—over as much uninhabited terrain as possible—to the farm where they believed the Lion to be. Rebecca coordinated the assault from the conference room, keeping in touch with Latisha and tracking events from there. It wasn't long before she was into Latisha's network and those of her foreign associates, so the status of thousands of little dots showed on Rebecca's screens. Some dots were the Lion's people, some CIA, some MI6, some Interpol, and others were the Russian Federal Police, whom Rebecca would be monitoring to see if the girls were being tracked. I looked up at the blinking screens and moving dots in amazement, as if they were the coolest video game I had ever seen.

I watched one dot in particular, as it tracked Allie's plane out over the Atlantic. Her leaving so abruptly burned in me, as did the custody paper in my pocket. I understood her logic and appreciated her concern, but not being there with her felt like something I knew I would soon be regretting. Despite her powers (and all evidence to the contrary), I thought of Allie as a woman I wanted to shelter and protect. I worried about her facing the Lion. I worried about her powers burning out. I worried about her getting trapped in a foreign land. I worried about her being injured with no aid in sight. I worried about not being there for her. Remembering the way I had disabled Shamil's man during the battle at the hotel, I felt certain I could help somehow.

But most of all I worried about where the closest place was to get some beer. I hadn't been much more than a social drinker since moving in with Allie, but I decided this was the perfect time to end all that.

The hit wasn't planned till the next night, so I had plenty of time to tie one on. The big question was, what was the appropriate snack food for watching a battle that would affect the future direction of the entire world? And dips, you needed to get just the right dip for a conflict involving world domination. Heck, where did I put that giant we're-number-one foam finger? I could use that to cheer as I watched Allie's little light blink on the screen, moving in on the Lion's, and hoped Allie's light never went out. I couldn't have felt more useless unless I were a member of Congress.

Paige and her friend Kelly were watching TV when I came home. I stuck my head around the corner of the TV room and prepared to break the news to Paige that her mother was out of town…again.

"Don't bother," Paige said, holding up her hand. Her stare at the TV told me she was angry. "The queen already called. I know she's off to…somewhere on business for a few days. I know she's sorry. Ha. Can you believe she actually told me to listen to you as if you were my dad?" she said, glancing over at me with disbelief to demonstrate the absurdity of that concept. Then she refocused on the TV and shook her head. "Why is she getting all mushy all of a sudden? A little dramatic, don't you think?"

That made Kelly laugh. "Drama City, just like my house."

"No, not dramatic," I said, coming to Allie's defense. "It's hard for her, spending so much time away from you. She feels guilty, I think." Then I thought for a second. "Did she really say, 'As if he were your dad'?"

Paige laughed. "Yeah, isn't that hi-larious?"

My faced dropped. "Well, I don't think it's that funny."

Paige looked at Kelly, and they both snickered.

"I mean, we do things together, and we're cool…right?" I asked uncertainly.

Paige nodded without looking away from the TV. "Sure."

I slowly backed away and went into the kitchen, knowing that this hadn't gone well. I paced around and wondered where Allie was and how it was going. I opened the door to the refrigerator and peered into it, waiting for some battle-for-world-domination snack food to leap out at me. When nothing happened, I closed the door but then opened it again, convinced I must have missed something really good.

Then Paige and Kelly came out of the TV room and proceeded across the great room to the front door.

"Where ya goin'?" asked Daddy-o.

"Megan's. See ya, Dad," answered Paige sarcastically without even looking at me.

The door slammed, my heart sank, and worry slowly descended like a black cloak over my head. I had pined for Allie before. I was used to that. But this heightened level of concern was new. I had always felt confident before. I hadn't even concerned myself with the dangers Allie faced. I'd known in my heart everything would be fine. Now I was scared shitless.

FORTY-FOUR

Everyone Gets Ready

ALLIE

I stood on a hilltop looking up into a Russian night sky peppered with clouds and a glowing full moon. The stars flickered in the midnight blue between the clouds, a serene sight that should have made me feel tranquil but didn't. I took a deep breath and tried to calm myself, but it worked for only a second. The engine of my nerves was running, and I couldn't stop it. I checked the NAV system on the wrist of my B.I.B. suit, trying to figure out how far away from the Lion we were.

Finally, Iyla emerged from the brush, her feet crunching the rocky ground. She wore jeans and an I-love-Scranton hoodie, looking more like she was on her way to go shopping than preparing to battle the world's foremost villain. "There now, did that take so long?" Iyla said, rejoining Jennifer and me.

"I told you to go before we left Turkey!" said a crabby Jennifer.

"Yeah, remember?" I scolded Iyla as well. "We're time critical here."

"What am I supposed to do? Lately, I have the leaky bladder of an old lady. Yesterday I laughed while watching a *Sponges Bob* cartoon and peed my pants. I'll just bet this is from your American food. Yes, I blame it on Coca-Cola!"

"Coca-Cola, my ass!" declared Jennifer. "Did you really need to drink three bottles?"

"I was thirsty. Would you rather me be guarding your back dehydrated? Or with full bladder?" Iyla said, defending herself.

"Can we go now?" I adjusted my COMM headset and lowering my night-vision goggles.

"You had better check with Miss Puckered Ass over here to see if it's okay," said Iyla, pointing at Jennifer, but then she too adjusted her waistband and headset.

I grabbed one of them in each arm and shot into the sky as fast as I could go.

"Whoa!" said Iyla through her COMM. "I think I have to go again!"

"Me too," said Jennifer in a discomforted voice.

"Get used to it," I told them. "It's called flying."

"Can I just go back and get my stomach?" Iyla asked.

I checked the NAV unit on my wrist for course, speed, and arrival time, and then dropped into a dive to treetop level to pick up some additional speed. The increased velocity made me think of what Logan had said, asking me to slow down. I thought about it, considered the job ahead of us, and decided to speed up as fast as I could. "Looks like we'll be there in seventeen minutes. That'll be cutting it close, but we should be okay."

* * *

LOGAN

I arrived at the conference room early, a good hour and half before all hell was scheduled to break loose. I dragged Jones along with me instinctively, without a plan, as was my method. (I don't know, it just felt weird watching the end of the world by myself, and who knows? His expertise might be of use.) When I gave him a rundown of the night's events and he realized the magnitude of them, he wasn't hard to convince. It was history in the making, and we would have a front-row seat.

Rebecca was hard at work, perspiration dotting her forehead, and looking like she hadn't showered or slept in a day or two. After hours of thought and research, I had determined ideal battle-for-world-domination snack food was a cheese-crust double pepperoni pizza with a side of garlic dipping sauce. Her severe expression changed instantly to gleeful upon seeing the pizza and two-liter soda I'd brought her. She mouthed "thank you" to me as she listened to Latisha on her headset and dug out her first slice.

Jones wandered about the transformed conference room, marveling at the video and computer screens. "This is all happening live, right now?" he asked. I nodded. "What is this?" he asked, pointing at a group of dots on the video map of Europe.

"Those are green, so I'm guessing a SEAL team," I told him, though I really had no clue. I wanted Jones to think I'd been an integral part of the planning.

"Oh, they just blinked yellow! What does that mean?"

I stared at the dots for a moment in thought with my mouth open. The dots turned back to green. "False alarm…I guess."

"Wow!" said Jones, spinning in a circle as he admired the screens. "There must be thousands of variables displayed up here. Coordinating this all must take a fleet of supercomputers at least…amazing organizational software."

"We do our best," I said modestly, trying to take some degree of credit for our supercomputers—Rebecca and Latisha.

"Lot of green on this map of England. You sure those are SEALs?"

"Look over here," I said, diverting him. "This speck in southern Russia is Allie." I pointed to a rapidly moving icon.

"Look at that sucker movin'!" Jones' expression changed as he turned to me and spoke in a low tone, "Did you tell them? She is burning her powers like a *mofo*! You didn't tell them, did you?"

"They know," I said with my head down. "They all know."

Jones threw his arms in the air. "And they're burning themselves up like this? It's insanity!"

"It's commitment."

"It's foolishness!"

"It's heroism," I said, poking him in the chest with a finger.

"It's suicide!" Jones said, poking me right back.

"It's courageous," I said, moving in closer and poking him harder.

"It's absurd!" countered Jones, pushing a palm hard against my chest.

"It's valiant," I said, knocking him two feet back with both palms.

"It's poppycock!" Jones said, trying to do the same to me. I barely moved.

"It's...it's whatever a *female* poppy is called!" I stammered. Jones flinched as if I was going to hit him, but I didn't.

We both stood breathing heavily for a moment. Jones looked around the room at the video screens and then at Rebecca, who was sliding her chair around the throng of computer screens while speaking constantly on the phone. "You know, you're right, what these women have done is amazing. We're literally standing in a room that holds the fate of the world in its hands."

I thought about Allie. I felt the sincerity of her heart. Then I imagined her thousands of miles away in peril. "Yeah, but the risks they're taking are frightening."

"It's the price that has to be paid if the world is to evolve," Jones rationalized.

"Yeah, but why does it have to be Allie?"

Jones turned up his palms and raised his hands. "It's what she was born to do. Fate, my friend, has pointed its bony finger at her."

"Yeah, but what if I never see her again?" I said, moving in closer to Jones.

"It's the price committed people pay to change the world. Without the courageous, the world will never progress."

"Yeah, but losing Allie is too high a price."

Jones looked at me with frustration. "What happened to committed and heroic? I thought you supported them burning themselves out for this?"

"Listen, a-hole, I support everything she does!"

"Then quit your childish moping…shit for brains!"

"Listen, dickhead, I don't mope, I pine!" I countered. "There's a difference." (I hoped.)

"Well, moron, when did pining ever change the world or get you ravished by a harem of horny cheerleaders?"

"Plenty of times!"

"Okay, name one!" Jones challenged me.

"You mean besides last Tuesday?" I said, getting in his face.

"Could you girls tone it down?" interrupted Rebecca. "I can hear you over here, and I've got headphones on! Little busy, ya know?" she said without stopping her frantic flitting from screen to screen and keyboard to keyboard.

Jones made a sheepish face and waved an apology to Rebecca as I stared at the tiny video-screen light blinking its way over southern Russia. *Allie*, I thought, *Allie*. Then I thought of Paige, oblivious to the danger her mother was in, somewhere giggling with her friends while the custody papers Allie had given me sat in the drawer of my desk. Then I thought of the millions of people whose lives would be changed by this night, unburdened by the gravity of events taking place while they watched TV, ate a burger, or shopped for toothpaste. *Wow, so this is what being a grown-up feels like.*

FORTY-FIVE

The Farm

ALLIE

Under the light of the starry night, we stood in the cover of a small grove of fir trees and stared at the dark, lifeless farmhouse. It stood across a narrow dirt road from where we were concealed. Beyond the house was a yard and then a barn and a number of sheds, including a small pen full of pigs. The drooping siding and peeling paint on all the buildings told a woeful story of years of neglect. An old swaybacked horse stood alone in the corral next to the farmhouse; it appeared as tired and neglected as the rest of the farm.

"This can't be it!" Jennifer complained for the second time. "You've taken us to the wrong place!"

"Lion's den? Looks more like termites holding hands," said Iyla, digging in her backpack.

I checked the satellite feed from Rebecca. It reassured me that we had arrived, but my eyes just didn't agree.

"You know, that horse does look like a pretty shady character," Iyla joked, munching on a banana. "I suggest we go in with guns blazing. No need to take chances. You divert him while I sneak up from behind. I doubt he'll let us take him alive."

Jennifer kicked a stone out of frustration. "Christ, how did we screw this up?"

"Quiet, the horse will hear!" Iyla said putting a finger over her lips and taking cover behind a tree.

I put out my hands and made a gesture, lowering them. "Let's all just chill, shall we? Iyla, do you sense anything…any thoughts?"

"From the horse?"

"From anything," I said.

Iyla put her fingers to her head. "I'm getting something about hay and oats."

Jennifer laughed in disgust. "Let's get the hell out of here."

I checked my GPS again and then focused on the farmhouse. In the green light of the night-vision visor of my suit, I saw a sudden flare of light as the door to the house opened and two dark, bearded men emerged. They walked toward the barn, calling for someone. The side door of the barn opened, and one by one, four other men appeared and stood in a line. The other two appeared to give them instructions verbally and with their hands.

"I told you," I whispered.

"Holy…horse is just a decoy," Iyla murmured.

"How'd you miss them?" complained Jennifer, changing her target to Iyla.

Two of the men opened the large front door of the barn and drove off in a small jeep as two more began to walk across the pasture and the first two men returned to the house.

Jennifer and I both looked at Iyla. "Well?"

"Those two," she said, pointing to the men in the pasture, "are supposed to check an antenna because the signal isn't strong enough. One is pissed that they have to do it. The other is thinking about a woman in the house he is supposed to meet later for a little…'bouncy bouncy.' The two in the car went to open a gate to let the others in."

"Others?" I asked.

"I can't explain, I just am telling you what they are thinking. Those two are also pissed off. Man, everybody here is angry, pissed-off people."

"The four of them are gone. Maybe we should hit the house now?" Jennifer suggested.

"Not without knowing what's in there," I said.

"Pussy," mumbled Iyla before taking another bite of her banana.

"What'd you say?" I asked.

"There is a cat by front door," Iyla answered with her mouth full, but I didn't see anything.

Jennifer looked at her wrist. "Twenty minutes until Latisha starts hitting them. We've got to move or we lose our surprise!"

Iyla took a couple steps and then pointed to a curve in the road that led to the farm. "Guys, you might want to be waiting a minute," she said apprehensively as a string of eight sets of headlights appeared in the dark, snaking around the corner.

"Crap!" said Jenny.

I changed the focus of my goggles to get a clear view of the eight pickup trucks, each of which appeared to have four to six people loaded in the back. Small pickup trucks being the main battle tank of terrorist groups, in my experience, this convoy was the closest thing I could imagine to a terrorist army.

"Now what?" Iyla asked. Then she turned to look at the little farmhouse. "I warned you! The horse is the mastermind and not to be trusted."

We all crouched down in the trees as the convoy approached on the road between us and the farmhouse. Each truck stopped, unloaded its riders, and then drove into the barn, where the trucks were parked side by side and nose to tail until they had all disappeared and the barn door was closed. The mob of riders from the trucks chattered amongst themselves as they headed for the house. A sudden burst of light shot up from the ground as they approached the side of the house. We watched as they slowly shrank out of sight down a flight of stairs we hadn't seen that led into the ground—all except one thin young woman with a dark scarf wrapped around her head, who broke off from the group and hurried over to the corral.

She stroked the horse on the nose, spoke sweetly to him, produced an apple from her pocket, and fed it to him.

"I told you! The horse is in on it!" Iyla declared.

"Forget the fucking horse!" Jennifer commanded.

"No, that's our way in," I said, rising up and moving to the edge of the trees.

"What are you doing?" Jennifer asked.

I didn't wait to answer, just flashed across the road to the corral, put my hand over the woman's mouth, lifted her up, and hurried back into the woods while the horse whinnied a complaint. I pinned the wide-eyed woman to the ground covered with pine needles. "Iyla, have her tell you what's down there."

Iyla put her hand on the forehead of the woman as she futilely tried to resist. Within a few seconds, she was calm and her body went limp. Seconds later Iyla took her hand away, and the woman's eyes closed.

"You can let her go. She thinks she is a baby sleeping on her mother's lap," Iyla said calmly.

"Well?" asked Jenny.

"The Lion is here," Iyla said warily. "This woman works in the control room. Brother was killed in Iraq, father and sister in Syria. So she is pissed too. There are many rooms underground. The big room at the end of the hall is the control room. Thirty or forty people are in the control room tonight. The room to the right is where the Lion is. He always is with four guards. The house has only a few people in it. Ten more guards are outside, around the house and on the road. All are here tonight to launch a big attack."

"Attack? What kind of attack?" I asked.

Iyla looked at me with an expression of dead calm. "Scrantone," she said. "They are not after the world. Tonight they want to burn us. Just us."

* * *

We followed shadows to the side of the house and located the handles of two earth-colored doors, barely visible in the ground. We swung open the doors to reveal the stairs that led into the ground beneath the house and slipped down them to the portal that led into the basement of the farmhouse. I gestured for Iyla to check to see if she could sense anything inside. She pressed her hand against the entry and then turned to me and shook her head. I tried the door, found it bolted shut, and then opened it as if it wasn't. We lifted our night-vision goggles and crept into the crude hallway with its dirt floors and dirt and cinderblock walls. A string of bare light bulbs hung from the ceiling providing gloomy lighting, making it feel more like a tunnel than the inside of a house. Along the wall every few feet hung a prism-shaped mirror unlike anything I'd ever seen. The air was stale and musty and filled with chatter from the control room at the end of the hall.

I crept along the right wall, pointed at the door, which we'd determined would lead us to the Lion, and then held up one finger. I pointed at the control room and held up two fingers so Iyla and Jenny would know I was planning to take the Lion out before hitting the control room. Iyla flipped off the safety of her pistol and held it barrel up in front of her. Jenny held her arms out before her with her fingertips glowing crimson. I looked at her, and she nodded to me that she was ready.

I looked at Iyla, pointed at her gun, and then shook my head. She gave me a questioning look, so I pointed at my ear several times and mouthed, "too loud." Iyla rolled her eyes as she lowered her gun.

I felt my heart suddenly begin to pound in my neck. The feelings of being shot by Shamil's men replayed in my mind; the thud of the bullet exploding as they hit my suit, followed by the bitter face of someone hoping to watch me die played over and over. I reached for the doorknob with a sweating palm, flexed my fingers, and then froze. A memory surfaced: lifting that gunwoman and dropping her over the railing onto the floor below at the hotel. I heard her screaming cut short by her death…but most of all, the thud. Man, the memory of that thud made me cringe inside. My heart was racing wildly.

Jenny saw what was happening and motioned for me to move. So I did. I threw open the door and flashed into the room to the right side of the door. Jenny stood in the doorway, covering me. In a fraction of a second I sent my fist into the belly of a heavyset guard, knocking him into a silent pile against the wall, and Jenny turned another guard into a charcoal cloud with a red, searing flash. Across the room another guard rose from his chair and reached for an AK-47 leaning against the wall. Soon he was indented into the cinder-block wall of the room with a quick twist of my wrist.

Jenny and I stopped and studied the small room as Iyla followed us in and closed the door. Bare bulbs lit this room as well, and there were the same prism-shaped mirrors in each corner. There was one other door leading out of the room, so we moved in on that. As we did, another man cracked the door to check on the noise we had made. Jenny made a quick flash and the man disappeared in a charcoal cloud before Iyla could raise her gun. The door hung open where the man had been. Suddenly it was full of holes from the fire of an automatic weapon inside the room. When the firing stopped, Jenny and I got down low, eased the door open a bit, and burst into the room. I caught another guard by ramming my shoulder into his chest while he feverishly tried to reload his weapon. He groaned as I drove the air out of him and then slammed him into the wall. After that, he wasn't moving anymore. The adrenaline was so rampant in my veins by then I shivered, craving another target.

The room appeared to be an office. There were video screens on the walls, and it contained a large desk, communication equipment, and a twin-sized bed tucked in the corner. Jenny and Iyla paced around the room inspecting it and discovered a well-dressed Arab man cowering beneath the desk. Jenny tapped him with her foot and gestured for him to get up. He appeared indignant and straightened his jacket as he rose.

"I expected a little more of a fight from you," Jenny said.

"I wasn't expecting guests," he said indignantly.

"Oh, we are about as far from guests as they come," said Jenny with a laugh.

"Stop the attack or we finish you right here, right now," I said, moving in on him.

"I can't do that."

The chemistry of my blood fired. I grabbed his neck in my hand and lifted him off the dirty floor. "Yes, you can, and you will."

His eyes flew open, and he gasped for air, so I put him down.

"How about now?"

"I can't."

"Won't!" I said, reaching for him again.

Iyla came up to me and tried to lower my arm. "This is no Lion."

"What?"

Iyla appeared frustrated. "What can I say? I don't think the thoughts, I just report them. This loser ran a food stand in Beirut. Just look at the poor bastard. Does a man who kills forty thousand people for fun hide under a desk? Does he look like a sadist who gets off sending people to their deaths with suicide bombs? But he's great at making you falafel. You hungry?"

"Crap!" Jenny said.

I turned to interrogate the man, but then stopped and turned to Iyla. "He knows where the Lion is. Get it out of him!"

Iyla approached the man, who backed away and then turned and bolted for a door behind the desk. The lights in the room suddenly went out, and there was a long burst of gunfire from the doorway that dropped us to the floor. Judging from the sound of it, the man we had thought was the Lion moaned and fell before he could reach the door. I turned on the night-vision in my visor, but in an underground room with no windows and no light source at all, there was nothing to see. The three of us felt anxiously around in the dark.

"Which way is the fucking door?" Jenny whispered.

"That is not the door!" Iyla declared.

"Sorry," I whispered. Then I saw the faint outline of the door we had come in through. "Let's fight our way back to the hall."

Just as I said that, the door toward which the man had run swung open, letting light in, and a thin woman about our age with long, dark hair appeared in the doorway. "This way," she whispered, waving her hand. Then she looked down at the body of the man we had thought was the Lion lying in the pool of light coming from the door. "Oh," she said, "I see you have met Asad. Pity, poor man," she said in English with a Russian accent.

I didn't understand a bit of what was happening. I was ready for a fight, but not this. I studied the woman's face and saw glowing gray eyes. *My God*, I thought, *she's a Super Born*. We heard the sound of footsteps and raised voices outside the office, hesitated, then all turned together and ran toward the woman in the open doorway.

* * *

IYLA

"Come, hurry!" the woman said, waving her hand like a crazy lady.

I looked past her down the long tunnel with lights hanging down from wires, little mirrors shining in the ceiling, and a dirt floor. There was a door at the end, but something made me afraid to go in there. Maybe it was because I didn't know who this woman was or why she would help us. I didn't know why, but I didn't feel safe. Still, when Allie and Jennifer ran into the hallway with her, I reluctantly decided to follow and locked the door behind us.

"Who are you?" Allie asked the woman. It was a good question, and I wanted to hear her answer.

"No time for that," she said roughly in a Russian accent and then pointed at a doorway at the end of the hall. "The control room is there. You must stop them. Go. Go, now."

"Where is the Lion?" Jenny asked.

"He is in there," the woman said pointing at the door. "He is controlling the launch. Hurry if you want to save your town and your family!"

Allie and Jennifer looked at each other. Then Allie gestured with her head toward the control room door, and Jennifer nodded. They ran down the hall, but I stood for a moment, watching. What I saw was the woman's hand sending out a see-through energy wave I could barely make out. It came up behind Allie, overtaking her and sending her crashing headfirst into wall by the control room door. She fell like a limp rag doll, sliding down the wall to the floor, not moving. Jenny turned and fired a bolt of crimson energy at the woman, but the same barely visible energy wave blocked it and sent it exploding back at Jenny. She flew through the control room door and landed, twisted, on the ground. Neither of my friends moved, and the tunnel became silent. I couldn't believe that powerful women like Allie and Jenny could be taken out in a flash like that. I lifted my gun and pointed it at the woman who had done this. I didn't know why she didn't crush me too.

"You won't shoot," the woman said in Russian, smiling calmly at me. The voice was eerie and familiar. It raised the hairs on my neck and knotted my stomach.

My finger reached for the trigger but then stopped. Maybe this woman was right. "Who are you? Why did you do this?" I responded in Russian, gesturing to my friends with my head.

She didn't say anything, just held out her hand toward me. I crept toward her like a frightened, hungry dog, but then pointed my gun at her head so she knew I meant business. I touched her hand for only a second and then jumped back as if hit by an electrical shock. I stared at her with disbelief on my face and tears forming in my eyes.

"You understand now, my little Iyla?"

I kept my gun pointed at her, but now it shook like I'd had too much vodka. "Mother? How can it be? You are so young."

She sighed and said nothing.

"And how can you be here with the Lion? He is burning the world and wants to control women born like us! I know, I have seen his plans!"

The mirrors in the ceiling flashed a brilliant white light that was brighter than sunlight. I lifted my arm to protect my eyes. Then the mirrors flashed a blinding blue. When I could see clearly again, I watched as the image of the young woman flowed down like a waterfall to reveal a frail woman in her seventies. "Does seeing me as I am make you feel more comfortable?"

"No! Why did you do this to my friends? You should be helping us! The Lion will try to control you too."

"I seriously doubt anyone will be controlling me." My mother began to pace around the hall stiffly with her back hunched over. "We gave you four times the epsilon I had, four times!" She held up four quaking fingers and pointed them at me as if they were swords. "Yet here you are," she said, shaking her head. "You always were a disappointment."

"Is that why you sent me away? Why did you treat me like I was never good enough to be the daughter of Olga Settchuoff?"

She turned on me like a snake with burning eyes. "Because you weren't!"

I tried desperately not to let them, but tears began to fall from my eyes, and I totally lost focus on why I was there.

"Back then, I am setting records in space. Everyone knows me. Everyone loves Olga. Everyone is so happy when you are born…but my daughter? Disappointment. I leave you in the cradle because you will never be me. I give you to others because I am ashamed of you. Can't you see how you hurt me? I give everything so that you will have greater powers, better life, than me, and what do you do in return? You are nothing—no Olympic medals, no space records. You are too ugly to be a model, too stupid to cure cancer. You are not the best at anything, not even cheese rolling! All you can do is stupid parlor trick and guess what people are thinking. You embarrass the name of Olga Settchuoff."

I turned to jelly. Not the good kind like strawberry or grape, no—I became like a shapeless lump sliding down the wall until I sat on the ground and dropped my gun, blubbering with my chin on my chest.

Mother looked at me with disdain and threw her arms up in frustration. "Ah, see? See what I am talking about?" she said, pointing at me. "Useless. When they tried to tell me I was finished, that they didn't need Olga Settchuoff anymore, did I cry like a little girl? No, no, let me tell you what I did," she said, bending over me. "I cut their throats. I deposed entire governments. They didn't tell Olga she was finished. I told them." She stood over me closely. "You ever do anything like that? Huh?" When I didn't respond, she slapped me across the face. "Huh?" she asked before hitting me again. "Of course you haven't. You don't have it in you," she said, smirking. "What do you do? Play guess-what-number-am-I-thinking?"

She paced for a moment in silence with her arms behind her just like Demetri used to. She took several deep breaths while I cried and shook, just as I had done with her as a little girl. After a moment she seemed calmer. "You need to understand this. Do you think you can try?" she asked, stopping in front of me and leaning over.

I wiped the tears off my cheeks and nodded. "Yes."

"Your days of…experimentation with those American Super Born," she said, pointing over at Allie and Jennifer's bodies, "are over. You'll work with me now."

"For you? Doing what?"

Mother stared at me and smiled. "Doing what we Super Born were made to do—rule the world."

"Controlling the world by burning it down?"

Mother gave me an icy stare and then smiled. "Precisely."

"I think maybe you have been sniffing too much epsilon. Your mind is backward. You improve the world by building, not destroying!"

Mother strutted in front of me. "Oh, but destroying is so much easier."

"How can you control the world if all you do is burn it?"

"We—the question is how can *we* control the world, my little Iyla. The formula is simple. One Super Born, even someone like me, is not enough. So first of all, you need an army, an army willing to die for your cause, an army so full of emotion they sacrifice all else."

"Good luck with that," I chuckled.

"Why do you laugh?" Mother held out her open arms. "Look around you. As the world globalized, millions in the Middle East were left behind. No one was there to tell them their outdated social and governmental structure was making them fall behind. Things like theocracy, tribal allegiances, sheikhs, and oppression of their own people, including their women, had brought to them a Dark Age, just as these same factors did in Europe centuries before. They fought amongst themselves in splintered little groups while the world passed them by."

I looked at her, hypnotized by her calm, reasonable tone. Her tranquil side had always tantalized me with the hope of communicating with a real mother. Then she sat down against the wall across the hall from me, groaning with the effort of folding her creaking knees.

"Then oil was discovered and a tiny few of the people had incredible riches—they wouldn't share it with their people. This has created tribal and class bitterness enforced ruthlessly by oppressive governments the West supported. There's the key," she said, pointing a finger at me, "bitterness with no outlet. This was the opening we used. The forgotten, hopeless ones whose houses are on fire are full of vengeance—ripe recruits."

I shook my head.

"This bothers you, Iyla?"

"You use them," I said with a sour face.

"You're damn right!" Mother said with excitement returning to her voice. "What do you think we told these oppressed, vengeful people was the answer to their problems? We told them to run back into their burning houses, and they did it! We said the only answer to oppression and violence is even greater oppression, intolerance, and violence, and they believed us! The world has left you behind, so here, drink more of the poison that has made you as you are! We tell them, 'It's not your outdated social structure that has not been competitive for hundreds of years that's at fault. No, no, it's the West that is the root of all your problems. I love that term, 'the West,' because I can use it to include just about anyone I want. So it's easy to get them to sacrifice themselves to serve our purposes."

"You lie to everyone? That's your solution?" I asked.

"Lucky for me, others aren't as spineless as you," she said, pointing a bony finger at me. "Osama couldn't believe I could tell an angry, hopeless person to blow himself up along with a crowd of our enemies and he would do it. When he saw it working, he got off on it like a boy with a toy. Having that power to make people jump up and die just because he said so made him giddy. Those with no life and no sense of a future are so easy to control."

"So how does that make an army?"

"It's enough to instill fear and doubt in your enemy. The panic and desire to be safe makes your enemy more like you. They begin to oppress their own people—anything to feel safe again. But of course they never will. This draws even more recruits to us."

"What does that accomplish besides creating fear?"

"Instilling panic is just phase one," she said, holding up a finger. "As our power grows, our assets grow, our funding grows. Now we bring in millions of dollars each day from the black-market oil in the Middle East. Westerners buy our oil, and we use their own money to destroy them. The more money, the bigger the operations we can muster. Now we have drones from the design the Iranians captured from the United States, along with helicopters, trucks, and advanced weapons. Our range grows. Now we can strike our enemies where they live. Their panic grows. The desire to feel safe again will come at any expense."

"But that just stirs up the world. You will never control it."

Mother smiled again. "No imagination. Do you know your teachers told me that about you when you were four? Wait for the next phase to come. My technicians are working on a device to control and unite all the Super Born behind me. Poor Demetri got me the design just before his unfortunate murder. Once I have the device, no country can stand against the power of all the Super Born. Together we will burn anyone who stands in the way of us taking our rightful place." Mother slowly stood, leaning on the wall for support. She came across the hall to me.

"So then, what does my daughter, the fruit of all I hold dear, decide to do? Huh? On the eve of my greatest triumph, does she join her mother? Does she apologize for being such a massive disappointment and beg my forgiveness?" Olga shouted in my ear as I trembled. "No, she brings those disillusioned bitches to my doorstep! She helps them try to give hope to the hopeless, comfort to the angry, opportunity where there shouldn't be any! How can I tell a man who has a future to be angry and go kill somebody? Does that really make any sense to you? Does it?"

My lack of response made Mother even angrier. She took hold of my arm and struggled to slide me along the floor, foot by foot, toward the control room. "Let me show you what makes sense," she said, stopping to kick Allie's body out of the way, then doing the same to Jenny's, as it blocked the doorway. She left me on a raised platform overlooking the control room. "Get up! Get up, you waste."

I strained to get to my feet. There was nothing wrong with my legs, but my mind was spinning in circles. Through eyes blurry with tears, I could see dozens of people at flimsy tables guiding drone aircraft via laptop computers. On some of the screens I saw explosions, which were followed by cheers from the operators. Then I suddenly sobered and focused when I recognized an image on a screen. It was the plant in Scranton where the generators were made and where Rebecca and Logan must be. Then it dawned on me that it was where Mother expected all of us to be. She had planned to kill us all there. I gasped at the image of one of the massive mountain-top generators that powered the plant suddenly disappearing in a ball of fire—its tower dropped to ground like a falling giant. The drone operator who had hit the tower cheered and raised his hands in victory, and it made me feel sick.

"The future!" Mother said with pride. "Mine—ours."

FORTY-SIX

The Lights Go Out in Scranton

LOGAN

Zero hour hit, which meant it was Latisha's time to launch hundreds of raids across the globe. Rebecca put her feet up, took off her headset, and put the audio from Latisha on speaker. Rebecca took a deep breath and said, "Here we go."

I looked at the Asian video screen at Allie's blinking light in southern Russia. It hadn't seemed to move in a half hour. I didn't know what that meant, but I was worried regardless. Lights on all the other screens began to flash and move wildly, as if an army of kids were playing a giant online video game. Over the COMM speakers, we heard Latisha talking to operatives in a calm, business-like voice, which contrasted with the operatives, who had energy, expletives, and sometimes fear in their voices. As moments passed, the pace of the communications accelerated, and Latisha's tone rose in volume and became more commanding. "Just do it, or I'll fry your fat ass!" I heard her say.

Jones stood beside me and watched the screens in awe. "Is this really happening, live?"

I nodded. Lights disappeared from the screens everywhere, and Rebecca was starting to smile, both of which I took as good signs. But when I looked at southern Russia, Allie's light wasn't moving. I was just about to ask Rebecca how it was going when the lights and boards in the room flickered. Rebecca looked up at the lights and then turned her attention back to her screens. "Holy shit!" she said.

"What is it?" I asked, running over to her. She was typing frantically.

"They're here!" she said, flipping from one security camera screen to the next. They showed explosions at the generator towers on the mountains above the plant.

That was when I heard the first explosion. It wasn't close, but it made the room vibrate subtly. Rebecca accidentally knocked over a computer screen that portrayed the activity in Europe as she rushed to slide her chair over to the screens showing the events in the United States. She clicked the keys until the screen was focused on Scranton and then let out a loud groan. "You can't be doing this! Not to everything I've created!"

"What?" I said, not understanding how everything could suddenly be going wrong. After all, we were the hunters, right? On the screen Rebecca was focused on, I saw the streets around the plant with dozens of small, fast-moving dots approaching. "What are those?" I asked.

"Drones! Fucking drones!" Rebecca replied. She pushed herself away from the computer and leaned her head back. It was a look I had seen just before Carmine Camino was vaporized. Her body went calm and her eyes turned black just as a much closer explosion shook the room. Part of the plant was certainly rubble now.

As I watched the screen, approaching drones seemed to be slowly disappearing. With each one Rebecca made vanish, she murmured a low groan. Her arms began to shake as her pace quickened. Her entire body began to quake, until even her head started to swing back and forth madly.

Jones came up beside me. "She's doing it, just as I told you. She can't keep that up! It's killing her!"

"No! No!" she screamed; she seemed to be struggling against herself. Still more drones disappeared.

I could hear more distant explosions and then one close, very close. *That was the assembly building*, I thought. I looked up at the ceiling as if I could see the drones gathering outside.

"No, you bastards!" Rebecca screamed and then made guttural sounds as if she was struggling with some invisible bonds that held her.

I watched the drones flicker off the page and then looked back at Rebecca convulsing in the chair. I was surrounded by the sound of explosions and Latisha's oblivious audio. If I tried to stop Rebecca, the drones would have their way and perhaps bring the building down around us. If I didn't, we might lose Rebecca. I wondered if the drones or Rebecca would give out first.

I heard the garbled tones of Latisha calling for Rebecca on her headset, so I picked it up. "Latisha, this is Logan! We're under attack here! There are explosions everywhere! Drones came out of nowhere," I told her in a panic.

"Don't worry, I've got the Air Force on it. The drones didn't show up on radar, but now we've got them on thermal. You should have help soon. And I'll have attack choppers in the air any minute."

I sighed, looking at the screen and at Rebecca. "I don't think 'any minute' is gonna work for us," I said as another explosion rattled a building nearby.

FORTY-SEVEN

Mommy Dearest

IYLA

As the control room became full of the noise of gleeful destruction, I looked around, feeling like a lump of crap. I could not stand that I was helplessly watching this calamity happen. Mother stood next to me shouting instructions and encouraging the pilots to create the most carnage possible. "The rest of them must be in that building with the offices. For the sake of all those we have lost, bring the building to the ground!"

My mind slowly began returning, and I took inventory of the room with a long look. "Where is the Lion?" I asked.

Mother looked at me with disbelief. "Are you really that stupid?" She pounded her chest. "I am the Lion. I am in charge. The man in that room was just a face to lead everyone off the scent. Some need the face of a man to believe in, so I gave it to them." Mother gestured to the screens. "Do you like what you see?"

"I think it is…disgusting," I said with a hapless sneer.

Mother leaned down and slapped me across the face where I sat. "No one speaks to me like that!"

I shook off the hit and moved my face into hers. "For years I wished I could be like you. I ripped at my heart because I wasn't someone you wanted. No more. This," I said, pointing at the screens full of violence, "is not the future. This is clinging to the past in anger and being consumed by it. This takes the world backward into hate."

She came at me and got in my face. Her eyes burned out of control. "The same way the Super Born killed my men and Shamil? The same way you came here to kill the Lion? I am trying to show you we are the same—same blood, same anger."

"Mother, you killed forty thousand innocent people!"

Mother smiled. "More than that!"

"We wouldn't come to kill the Lion if there were no Lion. The Super Born were influencing the world through cooperation, not oppression."

Mother shook her head."Believe me, oppression works better, has for centuries. Ask Stalin or Hitler."

"In the past, maybe, but not the future. The world is changing and will pass you by," I said, lifting a hand toward her as she passed.

Mother slapped my hand away. "Don't try your feeble mind games on me."

"I just wanted to find out what you are going to do with me."

Mother looked up in thought for a moment. She smiled, and it seemed that the question intrigued her. "I don't know. When the American Super Born are all gone, maybe I can find a place for you, some little thing that you can handle. After all, you are my daughter…though maybe no one needs to know that," she said, thinking out loud.

I took a deep breath and felt like giving up. Then the things Allie had told me about Dr. Jones' theory—about the Super Born being fireworks—entered my mind. My mother was old and frail, yet she was alive and well. At first I thought Jones must be full of shit from a bull, but then I wondered. "Mother?"

"What is it?" She answered as if bothered by my voice.

"They tell us if we use our powers we will burn up and won't live long. How is it…"

"That I'm old?" she said, almost laughing.

"Yes. What they say isn't true?"

Mother turned to me and acted like a real mother for a minute. She stood with her arms folded and said earnestly, "I almost died several times, little one. Every time I realized it was when I use my powers that I become weak. Others, my friends from the Olympic team, never understood, so now they are gone. They thought they were invincible. That's how the powers make you feel, but it is a cruel lie." She bent down to my level as I sat against the wall. "Epsilon eats you for dinner, makes you feeble, brings you years of pain as your body wears out. You cannot imagine the constant pain or what it does to your mind. Day after day the pain is there, and it never goes away. It never stops, and there is nothing you can do. It changes how you think, how you feel." Then she stood up and began to pace in front of me. "I was like you when I was young, ready to save the world. Now I know the only way to get people to listen is to conquer the world instead. Saving people just eats your powers up until they are gone. You must learn to use your powers only when you need them. You need to use people and machines to do your work so you don't have to burn yourself up. I will teach you. It is like having three wishes from a genie: don't use them all at once."

"You used those mirrors to make you seem like a young woman—is that what you mean?"

"And more. You use your powers enough to let people know you have them, to fear you, like these," she said, pointing at the drone pilots. "They do anything I ask because they know I have the power to crush them. A little demonstration of strength goes a long way."

"So you make an example of someone."

"Sometimes it is the only way to get your point across."

"But what if that someone is someone you love?"

"You think I care?" She shook her head. "You are so weak it sickens me. Everything has a price—just be sure someone else pays it." Then she noticed a female drone pilot who was hesitant to launch her missiles. "Like this," she said to me, pointing at the pilot. The mirrors in the ceiling glowed, and mother sent out the nearly invisible waves of energy she had used on Allie. They lifted the female drone pilot into the air and then crashed her into the wall. When the woman hit the floor, she was half the size she had been. "You!" mother said to another woman at the back of the room. "Are you afraid to do as I say, kill these infidels?"

The woman shook her head. "I am not afraid!" But I could tell she was when she looked at the other pilot's body on the floor. Still, she hurried into the first drone pilot's vacated seat.

Mother held out her hands. "See? It is as easy as that."

"Infidels? Mother, you're not Muslim."

"Of course not," she said, perturbed.

"Then how can you…"

"Nothing lights the world on fire like religious intolerance. Muslims, Christians, it doesn't matter. Did you know Islam, Christianity, and Judaism all come from the same source writings and share the same prophets? Jesus and Moses are prophets of Islam. But even with that same base, these fools are ready to kill each other over religion. Sunnis and Shiites even share Islam, but I can put them at one another's throats. All it takes is pain and anger, and giving people a target for them. Once you can get people to believe they are better than someone else because of their beliefs, it is easy to use them to kill and oppress any people you choose. With someone to vent their pain on, the inconceivably cruel becomes possible. Then, once the cycle of revenge starts to roll, an eye for an eye, there is no stopping it."

"But how can you support policies that oppress and degrade women? You are a woman."

Mother stopped pacing and leaned in toward me. "Do you think I care who is the target as long as it not me?"

"That's horrible."

Mother moved close to me, seeming excited. "Yes, yes, it is, but it is child's play compared to what I have planned."

"You? You are the one who wants to control the Super Born?"

"Of course. Thanks to Demetri, I am this close to the kind of control the world needs. Once I control all the Super Born, they will be invincible."

I didn't know if I should tell her the plans she had for the Interrupter were a piece of crap Rebecca had planted. I wanted to throw it into the face of Olga Settchuoff that her daughter had fooled her and ruined her plan. Should I tell her that I had put the gun to head of Demetri and Shamil? Part of me thought I should hurt her with it, part of me was afraid to face her reaction, and yet another part of me thought she might be proud I had done such devious things. The words danced on my tongue and then floated away.

Mother ignored me. She stamped her way down the aisle of drone pilots, chastising and encouraging them to do more.

I climbed into a folding metal chair and watched my mother intently focused on the devastation she was reaping on the computer screens. I felt hopeless. Allie and Jennifer lay still on the floor of the hallway outside. Rebecca and Logan could be lying in the rubble of the plant that was meant to bring hope to the angry people who were now destroying it. Here I sat, powerless, like a moldy piece of week-old bread that no one wanted. I couldn't stop my mother, and I couldn't join her, the same old story since I was born.

That was when I noticed a man coming up to Mother and whispering in her ear. "All of them?" my mother erupted. The man took a step back but continued to speak to her. I knew it was bad news when she turned and glared at me with the face of six devils. She stormed at me and then lifted her hand and sent out waves that knocked me out of my chair and against the wall again. "You don't just come here, you attack my entire network! What have you done?" She picked me up with her shock waves and slammed me against the wall over and over like a bouncy ball, until I could only lie in the dust with pain in every inch of my body. I could tell how much she loved her daughter; otherwise, I would have been like the drone pilot on the floor. She took a step toward me but then stopped and returned to her work with increased zest.

It took several minutes of dizziness before I could think again. I decided moving was not a good idea. She would just knock me down again. So I lay in the dirt—to rest and think. Nothing was clear to me anymore. This side or that didn't seem to matter. Pain was something I was certain of, and my mind was full of it: pain in my body, pain in my memories of my mother, pain for Allie, pain for Scranton.

I sensed the anger of the pilots in the room. I felt hatred, anger, loss, and hopelessness. There were so many of them that their thoughts and feelings came at me like a wave of confusion. It all began to overwhelm me. Together, my thoughts and theirs formed a massive cloud of hate, theirs for the world around them and mine for my mother. But in the back of their thoughts I felt sadness, reluctance, and the wish for things to be different.

Suddenly I felt a little presence in the background behind the anger and the thoughts of the drone pilots. It was quiet at first, but then it got louder, and I knew it was Allie's mind trying to work. She wondered what had happened. She felt pain in her head, her neck, and back. She opened her eyes and saw a dirt floor, felt the dust in her mouth. Then she sat up. I smiled just knowing she was still alive. I told Allie about the prism mirrors in the ceiling that Mother used. I warned her about the energy waves that had sent her into the wall. I told her about the attack on Scranton and asked her what I could do. Naturally, Allie thought, *What?*, the same thing everyone thinks when I crawl into their mind for the first time. But finally she understood, and I felt her getting stronger. She stood up. She looked at Jennifer and was worried and frightened. I told her there was no time for that: *Every minute another missile strikes.* Allie looked at the mirrors in the ceiling and hurried down the hall, jumping and smashing them as she went. I sat up and tried to breathe.

That is when Mother turned from the destruction of Scranton. She saw me moving and heard Allie in the hallway. She hurried across the room toward the corridor (not bad for an old lady) and glared at me. "You are not a Settchuoff!" she yelled as she passed me. I limped after her. I felt anger release drugs into my blood, and suddenly I was full of energy and fight. I remembered my gun lying on the floor and was determined to fight Mother this time. My pace quickened, and I chased after her. Maybe I was not Olga Settchuoff, but I was Iyla.

As soon as she sped out of the control room to confront Allie in the passageway, I saw her quickly begin to change. Without the mirrors in the ceiling powering her, she appeared as she truly was. Within a few seconds she turned from a woman in her seventies to a gray, skeleton-like husk with only a few tufts of white hair and muscle-less skin. This was my real mother, without the mirrored prisms to disguise what epsilon had truly done to her. She was barely able to move. Mother turned slowly and tried to stagger back into the control room, but there I was, blocking her from the door. She made a futile attempt to get by me, but I pushed her back into the hall. Without the mirrors she was a small fragment of the super-woman who had crushed Allie into the wall.

"Look what epsilon has done to you," I said. "All the pain you feel has made you bitter. All you know is pain and how to use it to bring more." She tried to speak and tried to get by me, but not this time. "Mother, I forgive you for all you have felt and inflicted on the world, and I release you from it," I said, striking her with a sweeping flurry of my arms. With each blow, Mother broke into brittle pieces and into a cloud of dust as the pieces hit the ground.

Allie stared at me without knowing what to do, what to say. I stood over the dust of my mother and breathed deeply. After a minute, I looked at Allie with tears in my eyes and waved her toward the control room. "Go! Go! They are destroying Scrantone." Allie rushed by me, and I fell to the ground beside my mother and began to cry. How can there be sorrow for such a monster? *Or do I cry for myself?*

FORTY-EIGHT

Enough—Which Hand Will You Take?

ALLIE

I shot through the control room, knocking down the computers the pilots were using to control the drones, traveling down one row and then back up the other, leaving the pilots sitting at the other side of the tables in shock. I stood panting in the midst of their puzzled faces and then I lifted my arms before me. "Enough! Hasn't there been enough? That is my home that you're destroying!" I said, pointing at one of the computer screens. "Do you even know why you're destroying it? Do you know what that plant makes? It makes food, water, power, schools, hospitals, roads, but most of all, it makes hope and a future for thousands and someday maybe millions. It brings opportunity to people so they don't have to become angry, bitter, violent, and hopeless, the way you have." They all stared at me, intimidated.

"We do what we have to do," someone said, and others murmured in agreement, making me glad that at least some of them were able to understand English.

"I know you have lost loved ones to oppression and violence. Do you honestly believe the answer is more of it? When will the 'eye for eye' ever end? You've killed my friends and my coworkers, so should I kill you now?" I spun as I stood and spoke so I could look into the eyes of those around me. "The only thing that can stop this endless cycle of death is hope, love, and working together. The only thing that can stop it is you. You must remove the poison that's been placed in your hearts. No army, no matter how big or powerful, no number of bombs can end this horrible cycle. It is up to people like you." I paused to watch their responses and saw many whispering to others while some stared blankly at the ground.

"The Dark Ages ended in Europe when the people, the intellectuals, the artists, and the scientists banded together to embrace science and open minds to new possibilities, untied from the past. Are you the courageous ones who will end this darkness? Are you the future? Or are you running backward into what has caused your grief? Are you the ones who finally say, 'Enough is enough'?"

As I said that, a reactive armor patch in the center of my chest erupted, blocking a handgun shot fired by a dark, bearded young man in the back of the room. In an instant I had the gun out of his hand and pointing at his nose.

"I'll take that as a no," I said, tightening the grip on the trigger.

He tried to act brave, but I could see him trembling. There is something about shooting someone and having them come up and chat with you that triggers massive anxiety and concern for your future well-being. I played it up with slow, methodical movements to build up my image of invincibility to the crowd of pilots around me. I brushed off my suit with my fingers where the bullet had impacted.

"You got my suit dirty. I really like this suit. Now I'm gonna have to have it cleaned. That makes me really mad." The shooter cringed and backed against the wall, trembling. "What's your name, tough guy?"

"Anwar," he said, trying to be proud.

"You tried to kill me, but you don't even know me. Why would you do that?"

"I have seen the war the West has brought."

"Am I the West, or just a person like you? I wish you no harm. You destroyed my home, maybe hurt my friends and family.

You even tried to kill me. So should I kill you? Would that make the world better?"

"It is the way."

"Whose way? The way of what? Is this *way* something you made? 'Cause it's not in your religion."

"No."

"Then why don't you question it? 'Cause it's really a stupid way to live." I looked around the room and then got back in Anwar's face. "I see a lot people here who don't share your zest for murder. They look hurt, frustrated, and legitimately angry. They're here 'cause they don't know what else to do—yet. You, you look like one of those sadistic bastards who gets off on the hate and violence, not even thinking about what effect that it will have tomorrow. Is that true?"

Anwar bristled and stood up. He took a step toward me. "The world needs to change."

"Great! We agree on that. But think it through, Anwar. How does killing me or my killing you improve the world? Should I blow myself up and kill everyone in this room, the way your people would? How does that change the world for the better?" I could feel the pilots in the room cringing at my words as if they feared me carrying them out. "No, Anwar, your way is not the way. You need to think of a better one. Where are you from?"

"Al Hasakah," he said, regaining some decorum.

"Well, Anwar, I'll give you a choice. We can try to kill each other, right now. If you kill me, you can go home and tell everyone how you killed an infidel woman. If I kill you...well, what does that matter to you then? But I'm sure being killed by a woman isn't a good thing for your afterlife. *Or* I will promise you that I will go to Al Hasakah with you and together we will build a school or a medical center in your name and you can tell everyone that you did it for them. Either build something for a better future, or kill somebody and end it today. The choice is yours, right now, this instant." I lowered the gun and held it out for him to take with one hand, even as I held out my other hand for him to shake. "Which is it? How would you rather be known? One hand is the gun, and the other is my partnership in changing the world. Which will you take?"

Anwar looked at those around him who muttered encouragement for one choice or the other. A woman nearby said, "Anwar, maybe she is right." A man told him, "Take the gun, Anwar!" Another man chimed in, "I am sick of this, Anwar, and you have told me you feel the same. Let's end the killing now." Another screamed, "Yes, she is right. This is not the way of Allah!" Anwar froze.

"I'm serious!" I said. "Which is it?" Anwar wavered, so I yelled, "Now!"

He slowly reached for my hand and shook it.

I turned to everyone else in the room. "The same choice is there for all of you to make! All the horror can end here tonight with you. You can be the ones who finally say enough and begin the end of this madness. If you have the courage, I will be with you. What is it to be?" I said, holding out the gun and my hand in friendship to each of those around me. One by one they all shook my hand as I moved through the room. "You will not kill us?" some of them asked. When I reached the last person in the room, I pulled the clip from the gun, emptied the chamber, threw down the gun, and raised my arms in the air. "Enough!"

"We can go?" they asked. "You don't kill us?"

"I don't kill you. You don't kill me. We are not killers; we are partners in a global future. Together we can change this. Nothing will change without you taking the first step, which is to stop supporting those that use you and your religion for their own purposes." I waved toward the door. "Go, go in peace."

Some of them began filing out of the control room, but others came up to me. Some shook my hand and smiled while others shook my hand before giving me an air kiss to each side. Some held my hand for a long while. It made me feel hope. Maybe some good had come from the night.

FORTY-NINE

Rebecca?

LOGAN

The sounds of the drone strikes grew closer. This wasn't the way it was supposed to be. The Super Born were supposed to toy with the rest of the world, not be attacked by it. I thought we would always be the unbeatable team and had felt safe and secure in that knowledge…wrong. Jones and I stood next to Rebecca as she strained through dark, hooded eyes to focus on the dozens of dots on her screen that represented the drones assaulting us. Rebecca made a mental connection with the drones, one by one, and lowered their numbers by crashing them, but they were still getting through. She began to quake even more, her skin became gray, and her breathing was heavy.

"You won't destroy what I've built!" she screamed, her voice strained. "You won't destroy it!"

I reached my hand out to Rebecca. "There's too many. Let's just get out of here. It's killing you!"

She struggled to sneer. "Not while there's one of the little bastards left."

Jones chimed in, "Rebecca, we must go. Let the Air Force finish them."

"Yeah, the buildings can be rebuilt but not you," I added.

We watched as she raised her head toward the ceiling and then collapsed down on the keyboard as the dots of ten remaining drones closed in on the plant. I gestured for Jones to help.

I looked at the screen of Rebecca's computer and watched the drones as an explosion shook the room, sending Jones for cover under the table. I looked up at the ceiling as if I could face the drones outside. *Come on, you mindless pussies*, I thought. But then suddenly all was quiet. All the dots of drones on the computer screen were gone. *They must not like being called pussies; who does?* "Rebecca, they're gone! We did it!" I cheered, hoping it might revive her.

Jones rose and searched for Rebecca's pulse while I lifted up her head. She fell back limply in her chair with her eyes to the ceiling; the blood vessels in her face looked like black spider webs. Jones looked at me for a long moment and then shook his head.

FIFTY

If?

ALLIE

I made Anwar wait while I offered my contact information to any-one who wanted it. Most of the pilots feared me, it was clear, but a few spoke to me without hatred. I doubted I would hear from many of them, but it was worth a try. I got more specific with Anwar and made a firm arrangement of a time and place to meet him in one week. Again, who could be sure what would happen? Maybe when I reached him, it would be a trap, but we would see. Even if one of the drone pilots had gotten something out of what I'd said, maybe the tide could start to turn and the Arab Spring would grow into an Arab Summer. If nothing else, we had saved the plant in Scranton, and ap-parently Latisha had done some serious damage to the Lion's network.

I told the pilots that they would not be harmed but that they needed to wait in the control room until my friends and I were gone. Then they would be free to decide their own course.

I hustled back to the hallway to find Iyla bent over Jennifer. As I approached, Iyla looked up at me with an expression that was both drained and concerned.

"How's she doing?" I asked.

"Not so good. She is still breathing but…" Iyla stopped and carefully rolled Jenny over a bit so her back and side were exposed.

A piece of the doorframe she had been thrown through protruded out of the right side of her back just above a pool of blood. "I am not a doctor, but I don't think that is good."

* * *

LOGANs

After the attack was over, the medics came for Rebecca, and the sounds of first responders filled the parking lot outside. I stood calmly in the conference room. Though maybe it wasn't calm that I was feeling, just plain old shock and dismay, a couple of my old friends. I slowly moved to the video screen of southern Russia and put my hand over the unmoving, blinking light that represented Allie. All across the other screens, thousands of lights had disappeared, showing the success of Latisha's gigantic operation, but not my little blinking LED. It just sat there…blinking. *Move, goddamn it*, I thought.

Jones came over and put his hand on my shoulder. "I'm sure they're okay," he said.

"I hope you're right. I hope they're not hurt. I hope their 'fireworks' haven't burned out, like Rebecca…goddamn it. Why did I let Allie go without me?"

"So she wouldn't have your mangy ass to worry about too…perhaps," said Jones, trying to lessen the smack of his comment with a cutesy smile.

"Mangy what? I just saved Allie's butt from a gunman the other day. And as I recall, I was the one who got the Interrupter away from you and helped to defeat your 'mangy ass'!"

"Oh my!" said Jones, putting his hand on my forehead as if searching for signs of a fever. "You've gotten delusional! Where are you hit, son?" He jokingly looked me over for a wound.

I turned to Jones, readying for combat, when my phone rang. I almost broke my wrist struggling to quickly get it out of my pocket. "Hello?" I asked.

"Dad? Are you okay?" asked a girl in a panicked tone.

I had been hoping it was Allie and had to readjust my thoughts. *Dad?* I had to think for a moment. This must be a wrong number…or maybe that lady I'd known in Philly, but then I recognized the voice. "Paige?"

"Yeah, how many families do you have?"

"What's with the 'Dad'? You threw me there."

"Just thought I'd try it out, something new. Are you okay? I heard about the explosions on the news."

"I'm fine. I think it's over. The medics are here, and there's a lot of damage. But I'm okay," I said, still smiling about the "Dad" part.

"Good, I was worried. It sounded really bad."

"It was," I said, looking at Rebecca's empty chair. I don't know if it was denial or the uncertainty of what was happening, but I couldn't talk about what had happened to Rebecca or the damned light that wouldn't move.

"There are people saying the B.I.B. helped end the attack. Is that true? Was she there?"

I hesitated and looked over at my little unmoving Allie-light on the screen. "She was. She had a lot to do with it."

"I knew it! Thank God Mom's away on business. At least I didn't have to worry about her."

"Yeah, thank God," I said, finding it hard to disguise my sarcasm.

"Isn't it amazing that every time something big like this happens, Mom is off on a trip somewhere? She misses everything."

"Yeah, unlucky her. We get all the fun."

"Ain't that the truth." Suddenly Paige's voice sounded a bit weak. "You be home soon?"

"Scared?"

"Kinda."

"I'll be home as soon as I can."

"Good…there might be a hug in it for ya."

"Hey, I'll be right there!" Paige never talked like that, so I knew she was bravely hiding her concern.

"Bye."

"Bye, see you soon."

When I clicked off my phone, I could see Jones struggling with the various headsets and phone lines Rebecca had used, trying to determine where a muted voice was coming from, so I hurried over and retrieved Rebecca's headset from the floor.

"This is Logan."

"Thank God someone is answering," Latisha said, obviously upset. "You guys okay there?"

"Peachy," I said, looking down at the half-eaten pizza I'd brought for Rebecca. The sight made me feel a tragic loss of innocence and sincerity that had existed only moments ago.

"I assume you can see that we did it. Our success rate was way over what I projected. The targets that launched the drone attack on you were on a ship anchored offshore in Lake Ontario. Coast Guard and Navy SEALS got 'em. They were on our target list; we just got there twenty minutes too late to stop them from launching the drones." She paused then sounded agitated. "You listening to me, Logan?"

My detached silence bothered her, I suppose. "Yeah."

"Any of the Super Born there I can talk to?"

"Not at this second."

Latisha paused for a moment then came back sounding aggravated, "It's funny. We did really well, but the lead Rebecca gave us wasn't the Lion, and now the girls aren't there. You wouldn't know anything about that, would you?"

"Me? No, I'm just the pretty face, remember?"

"I would hate to think they took on the Lion without me. That didn't happen, right?"

"You're asking me? I don't know what they're doing," I said, glancing over at my little map light.

Now Latisha was pissed. "Cut the crap! Logan, you may be the worst liar I've ever met."

"That's true, but I keep trying. You know, practice, practice. You did a great job, by the way—I'm sure the prez will be happy."

"Yeah, right! You think I'm gonna tell that bozo what's going on?"

"Oh," I stammered. (Who was running this show, anyway?)

"Well, I need to hear from one of the Super Born, especially Rebecca. That flash data feed she was giving me has stopped for some reason. Will you have them call me when you hear from them? Or is that too much for your pretty face?"

I looked down at the Rebecca's empty chair and my little Allie-light that refused to move. "It's not *when*, Latisha, it's *if*."

FIFTY-ONE

Escape from Russia

ALLIE

The drone pilots crowded in the control room doorway behind me. I could tell they were captivated by the events taking place in front of them by their wide eyes and open mouths. A couple of them even offered to help care for Jennifer, but I declined with a shake of my head. I lifted Jennifer carefully with both arms. Her body was cold, seeming more like a thing than my friend. I gestured to Iyla with my head. "Get the door. We have to get her back to Turkey."

We hurried back the way we had come through the maze of rooms and then toward the stairway leading back up to ground level. When Iyla opened the door to the outside, I heard the familiar whirl of helicopter blades coming closer. Then, when we reached the top of the stairway, I saw the shadowy shapes of the helicopters closing in. Tracer fire shot out of their machine guns and peppered the ground around the farmhouse. The terrorists around the barn began returning fire with small arms and RPGs. Iyla and I began running for the same woods that had sheltered us before, and the barn erupted in an explosion from rockets fired by the choppers. The blast ignited the gasoline in the trucks inside the barn, creating a series of fiery explosions that lit the yard like daylight. Behind us a steady line of drone pilots rushed up the stairs in an effort to escape. Three 'copters landed in the pasture nearby and released a dozen or more men who immediately began firing at us with automatic weapons as they charged the farmhouse.

I was speeding to the trees as fast I dared with Jennifer in such horrible condition when I heard Iyla let out a scream behind me. I turned to watch her crumble to the ground, reaching for her leg. "Iyla!"

"Those fucking assholes shot me. Me!" she complained, trying to stand on one leg—bullets were still impacting the ground around her. "Shoot someone else, you morons!"

I changed to a one-armed grip on Jennifer, ran back, and took hold of Iyla around the waist. I hurried them back across the road into the tree line and put Jennifer carefully down. I pulled the belt from Iyla's jeans in one quick motion and then began tightening it above the wound in her thigh. "Who are those bastards?" Iyla asked. "How dare they shoot me?"

"I'd like to know too. We didn't share this location with anyone. My guess from their equipment is Spetsnaz, you know, the Russian Special Forces."

"They don't seem very special to me, dick for brains shooting the wrong people," Iyla said raising her fist at the helicopter nearby. Then Ilya looked down and shook her head. "You don't think Latisha told them about this place?"

"We didn't even tell Latisha," I said, finishing my tourniquet.

"So what are they doing here?"

"Your guess is as good as mine."

"Too bad, cause my guess stinks," Iyla admitted.

I looked out at the farmhouse and saw the drone pilots running in a panic in all directions as they exited the basement. Many were immediately mowed down by the helicopters, and those who escaped became victims of automatic-weapon fire from the ground. I watched them fall and felt the urge to run out and save them. This was not what was supposed to happen. I'd had a moment with these people just minutes ago. I felt I'd reached some of them.

"This is wrong!" I told Iyla.

"What?"

"We're doing the wrong thing! We have to save those people, not kill them. It's our only hope to stop this!"

"What? Did a bullet hit you in the brain? Let's get the fuck out of here!"

I looked at the woman who'd fed the horse, who we had left in the woods unconscious. She still rested comfortably on the soft pine needles. I pointed at her. "Iyla, wake her up. Let her know that she's coming with us. Tell her if she stays, she dies."

"What's the point?"

"Just do it!" I said. Then I turned my attention to the carnage around the farmyard. A terrorist hid behind a small wooden shed and fired a RPG into a helicopter hovering over his head. The explosion sent it dropping straight down to the ground in flames. Seconds later the terrorist and the shed were no more than splinters as another helicopter found its range. Small pockets of terrorists fired AK-47s from the farmhouse, the barnyard, and pastures, trying to cover the terrorists who were struggling to escape from the basement. Each attempt was greeted by fire from the attack helicopters and the soldiers that had landed on the ground. The pigs broke out of their pens and began running around in the chaos. The swaybacked horse ran through the destroyed fence of his corral and down the road. I watched as more drone pilots ran from the farmhouse to become victims as the soldiers closed in on them. One looked like he would get away as he ran toward us in the woods. I recognized him as Anwar and felt myself smile with relief. At least he had made it. He saw me, and I could see the recognition in his face.

I had begun to move toward him when I saw the trail of machine-gun fire chasing after him. It caught up to him, and he collapsed in a fraction of a second.

"No!" I screamed as I bolted from the tree line toward him.

Iyla screamed from behind me, "Allie! You're my ride home!"

I reached Anwar and was glad to find he was still alive. He panted and looked up at me. "You? Why would you come for me?"

"Remember, we have a school to build."

Anwar's face softened. "Yes, maybe someday," he said, letting out a deep sigh and dropping the side of his face to the ground.

"Not someday—tomorrow," I said, lifting him off the ground. Just then four of my armor patches exploded on my leg and back and other bullets buried themselves in the dirt around me. I flashed Anwar back to the woods to find the female drone pilot looking afraid of us and of the fighting nearby. She nervously paced from side to side with her hands on her head, watching the carnage in disbelief.

Iyla was obviously upset. "Can we go now?"

I put Anwar down. "I can save two more at least," I said, turning to run back into the battle.

Iyla put her hand on my shoulder. She pointed to the many exploded tiles on my suit. "If that was heavy gunfire from a helicopter that hit you, we would be walking home without you."

"Just two more. I can save two more!"

"Sure you can, but if you do, maybe Jennifer bleeds to death. Maybe you are shot dead. Worst of all, what becomes of me? You want to take that chance?"

I looked at Jennifer and knew Iyla was right. Every second mattered. I flipped Anwar onto my back and pinned his arms against my chest with my left hand. I knelt down beside Jennifer and lifted her around her waist with my right. I glanced over at the female drone pilot. "Climb on my back, and Iyla, you grab onto my left side."

The drone pilot was confused and hesitated until Iyla pushed her onto my back. "I don't know why I have to save everyone's ass," Iyla complained.

As I got ready to take off, the woods erupted with the explosion of a rocket, downing several large trees. A hail of bullets slammed into the nearby firs and severed dozens of branches, which fell all around us. Someone had discovered our hiding spot. I waited for a lull in the shooting and took a deep breath. We shot into the welcoming sky just before the woods disappeared in a ball of fire.

FIFTY-TWO

My Little Allie Light

LOGAN

It was hard for me to move. I sat still in the conference room in a chair like I was part of it, waiting for the truth to catch up—it felt like the reality of the night's events had yet to hit me. I heard the sirens and helicopters outside like it was just the sound of a TV I had left on in the other room. I took some deep breaths and gave the wall in front of me a penetrating look, but it was only a wall. I knew I wouldn't find any answers there.

The memory of Paige's frightened voice resurfaced in my mind and motivated me to rise. I decided to check the video board one more time before I left to see if Allie had moved. I needed to take care of Paige right now. That's what Allie would want.

I put my fingers over Allie's little light in southern Russia and sighed. But when I pulled my fingers off the screen, I saw the light moving—and moving fast. Was I imagining it? (It had been known to happen, but this time I was sober.) Then as the little bugger flew toward the Turkish border, I leaped into the air and yelled, sending my fist joyously over my head. "Yes!" I spun around and did it again. I smiled and let out a laugh. I dug my phone out of my pocket and stared at it willing it to ring. I waited for a moment but then realized I'd better get back to Paige—standing there wouldn't make Allie call a second sooner. As I exited the conference room, I jumped and slammed my open palm on the jamb above the door. "Yes!" Then I stopped. Paige was safe, after all. A few more minutes wouldn't hurt. I went back into the conference room. I pulled up a chair and watched the little light stop in Turkey. I stared at the phone in my hand, waiting for it to ring. *Way to go, little light,* I thought.

* * *

ALLIE

The flight from Russia was agony for me. As the adrenaline waned, I began to feel a steady pain in my neck, my shoulder, and my back from being slammed into the wall by that Russian bitch. (Carrying all these people really brought new meaning to the phrase "get off my back.") I couldn't tell if the nausea I was feeling was a symptom of a concussion or just a natural reaction to the bloodbath I had witnessed. Then I began to feel a burning in my back and leg where those bullets had hit me. Maybe this suit had saved my life, but the process wasn't painless. I wanted to stop but knew I just had to stick it out for everyone's sake, like holding your breath when all you want is a lungful of oxygen.

When my NAV system told me I was over Turkish air space, I contacted Jennifer's security people at the airport and put them on alert that we were coming in hot, hurt, and overloaded. I made it clear that we needed immediate serious yet discreet medical aid for three—two beyond critical. (I wanted to include a hot tub for me, but that would have to wait.) Damn, the sites of the bullet impacts on my leg burned like fire. Rebecca would hear about that the instant I saw her.

The glow of the shining silver Lowe jet in the predawn tarmac lights was a welcome sight. It was the first instant I began to feel we had made it. I flew the last mile like someone hobbling to a bathroom with their legs crossed.

I was glad to see two ambulances waiting beside the plane along with a full crew of security guards and the ground crew for the jet. (But wait, where was the catering truck?)

I landed on the tarmac at the nose of the plane and squatted while Iyla and the female drone pilot jumped off. I stood up and hurried toward the two approaching ambulance gurneys. Two attendants helped me settle Jennifer, who wasn't moving, onto one gurney while another helped me slide Anwar off my back and lay him on the other—at least I heard Anwar groan. They hurried them into one of the ambulances and began attaching IVs while the doors closed and the ambulance pulled away.

I took a few steps and then dropped to my knees, exhausted, as Iyla limped her way over to me. "Her name is Raja. Her Russian sucks, but her English is okay. Be nice to her; she is scared less than shit," Iyla said, gesturing to the woman who had fed the horse. Other medical people began inspecting Iyla's leg and helped her onto another gurney.

"Okay," I said, nodding. "I'll take care of her…you'll be fine." I slowly stood up and waved to Iyla. "I'll check on you in an hour or so."

"I hope by 'check on you' you mean bring me a sandwich," she said as they wheeled her to the other ambulance. "Extra cheeses but no mustard," she added. I waved again and watched till the door to the ambulance closed.

Then I turned to Raja. "I'm Allie," I said, offering my hand.

"Raja," she answered, weakly gripping my fingers.

It was the first time I'd gotten a good look at her. She seemed small, almost frail, with a petite body under her robe. Her dark hair was mostly hidden under a wrap, but I could see the smooth, tan skin of her face, which was broken only by the dark circles of her eyes. Overall, she seemed forlorn and uncertain yet passive, contrasting markedly to her role as a terrorist who had been ready to destroy me. "Don't be scared," I said, putting my hands lightly on her shoulders and trying to convince her with a smile. "We just wanted you to be safe from that battle. You're free to go wherever you want. I'll make sure you get there personally. Okay?"

"Okay," she said, trying to smile.

"The important thing is that you're safe. You have a home to go to…a family?"

Raja said, "No, no family."

"Well, we'll find a place for you," I said, trying to sound cheery.

Raja reached out her hand to me but didn't touch me. "Horse…do you know what happened to the horse at farm?"

I smiled, amused that this would be her top concern. "The fence of his corral was destroyed in the fight. So the last I saw him, he was running down the road away from the farm, frightened but fine."

"Good," she said, nodding, but without any emotion on her face.

"You hungry?"

Raja nodded again.

"Come on," I said, wrapping an arm loosely around her shoulders. We stepped over the power cords that ran to the jet, and I led her up the steps to the cabin. "I'm sure we can find you something to eat and drink in here, and I am way overdue for a change of clothes."

I gave Raja her choice of items in the fridge, and she chose some kebabs, stuffed vegetables, and bottled water. I nuked the food to warm it up for her in the microwave. She settled in at a small table between two rows of facing chairs and began to eat daintily.

"I'll be back in a minute," I said. Raja nodded. Then I turned to change in the back bedroom. When I glanced back, Raja was voraciously scooping up her food and guzzling water.

I peeled off the suit, which clung to me with determination and sweat. Everywhere I'd been struck by bullets on my legs and back, the suit seemed especially determined to stick to my skin. I gingerly peeled off the suit, revealing large pink areas that I bet would soon be bruises. I wiped them with a washcloth, put lotion on them, and then put on a pair of jeans and shirt. I glanced over at the suit lying on the ground and saw tears down to the inside layer that marked where bullets had triggered reactive armor tiles. I counted six. In some weird way, I was becoming numb to the fact that each of them might have killed me. I swallowed a couple of pain relievers and then palmed two more and gulped them down.

When I joined Raja at the small table, I found her plate and water bottle empty. We sat in awkward silence for moment.

"So, you're a drone pilot?" I asked.

Raja shook her head no and looked down at her feet. "Programmer…what you call…hacker."

Only knowing about the drones being controlled from the farm, I was surprised. "You were hacking my company's network?'

"We tried. I try too, but your network is tough. I was working on knocking out GPS network of United States," she said without emotion.

But I couldn't hold back mine. "What?" I exclaimed.

Raja nodded. "That and making big internet outages," she added dryly.

My right hand wanted to smack her, but my left wiped my face as I sighed. Was her being a hacker any worse than piloting a drone into our plant? "Well, it's a different world we live in—different kind of war we inflict on one another for some useless reason. Destruction is such a waste compared to building."

She nodded. "I don't think I understand that until tonight—until I meet you. Now I can't believe I was doing those things." Raja looked up at me and studied my face before she said, "You can fly. Many people fly like you?"

"Nope, I'm the only one I know," I said smiling.

"It was amazing. You are hero. You save us. I thank you."

"I just wish I could have saved more of you. I wanted to," I said, suddenly finding my eyes beginning to tear up, "but I had to save my friends."

"My friends, they are all dead now. I would be too, if not for you. Why would you do that—save someone who would try to kill you?"

"Raja, all this killing must stop." She nodded silently. "Do you know Anwar?"

"Yes."

"He tried to kill me. The Russians tried to kill him. Now he's here with us fighting for his life. This is all crazy."

Raja nodded. "If I had been in that farmhouse, I would have been among them trying to kill you, yet you have saved me. There must be a reason for this."

"Maybe there is."

* * *

It wasn't long before Raja curled up in her leather chair, and I gave her a blanket. Within a few minutes she fell asleep, just as the sun was beginning to show through the jet's windows. But even as she slept, I could see her fingers occasionally shake, her foot twitch, or the muscles in her neck tighten.

I stood up and began walking back to the bedroom with my adrenaline gone, my back and legs turning stiff, and my shoulders hunched. I thought, *I never felt like this after a day of work at the phone company.* I closed the bedroom door and dug in my bag for my computer. I made a mental checklist: Jenny, Anwar, and Iyla to hospital—check. Raja settled in—check. Follow up on Jenny—no check. Talk to Logan and Paige and find out what happened in Scranton—no check. Time for Allie to calm down and to get some sleep—double no check.

I started up a video call on the computer. Maybe I could hit two birds with one stone: talk to Logan and make myself feel better. Remembering the explosions I'd seen in Scranton on the drone pilots' screens, I felt an ominous dread as the call connected. Logan wouldn't have been at the plant at that time of night. I was crazy to worry. When I saw his face on the screen, my heart leaped, a smile exploded on my face, and I forgot about all of the pain in my body.

* * *

LOGAN

Paige's next call came in after I'd decided, finally, to leave the office and was walking down the hall outside the conference room. So I ducked into a nearby office to take it. Which worked out great because it was our CFO's office and she always kept a bowl of chocolates there, bless her bulging jeans. I took the call, sat at her desk with my feet up, and popped a chocolate into my mouth.

"Are you coming home or what?" Paige's voice rang in my ear.

"I'm on my way. You caught me walking out," I said with my mouth full of chocolate.

"What's taking you so long? You at O'Malley's?"

"I am not at O'Malley's. I was just waiting for your mother to call, but I gave up."

"Yeah, I just tried to call her, like, a million times. She won't answer."

"It's probably the time difference. It's just late there."

"Or she's in a gutter—dead."

"They don't drop bodies in gutters anymore," I said, popping another chocolate.

"Okay, great, then she's in a shallow grave. That better?"

"Much, helps keep the litter down…I'm gonna go right now. Be home in fifteen."

"I hope you mean minutes!" she said and hung up.

Before I could get my feet off the desk, the video call came in from Allie, and I felt my heart stop before it began bursting through my chest. "It is soooo good to see you! I was so worried. You okay?"

Allie paused, her facing rippling with emotion, and then she nodded. "I'm okay." She put her palm toward the screen and I did the same.

"You did it? You got the Lion?"

Allie nodded. "How about you? I heard about the attack over there. Have you been to the plant?"

"I'm here now. It was really bad. I was just about to walk outside and see for myself. The offices are okay and the power's still on. Paige is pretty scared."

"Paige? She wasn't there, was she?"

"No. It's just all over the news, and she was home alone. I'm gonna get home after we talk. She's fine."

Then we both paused and looked at one another. We said simultaneously, "There's something I gotta tell you…" We both chuckled.

"You go first," I said, not wanting to tell her about Rebecca until I had to.

"No, you."

"What is it, Allie?"

"Okay." She took a deep breath and tried to look brave, but her face gave her away as she spoke. "We might have lost Jennifer, and Iyla was shot."

"Holy crap!"

"The medics took them away a minute ago. So I don't know yet."

"That's horrible," was all I could think to say.

Allie looked down and began to sniffle and then looked up at me in the screen. "I had to carry Jenny all the way from Russian. She was like…like cold…like…" Then she began to cry.

"Babes, I am so sorry."

"And I am so tired. I ache…the things I saw make me just want to…"

"It's okay. Just come home. Just get back here."

"That's the thing. I can't leave them here. I can't rest. I've got to find out how they are and stay here till they can travel or…bring Jenny home. Then I've got Raja and Anwar to worry about…"

"Who?"

"Raja and Anwar. They were two of the terroists at the Lion's farm."

"What? These two were trying to kill you...hell, they were trying to kill me! Now you're buddies?"

"It's complicated. We aren't—buddies. They're people just like us. They want the same things. They just don't know how to get there. They're angry and frustrated. Killing them isn't the answer. Working with them is."

"Are you crazy?"

"Logan," she said wiping her eyes and seeming to regain control. "We've been doing the wrong thing. This eye-for-an-eye has to end or this agony will never stop. I stopped the drone pilots attacking you."

"I knew that was you!"

"I talked to them. I reached them. But then the Russians came to kill them, just like Latisha was doing everywhere else. That's when I knew it was wrong, so I tried to save them, but I could only save two," she said, her voice becoming emotional again. "Just two, Logan, just two—Raja and Anwar. Now what do I do? What can I do?"

I sighed. "You're right. You need to stay there. I want to reach through this screen and hold you in my arms more than anything, but you do what you have to do."

"I know. It's just really hard sometimes."

"You'll do fine."

"How about you? What did you wanna say? How incredibly you miss me?"

I tried to laugh. "Yeah, the bed isn't the same without you." It was my turn to sigh. "Allie, my news here isn't any better. The EMS took Rebecca away too—Jones isn't a doctor, but he thinks she's gone. The EMS worked on her for a few minutes and then hurried out of here."

"I thought you said the offices were okay. How'd she get hit?" Allie asked in alarm.

"She didn't. I was standing right next to her. It was the 'firework' thing. She burned herself out defending everything you guys built. There were just too many of those drones at once."

Allie was silent for a long moment.

"Allie? You hear me?"

Allie's head went back and her lips began to tremble.

"Allie, don't do this."

"Fuck!" she finally yelled. "Fuck, fuck, fuck!"

"It's not your fault!"

"I could have stopped those drones a goddamned minute sooner!"

"You did your best."

"Tell that to Rebecca! Goddamn it!" she said, lowering her head. Then she said in a lower tone, "Goddamn it."

"Listen, Allie, we both have a lot to do. I'll make sure Paige is okay. I'll find out where they took Rebecca and get a report on her condition. As soon as I know, I'll let you know, okay?"

"Yeah."

"I'm sure Jennifer will be all right. And Iyla's too tough to kill. You know, meat loaf keeps forever."

"Sure."

"Sounds like you've been through hell. Take some time off from helping everybody else to get some rest."

"I'll try."

"Just get back here as soon as you can," I said, as if I had some control. "I love you."

"I love you too…I'm just having a hard time with all this. I'm so glad you're there. I don't know what I would do if you weren't. I want to be there with you so bad."

"You will be soon, and I'm gonna give you the greatest back rub ever."

"Yeah, right. I know what you're gonna rub," she said, rolling her eyes. Then she smiled, "And I can't wait."

We both put our palms out in front of the camera. "See you soon. You'll be okay," I said.

"Take care—and take care of my girl," Allie said.

"Yeah, I'm picking her up from rehab Thursday—hope it took this time. And I'll let you know how her ultrasound goes."

"Logannnnn."

"You want it to be a boy or a girl?"

Allie sighed. "I want it to be you and her sitting next to me watching a movie in front of our TV sharing a big bowl of popcorn."

"That's what I want too. And that's what we'll do. Get your sweet ass home."

* * *

I was unable to move for a few seconds after Allie hung up. I reached for another chocolate and found myself taking the last one from the bowl—oops. I went down the stairs into the main office lobby to find the windows at the entrance blown in and debris from outside littering the floor. I crunched my way out of the foyer without having to open a door to do it and took a walk to inspect the plant. Fire trucks and EMS vehicles were parked around the assembly building and the shipping docks. Small fires still raged in piles of rubble, and there was nothing but dark sky where three-story buildings had once stood. I walked past the manta-ray-shaped wing of a downed drone sticking out of the ground in front of the office building and smelled the aviation fuel that had leaked from it. I stopped and ran my hand over its smooth, rubber-coated edge, thinking how just moments ago it was trying to end my life. Now, thanks to Allie—or Rebecca's last act in life—it lay in pieces rather than me. I stood for a silent moment in disbelief and then, remembering my promise to Paige, hurried toward my car in the distant parking lot.

As I got near Old Reliable, a small compact car sped into the lot, rattled its way into a spot near mine, and stopped with a squeal of its brakes. A tall, thin young man hurried out of it, slammed his door, and ran over to me. As he approached, a line of police and

EMS vehicles came flashing down the road beside us with their lights on and sirens wailing.

"Hey, dude, you work here?" he asked frantically.

"I did," I said, pointing over at the fires.

"Do you know her?" he said, holding out a picture from a magazine and lighting it for me with his phone.

"That guy's a her?" I asked, referring to the old gentleman in the center of the picture from an oil-trade magazine.

"Not him! Her," he said, impatiently pointing to a woman in the background. "She's supposed to work here."

There is no way I could mistake the face (and rack) of Jennifer Lowe, especially when she was decked out in a cocktail dress. (I wondered what kept that sucker from popping every seam.) Dare I tell him what she looked like now? I studied the man's face to see what his game might be. His blue eyes seemed wild and frantic. His hair and his goatee were dark and unkempt. His clothes seemed wrinkled and strained from a long day. *Guy dresses like a loser*, I thought and then remembered the days when one pair of jeans and two shirts were the only clothes I'd owned. "Maybe. Who is she to you?"

"Don't play games with me! Do you know her or not?"

"Listen, bucko," I said leaning in toward him. "You're the one who's looking for a favor here."

The man held out his raised palms. "Sorry."

"So let's start with who you are and what you want with her."

"Name's Michael. She's just a chick I met."

"Just a chick? You think I was born yesterday?"

"Okay, I met her back in New York. We've been together a few times."

"And you're still alive!" I said, unable to control my surprise. "You often drive a hundred miles for 'just a chick you met'?"

"For her. What can I say?"

I gave him a disbelieving raised eyebrow. That was telling him.

"What? You've never had a woman bring you to life?" Michael asked.

"Never," I lied and quickly moved on. "What's so great about her?"

Michael stroked his goatee while his smile just kept growing. "She's, like, amazing. She's smart, and super strong, but with this funny little-girl side. But then she has this darkness. I can tell she's got problems in there. She's like this addictive mystery novel you just have to keep reading."

"You like train wrecks, do ya?"

Michael's eyes drifted off like he was reliving a memory. "She can wreck me anytime."

"Holy crap, sounds like you've got it bad."

Michael smirked. "You ever have a woman after you for, like, hours and hours?" Michael studied my face. "No, I doubt you could understand."

I resisted the urge to smack him a good one, secure in the knowledge it was he who couldn't even begin to understand the tip of the iceberg that was just beginning to push its way up his ass.

"But she'd never give me her number. I found this picture a friend of mine took last summer. I know that's her and she works here."

"You found her? You went through all this effort to track down some chick you just met?" *What an asshole*, I thought until I remembered all I had been through to find Allie.

"Sounds crazy, right?" confessed Michael.

"How'd you find her? What are you, some kind of stalker?"

Michael appeared to calm a bit and leaned back against the car behind him. "No, journalist, freelance."

"Holy crap, couldn't you get a real job?" I said, laughing, until I remembered what I had done before I met Allie.

"Funny. Real funny. Listen, I know the photographer who took this picture, and the caption says she works for this company. I came up to find her, and then I heard this place was involved in a terrorist attack. Before I wanted to see her, but now I just wanna know that she's okay. Was anybody hurt?" Michael said, gesturing to the plant.

I pointed at the plant, the fires, and the EMS vehicles. "Duh." My mind raced with how far ahead of this poor sap I was. I knew who she was, where she was, and that Jenny wasn't hurt in this attack, but that she was hurt halfway around the world. I knew odds were that she was dead. And I knew exactly how this pitiful rookie was feeling inside, the agony and uncertainty of the search, and taste of the stomach acid sloshing up into his throat.

Michael stood up straight. "Well, that's my story. Are you gonna help me or not?"

I considered all of the options of what I might say. Should I just blow him off for his own good? Let the chump know she was the president of a global company? Let him down easy by explaining that she was a sexual predator and he was just one of her many toys? Clue him in that the darkness he'd glimpsed wasn't just a side of her? Prepare him for her death? Prepare him for *his* death, however happy it might be? Warn him to look out for energy fields floating over her bed that might send him flying into a wall? (This night was just too wild and weird—even for me.)

"Okay, guess not," said Michael as he began walking toward the plant.

I turned and called after him, "Hey."

Michael stopped and turned confrontationally. "What?"

"You look like you've had quite a day. Maybe you could use a drink and a little conversation."

"Listen, do you fucking know her or not?"

"I do. I know her very well, but it's not a simple story."

"Oh, there's a shock!" said Michael, walking back to me. "I'm searching everywhere and driving to fuckin' Scranton looking for some mystery chick. She doesn't even act like I exist unless it suits her libido. And now I have to deal with a douche-bag like you. Who said it was simple?"

Knowing his frustration firsthand, I sighed and cut him some slack. I had vaporized lesser men for calling me a douche-bag—but hey, it was Tuesday, and I was feeling merciful. "I've got to take care of my daughter…"

"A dick like you has a daughter? I thought there was a law or something."

"What, et tu, Michael? You won't find your mystery lady in there," I said firmly, pointing at the plant. "Listen, I've got some things to take care of and a few calls to make to find out exactly where she is. Give me time, and we can talk about it over a beer. You're buying. I know the perfect place. Personally, I think you should save yourself a lot of grief and just get in that heap of yours and hightail it back to New York. But if you really want to know—and I mean *reallllly have* to know—meet me in two hours at a place called O'Malley's on Penn Ave."

Michael moved in close to me. "Okay," he said, nodding his head. His eyes lit up like he had just won the lottery. I knew just how he felt. And I knew the iceberg had just moved in a couple more inches, the poor jerk.

CPSIA information can be obtained at www.ICGtesting.com
Printed in the USA
BVOW05s2036160416

444385BV00011B/110/P